Espiona

AL Sowards

Espionage

a novel

A. L. Sowards

Covenant Communications, Inc.

For Jay & LaRee,
loving grandparents and members of America's greatest generation

Acknowledgments

A BIG THANKS GOES TO Melanie, VaLynn, Teresa, Laurie, and Josh for their helpful reviews of my manuscript. This book is better because of your suggestions. Thank you, Bradley, for your insight about Nazi-era German words. Thank you, Grandpa George, for sharing stories about growing up on a farm during the Great Depression.

I would also like to thank the many teachers who have taught me and encouraged me to love reading, writing, and learning new things. If you remember me as a student, I guarantee I remember you as a teacher. Special mention should go to Mr. Frederick for bringing *Fortitude South* to my attention for the first time.

I will always be grateful to the team at Covenant for taking a gamble on my work. Thank you to all the staff for their professionalism and amazing talent. Thank you, Sam, for your wonderful edit and your unfailing patience.

A special thanks goes to my husband. Thank you for pointing out plot holes, asking hard questions, and helping me hear and visualize scenes. Thank you for letting me pursue my dream. Love you!

And to those of you reading this book, thank you for picking it up. I hope you enjoy it.

Useful Terms

Abwehr—German military intelligence agency that operated before and during WWII—until early 1944, when Hitler turned all Secret Service activities over to the SS

Feldwebel—Noncommissioned officer in the German Army; rank similar to a sergeant in the US Army

G-2—Intelligence staff in the US Army

Gefreiter—Soldier in the German Army; rank similar to a private in the US Army

Hauptmann—Officer in the German Army; rank similar to a captain in the US Army

Hauptsturmführer—Officer in the Gestapo; rank similar to a captain in the US Army

Milice—French police. Their main task was to find and arrest the French Resistance. They generally cooperated with the Gestapo

Oberleutnant—Officer in the German Army; rank similar to a first lieutenant in the US Army

Oberst—Officer in the German Army; rank similar to a colonel in the US Army

Obersturmführer—Officer in the Gestapo; rank similar to a first lieutenant in the US Army

OSS—Office of Strategic Services. US intelligence and sabotage agency that operated from June 1942–January 1946

RAF—Royal Air Force (British)

SHAEF—Supreme Headquarters, Allied Expeditionary Force. Headed by General Eisenhower, this group planned the Normandy invasion

SOE—Special Operations Executive. British intelligence and sabotage agency that operated from July 1940–January 1946

Standartenführer—Officer in the Gestapo; rank similar to a colonel in the US Army

Sturmmann—Stormtrooper in the Gestapo

Chapter One
Switchblade

Early April, 1944

Private Peter Eddy felt the cold ocean water soak through his pants before he'd even had a chance to grip the oars. He looked up through the rain to see Captain Ducey laughing at him.

"You can still say no, Private."

Peter slipped the oars into the channel, feeling rainwater trickle down the back of his neck. "And let the Nazis get away with it? No, someone has to do this. I just wish the waves weren't quite so high tonight."

The gray-haired captain gave Peter half a grin. "Bad weather can be an ally. Use it. You have three hours. You should be done in half that time. You say you have never done this sort of thing before?"

Peter smiled. "Haven't even shoplifted." He thought about telling the old sea captain that for three years straight he had led his high school baseball team in stolen bases, but that wasn't the type of theft Ducey was interested in. Besides, Peter found that most of the English didn't *get* baseball.

"I thought not. Best of luck, then. You Americans are a crazy lot."

Peter nodded his farewell and began rowing. It wasn't long—maybe four strokes—before Ducey and his ship disappeared from sight. *I'm not crazy*, Peter told himself, not for the first time that night. *Inexperience doesn't mean I can't burglarize a Nazi garrison.*

Peter had met Captain Ducey just that night. The tough old sailor hadn't been willing to talk about any of the previous missions Peter suspected the man had been on, but he had taught Peter the basics of navigating his small, stealthy ship. Ducey seemed to know the English Channel as well as Peter knew his family's farm back in Idaho, even if his half dozen voyages during the Dunkirk evacuation were the only trips he was allowed to tell Peter about.

Peter's mission, Operation Switchblade, was his first for the US Office of Strategic Services, and it was extremely important. As he rowed, Peter reviewed the information he had learned during his briefing. Three days ago, a German spy stole one of the code books the American military used to communicate with sources in German-occupied territory. It was always bad news to have a code book stolen, but the military normally reissued code books so frequently that it wasn't a significant loss. This particular code book, however, was used to communicate with deep-cover agents in Belgium, Denmark, and Northern Germany. Peter was told that some of the agents were so entrenched in the German military hierarchy that issuing a new code book to them was deemed a risk of unacceptable proportions. The code book's loss was devastating to the Allied cause. If the book stayed in Nazi hands, they could set traps to capture and kill valuable sources of information.

One little book—that was why Peter was alone in the dark, in the rain, on the English Channel, hoping not to run into sea mines or be shot by a Nazi patrol when he landed on the beach. It was his job to find the book and destroy it before it left the French fortress.

When Peter's dinghy hit the beach, he wasn't sure he was ready. The OSS man, Captain Knight, had assured Peter he was the right man for the job, but Peter still wasn't convinced. He had grown up just a farm boy. Since then, he'd been one of thousands of new recruits, then a tank driver, then a very junior member of General Eisenhower's staff. *Too late to turn back,* he told himself. *Now you're a spy.*

The beach was rocky, but the man-made barriers dwarfed the natural ones. The German Army was expecting a cross-channel invasion sometime this year, and they had turned the beaches of Northern France into a soldier's nightmare. Peter prayed that he wouldn't step on a mine as he pulled his boat from the surf, past rolls of razor-sharp barbed wire, and around wooden poles stuck into the sand to slow down any invasion force. Peter could make out the glowing end of a cigarette not too far down the beach, and wondered how many patrolmen he could expect. He smiled as he remembered Ducey's advice. *Bad weather can be an ally.*

The night was dark, windy, and wet. The few German patrols he saw seemed more focused on staying dry than on looking for phantom enemies. Who, after all, would try to invade on a night like this? It was the type of weather that made sensible people want to stay indoors. Peter usually thought of himself as sensible, but as he climbed the steep hill off the beach, he was grateful for the tempest. The clouds obscured nearly all light from the moon and stars, and the rain dimmed the sound of his footsteps as he circled the Nazi base. The threat of an air raid kept the fortress dark; the time of night kept it quiet.

He avoided the compound's carefully guarded main gates and went instead to a smaller gate, almost hidden. His briefing for the mission had included a map of the complex made by a French refugee who had long ago served on this base. Peter waited while a patrolman walked past and checked the gate then noiselessly slid toward it when the man moved on. The side gate was secured with an old lock—which took approximately thirty seconds to pick. Peter locked it again behind him, sure a patrol would check it again before he was finished and ready to leave.

Once inside, it was easy to avoid the solitary, huddled soldiers on patrol. Their flashlights gave Peter plenty of warning that they were approaching. Besides, the building he sought was not far from the gate he had forced, and he soon found an unlocked window that allowed him inside. Peter entered the compound swiftly and found the rooms he sought at the end of a long hallway after backtracking only once.

At that time of night, few people were about; the staff room was deserted when Peter arrived. The walls were covered with maps, silhouettes of friendly and enemy planes for identification, a picture of Hitler, and a medium-sized Nazi flag. Beyond the staff room was the commander's office, which Peter managed to unlock, even without a key. In the office, the wall decor again included a picture of the Führer, but there were fewer maps. Rummaging through the pile of undone paperwork on the commander's desk, Peter located a book and verified that it was the one he'd been sent to retrieve. It wasn't very big—several dozen pages thick, with a soft, well-worn, red leather cover. It had no title, but the first line of text matched what he had memorized earlier that day. *Had it really been that easy?* Peter wondered. His biggest hardship in retrieving the book had been the weather. He'd been expecting something more difficult.

He looked at the clock and realized he still had plenty of time until Ducey would consider the rendezvous broken, so he took apart the commander's phone and snipped a few wires before putting it back together.

* * *

Gefreiter Hess was halfway through his patrol. His shiny, recently polished boots struck the floor and squeaked slightly as he walked—the polish a result of strict grooming standards for members of the German Army, the squeak a result of walking through the rainstorm earlier in his patrol.

Hess yawned. He still wasn't used to being up all night, and patrol duty from 0000 until 0600 hours was not as exciting as he once imagined war would be. There were no Soviet snipers within a thousand miles, rarely any British pilots sighted, and the last French Resistance fighter to enter this base had been caught and executed more than two years before. No one had breached his base's security since then.

Hess continued his patrol through the staff room, pausing there to glance at the maps on the walls, tempted to sit in one of the relatively comfortable chairs and put his feet up on a desk. But the desks were covered with charts, orders from Berlin, and dozens of contingency plans for defending France from the cross-channel invasion everyone thought the Allies would begin that spring. *And if the patrol leader were to catch you . . .*

One of the other new guards had made that mistake. The hauptmann in charge of the nightly patrols had walked the halls silently—in socks—and found the guard sleeping on duty. The punishment had been severe. Reluctantly, Hess left the staff room and continued his patrol into the base commander's office. He walked into the room with a slight smile on his face. Usually the room was locked during his patrol, and he was eager to enter. Even when empty, the office was the center of power on the base. He could almost taste it as he breathed.

Then something heavy hit the back of his head, and his body fell to the floor with a thud.

* * *

Peter put the ammo box down and leaned over to check for vital signs. He had lost his blood lust for German soldiers several campaigns ago and was somewhat relieved to feel a pulse. He gently dragged the unconscious gefreiter around to the other side of the desk, where he would be concealed from the hallway, and continued his work, grateful the dark clothing he wore and his hair—almost black with water from the storm outside—had helped him remain invisible to the patrolman.

Peter was bent over the desk, putting a waterproof covering on the code book, when he heard the sound of a gun leaving its holster, followed by a German exclamation. In addition to English, Peter spoke near-fluent French because his uncle was married to a French woman. Peter's German was very limited, but he could guess that what he'd heard, if translated, would have earned the wrath of his mother and the bitter soap she'd kept on hand for washing out Peter's mouth when he was younger. He slowly turned around and faced the German hauptmann, glancing at the man's socks and recognizing that as the reason he had heard no warning footsteps.

"Turn around; hands on wall," the hauptmann said in rough French.

Peter gave the pretense of cooperation, turning around at a calm, slow pace. Then he brought his Colt M1911 up suddenly, swung toward the hauptmann as he dropped on one knee, and fired a shot into the German officer's chest. The hauptmann got a shot off too. It hit Peter's upper left arm, not hitting anything that would cause lasting damage but hurting nonetheless. The German officer dropped his weapon and fell to the floor. Peter's wound began to bleed almost immediately, and when he put his hand over the injury, he felt the warm sticky blood seep through his fingers. He didn't bother to see if the officer was unconscious or dead. He knew gunshots made enough noise to be heard over a rainstorm, and he was suddenly in a hurry to get out of the base commander's office. Using the same tool he'd cut the phone wires with, Peter cut the bottom of his shirt off and wrapped it tightly around his wound.

The code book was too big for Peter's pocket, so he stuck it inside the waistband of his pants. He looked around the room for an escape, knowing he needed to exit quickly. There was a single window in the office, but opposite that window, about twenty-five yards away, were the barracks that housed two German companies. Peter thought it would be wise to avoid the barracks if he could.

In the room were two immobile German soldiers and two doors. Peter knew the door he had come through led through the staff office to a hall with guards patrolling outside. So he went through the second door. As he closed it behind him, he heard loud voices and heavy footsteps rushing down the hallway, reacting to the gunshots. The door locked from the inside, so Peter locked it and turned around. The room he had just entered was a storage room. Filing cabinets lined one side, there were cleaning supplies in another corner, and shelves with rolled-up papers and unlabeled boxes took up the rest of the room. It had no windows and no doors, save the door Peter had just come through.

Somewhere on the base, an alarm bell sounded, and the German guards began yelling at him through the door. Despite having been raised in a strict Mormon household where vulgar language was prohibited, Peter nearly swore. He thought he was trapped until he noticed a puddle on the floor, looked up, and saw the grating on the ceiling that was part of the room's ventilation system. He guessed it was about two feet wide by two and a half feet long. He climbed onto the shelves rather clumsily because of the now-numbing pain in his left arm. As he climbed, German soldiers began banging on the door with something. He couldn't see what they were using, but based on the sound it made when it collided repeatedly with the door, he guessed it was something solid. The screws holding the grate to the ceiling were old and rusty. He tugged two of them loose immediately, and two more pulls rendered the remaining ones useless as well. Then he yanked out the fan. Peter glanced over his shoulder. The hinges on the door were showing signs of strain.

The ventilation system's second, mostly solid grate was hinged to open out onto the roof. Peter jumped to the ground, grabbed a broom from the corner, and used it to knock the second grate open. He climbed back up the shelf, nearly fell off the unsteady furniture, then regained his balance and used both hands to grip one end of the hole in the ceiling and swing his legs into the other end. It wouldn't have been a problem at all if both of his arms had been fully functional. As it was, his left arm gave out, and he found himself hanging by his legs. By that time, the German soldiers had nearly broken the door down, but all the sit-ups and pull-ups Peter had done during recovery from his last set of war wounds now proved beneficial. He swung his good arm up and managed to slither through the hole just as the door's hinges gave way.

The lights surrounding the complex had been turned on, casting alternating shadows. The view from the roof would have been extraordinary, but it was still raining far too heavily to see more than a few yards beyond the base's fence. Peter hardly noticed the rain, focusing instead on survival. He located the side of the compound nearest the beach and dropped from the roof.

By this time several dozen guards were roused. Most of them were heading into the front of the building Peter had just left, but some of them were patrolling the fence that surrounded the base. Peter crawled on his stomach the twenty-five yards to the troop housing, glad the rain masked his movements. Although he'd planned to avoid the barracks, the shadows at their base now seemed a safe haven. Out of breath, Peter paused in the darkness, lying on the soggy ground next to the barrack wall, hoping his pulse wasn't really as loud as it sounded in his ears. Looking back, he could make out dark silhouettes walking along the roof he had crawled from moments before. Getting out of their sight by crawling to the other side of the barracks was fairly easy. He stayed low and stuck to the shadows of the building.

His movements were glacial. He longed to escape from the compound as quickly as possible, and he knew if he was late getting to the ship, Ducey would leave without him. Still, Peter felt stealth was necessary for the present. Fortunately for him, the soldiers were sleepy and confused—most of them didn't know what they were looking for.

On the other side of the building, not quite fifteen yards from the fence, Peter spotted a thick electrical cord fastened neatly to the side of one of the light poles. Silently he unsheathed his knife and brought it up to throwing position in his good hand, thinking he could sever the cord and extinguish the lights. Then he could make an unseen exit. Peter was no expert in knife throwing, and it missed the cord by two inches, embedding the blade firmly into the wood instead. This time Peter did curse; he was running out of options.

Two patrolmen were walking along the fence, coming toward the shadow Peter was hiding in. *They'll see me when they pass,* Peter thought. He racked his brain, trying to think of a way to distract them, but the best idea he came up with was throwing something in another direction to divert their attention from his location. He searched the ground for a rock or a stick, but he only felt wet grass and mud.

Peter mentally cataloged his choices and checked his pockets: he had the book, his Colt pistol, an empty knife sheath, and his clothing. He couldn't find his lock-picking tools—they must have fallen out when he'd escaped to the roof. Peter knew he couldn't throw either of his shoes; he'd have to run like an Olympian to make it over the fence and to the beach. He couldn't get rid of the book—it had to be destroyed, or the lives of Allied agents in northwest Europe and the lives that depended on their knowledge would be in grave danger. The empty knife sheath was thick canvas and wouldn't make much noise, nor would any of his clothing. He didn't want to get rid of his pistol, small though it was, but he was desperate.

He spotted a patrol of four soldiers coming from the other direction. He didn't have enough bullets to fight them all. He fleetingly wished he were back in his tank in Northern Africa with his turret aimed at a Panzer rather than here on the northern coast of France with his little handgun aimed at six guards who each carried rifles or submachine guns. He wouldn't survive that shootout.

The shot he'd made earlier had been the first time he'd used his Colt in combat. Peter sighed, quickly unloaded it, and threw it and the bullets over his head so they landed on top of the building. They made enough noise that the soldiers heard them over the rain. The patrols both turned to the building and ran to the other side. One patrol ran along the west side of the building; the other patrol ran along the east side.

The moment they were out of sight, Peter sprinted north to the fence and jumped as high as he could. The chain-link fence was eight feet high; he still had a bit to climb. The top of the fence had three strands of barbed wire, but fortunately, the strands were similar to the type used to make cattle fences instead of the more dangerous razor wire the military normally used. Favoring his left arm, Peter reached the peak of the fence, found handholds without barbs, and swung his legs over just as someone saw him. The barbs caught his shirt and tore into his skin, but his weight was enough to free him as he dropped to the other side. Peter fell to the ground, hitting his left arm in the process and sending a new wave of pain through his body.

He winced. But what alarmed him far more than the pain was the sound of German soldiers rushing toward him; a few shots kicked up mud on the ground just behind him. Peter stumbled through some low-lying bushes and weeds, away from the fence and the shouting patrolmen. About a dozen yards beyond that was a steep hill that sloped down to the beach. He ran as fast as he could toward it—an eight-month-old ankle wound preventing him from achieving the speed he'd once been capable of—but he reached the crest of the hill just before the compound's pillbox-encased machine guns opened to full fire. He slid down the hill, below the guns' firing level, and made his way onto the sand.

He gritted his teeth to hold back a groan of pain and made sure the code book was still in his waistband. His hands were shaking, but the code book was there. So were a dozen new scratches, scrapes, and bruises. Peter headed for the rocks, knowing they would give him partial protection from the eyes of searching soldiers. He saw the headlights of several military jeeps about half a mile down the beach coming toward him from the east. It was too far and too dark for him to see how many troops were in them, but they drove slowly and shined lights into the rocks. Two other jeeps were headed toward him from the opposite direction, and a third, also heading west, appeared to have just passed his current location. They too were making careful, slow searches.

Peter found his dinghy and dragged it to the ocean, navigating his way through the maze of man-made obstacles. His arm ached horribly; it had felt like it was being torn off on the slide down the hill. He stumbled over the sand, tripping first on a piece of wire then on a boulder. Even the wet weeds clung to his legs as if they were part of a conspiracy to prevent his escape. He struggled to get the dinghy into the water, fighting against the frigid waves and his own fatigue. He reached chest-deep water a few minutes later and crawled into the boat. Peter was wounded, exhausted, frightened, and cold, but he was also on a strict time line. So he began to row, and despite everything, he kept going.

* * *

About one hundred kilometers to the east, in the Calais harbor, a man known as Pierre waited in the storm. He watched his contact, Philippe Laroux, arrive in the dark alley between two warehouses, close enough to the harbor that they could hear the rain hitting the water. Laroux was right on time for their rendezvous.

"Pierre?" the lanky Frenchman whispered.

"Right behind you," Pierre answered.

Laroux turned around, a look of surprise on his face. "They told me you would appear like a ghost, but I didn't believe them."

"Do you have it?" Pierre's voice probed.

"Yes. You know how to use the device?" Laroux asked.

"Of course. I only lacked access."

Laroux was holding the object in his hands: a limpet mine. "And you know the ship?"

"Yes," Pierre answered confidently. "The *Umsicht*. I watched her sail in this evening. She is scheduled to unload her supplies at the dock tomorrow morning."

"What is she carrying?"

"Munitions, mostly."

Laroux paused before continuing. "You are well informed."

Pierre nodded.

"Do you know what we went through to get this?"

Pierre could guess, but he didn't interrupt.

"My team and I broke curfew and risked execution to make the supply drop a success. We held up flashlights to alert the plane that it was passing over the right location then worked all night to hide the supplies. Then yesterday I was told to bring the mine to the harbor and assist a stranger with a sabotage assignment." Laroux lifted the mine to look at it more closely. "We have gone through considerable risk to retrieve this and smuggle it into Calais, so I must ask, Pierre, what is your vision for postwar France?"

Pierre knew enough about Laroux, even though this was their first meeting, to assume the man wanted to hear something about the end of both Fascism and Capitalism. "A France with no Nazis," Pierre replied.

"A return to how things were before the war?" Laroux asked.

"Not necessarily. "

What do you believe in, Pierre?"

Pierre chose his words carefully. He knew Laroux was the chief coordinator for a Communist cell with five other members. Most of their work was what they called "technical matters": secretly printing and distributing pro-Communist and anti-Fascist literature. They had only recently been asked by a member of the regional Communist party to cooperate with SOE contacts in sabotage activities. Pierre had no plans to join the Communist party, but he didn't want to offend them. For now, they were a useful ally. "Liberty, equality, and fraternity." Pierre hoped the slogan would ease Laroux's mind. If not Communist, it was at least revolutionary. "Does anyone on your team know how to place the mine?"

Laroux looked away. "No."

"Then may I have it?"

Laroux nodded. "Would you like me to keep lookout?"

"Please," Pierre was already removing his shirt and shoes. The rain was cold, and the water in the harbor would be even colder. But this was not the first time he had attached a limpet mine to a ship and blown it up. He could tolerate the cold water well enough. He carefully studied the explosive device Laroux had handed him. It was the same type he had used two weeks ago on a similar assignment. The mine didn't weigh much, and its buoyancy was such that Pierre would be able to easily handle it in the water. There was a timed fuse, and the mine was magnetic. He would stick it on the ship's hull about two meters below the waterline. He planned to set the fuse for an hour and be far away from the harbor when the *Umsicht* blew. Pierre tied a rope around the mine so it would be easier for him to tow out to the ship.

"You don't mind the rain?" Laroux asked.

Pierre almost laughed. The rain had long ago penetrated his clothing, soaking through to his skin. "I would be wet anyway. The rain will make me harder to see and harder to hear." Pierre noiselessly slid into the water with the mine, leaving Laroux behind as he disappeared into the dark, rainy night.

Pierre had lived near Calais his entire life, and he had grown up swimming in the ocean. One August, when he was twelve, he'd told his younger sister he swam all the way to England and back. It had been a lie, but she had believed it and reported his story with pride to their father. His father hadn't reprimanded Pierre for dishonesty; he had simply told him he should never lie to flatter himself. Pierre had thought it strange at the time; his father hadn't told him to avoid lying, only to avoid lying for the wrong reason. Years later, he'd learned his father had been a spy during the Great War of 1914–1918. Espionage and sabotage were in Pierre's blood.

His muscles cooperated easily, remembering the motions of how best to swim in open water. Pierre knew he would be a little sore the next day, but that wouldn't matter. Sore muscles were a small price to pay for the opportunity to anger the occupying army. The storm made the water choppy, and for every five feet forward, he felt he was pushed two feet off course. He slung the rope holding the mine over his left shoulder and under his right arm. Working with the mine was dangerous, he knew. If the explosives were agitated too much or if the quality of the workmanship was substandard, the mine would go off even without a fuse. The limpet mine was not large, but a premature detonation would put a quick end to Pierre's sabotage work.

He reached the *Umsicht* after about twenty minutes of swimming. He knew there had to be at least one sailor standing watch, but he could see no one. He was also confident no one could see him. He set the fuse and attached the mine to the hull in about two minutes, just as he had planned. Twenty-five minutes after that, he was pulling himself out of the water and accepting a blanket from Laroux.

"Will I see the ship explode?" Laroux asked.

Pierre was still breathing hard from the cold, the exertion, and the thrill of accomplishing something dangerous. "The explosion will take place underwater. You won't be able to see it—not at night, not in this weather." Pierre studied Laroux carefully and decided that perhaps he could, after all, stay to watch the *Umsicht* sink. Laroux would want to have an eyewitness account to give his comrades. Knowing what their efforts had helped accomplish would be their only reward. "There is an empty room in the top corner of this warehouse. If you have binoculars, we should be able to detect panic on the ship's deck. If we're lucky, some of the ship's cargo will ignite and we'll have ourselves a little fireworks display."

Laroux nodded, looking pleased, and handed Pierre a thermos of lukewarm liquid—it wasn't really coffee, but it was the closest thing a French civilian could get in wartime France—and the men entered the warehouse through a window to wait for the mine's detonation.

* * *

Peter was thoroughly worn out and dizzy when the starboard side of Ducey's fifty-foot-long ship came into view. Peter guided the dinghy to the side of the ship and tried to reach up to the railings, but it was difficult in the choppy seas. The slickness caused by the rain and the waves did little to help. He tried once more, failed, and decided to ask for help.

"Hey, Ducey! I could use a hand." Seconds later, a hand reached over and gripped his right hand, and then a second hand came down and grabbed his wounded left arm. Peter grunted in pain and tried to jerk away, but the grip was too strong. Despite Peter's movement, the hands continued pulling him up onto the deck, and the process sent horrible undulations of pain through his body.

"Wrong arm. Let go, or I won't be able to do anything with it for—" Peter didn't have time to finish before he'd been set down face-to-face with a very large, brutal-looking man. He had stubble on his cleft chin, and on his faded green-gray feldwebel's uniform was the emblem of the swastika. He was a beast. He didn't let go of Peter's arm; he pulled him over the railings and squeezed even harder. Peter gritted his teeth to keep from crying out in anguish, and his silence took every ounce of self-control he possessed. *Where is Ducey?* Peter thought as he stared up at the Nazi soldier.

After what seemed like a very long time, the feldwebel loosened his grip slightly as he spoke to someone out of Peter's sight and turned, bringing Peter around with him. There was another German soldier there, a teenager, by Peter's estimation. Peter caught the younger man's name, Himmelstoss, but didn't understand the German instructions. Peter's eyes didn't linger on the second soldier, however, because sprawled on the deck was Captain Ducey. Peter couldn't see his face, but he knew Ducey was dead. His neck was bent at an odd angle, one Peter had never before seen that portion of the human body take on. *The work of German nightmare number one*, Peter assumed. He looked back at the second soldier, who looked slightly ill. Peter concluded that the second man was either seasick or he didn't like the sight of Ducey's neck. Peter didn't blame him; Ducey's neck hurt him more intensely than his arm did.

The large German drew out his Mauser, stepped back, pointed it at Peter, and threatened him in German. He wiped Peter's blood from his hand onto his pants. The younger soldier frisked Peter and discovered only the book and an empty knife sheath, which he handed to his superior.

Himmelstoss then proceeded to tie Peter up, tying his hands together at the wrists then his upper arms to his chest. Peter thought that perhaps the young German soldier was not a vindictive person because he avoided putting a rope across the bullet hole in Peter's arm. Next he directed Peter to a chair, tied his legs at the knees and ankles, and tied his torso to the chair. Peter didn't struggle. He had no doubt he would be shot if he resisted. The look in the feldwebel's eyes hinted that at even the slightest provocation, he would execute his prisoner and feel no remorse.

Peter watched Himmelstoss check his work, which was quite secure. Then Himmelstoss stepped away from Peter and away from Ducey's body, drawing out his own handgun as he did so. He didn't point it at anyone. He just held it and looked pale and worried. Peter noticed the worried expression, and it confused him. He felt well cornered; surely his captors had nothing to worry about.

The older soldier spoke. "You and your friend have caused us a great deal of trouble." He spoke nearly perfect British English. "A pair of English spies. I hate spies, and I hate the English."

Peter thought about telling him that his few English ancestors from his father's side of the family had all left England before the rise of Napoleon but decided instead not to talk at all. He had said only a few things in English and thought perhaps he could still convince his captors he was French. British and American commandos were generally executed when captured. French Resistance men were usually treated the same but were expected to have less information worth teasing out during the predeath interrogation. Peter didn't consider himself a coward, but he still didn't want to be tortured.

Peter was grateful for his decision to remain silent as the feldwebel continued his rant. "The only thing worse than an Englishman is an American. I prefer to kill Americans on the spot. They ought to mind their own business and stay out of Europe." Peter believed the threat and held his tongue rather than point out that Germany had been the one to declare war on the United States. The man bent himself at the waist and brought his face down so it was level with Peter's. "What is this book, and who are you? You will tell me these things, or I will break every bone in your body."

Peter hoped he wasn't serious.

"Say something!" the Nazi yelled.

Peter took too long thinking through what he should say and which language he should use, so his interrogator kicked his chair over. Peter fell on his bad arm, and pulses of pain shot up and down the left side of his body. Milliseconds later his head hit the deck with a crack, causing bright lights to swirl across his eyes. Peter shook his head to clear the lights away, but he couldn't move much. Then the waves picked back up, causing the ship to rock up and down. Peter's head spun, and his stomach lurched. He wished he were anywhere but on the ship.

"Answer me," the huge German demanded.

"What do you want me to say?" Peter asked in French.

The man's face grew red as Peter's French words reached his ears. Peter momentarily worried he would be shot out of frustration. He didn't get shot, but he did get kicked, hard, in the chest. It knocked the wind out of Peter. While he struggled to fill his lungs with air again, the two soldiers had a small conference in rapid German; then the younger one took over the questioning.

The large German picked up the chair, with Peter still tied to it, and slammed it down onto the deck so it was once again sitting on all four legs. Himmelstoss spoke awkward and slow French. He repeated the questions about the book, which was now in his possession, and the questions about Peter and his intentions. Himmelstoss wasn't as bold in manner or in voice as the feldwebel, and Peter felt his situation grow ever so slightly less desperate.

He decided that if he didn't talk, their tempers would take over. "I am a member of the French Resistance. The English sailor and I have come to France to find out if there are sufficient troops at that compound to warrant an air raid." Peter spoke in French, so only the younger, less-intimidating soldier could directly communicate with him.

There was again a conference in rapid German.

"Why did you take book?" Himmelstoss asked in broken French.

"It looked like something good to read on the way back to England."

Himmelstoss translated Peter's answer to his superior, who was still standing behind the chair. The feldwebel didn't seem to like Peter's story. He slapped the back of Peter's head, grabbed his hair, and pulled his head back to face him. He muttered something in German that Peter didn't understand, but he assumed it was another threat to his life.

"Tell your name," Himmelstoss ordered in French.

"Captain Jean Valjean." Peter gave himself a promotion and blurted out the first French name that came to his mind. He waited for the translation and hoped that neither of his captors was a big fan of French literature. Then he asked a question of his own. "Why did you kill my associate?"

The young soldier was surprised at the question but was not experienced enough to recognize that he was letting his role as interrogator slip. "Your friend attack Feldwebel Keller. He hid, we came to ship, then he jumped on Keller; they fought. The feldwebel won." Himmelstoss turned to look at Ducey's body, and some of the color faded from his face.

"When did you get here?"

"Before you, ten minutes. We were on patrol and hear alarms, hear of spy. We got boat with motor and found your ship."

Peter inwardly cursed his slow rowing. *If I had arrived earlier, could I have prevented Ducey's death?* Rather subdued, Peter asked his last question. "What will you do with me?"

"We were to capture you, question you, bring you back to headquarters." Himmelstoss paused. "We were ordered to capture everyone, but Feldwebel Keller say one person enough to interrogate. He also say prisoner only needs to be half alive."

Keller broke in then. Peter wasn't surprised. Himmelstoss, at Peter's urging, was talking too much and not translating anymore. The younger officer nodded at Keller's instructions and was about to speak but paused, looking startled. A second later, Peter figured out why. The strong hands that had yanked Peter from his dinghy to the deck were now wrapped loosely around his neck. Peter thought about Ducey's mangled body and wondered if the enormous soldier standing behind him would obey his orders to bring back a live captive. The phrase *our prisoner only needs to be half alive* made Peter shutter. He wondered if Keller's taste for killing prisoners despite orders was the reason behind Himmelstoss's look of concern.

Himmelstoss spoke. "You will tell me why you took book, or Feldwebel Keller hurt you badly."

Peter thought desperately of something believable to tell him. "It is a list of compromised British officers and enlisted men who are giving information to the Germans." Peter sensed that Himmelstoss believed him. He also guessed that Keller found the lie plausible because he moved his hands from Peter's neck to his shoulders. His grip, however, tightened. He spoke to Himmelstoss, who then resumed translating.

"Now tell about your friend. Then we go ashore, and you talk with base commander."

"He's an English sailor. His job was simply to be the transportation." That was true enough. The young soldier translated, paused, and ran out of things to ask. Peter felt his time was running out; he knew his chances of escape were slim on the ship but even smaller on land. The prospect of talking with the base commander that he'd just stolen the book from didn't sound pleasant. The thought of spending the rest of the war rotting in a POW camp—or being executed—sounded even worse. Himmelstoss and Keller spoke to each other in German, and then Peter was cut free from the chair. The large feldwebel once again grabbed Peter's sore arm and pulled him to his feet. Then the German soldiers dragged Peter to the bow of the ship.

Tied to the front port side of the ship was a second dinghy, this one with an overboard motor. Keller released Peter as a gigantic wave and a powerful gust of wind hit the ship. With his legs and arms tied and not a single dry patch on the deck, Peter quickly lost his footing and fell. Fortunately, the fall bruised his pride more than his body.

Keller yanked Peter to his feet and yelled at Himmelstoss. The young soldier cut the ropes and retied them around only Peter's hands, leaving his legs free and cursing in German all the while. Keller shoved his prisoner to a sitting position against the wheelhouse cabin and threatened him with his Mauser. Then he left him in the younger soldier's charge and disappeared from view into the dingy. Another wave crashed onto the deck. Because Peter was sitting, he didn't fall this time, but the effect was worse on the dinghy, and the feldwebel did fall. Himmelstoss stepped away from Peter to investigate.

When Himmelstoss retied Peter he hadn't tied him very tightly. *Perhaps the boy's seasickness is catching up with him; he didn't cut off my circulation this time*, Peter thought. Himmelstoss had tied Peter's forearms together a little above the wrist. When he put his hands between his legs, Peter could pull the rope down to the narrow part of his wrists and, with a little help from his teeth, free his hands.

Peter kept his hands together as the young soldier turned around. "You jump down to our boat; no tricks, or the feldwebel will shoot."

Keller, however, was not in Peter's line of sight and would have to come back on board to be a real threat. Himmelstoss came toward Peter with his pistol in one hand and bent down to help him to his feet. He grabbed Peter's right arm to help him up. A swift, sweeping kick with Peter's right leg was all it took to knock the German soldier to the deck. A second later, Peter lunged on top of him and reached for his weapon. He wrestled the pistol away from him, rolled to the railing where Keller was waiting in his boat, and took aim. It was too dark for Peter to see where his shots hit, but he saw Keller fall.

Despite his exhaustion, adrenaline and the knowledge that he had a second chance of escaping kept Peter going. He turned to Himmelstoss, who was standing back up, his back to Peter, his hands raised slightly. Peter had every intention of killing him. He took aim, but then he paused. Peter started again—the pistol was ready to shoot, and his finger was tense on the trigger. But he stopped. Instead of shooting, he lowered the weapon and approached the cautious figure now turning toward him.

"Don't move," Peter said in French. With his attention still focused on Himmelstoss, Peter untied the German dingy from Ducey's boat and let the rope fall into the ocean. "Now, turn around and walk to the back of the boat." He kept his distance as he followed Himmelstoss, but the young German soldier didn't try to resist. Peter patted him down and made sure he had no remaining weapons. He did have a few spare bullets, which Peter took, and he also reclaimed the book. "You may step into the boat and leave. You will tell your superiors the feldwebel is dead, I am dead, and my ship is sunk."

Peter didn't know if Himmelstoss would obey the orders. Certainly the story would work to both their advantage. Peter wanted any search for him to end, and it was common knowledge that German soldiers who made mistakes usually received a quick transfer to the Eastern Front, where the German mortality rate was significantly higher than it was in occupied France.

Himmelstoss got in Peter's dingy, started rowing, and didn't look back. When he was out of sight, Peter went into the wheelhouse, found a match, and burned the book. There were other copies in intelligence headquarters; Peter knew the extra book in his possession was only a liability.

Mission accomplished, Peter thought. The code book was out of enemy hands and would remain that way. Now he just had to navigate the ship back to safety. Peter wasn't a sailor, but the ship was small, and Ducey had explained most of the controls to him on their voyage to France. Ducey had been teaching men how to sail for several decades, and Peter had been an avid student. *But he won't be teaching anymore*, Peter thought sadly.

Death was not new to him, and he had long ago learned how to push grief and sorrow aside in order to accomplish what he had to do next. It usually worked, at least until his memories returned as nightmares. As the ship moved away from France and back toward England, Peter had plenty of other thoughts to keep him busy. The sea was rough and getting worse by the minute, but Peter would have been willing to go through a hurricane to put some distance between him and Nazi-occupied France. The wind howled, his arm ached, and his exhaustion returned.

Peter was steering away from a ship to the west when a bullet whizzed past his head and flew into the glass window covering the front of the wheelhouse. The glass shattered, and seawater and rain splashed into the cabin. Wondering who could possibly be shooting at him, Peter dropped to the deck and drew his pistol. He was out in the open, so he rolled to the edge of the cabin, knocked over a thick steel table supporting a pile of navigational charts, and hid behind it just as another shot whizzed past his ear.

Peter still couldn't see his assailant. He slowly let out his breath, gathered his courage, and peered out from behind the table. He nearly took a bullet to the brain, but he finally saw who it was. Feldwebel Keller was standing just inside the doorway. He had two red splotches on his uniform, one on his upper arm and one on his shoulder. Peter's shots had not been as accurate as he'd first thought. *He must have climbed from the dingy back into the ship while I was getting rid of Himmelstoss and starting the engine.* Peter knew such an effort must have worn the feldwebel out, but he had never doubted that his opponent was tough, determined, and resilient. Peter noted the look of triumph on Keller's face now that the Nazi soldier again had the upper hand. He raised his gun and aimed for Peter just as a wave crashed onto the deck and water swirled around his ankles. His shot hit the table. "Come, little spy," he said in English. "It's time for you to die."

Peter ignored the remarks and the seawater soaking through his clothing. He checked the weapon in his hand and found it had only three bullets left. Quickly he loaded the two extra rounds he had taken from Himmelstoss and readied the pistol. Another bullet hit the table. Peter wondered how much ammunition Keller had. *More than you do*, Peter silently answered himself.

Peter peered over the table. Keller got a shot off that barely missed, and Peter fired off a round in return. Peter heard a grunt of pain from the German. *Not a fatal shot, but it was closer than his,* Peter thought with a bit of relief.

He took a deep breath and looked out from behind the table again. Once again, both men shot, and this time both hit their respective targets. Peter had hit the man's ribs. Keller's shot grazed Peter's temple, nicking his head and causing rapid bleeding but not injuring him seriously. Another shot hit the table, making Peter's nerves jump. Peter ventured another shot and hit his opponent's leg. Keller fell to the ground, and his next shot went wild.

Peter seized the opportunity and aimed at the Nazi once again. Keller was sitting with his body propped against the cabin door, too injured to support himself. Peter tried for Keller's head and missed. The storm heaved the deck up and down, making accurate shots difficult. Peter was starting to feel considerably light-headed as rain thinned the blood that ran into his face and blocked his vision. He had only one round left. Peter wiped the blood, rain, and sweat from his eyes and forehead and gambled a quick look. The feldwebel was on the ground but sitting up. Keller took a shot, but it missed high. Peter's vision was starting to blur again, this time because of blood loss; he knew he had to hurry. He aimed squarely at Keller's chest, right at his heart.

Peter's shot hit its mark. The German feldwebel fell to the deck and lay motionless. Peter hadn't realized he was breathing hard, but now he gasped for air. He rested with his back against the desk for a moment, breathing deeply, then decided to make sure his opponent was truly dead this time. He tried to stand up, but he was too weak. Instead, he crawled toward his enemy; Keller really was dead. Out of curiosity, Peter checked the status of the man's arsenal. His pistol had only two bullets left, but his pocket was full of extra rounds.

Peter crawled up to the wheel and checked the compass. He was heading nearly due north. Just as he breathed out a sigh of relief, the engine shuddered. Peter nearly cursed when he saw the fuel gauge. The tank was empty. He tried to check the other gauges, but he couldn't see them. He wiped the blood from his eyes but still couldn't see. He was losing consciousness and losing it fast. He ripped another strip of fabric from his shirt and pressed it to his head, but even that took extraordinary effort. He shook his head to try to clear it but only received a fresh wave of dizziness and pain. Everything was turning gray, and his peripheral vision blurred and then was gone. He could no longer see anything, could only feel intense pain and exhaustion. A few seconds later, he collapsed on the deck, and his consciousness faded completely.

* * *

Pierre was not his real name, just one alias of many. The man was certainly not a Communist—rather, he fully expected a war with the Communists as soon as the Fascists were defeated, a war in which he would be an active participant. His real name was Jacques Olivier, and he returned to his farmhouse east of Calais at about 0300 hours. He took off the glasses he had worn to the rendezvous with Laroux and removed the waterproof putty material he had on the end of his nose. Both were simply part of a disguise that would prevent Laroux from recognizing him unless Jacques wanted to be recognized. It was one of his more frequently used disguises, though Jacques had dozens of others he could just as easily employ when the need arose.

The house was dark, as it was supposed to be. He carefully checked the barn, the cheese cellar, and the bottom floor of the home before going upstairs to his bedroom. A light still glowed in his sister's room across the hall from his own. He slowly turned the doorknob and opened the door.

His sister, Genevieve, was asleep, lying on top of her blanket. An oil lantern burned on her bedside table. Beside the lamp was an old Enfield MK1 revolver. She normally kept it hidden under the false bottom in the table's single drawer, but something must have made her keep it out tonight. The revolver had been a gift from an RAF pilot several years ago. His Spitfire fighter had crashed not far from Calais, and he had been unable to use the revolver himself; he had broken his arm during the crash. The pilot had meant the gift as a show of chivalry and gratitude after the Olivier siblings hid him from the Nazis. He had a daughter—only a few years younger than Genevieve—and he wanted the young French girl in the war zone to be able to defend herself.

There was a need for the weapon, perhaps even more now than there had been at the time. Genevieve was nineteen. She still looked younger than her age, but in the last six months, she had begun to look less like a girl and more like a woman. Her skin had cleared of freckles and other imperfections, she'd developed a few small curves, her hair had darkened, and her cheeks had colored a little. The Olivier farmhouse was at times a safe house for Allied airmen or SOE commandos. Jacques noticed how the men followed her with their eyes. They no longer offered her weapons; now they offered her chocolates or wildflowers. Jacques had taken a few of them aside to make sure they understood she was off limits. He was a small man—five feet, seven inches high, and rather skinny. Still, he could be intimidating. The commandos usually understood his message quickly.

More disturbing to Jacques was the way the German soldiers watched her. *Heaven help the man who tries anything,* Jacques thought. Concern for his sister in their very dangerous world often kept him up at night. He was glad she had a revolver but wondered if it would be enough. *And what will happen when she returns interest?* Jacques didn't want to think about that.

Sighing, he adjusted the wick in the lantern on Genevieve's table until the flame disappeared.

"Jacques?"

"Yes, sorry I woke you."

"Did you sink it?" she asked sleepily.

"Of course." The memory of the ship blasting into an inferno flashed through his mind. The secondary explosions had thrown out enough light that Jacques had seen them through the rain, even without binoculars.

"You should have let me come. I could have helped."

Jacques knew that was true. She had assisted him in the past with his sabotage projects, and she would have been useful as a lookout at the harbor.

"I was working with someone new. I don't trust him yet." Jacques admired Laroux's skill—and appreciated his access to explosives. He doubted Laroux had any Nazi sympathies, but as they'd sat in the warehouse, Jacques had noticed that Laroux had seemed prone to bragging. One word to the wrong person . . . and he might as well be a Nazi agent. In addition, Laroux considered himself a Casanova and was rumored to visit the local brothels quite regularly. Jacques had no desire to introduce someone like that to his sister.

"You don't trust anybody," Genevieve said.

"You're exaggerating."

"Only a bit."

"Good night, little sister." Genevieve was accurate in her accusation; Jacques trusted very few people. The pattern of their conversation was familiar. Genevieve always offered to help, sometimes insisted on it. Jacques usually found a way to exclude her—not because she lacked the ability but because he was worried about her safety. Jacques sighed again and left her room, glad his sister was too sleepy to argue.

* * *

A few hours later, Peter awoke to the sound of a ship's horn. His head ached and so did his arm. He slowly rolled over and pulled himself to his feet, unsteadily stepping through the door of the wheelhouse. It was still mostly dark outside—the eastern sky was light, but the sun had not yet risen above the horizon. Peter could tell that the sound's source was a vessel larger than the one he was on and that it was heading toward him, but he couldn't make anything else out. He bent over the dead German, took his Mauser, and reloaded it. His head swam as he shuffled onto the aft deck and knelt down out of obvious view. Peter might have compared the feeling to a horrible hangover, multiplied by influenza, but he had never been drunk so he couldn't be sure.

This is ridiculous, he thought. *An injured, half-conscious agent armed with a single dinky handgun against an entire ship and her crew.* Peter tucked the pistol into his belt and weighed his options of surrendering or swimming the English Channel. The ship was closing in, and he knew it would overtake him soon. He thought seriously about jumping overboard but knew he wasn't accomplished enough as a swimmer to make it to the shore beyond the horizon, especially in his current state. And so he waited and worried. As his anxiety rose, he suddenly saw the most beautiful sight he had ever seen—his country's flag. *By the dawn's early light,* he thought. *Is this how Francis Scott Key felt when he stared across Baltimore Harbor?*

Peter waved his right arm as energetically as he could. As the ship cruised closer, he realized it wasn't a large ship, just a patrol craft, but size didn't matter to him. He went into the wheelhouse to hold Ducey's ship steady as the patrol craft pulled beside it. A smiling, redheaded captain jumped onto the deck, followed by a few other navy men.

"Are you Private Eddy?" the captain asked, looking at the dead bodies on the deck and at the blood Peter knew was smeared on his face and clothes.

"That's me, sir." Peter gave a sloppy salute and broke into a grin. "Boy, am I glad to see you guys."

"We've been keeping our eyes out for you the last few hours. My name is Captain Flanney." He extended his hand, and Peter gave him a weak handshake. "I was going to debrief you, but I think you'd better see our corpsman instead. I do need to ask you one question first: was the item you went after destroyed?"

Peter nodded but instantly realized his mistake. Dizziness flooded his head, and gray patches clouded the edges of his vision again. He reached up to hold his head, and the captain put out a hand to help steady him. But Captain Flanney had grabbed Peter's left arm, and the resulting flash of pain was enough to send Peter back into oblivion.

Chapter Two
Unpleasant Places

April–May

THE NEXT THING PETER REMEMBERED was waking up in a hospital. At first, all he could see were bright lights. He thought briefly that he might be in heaven, but he didn't think heaven smelled like disinfectant. *And if I were dead, I wouldn't be hungry.* His eyes gradually focused on a nearby nurse. His throat was too dry to talk, but she noticed he was awake.

"Welcome back," she said. "We were wondering when you were going to finally wake up." She helped him sit up and brought him some soup.

Sitting up made Peter realize his head still ached a great deal, and steadying himself with his hands confirmed that his arm was still injured. He ate about half his soup but couldn't finish it. The food slowed the pounding in his head, but Peter would have preferred it to halt completely.

He realized the nurse was speaking to him again and looked at her more carefully. She was a pretty girl with blonde hair, blue eyes, and perfect teeth.

". . . no damage to any of your tendons, but do not expect to get out of bed for at least ten days," she finished.

Peter let out a scornful huff. He didn't like hospitals, and he certainly didn't plan on staying in bed for that long. "How long have I been here?"

"A day and a half," the nurse said before hurrying off to the next patient.

As far as hospitals went, Peter knew this one wasn't bad. It was a real building rather than a tent—a nice upgrade from his last hospital. His fellow inmates looked like they were in stable condition, so unlike his previous stay, he thought he would be able to sleep without being awakened by moans or shrieks of pain. Large windows on both sides of the long room let in plenty of light, and it looked and felt clean. Though it was a nice hospital, it was still a hospital. Peter's last hospital stay had been in Sicily after a German shell hit his tank and it caught fire. He felt like he'd just barely gotten back to his full physical strength about a month before Switchblade. And now he was back in bed again. He was glad to be alive, but he'd had his share of hospital recovery time, and the thought of ten days in bed was a dire one. The windows let in bright, cheerful sunlight, but Peter's mood was black and stormy.

* * *

Peter's mood was marginally better the next day when Captain Knight of the OSS came to get a more detailed account of what had transpired during Operation Switchblade. Captain Knight was accompanied by a private, and together they wheeled Peter's bed into a separate room where no one would be able to hear their conversation. Knight directed the private to take careful notes of everything Peter said as he related all that had happened since he'd set sail with Ducey. When he finished, Captain Knight told his assistant to read the notes back to Peter to ensure everything was written accurately.

"Pity you didn't bring Himmelstoss in. German prisoners can sometimes reveal useful information," Captain Knight said.

"Sorry, sir. I should have thought of that," Peter said, not wanting to describe the powerful feelings that had barely prevented him from shooting Himmelstoss. "But having him aboard could have led to complications later."

Captain Knight nodded and told Peter he could consider himself debriefed. "Switchblade is closed," he said. Then Knight warned—threatened—Peter to keep all that had happened secret, and after that, Knight and the private wheeled Peter back to his original location. Peter saw them speak briefly with the doctor on duty before they left. He found the whole debriefing a bit melodramatic. *But I am a relative novice at the spy business*, he thought to himself.

Peter had reached two conclusions the day before: he wanted to become better at throwing knives, and he wanted to learn German. Knife throwing was not an option at the moment, so Peter asked one of the nurses about getting some German books. The next day, Captain Knight sent an English-to-German dictionary and an old, well-used high school German textbook. It gave Peter something to do when he wasn't sleeping.

* * *

Laroux collapsed on the floor of his cold, damp cell. *Maybe they'll give me a break now*, he thought. But Obersturmführer Prinz and the other Gestapo guard who had beaten him for the past two hours showed no signs of stopping, even though he was no longer physically capable of standing. Laroux held out a little longer and then caved.

"I'm ready to talk," he gasped.

"What was that?" Prinz's voice was deceptively smooth.

Laroux repeated himself. "I'm ready to talk." As he said it, he was stunned by how different his voice sounded. His throat had swollen from the beating he'd received, and he was now missing three teeth.

"Fine. Tell me who your contact is with the regional Communist party." Prinz squatted to put his face just inches from Laroux's. He ran a hand through his blond hair, which had fallen out of place while beating his prisoner.

Laroux didn't want to give that information away. Instead, he offered something he thought the Gestapo would find just as useful. "I'm supposed to meet with the man who sunk the *Umsicht* at four o'clock this afternoon. I was going to give him some detonators."

Laroux watched the interrogator's face. Laroux could tell that knowledge of the man responsible for sinking the *Umsicht* was tempting, but he wasn't sure Prinz believed him. *How can he not believe me? I was arrested with nine detonators, and I've nearly been beaten to death.* Prinz pursed his lips, twisting them to the side. Then he checked his wristwatch.

"Where?"

Laroux gave him the address. It was the basement of a little house near the town center.

"Name of the contact?"

"Pierre—that's all I know about him."

Prinz jerked his head at the other guard, and they were gone.

Laroux had no idea what time it was. He felt bad giving Pierre away, but he couldn't handle the pain any longer. *I'm too weak*, he confessed to himself. He knew that when the guards came back they would ask him for his regional contact again. If he gave that name away, it would be devastating to the cause. But he knew he wasn't strong enough to resist the torture anymore.

This was the first time he had been left alone since his arrest. His hands were shackled in front of him, but he could reach the collar of his shirt. He broke a few threads and fished out what he was looking for: an L-pill. The *L* stood for lethal. He put the pill in his mouth and hesitated for a moment. He knew if he lived, he would eventually betray the cause. Then he would probably be executed or sent to a camp that virtually guaranteed his death. Even if he survived the war, he would have no future in the party. He would be known as a traitor and a coward. Laroux decided it was better to die as a hero than live as a traitor, so he bit the pill, breaking the capsule and releasing the poison.

* * *

Jacques Olivier pulled out his pocket watch again. Laroux was seven minutes late. Jacques was eager to get the detonators, but his gut told him something was wrong. *You can steal detonators from the Nazis,* he thought to himself. He had done that before, many times, but he preferred the quality of British and American explosives to what he could round up from the German Army. Jacques closed his watch and decided it was time to go.

Jacques left the small home's basement and began walking away from the little neighborhood. Then he paused and darted across the street, where he hid in the second story of an apartment complex to see if Laroux showed up. Laroux never came. Several other men did.

Schneider, Prinz, and six guards, Jacques thought. *Laroux didn't know I'd be that important to the Gestapo, did he?* He watched the Gestapo surround the building he had exited only a few minutes before. He removed his glasses but kept the putty on his nose. He no longer matched the physical appearance of the man Laroux had known just in case Laroux had given the Gestapo a description of him. Nor would he look quite like Jacques Olivier. He made sure his pace was unhurried and unsuspicious as he exited the back door of the apartment building, a street away from the Gestapo roundup.

* * *

Hauptsturmführer Schneider was angry that they had missed Laroux's supposed appointment. And he was even more furious when he was informed of Laroux's death. He'd been working up to the day's arrests for weeks. Schneider had received a lucky break when his most trusted agent posed as an eager Socialist and then reported on one of the Communist's attempts to recruit her to the party. She had been introduced to another party member, and then the Gestapo had carefully tailed those two men until they led them to the other four members of the cell. Schneider had postponed arresting any of them until he could identify all of them. The last member, Laroux, had been discovered just that morning.

Schneider had ensured that all six of the Communists were arrested that afternoon, within hours of each other, before anyone could be warned. Schneider was familiar with how the Communists organized themselves. Philippe Laroux was the leader of the cell he had just captured, and he was the only one with ties to the regional party. Schneider had planned to use Laroux to get to others more important than he. Now Schneider was once again up against a dead end. *Unless this Pierre shows up next week for his follow-up appointment.* That was the pattern most of these groups employed: if the contact missed the first appointment, they were to try again at the same place exactly one week later. Somehow Schneider doubted that would happen. He would make arrangements, just in case, but he held little hope that the day's arrests would remain a secret. Pierre would no doubt be warned off. All of Schneider's work would produce only six prisoners, all relatively unimportant political dissidents who posed little threat to the Nazi empire.

"Find out who searched Laroux when he was put in his cell," Schneider commanded Prinz. "Tell Standartenführer Tschirner I want the man demoted and transferred."

"Yes, sir," Prinz replied. Tschirner outranked Schneider, but neither of the men doubted that Tschirner would fulfill the request. Tschirner was just as vindictive as Schneider was. He too would want severe punishment for such a serious oversight.

* * *

Peter had been in the hospital for four days when he received two letters, both in the same envelope, both from home. The first was from one of his sisters. Peter had one older brother, Robby, and three younger sisters: Pearl, Ruby, and Opal. Of his sisters, Ruby was his clear favorite. They both seemed to see the world the same way. Growing up, they had always gotten into trouble for the same reasons—mostly for talking during church, having a smart mouth, or teasing another sibling too much. The two of them also looked more alike than any of their other siblings. Both had dark brown hair and eyes to match, just like their mother. The rest of the Eddy siblings had varying shades of light brown or blond hair—more like their father— and they all had blue eyes. Peter had grown up working and playing more with his brother, but when it came to finding new ways to tease their sister Pearl or coming up with pranks to play on the neighbors, Ruby was Peter's favorite co-conspirator. Since he had left home, she had become his most faithful correspondent, and despite the distance separating them and the length of time since they had seen one other, the war had actually brought them closer.

Dear Peter,

I hope you are doing well. How is your ankle? Have you met General Eisenhower yet? I'm glad you're not on the front lines anymore, but I still worry about you being stuck in an air raid. Everyone says the air raids in London aren't as bad as they used to be, but I don't believe them. I think they're only saying that because you're stationed there.

Life at home isn't all that different. Pearl's got a job as a telephone operator. She's part time right now, but she'll go to full time when she graduates next month. She buys a new dress every other week. They're all beautiful. I've never seen a closet so full, and I can't borrow any of them because she's so much taller than me. Despite my name, I'm green with envy. I'm sure you can imagine what Dad says every time she walks in with a new dress. He's still just as frugal as ever. Mama just rolls her eyes. I haven't figured out if the eye motion is about Pearl's spending habits or about Dad's reaction.

Mama and Opal are doing well. Well, Mama cut her hand with a kitchen knife yesterday when we were all peeling potatoes. She had the dull knife, so the cut's not too deep. I think Opal was more worried about it than Mama was. By the time you get this letter, she will be all healed.

Dad's busy with the farm and with Church stuff like normal. Uncle Pete and Aunt Anne-Laure are the same as always. Little Owen has decided he wants to be a pilot and bomb Tokyo. Well, this week it's Tokyo; last week it was Berlin. The war better not last the thirteen years it will take him to reach enlistment age! Opal and I both like our classes. Well, I don't like my English teacher, but other than that, school is fine. Opal is looking forward to the summer, but I'm not. Next year Dad thinks he will hire some extra help around the farm. But this summer I guess I'll have to be his field hand. Yep, that's right. Pearl gets to dress like a movie star, Opal gets to help Mama and Aunt Anne-Laure with the housework, Owen gets to pretend he's a pilot, and I get to be a trusty field hand for Dad and Uncle Pete. One more reason I miss you! Do you think you can win the war in time to help with the harvest?

Take care of yourself, and buy me something beautiful from London!

Love, Ruby

Peter smiled at his little sister's letter. He'd already bought her a Waterford crystal vase, and he was confident she would love it. Ruby was a bit of a tomboy, but she still liked pretty things: butterflies, daisies, hair ribbons. Peter paused after reading the letter, feeling a mix of guilt and amusement that his family thought his new job was relatively safe. Peter had been working on General Eisenhower's staff, but he had given up his desk job about a week ago. *Only a week ago?* He sighed. A lot could happen in a week.

All the nurses in the hospital wing were busy with other patients, so Peter had time to reminisce about life on the farm. He had left Idaho more than two years ago, and things had changed. Ruby and Opal had both entered high school; Pearl was about to graduate. The trying economic conditions of his childhood and teenage years seemed to have improved, and his aunt and uncle no doubt still doted on their only child, little Owen, but he was no longer the toddler Peter remembered.

Peter picked up the next letter, expecting it to be from his mother, but instead, it was from his father, Robert Eddy Sr. It was the first letter he had written to Peter since he'd left home. Peter's mother often wrote to him, and she usually signed her letters, "Mom and Dad," but Peter recognized her handwriting and knew who was really writing. The rather messy handwriting on this letter, however, was clearly his father's.

Peter's mind wandered back to December 8, 1941. He'd just returned home from joining the army and had gone into the kitchen for some lunch. He hadn't felt like eating breakfast that morning, and his hunger had finally caught up with him. Halfway through leftovers—none of the family had eaten much the day before, and most of their large Sunday meal was still in the refrigerator—Peter's father had come in and asked him where he'd been all morning. As farming went, December wasn't so bad. Peter had finished his chores before he'd left, and his dad had just been curious, not mad—yet.

Peter had grinned at his father and finished chewing before replying. "I joined the army."

Peter's father had been about to pour himself a glass of milk. He'd set the pitcher down hard on the counter and turned around. "You did what?"

"I joined the army."

"The army?"

"Yeah, they were the ones who could take me the soonest. I looked at the navy, marines, and the air corps, but the army had the soonest reporting date. Seth Jensen was going to report the week after Christmas, but he broke his arm, so the recruiter gave me his spot."

Peter's father had taken a deep breath before speaking. "I know you're upset that Hawaii was attacked, but making a decision about this without consulting me or your mother—"

Peter had cut his father off. "Yeah, everyone's angry, but I seem to be the only one doing something about it."

"Your brother might be alive; they don't have a list of survivors out yet."

Peter had shaken his head. "I wish I could believe that." Peter's older brother, Robert Eddy Jr.—his hero since he had learned to walk—had been a sailor on the *USS Arizona* when the Japanese had attacked. The family wouldn't receive the telegram confirming the bad news until a few days later, but ever since the attack Peter had been expecting the worst. He'd stood up and started walking out of the room. Leaving the kitchen without cleaning his own dishes was a minor felony in his mother's home, but Peter hadn't wanted to talk to his father anymore.

"Peter, what about your mission?" His father had served a mission to New England. So had Peter's brother. They'd even served in two of the same towns. Peter had been planning on serving a mission too, much to the pride of his father—but Pearl Harbor had changed things.

Peter had continued walking out of the kitchen.

"Peter, I'm not done talking to you," his father had said louder than he'd needed to. Peter had stopped, but he hadn't turned around as he heard his father continue. "Do you know how much we've all sacrificed to save up money so you could accept a mission call?" He'd been right, Peter had realized. The whole family had contributed to his mission fund, and Peter had been working full time on the farm and part time in town, restocking the shelves of the local grocery store every night for years to scrape together the money it would take. Even his older brother had sent money home for that purpose since he'd joined the navy. Bob had grown up with the local stake president and had been certain he could get Peter a recommendation to serve. "I can't believe you would put warfare— revenge—above serving the Lord. I raised you better than that."

"Joshua, both Gideons, and both Moronis were warriors," Peter had countered, "and I can't remember you ever saying anything bad about them." He and one of his friends had brainstormed scriptural warriors on their way home from the recruiting office because Peter had been expecting a heated discussion with his father. Peter had paused and turned around then. His father's blue eyes had glared back at him. "They aren't going to issue mission calls to men of draft age until the war is over anyway." That piece of logic had had no effect on Peter's father. "Look, I already signed. I'm old enough that I don't need your permission."

His father's face had turned bright red. Peter had never seen him so angry, but he hadn't been about to change his mind. Peter had waited for his father's temper to explode, but Bob had caught himself and managed to calm down. He'd walked past Peter and left the house. But right before he'd slammed the front door, he called back one final question. "Did you even pray about it, Peter?"

His father had been late for supper that night and barely spoke to Peter the rest of the week. His guess had been right: Peter hadn't prayed about his decision to enlist. He hadn't even researched which branch of the military would be best for him. Something inside Peter had known his brother was dead, and he'd been angry at the Japanese for doing it and angry at God for letting it happen.

In hindsight, Peter realized that anger toward the enemy had proven useful over the ensuing months and years; anger toward God had proven foolish and counterproductive. Fortunately, it hadn't lasted long. Peter hadn't spoken to God for about five weeks—from the time he woke up and said his morning prayers on December 7 until more than a month later at basic training. The day had been physically demanding. It had also been the first day in Peter's life—as far as he could remember—with no potatoes served at any of the day's meals. While growing up, he had often complained that potatoes were all the family ever ate, but for some reason, the strange lack of them had made him miss his family and the farm. Tired, homesick, and finally humble enough to admit his stupidity, Peter had found a quiet place and prayed for forgiveness.

Beginning that day, Peter had tried to be good. He always said his prayers—though, truth be told, sometimes while half asleep and rarely while on his knees—and he read his scriptures often—though not quite every day. Naturally he went to church on Sundays—as long as he could get permission from his commanding officer and find a nearby branch. Peter knew he was still short of perfect when it came to spiritual things. He had, however, managed to avoid the biggest pitfalls of military life: drinking and womanizing. His uncle Pete had warned him to avoid those. Coming from the man he was named for—his uncle, a war veteran, his bishop, and one of his bosses on the farm—Peter had listened.

Peter had, however, fallen into one common soldier's vice—in his first three weeks of military service, he'd picked up a mouth as horrible as any he'd ever heard before he'd joined the army. Two years later, he was still trying to break the habit. He had nearly succeeded, but things still tended to slip out in high-stress moments. Three weeks to form a bad habit; at the rate Peter was going, he figured it would take three years to break it.

Peter and his father had settled into an uneasy truce after Peter had joined the army. They'd both stayed busy and worked on different parts of the farm when at all possible. His father had shaken Peter's hand when the family had dropped him off at the train station. Everyone else had given Peter a hug. Six months after joining the service, Peter had written his father a letter, apologizing for their argument. Peter's father had never responded.

Since joining the army, Peter had experienced a few missionary moments, despite being a full-time soldier instead of a full-time missionary, and he'd shared those with his family. Peter had explained his belief in the Word of Wisdom to countless servicemen when he'd traded the cigarettes that came in their rations for chocolate bars or packs of gum. Peter also felt confident that his friend Lewis Lee would have joined the Church had circumstances been different. They had both been in the same company in Africa. Lee had given up smoking and borrowed Peter's Book of Mormon every day for three weeks straight. Lee hadn't survived the battle of Kasserine Pass, but Peter tried to comfort himself with the thought that at least Lee had known a little more about God when he went to meet Him.

His father usually replied to Peter's letters by having Peter's mother write something for him—one of his mission stories, an update on the farm, a scripture for Peter to look up. Peter still couldn't figure out if his father's inclusions were meant to chastise or encourage. Curious to find out what his father had written in his own hand—and a little nervous— Peter opened the letter:

Dear Peter,

Your mother cut her hand with a kitchen knife. She will be fine, but writing hurts her for now. I know I always have her write—she's so much better at it than I am. I never got the education she did. I want you to know your mother and I pray for you daily. We encourage you to stay close to the Lord in the path you have chosen. Since you were little, you've always wanted to choose your own way. Even though I named you after my brother, I never expected you to be as stubborn as he is. Well, maybe I should say determined instead of stubborn. Lucky for

you and for your parents, you've never made any really awful choices. I'd also like to thank you for the money you have been sending home. It was very needed at times. Now things are looking up for the farm. Our debts are finally paid. We are grateful for the help you gave but no longer need it. Your mother tells me to write that you should look for a nice girl to spend it on. I personally think you should save it for college, if you still want to go when the war ends. Should you want to farm, your uncle and I will, of course, welcome you as a full partner. Your mother wants me to write that she loves you. I love you too.
Dad

Peter read the letter over again a few times, surprised at its contents. For the past twenty-nine months, he had assumed his father was still angry with him for joining the army. After Peter's injury in Sicily, he'd been given the choice to stay in the army and do office work or be honorably discharged and go home. Thoughts of his father's continuing anger had been a strong factor in Peter's decision to stay. After more than two years of thinking his father still hadn't forgiven him, it was good to know he had been wrong. Peter looked past several rows of hospital beds toward the window. The morning had been overcast, but the sun broke through the clouds as the afternoon progressed. This time, as Peter gazed out the window, the weather mirrored his mood. He was grateful to be alive and grateful to have a loving family supporting him from half a world away.

Later that day, Peter convinced one of the nurses to let him get out of bed. She was a little hesitant, but he convinced her he was improving. He walked around the room, and it wore him out completely but didn't stop him from doing the same thing again a few hours later. It took Peter longer to heal than he would have liked, but he was out of the hospital three days earlier than the doctors had predicted. He was assigned to a nearby army base for the rest of his convalescence. While there, Peter continued his study of German and was finally able to master the skill of throwing knives at electrical cords and other small targets.

Chapter Three
Operation Sinon

Saturday, May 27

A FEW WEEKS LATER, PETER WAS ordered to report to Colonel McDougall, a man he had never before heard of. He arrived a few minutes early to the office located in an old London warehouse not far from the River Thames. After waiting outside the colonel's office for a few minutes, he saw the door open and someone exit. The man was wearing clothing that didn't fit, and he was smallish in stature. His hair reached beyond his collar, and his beard was nearly as long but not as thick. Both were gray. Peter was about to mentally dismiss the civilian as a common old man, but then he caught sight of the man's eyes. They were golden brown, and something about them gave Peter the briefest impression of a hardened and determined soul.

A voice asking him into the office broke Peter's musing. He promptly entered and took in his new surroundings. The office was not large, and it was dimly lit. A single, uncovered lightbulb hung from a cord in the center of the room's ceiling. There was a large window on the wall opposite the door, which would have allowed in enough light to illuminate the room, but the window was dirty and looked like it hadn't been washed for at least a decade. A bit of light made it through, but Peter couldn't see what was beyond the glass. Floor-to-ceiling cabinets hid two of the walls. Each cabinet had a sturdy lock. In the room's center was a plain rectangular table made of wood. The top of the table was the only part of the room not covered with a thick layer of dust. Instead, it was covered with piles of paper. There were four chairs around the table; two of them were occupied.

Peter examined the two men sitting at the table. The one who was facing the door behind the makeshift desk appeared to be in his fifties. His hair and mustache were neatly trimmed. The hair on his head was dark in color, but his mustache was infused with gray. His haircut suggested he was a member of the armed forces, but he wore civilian clothing. His shirt was well pressed, with the upper button undone and his blue tie loosened accordingly. He wore dark brown slacks, and a matching suit coat hung on the back of his chair. The other man, who sat off to the side, was much younger. He wore thick glasses and the uniform of a lieutenant in the British Army.

The man in civilian clothing raised an eyebrow in inquiry.

"Excuse me, I'm looking for Colonel McDougall," Peter said.

"You're speaking to him." The man had a noticeable but well-educated Scottish brogue.

Peter immediately saluted.

"At ease. I assume you are Lieutenant Eddy?"

"Yes, sir." Peter had been promoted two weeks previous.

"Well, Lieutenant Eddy, I commend you for your successful trip into France. I learned about your assignment while you were in hospital. I went looking for an old sailor named Samuel Ducey and was told he was gone. When I asked why, Captain Knight explained your mission."

"Did you know Ducey, sir?"

"We went back a few decades," McDougall replied.

"My condolences, sir. I knew him only briefly, but he quickly earned my respect."

McDougall nodded then moved on. "Ducey is not the first of my colleagues to perish, and his death is not the subject of our meeting. I know this building doesn't exactly advertise whom it houses. I am with the Special Operations Executive, currently assigned to work with the Office of Strategic Services; hence my familiarity with Captain Knight and his projects. Would you consider an assignment from our office?"

"Yes, sir," Peter said, somewhat surprised at his directness.

"Good, good." McDougall passed some papers to his uniformed assistant. "My office is pleased with the abilities you exhibited on your last mission. You certainly surprised the OSS group; they were not expecting you to return from France. You caused a great deal of confusion at headquarters." He chuckled. "But not to worry; they allowed another code book to be stolen."

"Excuse me, sir?" Peter hoped the shock and confusion he felt didn't show on his face.

McDougall laughed again. "Ah, perhaps you deserve a bit of an explanation." He looked down at his desk and stacked his papers as he spoke. "The code book you recovered was a fake. Knight's group was planning to use the code it contained to send out messages to scores of phantom agents. They'll use a new one now to give their pretend agents an assortment of orders that will not be followed but ought to create useful confusion for the Nazis. Rather exciting, really. False leads, mysterious agents that slip like banshees through their nefarious fingers. They felt they needed to send someone after the book to convince the Nazis it was of real importance. They didn't expect that the person sent after it . . . er, you, as it turned out, would be successful. They were surprised when Ducey didn't return on schedule. Everyone involved thought you would miss the rendezvous and Ducey would return to port alone. Instead, Captain Flanney picked you up.

"Of course, on the whole, I think it is better that you succeeded. The first time the code book was stolen, it was a clumsy job, one we were bound to notice. The second theft was more professional. Knight's group has not sent anyone after it, and most likely the Nazis will think we don't know it's gone." McDougall finished sorting his papers and looked up at Peter as if he were trying to read Peter's reaction to the news that no one had expected him to survive his first mission. "Sit down, Lieutenant Eddy."

Peter felt like he needed to sit down, so he obeyed and forced his lower jaw to meet his upper jaw. After what he had just heard, he wasn't sure if he should be angry or if he should laugh. Regardless, the story had stirred his curiosity.

"Are you still willing to accept another mission from us? I was not involved in the decision to send you on your first assignment, but that is only because I was preoccupied with other projects."

Peter was quiet for a few seconds, but a large part of him knew he wasn't ready to go back to manning a desk in the army's bureaucracy. "I suppose so, sir."

Colonel McDougall's face relaxed, showing relief. "You understand that everything I am about to tell you must never be repeated? Security breaches are punished swiftly and severely."

"Of course, sir," Peter replied.

"As you may suspect, we are planning to open a new front this summer."

"Yes, sir, everyone knows that. Even the Germans."

McDougall nodded then continued. "Yes, but as you also may know, an invasion of mainland Europe will not be easy. The coast of France is strongly fortified." Peter nodded, remembering the way the beaches had looked during his first mission. "Hitler's Fortress Europe will, I am afraid, cost the blood of many brave men to breach. Nevertheless, it must be done." Colonel McDougall stood up and walked to the window. He gazed out thoughtfully, as if he could somehow see the bloody assault being played out in the swirls on the dirty windowpanes.

"Our intelligence sources report that, as of last year, the commander in charge of the Western Front, General von Rundstedt, predicted that the main assault would be near the Pas-de-Calais. According to our best intelligence, most of the Germans still expect an attack on Calais after, or in conjunction with, several diversionary attacks. Currently, the Germans think we have twice as many men as we in fact do—enough for a massive invasion and a few sideshows. Unfortunately, we do not have enough manpower for any false assaults—just enough for the real thing. Our situation is really rather desperate. Our only hope is to convince the Germans that the main assault will come in Calais, and when we do begin our real assault elsewhere, our focus will shift to convince them that our initial engagement is just a ruse to distract them from the real thing.

"Unfortunately, General Rommel and a few other influential Germans are not completely convinced of von Rundstedt's prediction." McDougall paused and turned from the window. "We want them all—need them all—to be convinced that the main invasion will come in the Pas-de-Calais." He paused again and looked directly at Peter, who nodded his understanding. Peter immediately saw the genius of the plan—the Allies would convince their enemy that they planned to strike where expected, and while the enemy prepared for an invasion there, the Allies would surprise them elsewhere.

Colonel McDougall had Peter's full attention. "We're already having some success. There are more troops around Calais than in other areas along the coast. If we can get them to stay there for a few weeks—even for a few days—after the real attack, it might just be the edge we need to break through and begin the liberation of Europe. Then the end of the war." McDougall stopped for a moment, his face softening at the prospect of peace.

"We are currently getting information about our real invasion site from members of the French Resistance. Activity in that area is picking up, and someone in the German Army or in the SS is likely to take note. We would like to dramatically increase the activity around Calais—increase it enough that it overshadows all other activity. We've asked the Calais Resistance to increase their sabotage work, but we're not sure it will be enough. They are too few in number. So we want to send you in to help stir things up a bit.

"In addition, and more importantly for the purposes of your mission, we are aware that at least one of our sources in the city of Calais is working for the Nazis. When we do assault Fortress Europe, it will not be in the Pas-de-Calais. But it will be important to have accurate information about how the enemy is responding there—whether they have swallowed the hoax. The German Fifteenth Army is stationed near Calais. If they guess our ruse and reinforce the real front too soon, we might be in trouble. We need to know the moment they conclude there will be no invasion of Calais. We do not want a double agent reporting lies to us. We have the traitor narrowed down to three of our contacts, but beyond that, we don't know who it is.

"We want you to go to Calais and find out which of the contacts is confederate with the Germans. You are to contact each of our suspected double agents, tell them you are intimately associated with the plans for the coming invasion, and ask for their assistance. We are taking a gamble that the agent will risk his or her cover to bring you in. If the agent does not immediately try to capture you independently, we expect their Nazi handlers to make an attempt. When that happens, you will know which agent is the bad apple and which agents we can trust when we need them." McDougall stopped and looked at Peter.

"So I'm to be live bait?" Peter asked.

"Yes, but you will have support, so you shall not be captured. Your talents are impressive enough that we would like to retain you through the end of the war; you are not as expendable as you were a month and a half ago. Your task is simply to contact our agents. When one tries to bring you in, you escape, you allow them to escape, and they tell their Nazi bosses that American spies are snooping around Calais, asking questions about troop concentrations in preparation for the big invasion. Your mission is simple, effective, and quite safe. And, of course, under no circumstances are you to even hint that Calais might not be the real invasion site. If all goes as planned, your mission will be one more piece of evidence tying the Fifteenth Army to Calais, one thread weaving its way through all our other schemes, making the enemy think twice before sending the group elsewhere." McDougall paused, still watching Peter carefully. "Your mission will be called Operation Sinon, carried out as part of Operation Fortitude South. Have you heard of Sinon, Lieutenant?"

"No, sir."

"Sinon was the sly Greek that convinced the Trojans to pull the wooden horse into their city. After they built the horse, all the Greeks hid inside it or in their ships offshore and out of sight. Sinon remained alone on the beach. When he was captured and they discovered he was Greek, some of the Trojans naturally wanted to kill poor, crafty Sinon. He assured them he had been abandoned by his own army and that Odysseus had indeed been hoping he would be slain by the Trojans. Some versions say Sinon gave himself injuries so it looked like his abandonment was authentic. The Trojans spared his life, and he convinced them that the horse was an offering to appease the angry goddess of wisdom and cunning."

"Athena?" It had been awhile since he'd heard the stories, but Peter still remembered a little about Greek mythology.

"Yes, very good. Thinking that the horse would bring Athena's blessings to Troy if it were located within their city walls, the Trojans wheeled it in. I trust you know the rest of the story?"

"Yes, sir. I'm familiar with it. By night, the Greeks emerged from their hiding places and sacked the city. Troy was razed to the ground, and the Greeks won the war. But that was a long time ago, sir—if it really happened."

"Sinon's job was to convince his enemy that there was no danger, when, in fact, their doom lay waiting in the belly of a wooden horse. Dante assigned Sinon to one of the lower circles of hell for his trickery, but I admire him. Your task is to be opposite Sinon's. Instead of convincing the Nazis that there is no danger where an ambush awaits, you will try to convince them that there is significant, overwhelming danger where none exists."

McDougall paused and studied Peter's face. Peter looked back but didn't show any emotion. After a long minute, McDougall broke the silence. "I realize this is quite a lot to hear in a very short time. I have another urgent meeting to attend. I will be back in approximately an hour. You have until then to decide."

"Thank you, sir," Peter said, relieved that he would have time to think.

"Lieutenant Hatch."

McDougall's assistant stood and grabbed the files from the table. He unlocked a cabinet and put them away. Then Lieutenant Hatch followed Colonel McDougall out of the room, leaving Peter alone to contemplate what he had heard.

Peter was hesitant to accept the mission but not because it was dangerous. That didn't bother him. He had long ago accepted the possibility that he might not live through the war. Even as he enlisted in the military with five of his best friends the day after Pearl Harbor, Peter had been very aware of death, the fate of his brother fresh in his mind. He had enlisted partially to avenge his brother's death but knew that the same destiny might be his.

Just before coming to McDougall's office, he had received another set of letters from home. Ruby and his mother had both written to him. Peter was glad his mother's hand was healed enough that she could write letters again, but she had bad news to report. Lyle Morris's F4U Corsair fighter had disappeared somewhere over the Pacific Ocean. Peter and Lyle had been close friends since they'd gotten in a fistfight in the fifth grade. Lyle had said Peter had "girlie-thick" eyelashes, so naturally Peter had thrown a few punches—and received a few—before their teacher broke up the fight. After the two boys had escaped the multimonth groundings their parents imposed on them, they had actually started to like each other. The two had played baseball together for years, and Lyle had joined the navy the same day Peter had joined the army. Lyle had been the one to drive Peter to the nearest recruiting station, and he had helped Peter plan for the upcoming confrontation with his father. Lyle's death took the original gang of five friends from that December morning down to two.

Still, it wasn't the chance of death that made Peter hesitate. The prospect of being live bait to draw out a Nazi double agent made him nervous but not nervous enough to make him turn down the mission. What really made Peter uncertain was the fact that, on his previous mission, he had been told significantly less than the truth. In his mind, Peter put it quite bluntly: he had been spun a whopper. He'd been told that if the Germans possessed the code book, they would be able to set up meetings with vital agents all over Europe and trap them. But Colonel McDougall had just informed him that the intelligence officers in charge of the mission had *wanted* the Germans to obtain the code book. *My mission was just a trick to make the scheme a bit more convincing*, Peter thought. *I was just a throwaway agent*, the thought of being considered that worthless was tough to swallow. Peter had nearly died on a mission he hadn't been told the truth about. And Captain Ducey? He had given his life for a mission Peter suddenly didn't see the importance of. Ducey had been sacrificed by special ops so they could play a few tricks on the Germans that would cause some mild confusion. He felt betrayed and angry and doubted he could trust the OSS, the SOE, or Colonel McDougall.

Peter also wondered why McDougall hadn't told him where the actual invasion site would be. Was it just a precaution? He realized that for Operation Sinon to be successful, Peter didn't need to know the real invasion site. Perhaps a secret of that magnitude was told only to people who had a vital need of such knowledge. Still, he was suspicious. Was McDougall expecting Peter to be captured and interrogated? What if the invasion really was going to happen in the Pas-de-Calais, and McDougall was simply betting that Peter would break under torture and tell the Germans the invasion would come elsewhere?

Frustrated, Peter paced around the room. He couldn't see anything from the windows, so he looked more closely at the cabinets and realized Lieutenant Hatch had failed to turn the lock on the papers he had recently stored away. An oversight—or something more? Peter hesitated for a few minutes, carefully pacing to the other side of the room; then his curiosity got the better of him. He reached into the cabinet and pulled out a stack of files. He read the names on each folder: Fortitude North, Ironside, Zeppelin, Fortitude South, and Sinon. The first three names were unfamiliar to him. Peter opened the folder labeled Sinon and was surprised to find that it contained only two sheets of paper. The first page was a list of what the file should have contained: his own service record and information on four others named Olivier, Toussaint, Laurier, and Murat. The next page was the operational summary, which he quickly read. There was nothing there that Colonel McDougall hadn't already told him.

Next, Peter pulled out the thickest file of the bunch: Fortitude North. At first glance, it looked like it contained plans for an invasion of Norway from Scotland. There were maps, naval charts, and detailed lists of the German forces currently occupying the fjords along the North Sea. Then Peter read through a series of memos directed to British officers with radio expertise, asking them to postpone their retirement for another year and report to Scotland for a special mission. Following that were the instructions given to the elderly officers. They were to stay busy ordering thousands of skis from one another, arranging lectures from expert mountain climbers, and testing out new cold-weather gear, all within range of German listening outposts. Another page described the encoding method they were to use for their transmissions. Peter wasn't a cryptography expert, but even to him, the code looked rather elementary. The file went over details of Allied military units from the United Kingdom, the United States, Canada, New Zealand,

Poland, and several other countries, describing what their uniforms would look like, focusing on any identifying patches they could be expected to display. Then there was a list of several journalists—Peter couldn't make out if they were real or fictitious—writing from Scotland. He found newspaper clippings reporting football games—the British kind—between different divisions and a few reports of brawls at local pubs written by the listed journalists. Peter closed the folder with the conclusion that the Allies weren't really going to invade Norway, but they were doing everything in their power to make the Nazis think they were.

Partway through Ironside, Peter realized Colonel McDougall had been expecting him to read these files. Lieutenant Hatch had not left the cabinet unlocked by accident. The files contained information they wanted Peter to know but weren't supposed to tell him. Even so, they hadn't given him full access. Each of the files had been carefully picked through—the names of most staff members and the identities of key agents blackened out or missing. There were very few dates, and in some of the files, like Sinon, the table of contents revealed that more documents were missing than were present. Even so, Peter continued to read with great interest. Ironside was a fake attack by the Allies on the Bay of Biscay, Zeppelin a similar hoax in the Balkans.

Peter picked up the folder labeled Fortitude South. As he read, it became clear to him that the fake attack on Calais was the most involved of the schemes and the most important to the success of the real second front. He paused to think. The second front was critical—if it failed could another be launched? Certainly not in 1944. How much stronger would the German entrenchments along the northern coast of Europe be in another year? How many more people would die behind enemy lines if the assault failed? How many additional servicemen would die in the real attack with each month's delay? Too many.

Peter continued studying Fortitude South. The army had recruited Hollywood set builders to make the coastal city of Dover look like it was the staging ground for a massive cross-channel invasion. General Patton had been given command of the huge army preparing for the attack, but in reality, Patton's army consisted of a mere handful of men. Just enough information had been leaked to the right sources: ambassadors from supposedly neutral countries, journalists, loud-mouthed politicians, and known Nazi sympathizers. Peter also read through a list of code names for captured German spies. The agents had been given the choice to cooperate with the Allies or face serious consequences—sometimes a long prison sentence, usually execution. Through the turned agents, the British were feeding accurate information to Abwehr. The information was always dated or of little real use, but after several years, the Germans trusted the information they were being fed—including the new information warning them of a huge military build-up in Dover and the reports of an imminent attack on Calais.

It seemed that thus far, the Nazis were swallowing the hoax. General Rommel had placed his strongest army, the German Fifteenth, across the channel from the phony invasion force in Dover. The file also contained a telling map of northwest Europe. Peter assumed the map had been captured from the Nazis because the captions were in German. The map showed the estimated direction of the invasion: a straight line from Dover, through the Pas-de-Calais, into Belgium, and then on through Germany. Hitler's Atlantic Wall was being strengthened all along the French side of the English Channel, but according to reports from the French Resistance, the fortifications near Calais were being prepared with extra fervor.

Again, the file was missing half its contents. Peter had nearly finished skimming through the last page when he heard footsteps out in the hall. Though he was certain Colonel McDougall had wanted him to read what had been left behind in the files, he felt it might be awkward if he was still snooping through the papers when McDougall and his assistant returned. Reluctantly, Peter placed the files back in the cabinet. He was still standing when McDougall and Hatch entered. McDougall didn't immediately motion for Peter to make himself at ease. He opened the cabinet with the files and put a file of papers labeled "Eddy, Peter" back into the file labeled Sinon.

"Well, have you decided now?" McDougall asked after he had returned Peter's file to the mission folder.

"Permission to speak freely, sir?" Peter asked.

McDougall nodded his permission.

"Before I commit, I'd like to know if I've been told the entire truth about this mission." Peter said it as respectfully as he could, but he really didn't care if he was out of line. After Operation Switchblade and the confusion he felt about being expected to snoop through a stack of files he wasn't supposed to see, Peter felt his request was justified.

McDougall stared at Peter for a moment, as if he were trying to read him. Peter found McDougall's stare uncomfortable, but he met the colonel's eyes and did his best to remain impassive. "I can assure you, Lieutenant, that this time you have been told no lies. I will confess I have not told you everything I know. That would be unnecessary, and when a major invasion is in the making, the fewer people who know the details, the better. I myself am in the dark on many of the plans." McDougall sat in his chair.

"I apologize for my hesitation, sir," Peter said. McDougall studied him again, questioning him with his eyes. "I don't so much mind the danger, sir. I just don't care to be lied to, especially after my last mission."

McDougall nodded. "Understood. Are you willing to commit to Sinon?"

"Yes, sir."

McDougall motioned for Peter to be seated. "Hatch, go find Jacques." Hatch obeyed wordlessly as Peter sat on one of the wooden chairs.

"Your file says you are from Shelley, Idaho?"

"Yes, sir." Peter could tell McDougall had never heard of Shelley before, and he wasn't surprised.

"And you grew up on a farm?"

"That's right, sir."

"And you've completed high school but not college?" Peter thought he heard a hint of disappointment in McDougall's voice.

"That's correct, sir. Our high school was rural but had high standards."

"Tell me about your parents."

Peter complied. "My mother grew up in Logan, Utah. Most of her family still lives there. She graduated from college with a degree in English literature and couldn't find anywhere to work near her family, so she took a job in Idaho Falls, Idaho, and taught English for a few years at the secondary school. My father was born in Shelley; he's lived there on the same farm practically his whole life. They met at church, liked each other, got married, had five kids."

"It says in some of your early army files that you belong to a religious cult?" McDougall was trying to be straightforward, but Peter could tell he was slightly apprehensive that Peter's relatively unknown religion was going to be a problem.

"Growing up, sir, my parents took me to church, not to some weird séance."

"Yes, of course. I am not familiar with the Mormon Church, but it seems your commander during basic training strongly disliked it. SHAEF did not have any problems with your religion. I just want to make certain your faith will not have a negative impact on this mission."

"We're taught to obey the law, sir."

"But you were not drafted; you volunteered." McDougall leaned forward, resting his arms on the table.

"Yes, sir. I believe the scriptures teach that some things are worth fighting for. Freedom, family, and country certainly fall into that category."

"Yes, well, your religion doesn't seem to have affected you negatively in your past service," McDougall continued, evidently relieved to be moving on. "You drove tanks in Northern Africa and Sicily?"

"Yes, sir."

"Were you there for the amphibious landings in Sicily?"

"We landed the second day, sir." There were few days Peter remembered more clearly than that one.

"Difficult landing, carried out rather well. We expect our next amphibious assault to be much larger and much deadlier. Perhaps knowing what you now know, you can find it in your heart to forgive the officer who sent you to France with the expectation that you would be executed. When planning an assault that will have an estimated casualty count in the tens of thousands, one more death can seem insignificant."

"There were two of us, sir," Peter said, remembering Ducey. "But I do understand the stakes of the upcoming invasion."

"How did you get into special operations?"

Peter wondered where all the questions were going and concluded that McDougall was either just curious or simply trying to pass the time. "Circumstances, I suppose, sir. Between Palermo and Messina my tank got hit and caught fire. Stuff just started exploding. Most of my shrapnel wounds healed quickly, but the medics overlooked a piece in my ankle until a few days later. It took a long time to heal. I could walk but not very quickly. So I was reassigned to a desk at General Eisenhower's office here in England."

"How is your ankle now?" McDougall glanced down at Peter's feet.

"I walk normally. I don't run quite as fast as I used to. The medical staff told me I've healed as much as I ever will."

"Do you know General Eisenhower?"

"No, sir, not personally. I was an assistant to an assistant to an assistant in the G-2 Department of SHAEF. I've met the general once and seen him often. I don't think he would recall who I am."

McDougall nodded.

"At SHAEF I was often asked to make car repairs. Growing up, I learned how to fix tractors, so fixing tanks came pretty easily in the armored division, and SHAEF's automobiles . . . well, they were even easier. One day I was fixing a flat tire for Captain Knight with OSS. He came out of a meeting with Major-General Strong and said he needed someone for a job. Since my ankle felt fine and I was bored with fixing minor car problems and shuffling papers, I volunteered. I suppose in hindsight, he just needed a body to drop into France and didn't particularly care whose it was."

McDougall smiled knowingly. "That has been your only covert mission thus far?"

"Yes, sir."

"Strange that you should be recommended for this assignment with so little experience. But recommended you were—by someone I trust. I sincerely hope the luck from your first mission holds."

"Thank you, sir . . . May I ask who recommended me?" Peter inquired, not sure if being recommended was a compliment or a curse.

"Major-General Strong." McDougall's answer surprised Peter. Major-General Strong was General Eisenhower's staff member in charge of intelligence. Peter had been assigned to one of Strong's assistants. Though Peter had tried to do his best during his SHAEF assignment, most of his tasks had seemed rather routine. But Peter's consistent efforts on even routine tasks must have made an impression on the major-general. "Strong was infuriated that Knight took the best French-speaker on his staff and sent him off on such a reckless mission. Had you not returned, I think the major-general would have demanded Knight's resignation."

"I didn't know he thought so highly of me."

"Yes, well, he has made a career of keeping secrets, has he not?"

Before Peter could agree, Lieutenant Hatch returned. With Hatch was a civilian in his midtwenties. The man was slender and a few inches shorter than Peter's five feet, ten inches. His straight, light brown hair was combed away from his face and cut above his collar. His eyes were brown. As he entered the room, he smiled slightly, like someone with a secret.

"Lieutenant Eddy, this is the support we promised you," McDougall said.

"Just one man?" Peter asked, looking from the man to McDougall. Then Peter looked back at the newcomer. He was not smiling anymore. He was staring straight ahead with his hands clasped behind his back. Peter looked more closely at the man's eyes and had the impression that his innocent schoolboy looks were just a cover for a highly competent and highly dangerous person.

"With Jacques Olivier, you will only need one man."

Olivier grinned and met Peter's eyes. Peter extended his hand and discovered that Olivier's grip was firm.

"I've seen you before," Peter said.

Olivier merely raised one eyebrow in inquiry.

"You left the office right before I came in, but you were dressed as an old man then."

Olivier smiled, looking pleased to have been identified. "Yes, you're right." Peter thought the man's voice was surprisingly soft, like a tiger purring.

"Jacques is a member of the French Resistance in Calais," McDougall said. "He has helped at least ten airmen escape from France to England; four of them had been captured by the Germans. Jacques managed to rescue them and then send them safely on their way. I am sure he has fascinating stories about how he managed their liberation, but he has refused to tell me the details of those excursions, and the men themselves rarely remember much."

"We may want to use those routes again," Olivier said by way of explanation.

"Yes, I can understand that, but I most certainly would not inform the Nazis about your escape routes."

"We all have our secrets, don't we, Colonel?" Olivier said in reply.

McDougall sighed and shook his head slightly. "Jacques is also an expert at crossing the English Channel undetected. Luckily for us, he is on our side and still free. I don't know how he has escaped suspicion for so long."

"Few people realize they have seen me more than once, Howard."

"Oh yes," McDougall said, "Jacques is also a master of disguises. Rather remarkable that you recognized him. I never do. Yes, the two of you will be sufficient for a simple mission like this. Jacques knows the area better than anyone. He has just come over to England for a few days to describe the fortifications and troop stations in Calais. Tomorrow night he will sneak you both into Calais by ship, and with any luck, Lieutenant Eddy, you will be back in England before the first of June. I imagine by then Jacques will be up to something else, but perhaps he will be kind enough to point you in the direction of home when your mission is accomplished. Also, for the purpose of this mission, Jacques will outrank you."

That was the signal that the meeting was finished. McDougall stood up and made a motion with his hand toward the door. Peter stood then paused.

"Colonel McDougall?" Peter asked.

"Yes, what is it?"

"Who has jurisdiction over this project?"

"Does it matter?" McDougall's eyebrows scrunched together, and he tilted his head to the side.

"I'm just curious, sir. You're an officer in the British Army. I report to OSS."

"You ask too many questions, lad. But I am glad your mind is inquisitive. The invasion is a joint operation; nearly everything related to it is considered a joint operation as well. That, and we thought an American would draw more of the right kind of attention than an Englishman for this particular mission."

"Why is that, sir?" Peter still hadn't moved toward the door.

"Everyone has stereotypes of the other combatants. The Germans are less likely to expect the Americans to build a Trojan horse."

"I still don't quite understand what you mean, sir."

"You will find out," McDougall assured him.

* * *

After Lieutenant Eddy left, McDougall turned to Jacques. "Well, Jacques, what do you think?"

"I think he'll do. If the report of his last mission is accurate, he seems tougher than the last man you set me up with."

"Laroux?"

"Yes, he and his group of Communists were good at getting supplies, but I heard he only lasted two hours in Gestapo prison before he broke." Jacques sat down at the table and propped his legs up on a spare chair.

"It is hard to predict how a man will react to torture." McDougall joined Jacques at the table.

"Communists are weak, especially the city dwellers. I'm glad you've got a farmer for me this time," Jacques said. "Whatever happened to Browning? I'd gladly work with him again."

"Browning is working in Marseilles. Unavailable. And, Jacques, you really should stop being so critical of the Communists. We need the Red Army."

Jacques laughed. "Yes—as long as they stop in Berlin and don't continue on to Paris. But I'll let politicians like you manage that alliance." Jacques knew it wasn't completely fair to call McDougall a politician. McDougall had been very involved in the previous war, and little of his efforts had been from the safety of a desk. Jacques only knew what his father had done in the last war because McDougall, Julian Olivier's one-time partner in espionage against the Kaiser's government, had told him about it after his father had died in 1938. "I'm sorry, Howard. I shouldn't call you a politician."

McDougall sighed. "I didn't sign up to be a politician, but sometimes I think I am turning into one nonetheless. Churchill said there is only one thing worse than fighting with allies, and that's fighting without them. I fear he was correct."

"Then Sinon should be a success for you. A mission arranged by a Scotsman and accomplished by an American and a Frenchman."

McDougall grunted. "How are plans coming for the other part of Sinon?"

"Finished," Jacques reported. "Before I left France, I delegated the work to five groups, each of them assigned two days of the week. Starting tomorrow, something big will explode every day: a ship, a tank, a railroad car. On Mondays, Tuesdays, and Fridays, two targets should be destroyed. And you have other teams too, don't you?"

McDougall nodded.

"If the RAF can keep my teams supplied with explosives, they'll keep it up until the invasion begins, otherwise they'll run out of supplies the second week of June. If Eddy and I have time, we'll do something too, but either way, Calais is going to be a little busier than usual."

McDougall laughed. "I suppose I shouldn't be surprised that you've already sorted it out, but I would have expected you to keep more of a hands-on approach."

Jacques smiled. "I do love blowing up Nazi ships. But I want things to move independently while I get used to my new partner."

"I may have told Eddy too much; try to keep him out of trouble. I expect this mission will be simple, but if something goes wrong, be prudent and follow standard procedure."

"You had me blow up prudence, remember?" Jacques said, referring to the *Umsicht*. In English, the ship would have been called the *Prudence*.

"That sounds like something your father would have said," McDougall commented. "Have you told your sister about your father's war history?"

Jacques shook his head. "No, I don't want to give her any encouragement." Jacques knew McDougall didn't approve, but Julian Olivier himself had set the precedent of not telling his children about his past.

"How is Genevieve?"

"Alive and not in prison. That seems to be the best any of us can hope for at present. She wants to help the Resistance. Usually I find a reason to exclude her. She'd be safer here in England, I think."

"I could find somewhere for her to live, secure a job for her."

"She won't leave France," Jacques said. "Not unless a lot of things change." He leaned back in his chair and bit the inside of his lip. Besides, he suspected McDougall would get her involved in one of his missions should Genevieve come to England. And he didn't trust his sister to turn McDougall down if he asked for her help. He quickly changed the subject. "I don't suppose you'll tell me where and when the real invasion will come?"

McDougall smiled. "We all have our secrets, don't we, Jacques?"

* * *

That evening, Lieutenant Hatch gave Peter three papers. Each described one of the three agents he was to investigate: Charles Toussaint, Jean-Philippe Laurier, and Marie Murat. McDougall had larger files on each of them, but for security purposes, Lieutenant Hatch had selected only limited information about each person and typed it into a single-page statement for Peter's use. Most of the space recorded a summary of the information each agent had passed on, but each sheet also included some personal information.

The first page described Charles Toussaint. He was born in Calais in 1905. Both his parents had died of influenza before he was fifteen. Consequently, he'd moved in with his maternal grandparents in Boulogne-sur-Mer. After an extensive education in Paris, Toussaint had returned to Calais to practice law. He had never married. Toussaint had been supplying information to the Allies since January 1941. He claimed to be on excellent terms with the most educated German officers in the area and passed on any information he picked up while working and socializing with them.

Toussaint's reports did not come regularly but averaged about once a month. He sent his reports in letters to a friend in Paris. The friend delivered the letters to the Swiss embassy, and the information was then transferred to Switzerland, where it was delivered to the top case officer at the British embassy. Peter wondered how the reports were included in the letters so the Germans didn't recognize them, but Hatch's summary didn't elaborate. *Perhaps that is a secret between Toussaint and his friend*, Peter thought. Toussaint's method of reporting meant that most of his information was at least a week old but still highly valued by British intelligence.

Jean-Philippe Laurier, the second suspect agent, was born in Paris in 1893 and then moved to Calais in 1919 and married. There was little information about his childhood or his marriage. His wife died in 1934. His only son, Louis, was born in 1920 and disappeared in 1940. He also had two daughters. Both daughters were married; neither lived in the area. Laurier had been giving the Allies information since June 1940. Laurier owned a farm about three miles inland from the city of Calais. His travels into and around Calais gave him the chance to study German positions, and his reports were described as remarkably detailed.

Laurier made regular reports nearly every Saturday, weather permitting, by radio. Each week he sent the information from a slightly different location so the Gestapo wouldn't trace the signals. According to Laurier, the radio wasn't kept in his home. He moved it weekly from one place of concealment to another. Fortunately, the radio had not yet been discovered and remained in working condition.

Marie Murat had been born in a country estate to wealthy parents in 1919. Growing up, she'd attended a prestigious private school for girls and traveled throughout Europe during the summers. When she was sixteen, she had left her parents' home without their blessing and without their financial assistance. In 1939 she'd moved to Calais. She still lived there, one block south of German headquarters, and served as a waitress in a nearby café. She was not married and was still estranged from her parents. She had been supplying the Allies with information since May 1941—mostly what she picked up from German soldiers in the café.

Her reporting was also by radio. Most often, her information came in the morning before she began work. Her transmissions nearly always came from inside the city. According to the paper, her skills as a radio operator were considerable. Once contact was established, messages were transmitted quickly enough that there was little danger of the Nazis honing in on the signal. The report concluded by saying her reports were sporadic. Her handler in Dover once heard from her three times in the same week. At other times, it would be a month between signals.

Charles Toussaint, Jean-Philippe Laurier, and Marie Murat. As Peter drifted off to sleep, he wondered which one of them would very soon want him dead.

* * *

In the center of Calais, Marie Murat was finishing her shift at the café. Most of the patrons were gone, and the few who remained had all been served. As she began to wipe down the tables, Marie went through the few new people who had come into the café that day and mentally cataloged them: French, not a Nazi, too scared to do anything about the occupation; German officer, committed Nazi, but likely to give away information he shouldn't if it would make him look intelligent or prestigious; German enlisted man, uninterested in politics, glad to be in France instead of on the Eastern Front, unlikely to betray his country, equally unlikely to do anything beyond his basic duty; French, willing to work with whoever could help him maintain his profits; French, probably opposed to the Nazis, obviously suspicious, dimwitted, likely to be in jail by the week's end.

"Marie, a moment please."

She recognized the smooth voice without turning around. German, SS officer, devout Nazi, intelligent, efficient, ruthless. Obersturmführer Heinrich Prinz had been sitting with another SS man for the last hour, slowly drinking a beer.

"Another drink Obersturmführer Prinz?" Marie asked.

"No."

The answer didn't surprise her. Prinz came to the café often, and Marie knew his drinking habits. Prinz usually drank very little.

"That man over there," he said, pointing to the patron Marie had earlier labeled as suspicious. She glanced at him. He looked like a schoolboy; Marie figured he had barely started shaving. He looked nervous, though from his table, it was unlikely he could hear Prinz. "Have you ever seen him before?"

"No, I have not," she answered truthfully.

"How long has he been here?"

"About five minutes longer than you."

"Thank you, Marie."

"You're welcome, sir," she replied.

Prinz and the other SS man left then but not before arresting the suspicious young Frenchman. *He was probably waiting to meet someone, and his contact didn't show,* Marie thought. She felt sorry for him but also thought him foolish. *Don't get involved in the Resistance if you're going to be incompetent. Fools have no business trying to oppose the Reich.* The man should have left as soon as his meal was done. Instead, he had hung around waiting for well over an hour, looking rather conspicuous the entire time. The café was warm, but Marie felt a sudden chill. She knew enough of Prinz and his methods. She doubted she would ever see the young man again.

Chapter Four
Insertion

Sunday, May 28

PETER THOUGHT THE WEATHER WAS cool for May. But after thinking about the assignment he'd been given the day before, he concluded that it was his apprehension and not the temperature that gave him chills. He'd gone to church that morning before he'd had to report for duty then spent the rest of the day with Olivier going over documents, code phrases, and maps. None of the suspected agents were aware that the others were also reporting to the Allies. According to the information sheets, none of them socialized with one another, and none of them lived in the same neighborhood. They all spied in isolation from one another, and they all had other contacts. In every case, however, the majority of their contacts sympathetic to the Allies had been captured or had simply disappeared.

Olivier already planned to use his home, about six miles northeast of Calais, as headquarters. He had done that before with other assignments, and despite the risk, no one had yet been arrested at the Olivier farmhouse. Beyond that, the two men made few plans. There really weren't many to make. Peter would contact the agents, let them know he was an American seeking information about German forces in the area, and ask them for any information they had. Olivier would remain in hiding where he could easily come to Peter's aid when they ran across the double agent.

McDougall had promised them any equipment they wanted, but they packed lightly. Peter had a new Colt M1911 pistol and a new trench knife, both in waterproof coverings. He also packed a small pile of papers that McDougall had given him: mostly maps of the beaches and the city but also the addresses of the contacts and a few other things. All were wrapped in waterproof cloths. He grabbed a few changes of clothing, his serviceman-size Book of Mormon, and some rations. As he finished packing, Peter looked over at Olivier's pile: only a pistol and a duffel bag.

"What's in the bag?" Peter asked. Olivier showed him. The bag contained an American-made M1 rifle, extra ammunition, a bundle of French currency, some wigs, a few odd items of clothing, and an elaborate kit of make-up, glue, paints, loose hair, and other items one might want to help create a disguise.

"What's with the make-up? Want to look good for the Nazis?"

"The way I have managed to survive so long in occupied France is by blending in, remaining anonymous while I am working an assignment." Olivier closed the make-up kit. "Otherwise, I am the crippled son of a milkman. Everyone recognizes me and ignores me. My sister and I live on a small farm, and I only leave it once or twice a week. I don't get involved in anyone else's business, and they don't get involved in mine."

"I thought you knew the area . . ."

"I do." Olivier glanced at Peter with a smile. "As Jacques, I only leave a few times a week, but I leave quite often as someone else. It's amazing what a little make-up can do, eh?"

Peter was unacquainted with how much the right make-up could change someone's appearance, but he didn't confess his ignorance. His three sisters back in the States had still been too young and too poor to wear make-up when Peter had left, so he was skeptical about its usefulness until he remembered that Olivier had looked like a different person when Peter had first seen him exiting McDougall's office. Peter had recognized him later but only barely. He decided he would wait until he had seen a few more disguises before he came to a conclusion about their effectiveness.

"Don't you think we'll need something more than this? Just a disguise and a few weapons? Should we take more food or explosives? I only have a handful of extra rounds for my handgun. And maybe we should take some grenades, just in case."

"We have to travel light on the route we're taking. I have almost everything we need in France, including bullets for your .45," Olivier said.

"Everything except the make-up?"

Olivier ignored Peter's jibe and carefully began wrapping each item in multiple layers of waterproofing. His hands were steady and relaxed as he worked, as if preparing for dangerous assignments was routine. *Maybe it is routine for him,* Peter thought.

"How long have you lived in Calais?" Peter asked.

"My whole life." Olivier put the last item, his rifle, in his bag and placed it where he could reach it from his bed. He slipped his handgun under his pillow.

"So I imagine you know most of the people there."

"Not most, but many."

"Then why do they believe you're crippled? Surely you haven't been pretending to be a cripple your entire life."

"Not much gets past you, does it?" Olivier stretched out on his bed and put his hands behind his head. "Besides my sister and a few neighbors, everyone in France thinks I was injured in an explosion when the German Army began its occupation."

Peter nodded, his curiosity satisfied. Olivier spent the evening catching up on sleep. Peter spent the evening lying on his bed, but he didn't sleep.

* * *

Charles Toussaint knelt to survey his largest flowerbed. He pulled another weed then sat back when he found no others. He loved his garden. It wasn't at its best this year, but working in it still helped relieve stress. And this year there were many things aggravating the ulcers in his stomach. The war was not good for his legal business. He was keeping ahead of his bills but knew even a minor setback could cripple him financially. But as long as he had his garden, he had something good in his life, and he could live with the ulcers.

"I thought I might find you playing in the dirt."

Toussaint looked up and smiled. He liked Hauptmann Hans Wenders of the German Fifteenth Army. Wenders was well educated, honorable, and shared his love of flowers. Toussaint stood. "I would shake your hand, but perhaps I should wash up first. How was your leave, Hans?"

Wenders smiled. "I believe I have the most beautiful wife in all of Europe. I wish I could have stayed longer. I needed the break. Rommel is driving us hard to finish our fortifications before the Allies attack. The man won't be happy until every inch of beach is mined, from the Bay of Biscay to the North Sea."

"So you're not finished yet?"

Wenders shook his head and frowned. "Even if he gets all his mines and all his pillboxes, Rommel will find more to do."

Noticing the downward turn in Wenders's mood, Toussaint changed the subject. "And the tulips?"

Wenders smiled again. "The Dutch tulips were spectacular. I shall have some bulbs sent to you in the fall. In the meantime, in honor of my good French friend, I have brought some good French wine."

Toussaint laughed. "Then, in honor of my good German friend, we shall share it while listening to some good German music."

Toussaint led Wenders into his home. He let Wenders pick out a Wagner record while Toussaint went upstairs to wash his hands and retrieve two wine glasses.

* * *

At 2300 hours, Peter and his new partner left from Dover. The quickest, most direct route from England to France was the one between Dover and Calais, making it the obvious choice for a cross-channel invasion. Peter hoped his mission would succeed in making the Nazis believe the landing would come at the most logical location.

"You look somewhat distracted, Lieutenant. Something on your mind?" Olivier asked as they boarded the ship.

"I'm just remembering the last time I was on the English Channel," Peter said.

Olivier nodded and left Peter with his thoughts.

They traveled partway across the channel on a small patrol craft—a British vessel. Peter tried to talk to the crew about their past experience of dropping spies off in the middle of the channel, but the captain grunted, and the first mate just smiled. *Strong, silent types*, Peter thought, *with emphasis on the silent part.* The crew didn't get as close to the French shore as Ducey had. There were too many mines blocking the way.

The moon had already set by the time Peter and Olivier left the patrol craft. The two of them took a small boat with an overboard motor for the final five miles. Olivier navigated with a compass and flashlight. Each time he used the flashlight he was careful to conceal any extra light. Peter was grateful for the motor, but the ride was rough. The boat was only big enough for three people—or two people and their gear. It was a calm night, but even the calm waves were enough to make the little boat heave up and down, giving the men a saltwater shower. As soon as he thought he heard waves crashing on the shore, Olivier stopped the motor and handed Peter a pair of oars. They rowed, largely in silence, until they could clearly see the breakers.

Olivier carefully scrutinized the shore until he saw a faint light and smiled. "One of my neighbors left a light out for me. Quite often a German patrol will stop by and put it out, but occasionally the patrols get lazy and we get lucky. Louis was to set the light so it could be seen from the ocean but not the land. There is a hole in the cliffs—a cave you could say. The cave

is about a quarter mile east of the light. I used to play there when I was a
child. A couple years ago I decided it might be useful, so I dug it out a little
more. We'll hide the boat there."

Olivier directed the boat to the cave, and they rowed toward it. Near
the shoreline, they jumped out to pull the boat onto the sand. The beach
was deserted as they approached, or at least it was clear of people. But
large pieces of wood jutted toward the sea from the sand, standing in
unwelcome greeting to any troop transports that might try to land. Rows
of barbed wire crossed through the wood, across the sand, and into the
rocks. There was a lot of it, more than Peter had ever before seen in one
place. He looked around with a sense of foreboding. *I wouldn't want to be
an infantryman trying to take this beach,* he thought.

"There are land mines everywhere, so follow my lead," Olivier warned.
"My sister and I bribed some of the Serbian workers to skip small sections
of sand, but those sections are narrow."

With Olivier's warning, Peter allowed the Frenchman to determine
their path down to the inch. Olivier tied a rope to the bow of the ship and
pulled; Peter pushed from the back. The boat was heavy, but it was small
and manageable. The sand gradually turned to rock interspersed with
grass and weeds before reaching a short cliff that was the final transition
between land and sea. That was their destination.

Olivier pointed to a cluster of three large boulders then motioned
for Peter to help him move the second-largest stone in the group. It
was rounded and thin, so they carefully rolled it onto another rock that
prevented it from rolling out of control. They did the same thing with
another rock in the group. The last rock was too big.

"I've never been able move the last rock, but usually we can still get
the boats in. We'll want to keep the boat in good shape. Quite likely, it
will be your transportation back to England," Olivier explained.

They carefully maneuvered the boat onto its side so it would fit into
the narrow opening then pushed it into the hole and slid it back well out
of sight. Together they moved the two boulders back in front of the cave.
Peter grabbed some driftwood to help camouflage the cave, and Olivier
replanted a few weeds in the sand. Then Peter walked back to the waterline
and used his shoes and a handful of brush to soften the line in the sand
where they had dragged the boat.

After they were done, they moved from the open beach up the small
cliffs and into the cover of the grass, bushes, and trees. There, Olivier opened

his bag and checked his equipment. The wigs were slightly damp from all the sea spray, but his make-up and rifle were fine. Peter's equipment had similar luck: the clothes were damp, but the papers and weapons were dry. Olivier pulled an eye patch from his bag, placed it over his left eye, then pulled it down around his neck.

"My eye was injured in the same explosion that crippled me."

"So everyone remembers you and describes you as the cripple with an eye patch, and they don't take much notice of how tall you are or what color your eyes are," Peter said, recognizing the value of Olivier's disguise. "If they wanted to draw a picture of you or describe you to the Gestapo, they wouldn't recall much of your face—they'd just remember the patch and the limp."

"That's right. They remember the patch, not the person. And they don't recognize the same eyes peering at them as a salesman or a painter or a priest. Besides, if the occupying power thought I was healthy, they would have sent me to Germany to work in a factory years ago."

Peter was beginning to appreciate Olivier's methods. It was Jacques's eyes that had given him away to Peter the day before, but if the old man who had walked out of McDougall's office had been wearing an eye patch, Peter knew he wouldn't have noticed the tiger behind the eyes.

They followed a dirt road but stayed in the bushes and trees. It wasn't exactly the thick forest that would have been ideal for a stealthy entry into France, but there were enough trees and tall plants to hide in if they needed to. It wasn't pleasant for either of them to walk around in wet clothing at night. Peter's shoes were so wet he could feel the water sloshing around inside of them. His pants clung to his skin and seemed to rub in all the wrong places, but Peter reminded himself that it could have been worse.

They had walked only half a mile when Peter heard a motor. Olivier noticed it too. They dropped to the ground and cautiously peered at the road. The noise grew louder as a jeep with three German soldiers inside drove slowly by. The headlights were out, and they seemed to be looking intently into the trees. Peter wondered if the men had somehow found out about the mission. The car drove past them, and the noise faded then stopped. They heard the car doors open then shut.

"Did they see us?" Peter asked. *Surely they couldn't have seen us while we were on the ground,* Peter thought.

"No, they stopped at Marcel Papineau's home," Olivier replied with an edge to his voice. "Come on." He stood, grabbed his rifle, left his bag, and began to run. Peter followed. As they reached the home where the German vehicle was parked, Olivier motioned Peter to the side of the small house. There, Olivier loaded his rifle.

"Papineau is a member of the Resistance. He often shelters Allied airmen who have been shot down; his home is the last safe house before the channel crossing. But occasionally Papineau is too willing to trust potential recruits. I fear he may have made another contact who has turned out to be an agent provocateur. The Nazis will probably bring him and his wife out to the car and take them to their headquarters in Calais for questioning. But sometimes they like to perform interrogations away from their paperwork. If they come out with Papineau, we shoot the Germans before they get to the car."

"And if they don't come out?" Peter asked.

"We wait five minutes, then we go in."

Peter's handgun was ready. So was Jacques's rifle. A few minutes passed; it seemed like eternity. Then they heard a woman's scream. Peter looked to Olivier for orders. He cocked his head toward the back door, and they moved toward it. Olivier tested it, but it was locked. He fiddled with it and tried again, but the result was the same. He was about to kick the door in when they heard the screams again.

"Those screams came from the front of the house," Peter said. If the two wanted to maintain surprise, kicking in the back door was not their best option.

"Front door," Olivier said.

They ran around the house, and Olivier instructed Peter to take whichever soldier was farthest to the right. Then he kicked the door in. There were six people in the room. Peter shot the German soldier who had been holding his pistol to the temple of a middle-aged woman. Olivier shot the soldier on the left—apparently the man in charge; he'd had his rifle pointed at the remaining people in the room. And both Olivier and Peter shot the soldier in the middle, who had been whipping an old man.

The three bodies fell to the floor, and Peter calmly shut the front door.

"Jacques, you are once again a Godsend. Hélène was about to tell them you are the next house on the route." Peter thought Marcel Papineau looked to be at least sixty years old but realized the stress of the night's events could have made him seem older than he was. He was bald on the top of his head, and what little hair he had left along the side of his head was white. He was clean-shaven, and Peter thought his blue eyes seemed honest.

Olivier didn't smile, despite being greeted as a deliverer. "Marcel, I warned you to be more cautious with your recruiting. Now is not the time to be risky; we don't have time to prove new members. We just need to keep what strength we have."

"I didn't recruit anyone, Jacques, not today. I don't know how they found us. We were just trying to get this pilot to safety."

The pilot, sitting on the floor by Marcel, was American. His arm was wrapped in a sling, and there were several bandages on his legs. A large, bloody wound extended along the side of his head. He had sun-bleached, fair hair and injury-induced pale skin.

"What happened to you?" Peter asked in English.

The pilot focused on the English words. "I was shot down this morning," he said in a barely audible voice. "I landed in a tree and was stuck there for a while . . . and then I don't remember."

Peter switched to French and spoke to Papineau. "What has happened today?"

"This morning's raid lost several planes. I was out in the fields and saw one crash about a mile inland. I walked there and found one dead airman, and then I saw this one hanging in a tree, completely unconscious. I reached him at the same time another man did. He helped me cut the pilot down and bandage a few of his wounds. Then the other man said he heard a patrol coming and left. I hid with the pilot in a friend's barn until it was dark. The pilot woke up during the evening, but I speak little English, and he doesn't speak French. After dark, we made it back here by bicycle. The Germans have been searching areas near the crash site all day. I don't know how they found us here."

"Sounds like one of your friends was more interested in whatever the Germans were offering for the successful capture of an American pilot or Resistance member than they were in your safety," Olivier said.

"Or more scared of threats to their lives than of threats to ours," Hélène broke in. She was a pretty woman, despite the strain that lined her face. Her cheeks were tear-stained, and blood oozed from a small cut where the pistol had been pressed to her head. Her brown hair was glossy, streaked with gray, and at the moment rather disheveled. Peter thought she looked younger than her husband by about a decade. "Greed is not the only reason—indeed, not even the most common reason the Resistance is being betrayed. You can hardly blame even a patriotic Frenchman for selling out his friends if there is a Nazi soldier pointing a gun at his wife's head. You can't expect them to value the life of one Allied pilot over the lives of their family."

"Being alive under occupation is no life," Olivier said. "Today they had a reason to whip Marcel, but if they had wanted to whip him yesterday, they would have, even without a reason." Olivier examined the wounds on Marcel's back and the wounds on the pilot's head and arm. "You should leave tonight," he said to Papineau.

"But we can't find transportation that quickly. And our radio is broken. The Nazi you just killed found it when he found the pilot."

"Where were you hiding?" Peter asked, thinking that the house didn't seem big enough to have many hiding spots.

"Hélène and I were not hiding—we were in our bedroom on this floor when they came. We had put the pilot upstairs in the loft. We didn't make an attempt to hide him because his injuries are serious and we thought if someone did come, we would have time to warn him. There is a trapdoor under our bed that goes into a cellar. That is normally where we hide people, but the cellar has a half meter of water in it right now. The soldiers came in so quickly and quietly. I heard the car door shut, and I got out of bed. Then I opened our bedroom door, and there was a soldier there with his pistol in my face. He told Hélène and me to go into the front room, where his hauptsturmführer pig was waiting." Papineau motioned to the dead officer lying on the floor. "Then the third soldier came from the loft, dragging the pilot behind him. He had also found the radio and smashed part of it. Then the hauptsturmführer threatened Hélène and me and said one of us would die if he was not told the names of our Resistance contacts."

Peter watched Olivier think as he heard Marcel's tale. It didn't take him long to determine what needed to be done. "Marcel, you can use the boat we came in. I'm sure my new friend won't mind if we find a different way for him to return to England." Peter nodded his agreement. "We all need to leave. Someone will know these Gestapo thugs came here, and when they are missed, reinforcements will come to search. When these three are found dead, there will be little mercy for anyone still in this house. You have to leave now."

Olivier knew his way around the Papineau home. He grabbed a coat for Hélène from a closet, retrieved a compass from a drawer, and easily unlocked the complicated lock on the back door. "Eddy, will you help the pilot?" Peter slung the pilot's healthy arm over his shoulder and followed Olivier out the back door.

"Marcel, Hélène, we have to go now, for your own sakes." Olivier's request was forceful, and the Papineaus followed. Hélène was still crying as they walked out the door. Olivier turned to them. "And we must try to be quiet. Another patrol might come along at any time."

They journeyed back the way Olivier and Peter had just come. On the way, they collected their bags. Peter found out the pilot's name was Jonathan Walters and that he was from Mississippi, but he was badly injured and they needed to keep quiet, so Peter didn't bother him with too many questions. When the group reached the beach, they left Hélène and the pilot in the relative cover of the brush with their gear.

"So much for all the weeds we just planted, huh?" Peter said.

Half of Olivier's mouth pulled into a smile as he helped Peter move the first and second stones out of the way. Even with Marcel's help, getting the boat out of the hole proved more difficult than getting it into the hole had been, but the three of them managed to manhandle it until the boat was out of the cave and flat on the sand. Marcel and Olivier pushed the boat down to the water, and Peter went to get the other refugees.

"All right, one-way ferry to England leaving in ninety seconds," he said when he reached Hélène and the American pilot.

He helped Walters to his feet and instructed Hélène in French. She was calmer than Peter had seen her earlier, but she didn't look happy to be leaving her country. Tears still trickled down the side of her face. She bit her quivering lip as she looked back into the dark French countryside. "Hélène," Peter said gently. She looked up at him. "You'll be all right. With any luck, you'll be able to return before autumn."

Peter wasn't sure if she believed him or not; he didn't really believe it himself. But she managed to give Peter a half smile as she carefully followed him down the beach in the path Olivier had created with the boat.

Olivier helped load the three escapees into the small boat. He gave Marcel directions to keep the oars handy but to use the motor as long as it would work once they got past the breakers. He tied the compass to Marcel's wrist so it wouldn't get lost in the sea. Then Olivier and Peter kicked off their shoes and pushed the little boat into the channel until they could no longer touch the bottom.

"Marcel, don't start the motor for a while. Give us a chance to get on shore and off the beach. If the motor quits or if you run out of fuel, pace yourself. Row for five minutes, then rest for three. Try to keep this pilot alive so when you wash up on the English shore you'll have someone who can speak the language. Contact Howard McDougall with British SOE. Have the BBC announce you've made it safely so Genevieve and I don't worry. A verse from the Epistle of James. Good luck, my friend."

"Howard McDougall, SOE. A verse from James." Papineau repeated. "Good-bye, Jacques. See you after the war." But as he grabbed the oars and slipped them into the water, Peter saw fear in his eyes. Fear for himself, yes, but also fear for the young man he left behind. "Jacques, don't do anything crazy. Remember you can't win the war all by yourself."

Olivier laughed, gave the boat a final push toward England, and waded back to the beach. Peter followed.

"Well, nothing like a late-night swim to get the blood pumping," Peter said in an attempt to lighten the mood. Olivier didn't seem to be listening. They put their shoes back on, smoothed the path the boat had created, and replaced the rocks and driftwood so they covered the hole once more. As they tried to salvage enough weeds to camouflage the hole, Olivier stopped and gazed back at the sea. "Do you think they'll make it?" Peter asked.

Olivier sighed, and the two of them stood. "With a little luck. If the motor works for most of the journey. If they don't try to land in a highly guarded area and get shot by a nervous patrolman. If the weather stays calm." He punctuated each sentence with tense hand motions then shook his head slowly. "I don't like sending friends to possible death. But what they are leaving is certain death."

"I don't envy them. It will be a wet and cold night at best. At worst . . ." Peter stopped, not wanting to continue his thoughts on the worst-case scenario.

They had just reached the shelter of the trees when they heard the sputtering of an engine. "Marcel is cutting it a little close. I hope we've seen our last patrol for the night," Olivier said. The engine coughed but caught. Peter and Olivier stayed there, shivering and listening until the sound faded away.

Olivier grabbed his gear and began walking inland; Peter did the same. They took the same route as before because Olivier thought it would be wise to get rid of the three bodies in the Papineaus' home. It would be risky, but it might buy them more time before the Germans found out about the deaths.

Peter decided he strongly disliked walking in wet clothes through the French countryside, but then they heard something he disliked even more: a car. They didn't know who was driving it at first, but since few honest French people had petrol for their cars and even fewer drove their cars after curfew, they flattened themselves against the ground. They hadn't been walking on the road, but they were close enough to see the car speed by. It was a Nazi patrol car, and it wasn't patrolling at a leisurely pace. It was headed to a specific destination.

"Good thing we sent them to England," was all Olivier said when the car was out of sight.

They took a different route after they saw the second patrol car, one that Olivier explained would make a wide curve around the Papineau home. Then Peter heard explosions.

"What's that noise? We aren't anywhere near a front line," he asked as the detonations began sounding more frequently.

"Just the RAF trying to take out some train tracks or airfields. If you're here long enough, you'll get used to the air raids. They are fairly standard: Americans by day, British by night," Olivier explained.

After a few minutes, Olivier spoke again. "One of the men in Marcel's house was Hauptsturmführer Schneider. He's been in Calais since spring 1940. He was very good at tracking down Resistance members. He wasn't the highest-ranking SS man around—that's Standartenführer Tschirner, but Schneider has been here longer. Tschirner is probably the most feared officer in the northern half of France; Schneider isn't—wasn't—too far behind.

"I don't know how Tschirner and Schneider got along personally, but professionally, they made a rather lethal team. Schneider would track the opposition down and bring them in. If they didn't break quickly for Schneider, Tschirner would extract the information he wanted, even if it took days or weeks. Above all, Schneider enjoyed the thrill of the hunt. Tschirner thrilled in bringing men to their knees. I hope Schneider's death will at least partially cripple their effectiveness. But realistically, I think we can expect the local Gestapo to exert every effort in trying to discover who killed Schneider and his men."

"So they'll be looking for us?" Peter asked.

Olivier nodded.

"Tell me more about Standartenführer Tschirner."

"Tschirner honed his skills at repressing local populations in Warsaw before he was assigned to Calais. He rarely travels outside the city limits. I hear he fears assassination and wants to stay in the city where Resistance members have more difficulty operating. He was transferred here from Poland after someone in the Polish Resistance tried to assassinate him. It's a pity they didn't succeed. Tschirner was hit in the chest and spent several months recovering in a Berlin hospital before he came here. The Polish assassin hit him while he was outside of Warsaw; hence, he doesn't want to leave the more populated areas without strong protection.

"I don't know if he has any family. If he does, they are back in Germany. Tschirner is rumored to know Adolf Hitler personally. He rarely takes time off, and if there is something important going on, he can go days with very little sleep. He's obsessive and efficient. He always travels with his aide, Obersturmführer Prinz, and usually a few other guards. From what I hear, Tschirner's aide is much like him: ruthless, slightly paranoid, a loyal member of the Nazi party, a skilled interrogator, and suspicious of his own army. Like Tschirner, very dangerous."

They trudged through the fields and hedgerows until nearly dawn. Finally, Olivier pointed to a dark two-story home and indicated that they had arrived at the Olivier farmhouse. He told Peter to stay in a clump of trees while he checked the home. He circled the house slowly then disappeared into the barn. A few minutes later, he reappeared and went into the cellar then came out and went into the house. He was inside for a long time. Or at least it seemed like a long time to Peter, who had little body fat, was still wet from their swim, and was getting increasingly colder as he waited for Olivier to finish his inspection. He had been fine while they were moving, but inactivity allowed the chill to seep deep into his body. Peter had begun to shake from the cold when Olivier leaned out a door and motioned him inside.

The door led into the kitchen. It was small but clean. Olivier laughed softly when he saw Peter shivering. "Sorry, I know you're cold, but I didn't want to enter a trap. If the Papineaus were betrayed, I thought it was possible that my cover, too, had been blown. We have a secret room you can sleep in." Olivier bent down to take his own wet shoes off. "Well, it's more of a hole than a room." He handed Peter some dry clothes and lit a candle. "We have extra blankets, so maybe you can finally warm up, eh?" Peter tried to smile, but his teeth were chattering too violently. Once he changed, Olivier led him into the parlor, opened a closet, removed a broom, mop, and bucket and pulled a panel from the back wall. "The space under the stairs. It's not very roomy, but my sister keeps it clean and organized."

It was small. Peter had to crawl in, and once inside, he couldn't stand. But there was a narrow sleeping pad against one wall, and several blankets lay folded at the head. There was less than a foot of bare floor along the other wall. It was stacked with boxes of ammunition, an enormous radio, and some other items too far back along the wall for Peter to see. He carefully maneuvered into the crawl space, lay down, and wrapped the blankets around his body. Then Olivier put the panel back on the wall. Peter heard him replace the cleaning supplies and then heard him walk up the stairs.

It took Peter some time to fall asleep. His training had helped him stay calm and focused during the night's events, but there was no training on how to deal with the aftermath. He had helped kill three people that night. He tried not to think about it because, even knowing what he now did about Hauptsturmführer Schneider, it made him uneasy. *You also helped save three people tonight,* he told himself. *If they make it to England in one piece.*

Peter remembered to say his prayers. He prayed for his family and for the three exiles trying to cross the English Channel. Then he prayed for help with his assignment. He wanted to repent for the deaths he'd caused, but he knew he would do the same thing if the situation came up again, so he didn't mention it. It was just easier not to bring it up.

Early in the war, Peter had figured out how to shove unpleasant thoughts aside, so after he finished his prayers, he turned his thoughts to the next task: how to make his body stop shivering. The night hadn't been very cold, but the wind through his wet clothing had left him feeling like an ice cube. After he managed to stop shaking, he had to get over the eerie feeling that he was sleeping in a coffin. If he stretched out, either his toes touched the back of the far stair or his head bumped against the back of the closet. He also didn't like the fact that there was nowhere for him to run if someone found the hole in the back of the closet. Mentally, he tried to come up with a few ways to escape should he be discovered. In the end, however, he just crossed his fingers and hoped that any patrols would be small enough that he could shoot them before they shot him, and then he went to sleep.

Chapter Five
Olivier's Sister

Monday, May 29

PETER WOKE UP TO VOICES. When he and Olivier had arrived at the farmhouse, the night had been black. Peter assumed it was late morning now, but no light penetrated the secret hole under the farmhouse stairs. Visions of angry Nazi soldiers dragging Jacques down to their headquarters passed through Peter's mind, but though the voices were slightly angry, they were quiet. And one of them belonged to a female. As he listened more carefully, he could make out the rapid French.

"I've been saving sugar rations for that cake since Christmas," the female voice said. "It had only been in the oven ten minutes, and the gas went off. The cake was ruined."

"It's just a cake."

"It was for Birgit's birthday. Birthdays are big deals to five-year-olds."

"There's a three hundred and sixty-four out of three hundred and sixty-five chance it's not her real birthday anyway," Jacques's voice said.

"Well, it's the closest thing she has to a birthday, and I wanted her to at least have a cake."

"She wouldn't have been expecting anything if you hadn't built her hopes up so high."

"She's already lost most of a normal childhood. The least I could do is try to have a special celebration for her birthday."

Peter smiled at the female voice's intonations.

"Okay, I'm sorry she was disappointed. You know I like her as much as you do. But I don't see how the cake was my fault."

"If you would have told me you were going to cut the telephone wires or the electricity or whatever you cut, I would have been expecting them to turn our utilities off. I could have made the cake later or earlier or—"

"I haven't cut any lines for at least two weeks," Jacques said. "So your second reason is no good. What's the third reason you're upset with me?"

"You got the floor dirty, and I just cleaned it yesterday. Then there are all the wet clothes strewn about the kitchen. If the clothes line was too far of a walk, you could have at least spread them on the backs of the chairs."

"Sorry, it was a busy night."

"Jacques, I was really worried about you. For an entire day, I thought you'd been picked up until Marcel found me that night and told me you'd gone to England."

"He was supposed to come tell you first thing in the morning." Jacques sounded surprised.

"Well, he didn't come until sunset, and all day I was terrified you'd been arrested."

"I've told you a hundred times not to worry about that. They won't get me, not alive."

"Ever?" There was a pause before the woman spoke again. "Are you sure? They seem to be finding a lot of us lately."

"You're only saying that because there was a fool in the Communist cell. He trusted the wrong person and got his entire cell arrested. After those arrests, the Gestapo managed to extract the names of a few additional contacts, and half of those cells disappeared as well. You're just worried because it happened to them and it happened fairly recently. But as I told you when it happened, I only had one contact with a member of that cell, and he knew me as Pierre. Pierre with a large nose and thick glasses. He wouldn't recognize me without that disguise, and he thinks I live near the town hall. And no one will come get you because you don't have any contacts with any of the affected cells."

"I was still worried. And you still got the floor dirty."

"The floor wasn't entirely my fault."

"Oh, I suppose you brought home a secret army that you're hiding in the barn, and they got the floor dirty. Oh, but that can't be right because I was in the barn this morning milking the cows while you slept in, and there wasn't anyone there. I suppose they're under the stairs?" There was a pause, and then she continued in a slightly different tone of voice. "Did you bring another pilot in yesterday?"

When Jacques answered, there was a slightly playful quality to his voice. "There are no *pilots* under the stairs. And unfortunately, no secret armies in the stable or elsewhere."

Peter heard the closet door open and the broom, mop, and bucket being moved. Then the panel was removed, and light poured through the opening. Not a great deal of light, but there was enough for him to see a young woman's face and for her to see him. Peter's first impression was that she had a pleasant face—not beautiful in a glamorous sense but pretty. She had dark, smooth hair and clear skin with delicate lineaments. He thought her brown eyes the most striking of her features. They were dark, accented with full lashes and nicely curved eyebrows—eyebrows that were raised in amusement.

She studied Peter's face then spoke. "Welcome to France," she said in English with a polite smile. "You're not an airman?" she asked.

"No, mademoiselle, I've never even been a passenger on an airplane," Peter answered truthfully, running a hand through his thick, messy hair. He had crossed the Atlantic on a freight ship converted into a troop transport then had gradually made his way from Northern Africa to Sicily, then England and France on progressively smaller ships.

"Eddy, this is my sister, Genevieve. Genevieve, this is Lieutenant Eddy. He's from the United States and will be staying with us for a few days. He and I both prefer his visit to remain secret."

Genevieve looked at her brother, her smile gone. "Jacques, do you really think I'm so stupid that I have to be reminded that we could be executed for housing an American? Why don't you do something useful and clean the kitchen floor."

* * *

Genevieve was surprised when her brother actually followed her advice and carried the broom and mop into the kitchen. She had been angry with him for days, but she wasn't upset any longer. The cake hadn't been his fault, after all, and to be fair, she had been more disappointed than Birgit had been. *And he meant to tell me he was going to England.* She still thought he should have told her in person or sent someone more reliable than Marcel with the news. *Marcel used to be reliable*, she reminded herself. But the last year had aged him significantly. *The last few years have changed us all*, she thought. Still, it made her sad to think of the physical difference in Marcel Papineau. He had been strong and hardworking before the war; lately, he just seemed old and cranky.

Genevieve gathered the laundry that would be her next task and walked through the kitchen on her way outside. The American was helping Jacques with the kitchen, kneeling on the floor to scrub a stain away. He looked up at her with a smile as she passed. The smile was a little crooked, but she noticed the way it lit up his dark brown eyes, and those eyes held her attention a little too long; she stubbed her toe on a chair and almost dropped the laundry. Embarrassed, she quickly escaped outside. It wasn't until after she had all the laundry in the wash bucket that she realized she hadn't been breathing for the past thirty seconds.

Calm down, Genevieve, she told herself, *he's not the first handsome commando to drop into your house for a week or two. He's probably awful once you get to know him, and even if he's not, he wouldn't be interested in you.*

* * *

After cleaning the kitchen, Jacques and Peter went to relax in the front room. The parlor had a wooden floor, a couch, two chairs, and a small shelf of books. The walls were covered with oil paintings. Most of the paintings were of the ocean or the beach, but a few of them were of the fields and farmland. There were two framed photographs on the bookshelf. One was of a young couple in wedding clothes. The other was of the same couple, a little older, with a young boy standing by the mother and a baby in the father's lap. Looking more closely, Peter recognized Jacques as the little boy. The baby, he assumed, was Genevieve.

"Once or twice a week I go into town and sell cheese in the market and to the cafés," Jacques said. "It's expected that I wander through. I'll scout out the addresses of our contacts then bring you with me tonight so we can plan."

"Don't you think I should go with you now?" Peter said.

"Two people will attract twice as much attention. You should get some rest so one of us will be sharp tonight."

Peter thought about arguing with him but clenched his teeth instead. *Does he think I'm a security risk?*

Jacques's face softened. "Eddy, it's not that I don't think you're competent. I wouldn't have agreed to work with you if I didn't admire your abilities. McDougall let me read the report of your last mission, and I was impressed. And you were equally impressive last night. But I'm going into town as Jacques the crippled cheese peddler. If anyone went with me, it would be a break in routine. It might make someone suspicious. Rest up, and we'll get to work tonight."

Jacques retrieved some maroilles cheese—a regional specialty—from the cellar. He then wrapped several squares of it in cloths, placed them in a bag, and left for Calais.

* * *

Genevieve watched her brother leave then looked around in surprise when the American wandered outside and offered to help her hang the wash on the clothesline. She nodded her consent but didn't attempt to speak.

"The weather's nice today. Not too hot, not too cold." He handed her a few clothespins. "Of course, growing up, this time of year meant a lot of work on the farm."

"Yes, for us too," Genevieve replied. "Lieutenant Eddy, you didn't come to France to talk about the weather. What are your plans?"

"You can call me Peter."

She glanced at him, taking in his smile, and she smiled back. "All right, Peter. What are your plans?"

"Check on a few information sources. Make sure they're telling the truth."

"How long do you plan to stay?"

"It depends on how quickly I can get in contact with everyone. Maybe a few days; maybe a week," he said. "I'm sorry for barging in on you like this and making a mess of your clean floor. I'll try not to be a nuisance while I'm here."

"Oh, I don't mind visitors, especially interesting visitors who clean up after themselves." She allowed herself to study his face for a few seconds, taking in his tan complexion, defined eyes, and strong jawline. "Where in America are you from?"

"The great state of Idaho."

Genevieve frowned a bit, trying to remember if she'd ever heard of Idaho.

"It's in the northwest. My town's not very exciting or interesting, I'm afraid. Just a small place surrounded by potato fields."

"It's different from France, and that makes it interesting to me. Does your family still live there?"

"Yeah, my parents, three little sisters, an aunt, an uncle, and a cousin still live there."

"You have three sisters?"

"That's right," Peter said, smiling as he thought about them.

Noticing his smile, Genevieve asked about them.

"Well, first there's Pearl. She's the smart, well-behaved one. Naturally, that makes her the most fun to tease. Then Ruby. She's a little more like me—prone to sarcasm and practical jokes, but she knows how to work hard. The youngest is Opal. She's the nice one. She's also a little more fragile than the rest of us. She was sick a lot when she was young—ear infections, sore throats, that type of thing. She's a bit of a bookworm now. Then there's my cousin, Owen. He was really little when I left and spoiled rotten by all of us. He probably doesn't even remember me."

"Is that your whole family?" Genevieve wondered what it would be like to have three sisters and a cousin nearby.

"My mom lost a baby a couple years before I was born, so I guess the baby is part of our family too. I also have an older brother, but he was killed."

"In the war?"

"Yeah, at Pearl Harbor."

"I'm sorry," Genevieve said with real sympathy. She had seen and heard of many deaths since the war had begun, each one of them causing her pain.

Peter nodded. "I'm not the only one who's lost a brother, but I miss him. We were pretty close growing up. He was a good, solid guy, my brother. I was always trying to be like him. That was usually a good thing, but it also led to its fair share of trouble, especially when we were younger."

"So you weren't little angels?"

"No," Peter said with a laugh. "Typical boys, usually involved in some sort of mischief."

"What type of mischief?" Genevieve asked.

She noticed a mischievous look in Peter's eyes as he picked up a shirt to hang on the clothesline. "I remember once, the two of us were hanging the wash out to dry, and we decided to dress our calf in my dad's Sunday clothes. So my brother snuck back into the house to grab my dad's tie, and I tried to chase the calf down. I got one sleeve on its front leg, then it started running around and trampled my dad's good shirt and the rest of the laundry into the mud. Robby came out and started laughing; then my mom figured out what we were doing and came out and yelled at us. She was holding the baby, and then the baby started to cry. That brought Pearl out, and she started chasing the calf, trying to help it. Then it turned around and started chasing her. We tried to convince my mom that the calf had stuck its leg in my dad's shirt all by itself, but she was smarter than that."

Genevieve laughed, picturing the scene. "How old were you?"

"Oh, we were probably seven and eleven. We got in a lot of trouble for our efforts. My dad's shirt—his only good white shirt—had to be mended, and it was permanently stained. Our family didn't have the money to go right out and buy a new one, so our dad had to wear it that way for nearly a year. We were both grounded and given extra chores for weeks. And, of course, we had to redo all the laundry—and for a family of seven, that was a lot of work. Although, I don't remember it being much more than what you have here."

"This isn't all ours. I do extra laundry for people in town. Most of them can't pay cash, but they give me food, or we trade for something."

"Do you enjoy being a laundress?"

"No, I hate it," she said honestly. "And Jacques never helps. I can make bombs and cut German wires just as well as he can, but he's horrible at laundry—horrible on purpose. He can do anything he wants to and do it well if he tries for more than five minutes. But he doesn't want to learn how to do laundry."

"Have you been doing laundry your whole life?"

"Mine, yes, but not other people's. Until about a year ago, I made and sold lace. I'd sell it to the soldiers—convince them to buy it for their sweethearts or wives. It was beautiful lace." She smiled at what was for her a fond memory. Calais had a tradition of lacemaking, and her handiwork had served as a tangible tie to her culture. Then she sobered. "Jacques hated me being around the Germans so much, but none of the local people can afford lace, not anymore. Jacques hates the Germans so much, but they're just people. Some of them are rotten, but most of them are just normal people with normal lives and normal reichsmark. I thought being friendly with them would be a good cover for Jacques."

"Did your brother make you stop?"

"Not exactly. Last June one of the rotten ones followed me home and wouldn't leave. He didn't want lace . . ." Her voice trailed off, and she pretended to concentrate on the shirt she was hanging on the clothesline. She avoided Peter's eyes, thinking of the horrible memory, remembering how terrified she had been. She could still remember the soldier's face—almost handsome—but the look in his eyes had been so cruel. He had been halfway across the front room before she'd recognized the lust in his eyes and realized what he was planning. She had dropped her basket and run to the kitchen door, but the latch had stuck, and her trembling hands had been too slow. The soldier had grabbed her hair and thrown her to the floor. Then he'd been on top of her, had struck her face and ripped her blouse. Jacques had come home then and shot the man in the head.

Thinking about it again, Genevieve could still remember the fear and the panic. And she could almost feel the soldier's blood. It had gotten all over her, and she had felt like it was going to stain her forever.

"You don't have to talk about it," Peter said gently.

Genevieve ducked her head and looked away. She hadn't meant to leave such an awkward silence. "My brother wasn't far behind us. Jacques came home and killed him before much of anything happened."

They were quiet for a while. Then Genevieve started again, embarrassed by the silence and surprised she had told someone she barely knew something so personal. "Jacques doesn't think twice about killing Germans. He tends to stereotype most nationalities. Germans are evil and inhuman, the French deserve what's happening to them for not noticing what was going on sooner and not putting up a better fight in 1940, the Brits are intelligent and nice to have on our side—at least in this century—and the Americans," she continued, looking at Peter and trying to keep a straight face, "are easily distracted with their own affairs unless something knocks them out of their own little hemisphere. Then they become naïve idealists, but they generally have good intentions."

"Has Jacques always been such a keen analyst of world politics?" Peter smiled as he hung a shirt on the line.

"No. Before the war started, I don't think he knew Hitler's first name." She smiled at Peter but then became serious again. "He classifies himself with the rest of the French who didn't do anything until it was too late. He was too busy being in love."

"Jacques, in love?" Peter asked. Genevieve detected the surprise in his voice and knew why. Her brother had been very different before the war began.

"Yes, he was in love and happily married."

"Really?"

Genevieve smiled at Peter's doubt. "Yes, really. Her name was Mireille. They'd been sweethearts since they were young children. She didn't live around here, but she came and visited her Aunt Hélène and Uncle Marcel every summer."

"Hélène and Marcel Papineau?"

"How do you know their names?" she asked, surprised.

"Um . . . Jacques and I stopped by last night." Peter suddenly seemed extremely interested in the shirt he was pinning on the clothesline and refused to meet her eyes.

"You just stopped by?"

"Hmm, something like that."

"Right, I suppose for a little wine and a game of chess at two a.m."

Peter continued to concentrate on the shirt.

"Peter." Genevieve stopped her work and faced him with her hands on her hips, giving him a look she normally reserved for her brother. "I don't like it when people don't tell me what's going on."

"Yeah, I can relate to that feeling."

Something in his voice told her he knew exactly how she felt. "Then why are you doing it to me? I'll find out eventually."

"Your brother asked me not to tell you about it until we find out if they're safe. He didn't want you to worry."

"Well, you've already let enough slip to worry me, so you may as well give me the details. The Papineaus are good family friends; I need to know if they are all right."

Peter met her eyes briefly then nodded. "We sent them across the channel. Last time I saw them, they were fine, and they should be safe in England by now."

"But Hélène doesn't speak English, and her garden is always the prettiest in June, and now she'll miss it."

"What a shame," Peter said, picking up another shirt to hang on the clothesline. "What types of flowers does she usually grow?"

"It's not funny." But she guessed he was just trying to be sympathetic. "Did Jacques get them into trouble?"

"No, Jacques and I passed by their home last night and had to take care of a Nazi infestation that started before we showed up. Jacques thought it was best to get Marcel and Hélène out of the country."

Genevieve felt suddenly nauseated with worry and sensed herself swaying to the side. Peter gently grasped her arms and turned her around to face him. "Look, Jacques told Marcel to send a signal over the BBC, so after they arrive and the code phrase makes it past the normal scrutiny, you'll know. I'm sure they'll be fine."

Genevieve stepped away and fiddled with a few socks until her dizziness passed. After she was silent with her thoughts for a few minutes, Peter asked her more about Mireille.

She smiled faintly, knowing Peter was deliberately changing the subject, but she was willing to go along with it. "Let's see, where do I begin?" She paused, deciding where to start. "Mireille was amazing—beautiful and clever.

I think I started to idolize her when I was about four. She painted all the landscapes in our front room."

"She was talented."

"Yes, she was. She could paint, act, cook, sew, and make lace. Hélène taught both of us lacemaking in the summers, and Mireille was always sweet to me, even through my worst phases of childhood. When I was thirteen, she gave me this necklace." Genevieve finished hanging up the pillowcase in her hand and gently pulled on the gold chain around her neck. She usually kept the pendant, a petite gold cross, hidden inside her blouse. The ornate cross was encrusted with sapphires, rubies, and emeralds. None of the jewels was exceptionally large, but the cross contained a dozen stones. Genevieve kept the necklace hidden to deter theft, though to her, it was of value not because of the gemstones but because of the woman who had given it to her.

"It's beautiful," Peter said. "I've never seen one more lovely."

"Thank you," Genevieve said as she put it back inside her blouse. "Mireille said it was a family heirloom, and she felt like we were sisters, even before she married Jacques. We really were the best of friends, even though she was four years older than me. She was an only child and liked having other children to talk to and play with. Even when Jacques got tired of me hanging about, Mireille never did. She would teach me new poems and show me how to do my hair.

"Jacques always liked her too, of course; even though she's gone, he's never really stopped loving her." She paused, lost in the past for a moment. Then she looked up, smiled, and put the painful memory of her sister-in-law's death aside by reminiscing about happier times. "When we were little, the three of us spent hours exploring the beach and the fields. Then we'd act out the stories Mireille would teach us. She was a fantastic actress, and Jacques wasn't too bad either. I usually ended up being the villain."

"Did you ever get to be the heroine?" Peter asked from across the clothesline.

"Rarely, but it was more fun the other way. I didn't want to be rescued by Jacques anyway. I played an excellent witch, dragon, Medusa, or evil English lord. We'd stay out for hours exploring and pretending. A scolding from our papa would usually follow for being out too late and shirking our chores, but it never stopped us from doing the same thing the next day.

"There were a few years when Jacques pretended not to like Mireille. I think that was when he was thirteen and fourteen. He didn't like me much during those years either, and I don't think he was pretending about that.

He said he hated all girls, but he was lying, of course—trying to be tough. He would tell us we were just stupid girls and refuse to be in our plays. Then he'd hide behind a fence or a tree and watch us. Anyway, that phase passed. They got married in 1938, and they were happy. Both my parents had died by then, so the three of us lived here."

"How did your parents die?" Peter asked.

"My mother died in childbirth when I was three. The baby boy died the next day. Jacques remembers it happening, but I don't. I have a few memories of my mother but none of my younger brother. Papa died about ten years later. One spring he just got sick. We didn't know why. The doctor came but didn't know what was wrong. We were very poor then and had trouble paying him, so eventually the doctor stopped coming. My papa had bad days and days that weren't quite as bad. But he just kept getting weaker. He died the next winter, just as the new year began. So after that, it was just Jacques and me. And then Jacques and Mireille and me. Then the war came. And then she died."

"What happened to her?"

"She was hit by a car." Genevieve closed her eyes tightly at the memory. "It was raining, and they said they hadn't seen her. But I was across the road when it happened. I ran over to her and noticed liquor bottles in their car—I think they were drunk. I'll never forget the date. It was only a little before sunset on May 14, 1941."

"Who hit her?"

"German soldiers. That's another reason Jacques hated it when I would sell lace to them. He hates them so much. But we needed the money. We can avoid starvation with our garden and what we trade the milk and cheese for, but being involved in a major resistance movement isn't free of cost. It takes money to bribe guards to look the other way; it takes money to buy the weapons we can't steal. And all the airmen we hide seem to eat a lot."

Peter hung up another shirt. "How long have you and Jacques been involved in the Resistance?"

"That depends on your definition of involvement. In the early days of the war, there wasn't much we could do besides stockpile a few weapons and make life difficult for the Nazis. They'd come and want a cow, so we'd give them the one with the worst milk. Things like that. One night we punctured all the tires on their automobiles. Another time we dug a few potholes in the road before a large convoy came through, and, of course, we always gave them bad directions when they asked for them. That type of thing. We had to be careful, but it was mostly like a game for us during the first year of the war, seeing who could cause the most trouble without getting into any.

"Then Mireille died. Jacques thinks it might have been an arranged accident. We were waiting to meet a new recruit—someone Mireille knew from school, a girl she called Ophelia—when the car hit Mireille. I don't know if his theory is right, but we never saw her friend, and Jacques shot the soldiers as a precaution. After that, things were different. It wasn't a game anymore. Jacques decided it was too dangerous for us to trust anyone else, so now he usually operates alone."

"I noticed Jacques isn't very quick to extend his trust."

"He trusts you."

"He does? Did he actually say that?" Peter asked doubtfully.

"No, but he told me that I could trust you." *And he wouldn't have left me alone with you if he doubted your loyalty or chivalry,* she thought to herself. "I have almost no contacts in the Resistance," Genevieve continued. "Just Hélène and Marcel and our neighbors down the road a ways. Jacques has more than that, but they don't know him as Jacques. They always know him by a different name and a different face. I think some of his contacts actually think he's a woman."

"A woman?"

"Jacques is quite good with disguises. He can fool anyone but me." She laughed at Peter's facial expression. "Don't worry, he doesn't dress like a woman often. And I doubt he will make you dress up like a woman because you're too tall."

"Does he dress you up?"

"No, I can disguise myself. Besides, he rarely lets me go to meetings anymore." She sighed. "I just stay here and do the laundry and milk the cows. In between, I do a few dead drops and run airmen from one house to another. I do things with some risk, but I never make contact with anyone we haven't known since before the war." She grabbed the last piece of clothing from her basket. "Well, I guess I shouldn't say never. I have met some pilots. And a few spies," she finished, looking at Peter and feeling herself smile.

"That's the first time someone has called me a spy without it sounding like an insult."

Genevieve shrugged. "There is a war on. Spies are necessary. It would be naïve to think otherwise."

Peter handed Genevieve the empty basket when she reached for it; then they weeded the vegetable garden she was struggling to grow. The two of them shared stories and compared growing up in rural France to growing up in rural Idaho. After that, it was time to milk the cows again.

"Who was the cake for?" Peter asked.

"You heard that?" Genevieve asked, a little embarrassed but not surprised.

Peter nodded then laughed. "I doubt anyone but you could get away with scolding your brother like that."

Genevieve found herself returning the lieutenant's smile then told him the full story. "The cake was for the little girl who lives with our neighbors. Anne and Louis were in Paris a few years ago. They got caught behind a crowd of Jewish people being sent to a camp in Germany. Birgit was about three. She wandered away from her parents, and Louis started making faces at her, making her laugh. Louis searched the crowd and made eye contact with a woman; he thinks it was Birgit's mother. She started to wave him over when someone in the crowd tried to escape. The guards shot him in the back and warned that if anyone tried the same thing, they would also be shot. Louis said after that the woman changed her mind; she must have had some horrible premonition about what would happen to them. Birgit was wearing a yellow armband with the star of David on it. Louis took it off, and the woman nodded and cried, like she knew Birgit would be safer with them than with her. So Anne and Louis took Birgit, and the woman boarded the train. We don't even know Birgit's last name. Or her real birthday. But she's lived with Anne and Louis for two years yesterday. That's why I was so upset about the cake."

"Does she remember her real parents?"

"I don't know. She never talks about them. I'm sure Anne and Louis will try to find them after the war, but without knowing their names, it will be difficult. And Birgit's parents have no way of knowing where the LeBrases took Birgit if they're still alive at war's end. There are awful rumors about the work camps they send the Jews to." Her voice trailed off ominously.

Genevieve rested her face on the cow she was milking. "Birgit calls Anne and Louis her aunt and uncle. They tell everyone she is their niece from Paris, living with them in the country so she can get enough fresh food. She's a smart little girl. Anne and Louis absolutely dote on her. They were never able to have children of their own. They live just over there, in that house." She pointed through the barn door and across a field to the LeBras home, almost hidden among some trees.

"Their house is part of the escape line for downed airmen. Then our house, then the Papineaus'. When they have someone hidden there, they send Birgit across the field to our house to buy some cheese. If they have two airmen, Anne sends her with two coins. If they have five, Anne sends her with five. If I send her back with one block of cheese, we will pick them up that night. If I send her with three blocks of cheese, we won't be ready for them for three nights."

"It sounds like a clever system," Peter said.

"I suppose it is, but Birgit doesn't pass by any roads, so it's not like German soldiers are stopping her and asking her what she's doing. I don't think the system has ever really been tested. Come to think of it, I think the only time Birgit sees soldiers is when the LeBrases take her to church on Sunday."

"Isn't it risky to be in a chain like that?" Peter asked. "If the Germans caught someone earlier in the line, wouldn't they arrest everyone, one by one, until they got to Anne and Louis, then you and Jacques, and then Hélène and Marcel?"

"It is risky. But Louis picks the airmen up from what is essentially a dead drop."

"A dead drop with people?"

Genevieve nodded. "A few years ago a British agent helped Jacques set the line up. Jacques was in disguise, so no one would recognize him again. We are fortunate here because Calais is big enough that new faces aren't noticed. In smaller towns, the Germans would know most of the townspeople—if not by name then at least by face. Here, there are too many people. Not as many as Paris, but enough.

"The airmen come through the line until they reach the big Notre Dame church in old Calais. One of the priests there can hide them for weeks if he needs to. When he has someone who needs to be picked up, he leaves a cord hanging out one of the windows. Louis goes into town every day, so he knows when there is someone to be picked up. When he is ready for them, he leaves a rock on the wall by the church. The priest smuggles them out into a cave in the fields. They wait there, and Louis picks them up."

"Do you ever have anyone claim to be an Allied aviator who isn't?" Peter paused in his milking, stifling a yawn.

"Oh, Louis is very careful to prevent that. He asks them lots of questions to make sure they aren't lying. And so does the priest."

"What do they ask?"

"Louis told me that when they say they are American, he asks them to describe a football. If they say it's round, they aren't from the US. He also likes to ask about baseball and the World Series, whatever that is."

"You don't know what baseball is?"

"Some game," Genevieve said with a shrug.

"Oh, it's not just some game; it's the best thing ever invented."

Genevieve laughed at the passion in Peter's voice. "Yes, I expect that's what Louis looks for all the Americans to say."

"So they go from the church to the cave to the LeBras home," he summarized. "It doesn't seem like much progress to move them from the LeBras home to yours."

"Well, we aren't exactly in the line. We might keep an airman or two for a few days, but most of the time we just lead them from the LeBras home to the Papineau home. Neither couple knows of the other's involvement. Marcel used to arrange most of the transportation across the channel, but more recently, they've just been innkeepers for the occasional airmen who stop on their way through. Jacques has started doing more; they've started doing less. Now I suppose Jacques will have to do it all."

"How many airmen have you helped escape?" Peter asked. He was concentrating on his milking, giving her plenty of time to study him. She hadn't noticed earlier, but he had a scar on his left temple. It looked recent.

"Not really that many—perhaps a dozen. Other lines handle far more. I've gotten the impression that we're more of an emergency route when another line is breached. Most of the flyers get sent through Paris and across the mountains into Spain. But when they get shot down around here or get stranded somewhere near the border with Belgium, they often end up at the church. And then Louis goes to pick them up."

"It's as simple as that, huh?" Peter said as he finished milking a cow.

"No, nothing is really simple during war. I feel like everything is more complicated. Even milking a cow."

"How has milking a cow become more complicated because of war?" Peter asked with a slightly crooked grin.

"Well, if we start doing too well, and it appears that we have a very fine cow, the Germans might commandeer it. Too much milk might lead to the loss of our property."

"So you milk your cows less to prevent them from being confiscated?"

"No, we just take advantage of the black market from time to time."

Toward the end of the afternoon, Peter began to yawn again.

"How much sleep did you get last night?" Genevieve asked.

"About three hours."

Genevieve insisted that Peter take a nap and told him to sleep upstairs in Jacques's room. Another yawn broke Peter's protest, and he complied.

* * *

When Jacques returned home, Genevieve was kneading bread in the kitchen.

"Where's Eddy?"

"Upstairs sleeping," Genevieve said. "How was the market?"

"Same as always," Jacques replied. "I actually got a little real money today." He opened a cupboard and put a handful of coins and bills into their money jar. Then he pulled off a little piece of dough to snack on.

Genevieve was used to her brother eating her bread dough. She preferred cooked bread and didn't think the dough was worth eating raw, but she wouldn't have thought anything of her brother's actions if she hadn't seen something reddish-brown on Jacques's cuff.

"Your shirt's dirty," she said quietly. "It's not blood, is it?"

Jacques glanced at his shirt cuff and didn't seem surprised to find the stain there. "I ran into a German about halfway home. I guess this was his."

"What happened?"

"Nothing much. Our paths crossed, and I slit his throat."

"Was he trying to arrest you or something?" Genevieve asked, worried.

"No, not yet. He was just asking me questions I didn't care to answer."

"So you just killed him," Genevieve said, angry now, her voice louder. "What was he doing to you or to anyone else?"

"He was occupying my country, and he was stupid enough to be alone in the middle of nowhere. He also made fun of my limp. Don't give me that look. He might not have been harming anyone when I stumbled across him, but if I had given him a few days, I'm sure he would have. This war is far from over, and any Nazi I can take out before the invasion comes, the better."

Genevieve was upset but knew appealing to Jacques's conscience would get her nowhere, not when it involved Nazis. Instead, she appealed to his sense of self-preservation. "Don't you think you should be a little more careful? What if someone besides me had seen the blood on your clothes? What if they investigate? . . . Sometimes I get the feeling you would like to die."

"Come on. If I died, who would look after you? I could never leave my sweet baby sister all by herself. Don't worry so much, Genevieve."

"I can take care of myself, thank you. And I'm hardly a baby anymore. But you seem to forget that this war will end one day. I'm looking forward to peace; are you? Will you know what to do with yourself when you don't have an occupying army to loathe?"

"Once we're finished fighting all the Fascists, we'll have to fight the Communists." Jacques crossed his arms as if he were daring her to disagree.

"Maybe we can hold elections like a civilized democracy and settle our differences peacefully. Life might just go back to normal someday. Are you ready for that to happen? Ready for peace and happiness and maybe even love?"

Genevieve could see her brother thinking about her question. "Peace maybe. But not love . . . not after hating so intensely. One can't love after hating so deeply and killing so many people."

"That can't be true, Jacques. If it is, what are we fighting for? If we're already ruined beyond all redemption and there's not even the hope of a happier future, what's the point?"

"Oh, Genevieve, it's not too late for you or for most of the world . . . It's just too late for me. You don't like the person I've become since the war began; I don't like him much either. I just fight to fight, and you're right—I don't know what I'll do if peace really does come and I'm still alive. I've been motivated by hatred for so long I don't think I can be motivated by anything else."

"Jacques, you're worrying me."

"Worrying won't help."

Genevieve paused. "Then what will?"

"A time machine."

She paused again, trying to think of something she could say that would get through to him. "It's not too late for you, Jacques. If the only thing you felt was hate, you wouldn't care about me or the Papineaus or the pilots who get shot down. War is awful . . . but Odysseus made it back."

"The Trojans weren't as bad as the Germans," he said quietly. Then he left the room.

Genevieve blinked away a few tears and took her frustrations out on the bread dough, kneading it for much longer than was necessary. She hated it when they fought. *And we seem to fight all the time now,* she thought. She was torn between a very real and deep love for her brother and a fear of what he had become capable of. She knew he was fighting on the correct side in a struggle of good versus evil, but sometimes she wondered if he would still be counted among the good when all was said and done.

* * *

Peter heard most of Jacques and Genevieve's conversation from upstairs. He felt a little guilty for listening to their argument, but he couldn't help hearing the words they spoke. Peter didn't think Jacques was solely motivated by hatred, but the conversation did make him wonder if the world would ever be the same. He wanted to believe it could be, but there were times when he, like Jacques, wondered how the world could go back to peace. Peter had been filled with rage when Robby was killed. Since then, he'd felt some hatred, some apathy, and a lot of yearning for the war to end. Peter had always thought that once the war was over, things would be wonderful again. He would go home, see his family, help out on the farm again, maybe attend college, and start a family of his own. But now he wondered how he would do it, how he would get over all the strong, ugly emotions war had brought out.

War is evil, Peter thought, *and I've been entrenched in it the past few years.* Peter felt like he was standing waist deep in a mud puddle, but instead of mud, he was waist deep in darkness. It wasn't that the people he met were bad. He recognized that most of them—even his foes—were just normal people doing desperate things. His faith told him the Savior's Atonement could help, could make everything within him good and clean again, but he felt he had to get out of the puddle he was stuck in before any real cleansing could take place. With the way things were going, he wondered if he would live long enough to make an attempt at repentance, forgiveness, and a normal life.

Peter looked at the picture sitting on a small table next to Jacques's bed. It was a photograph of Jacques and a young woman Peter knew must be Mireille. She had a perfect smile, with straight teeth and full lips. Her fair, curly hair fell past her shoulders, and she was about the same height as her husband. She was facing forward in the picture, but her head and eyes were turned slightly so she was looking at Jacques and smiling at him. As Peter looked at the photograph, most of his attention focused on the man Mireille was smiling at. Physically, Jacques looked about the same as he did now, but there was something in the photograph that was missing now. In the picture, Jacques was standing up straight, his head tilted to one side, half of his mouth curled up in a grin. He looked completely and utterly happy, and the contrast between the joyful couple in the picture and the serious, methodical Resistance fighter Peter had journeyed to France with was dramatic. Jacques had survived four years of war. He had eluded capture and escaped serious physical injury. All the same, the war had taken a deep and heavy toll on him.

* * *

Jean-Philippe Laurier mentally cursed when Madame Rambures called out to him. He was in a hurry to get home but sighed and stopped outside her front gate, where she had come to wait for him.

"Good evening, Madame Rambures," he said.

"Good evening to you, Monsieur Laurier. I do wonder, have you heard anything from your Louis?" Laurier's son, Louis, had been a close friend to Madame Rambures's son, Gaston. Both Louis Laurier and Gaston Rambures had disappeared four years ago, both of them on the same day. They had not been heard from since, but Madame Rambures hadn't given up hope.

Laurier sighed. She always asked him that question. For four years, he had given the same answer. "No, I have not heard from my son."

Madame Rambures shook her head sadly. "And I have not heard from Gaston. You will tell me if you hear anything?"

"Certainly, madame. Good evening." Unlike Madame Rambures, Laurier had long ago accepted that Louis and Gaston were dead. He thought it was probably time she accepted that fact too, but who was he to rupture her false hope?

Laurier began trudging home, hearing Madame Rambures bid him farewell and making no acknowledgment of it. He hadn't always been so gruff, but enduring the war and being a widower had changed him. He was glad when he finished his journey. At times, his empty farmhouse seemed lonely, but not today. After a conversation with Madame Rambures, his home was a haven. Laurier began chopping some vegetables then sautéed them with chicken and spices in a little red wine. Laurier had learned how to cook since his wife's death, and he was getting good at it. He ate his dish with fresh bread he had purchased earlier that day at the market and then retired to his favorite chair. He would clean the kitchen later. He never used to procrastinate, but lately it had become a habit. He would paint the house next summer; he would weed the area between his house and his garage next week; he would dust the furniture tomorrow.

Laurier picked up an old novel but didn't begin reading it yet. He thought he would probably fall asleep in his chair, as he often did. Today was the tenth anniversary of his wife's death. He still missed her. Sleeping in the room they had shared was often difficult for him, and he predicted he would have no peace if he were to sleep there tonight. He sighed as he opened his novel. He had loved his wife, but sometimes he thought it was just as well she was gone. Louis was her favorite child. Had she been alive when he disappeared, it would have broken her heart. She wouldn't have approved of what the war had done to her only son, nor of what it had done to her husband.

* * *

Peter and the Olivier siblings ate Genevieve's bread and some chicken that night for supper. No one said much during the meal. Peter didn't think Jacques and Genevieve were still angry with each other, but they were choosing their words carefully, as if afraid they might spark another disagreement.

After the meal, Jacques went to his room to sleep, despite the early hour. Because of his late nap, Peter didn't feel tired, so Genevieve found some maps of the area for him to study. When she had finished her housework, she joined Peter, and they reviewed her maps and the maps McDougall had sent. While they looked over the maps, they listened to the BBC. Genevieve was distraught when she didn't hear a single verse from the Bible at all, let alone one from the Epistle of James.

"They'll want a little bit of time to verify that Marcel's signal isn't a Nazi code," Peter assured her. "Don't give up hope."

On the maps, Genevieve pointed out the roads along which she thought there were regular patrols. When Peter asked about her sources, she confessed that some of the information was old. Soldiers buying lace from her would describe their daily routines. She said the rest of her information was from listening to Marcel, Louis, or Jacques, and from personal observation.

"Before the war, the wall around Calais was solid. And a system of canals ran around the wall—acting like a moat," Genevieve explained.

"So is it hard to get into the city without passing through checkpoints?" Peter asked.

"The southern part of the city is built outside the walls. It's not a problem to get there without being seen. And between the German blitz and the Allied air raids, there are plenty of holes in what's left of the wall.

The canal isn't so swift that you can't get across—it's more tricky than our nearly razed wall but hardly prohibitive. When I go into town to deliver laundry, I just stay on the main roads and show the guards my papers. They usually let me pass without bothering me too much. After curfew, we usually swim in and out of the city. But even that depends on how much it's rained in the last few months and which part of the canal you cross."

She pointed out the areas where the canal was widest and the areas where the wall was most preserved. "But that's all subject to change with the next air raid."

"Or rainstorm," Peter said. They reviewed the normal process of getting through a checkpoint, and Genevieve declared the forged papers Colonel McDougall had provided Peter to be as good as the real thing.

Jacques and Peter left at about 2330, both dressed in dark clothing and darkened their faces with something black and oily from Jacques's make-up kit. Peter remembered that he had once thought Jacques reminded him of a tiger; now he thought a panther seemed a more accurate description.

The first location they scouted was the farmhouse of Jean-Philippe Laurier a few miles south of Calais. Though they traveled through fields and skirted the most populated areas, they still passed bomb craters, burnt buildings, and pile after pile of rubble. Some were old and some fresh—still smelling of fire and explosives—a vivid reminder to Peter that they faced danger from ally and enemy alike.

The Laurier farmhouse was run-down. The weeds were high, and the fence and house needed new paint so badly that the two men could see the flaking paint in the dark. The house had only one level and few windows.

"Have you ever met him?" Peter asked Jacques.

"No. We try to minimize the number of people we can identify as Resistance. My closest neighbors could be members and I wouldn't know."

"I thought some of your closest neighbors were Resistance."

"The Papineaus and Louis LeBras, yes, but others could be involved and I wouldn't know. I have never had the pleasure of meeting Monsieur Laurier as a citizen of the Calais area or as member of the Resistance. Nor had I ever been to his home previous to this afternoon."

They circled the house several times, becoming more familiar with the property as they formulated their plan. Jacques whispered to Peter. "When I came earlier, Monsieur Laurier was not at home, so I went inside. The house has two bedrooms—both of those on the left. To the right, he has a study in the front and a kitchen in the back."

"So when I meet him, he'll probably take me into the study. Which will mean we can be seen through that window." Peter pointed to the largest window in the house. "But there isn't much cover around the window, leaving you those trees to the left to hide in?"

"That's what I was thinking as well, but it leaves me exposed to the road." Jacques began walking toward the trees and motioned for Peter to follow. Then they walked over to a detached garage on the left of the house.

Inside the garage was a vehicle in much better repair than the home. "How hard would it be for him to get fuel for this?" Peter quietly asked.

Jacques shrugged and tested his line of sight from the inside of the garage to the house. "If I wait in here, I won't be seen from the road, but I won't be able to see you in the study. If he ends up being the bad apple, I don't suppose he'll kill you or torture you without first consulting the Nazis for some assistance, but I'd feel better if I could see what was happening."

"Where was he when you came earlier today?"

"Somewhere in his car. The garage was empty. But I did notice his radio is currently hidden here."

Peter followed Jacques's eyes and saw the radio. It was small enough to be carried on the man's back. It wasn't a very powerful radio, but the signal had fewer than thirty miles to travel. "It's not very well hidden in here, is it?"

"Maybe he's not worried about anyone searching his garage."

"He lives alone?"

Jacques nodded.

"You live outside the city; how often do Nazi patrols stop by your home?"

Jacques thought a moment before answering. "The frequency changes—most of the visits seem random, but I suppose we're searched about twice a month."

Peter looked more closely at the car and quietly inspected it. The fuel tank was nearly full. The oil was clean. The tires were full of air. "I think if there's a reason to, he'll either tie me up in the house and drive to get some backup, or he'll make me get in the car with him and take me to Gestapo headquarters."

"Or he'll bash your head in, drag you out to that pond, and drown you."

"Ah, but you will have an excellent view of the pond. And I'm going to be live bait, but I won't be unarmed. I might end up bashing his head."

It was a good distance from Monsieur Laurier's home to the city. The night was chilly, but since they weren't drenched with ocean water, the temperature was tolerable. On their way north, they passed through the newer, southern end of the city. Calais, in the middle of the night, was dark and mostly quiet. Many of the buildings were now craters or piles of rubble. Jacques had to point out the city wall to Peter when it came into view. It no longer presented an obstacle of any significance for two men trying to get into the city center unseen. The canal, as Genevieve had said, was more tricky. German patrols watched all the bridges. Jacques led Peter to a particularly shallow section of the canal, and they took off their shoes, held them above their heads with their weapons, and waded across. The water was chest deep and cold, but their heads stayed dry. Once they were past the canal and the piles of rock from the city wall, Peter couldn't help noticing that there were more damaged and destroyed buildings than unharmed ones. He also noticed several buildings with German soldiers standing guard, but other than that, the streets were empty, and few windows showed any light.

"Mandatory blackout curtains," Jacques said, explaining the darkness. They slid silently from shadow to shadow along the streets. Jacques led, and Peter followed, knowing his partner had determined the safest route to both of their city contacts when he'd come into town earlier.

Jacques stopped behind a building that looked like it contained several flats. He pointed to the second floor. "Marie Murat lives there." He spoke quietly so only Peter would hear him. There was a slit of light on the side of the window where the shade wasn't perfectly matched to the window frame.

"Is that her café across the street?" Peter asked, keeping his voice a whisper. Hints of bread and beer flavored the air.

Jacques nodded. "I saw her over there today. She didn't start work until late in the afternoon. Probably finished right as curfew began. Most of the people who eat there know her by name."

"What types of people eat there?"

"Do you mean, are they French or are they German?" Jacques stepped away from the window.

"Yeah."

"Both. And Marie seems friendly with each nationality."

"Does anyone live with her?"

"I don't think so. I didn't go into her apartment. But I saw the one beside it. It's a small apartment: bed, bath, kitchen. No one lives in the apartment next to hers because there is a hole in the wall where a bomb came through it." He pointed to a crater only yards from the building. "I'll probably hide in the empty apartment if we approach her while she's at home. But I think it might be better to contact her on the street."

"Yeah, too many people might notice a stranger coming in and out of the building. This looks like it must be about the center of the town."

Jacques nodded. The light in the window went out. "Good night, Mademoiselle Murat," he said quietly.

The last suspect agent lived three blocks away. In the middle of the night, the street was completely deserted, but it seemed that even in the daytime there would be significantly fewer visitors to this neighborhood than to Marie's flat near the café.

Jacques pointed to a narrow two-story building. "Monsieur Charles Toussaint has a law office on the street level, with his private residence on the upper floor."

"It looks perfect—a quiet street, lots of trees and bushes to hide in, large windows and a high fence."

"Yes, the only problem is when I walked by the first time, there were two German officers exiting his office. When I walked by the second time, there was another one just pulling up."

"Suspicious," Peter said.

"Yes, either he's a brilliant agent or he's practically under arrest or he's a full-blown collaborator."

"All those Nazis walking in and out of his office could make a meeting a bit awkward."

"Yes, they certainly could. Perhaps before or after business hours would be the best time."

"Right," Peter agreed. They opened the gate slowly and quietly to enter Monsieur Toussaint's yard. Peter walked around the house. The panes were a little dirty, but Peter could see shelves full of books through the front windows. There was also a window by the back door, but he could only see a dark hallway. He slowly went along the other side of the house, but curtains on those windows prevented him from seeing into the house. "Okay, let's go," Peter said to Jacques when he'd completed his inspection.

Jacques nodded and led the way back through the sleepy district to the even sleepier countryside.

Chapter Six
Agents and Enemies

Tuesday, May 30

DAWN OF THE NEXT MORNING found Peter standing in the same quiet neighborhood. *And so Sinon begins,* he thought. He sincerely hoped it was too early for Monsieur Toussaint to host any Nazi guests. As Peter looked around, carefully taking note of his surroundings and evaluating potential escape routes, he saw only a handful of French citizens and no German patrols. Curfew was over, but there was little activity. A few windows along the road were open, allowing a cool morning breeze to enter the small homes. Peter walked slowly up the block where Charles Toussaint lived, taking care to keep his footsteps as quiet as possible. Jacques had disguised him with a full beard and put gray streaks in it and in the rest of his hair. He had also used a little make-up to make Peter look older and given him the clothes and the toolbox of a carpenter. Peter thought it was nice to have a disguise to hide behind, but he was still nervous. Jacques, Peter knew, was already hiding beside Toussaint's home. He was disguised as an aging member of the fire brigade.

Peter opened the small gate in front of the yard and walked along the side of the house to the back door. Jacques grinned as Peter walked by him; Peter could barely make him out behind the thick green foliage. *The thrill of being in a dangerous situation.* Peter intuitively knew that was the reason for Jacques's smile. As Peter admired the flower beds, he thought briefly of Hélène Papineau and her beloved garden. He hoped she was safe in England.

The paint on Monsieur Toussaint's door was peeling slightly. Overall, the house gave Peter the impression that the man who lived inside was tidy but living with forced thrift. He didn't see anything that needed the obvious attention of a carpenter, but he doubted he would create suspicion should someone see him. Peter took a deep breath and knocked on the door as loudly as he dared. He heard nothing for a minute—a minute that seemed much longer than the normal sixty seconds. He forced himself not to look in Jacques's direction; Peter didn't want anyone to observe him and think there was someone else around. Finally he heard footsteps, and the door opened.

"Yes?" the man who answered the door said.

Peter carefully glanced at Charles Toussaint. He was not tall, nor was he particularly short. His hair was pale and thin. His shoulders were stooped, and his belly suggested that despite wartime rationing he was not going to bed hungry. His clothing included a pair of dark gray trousers, slippers, a white shirt, and light brown suspenders that were twisted on the left side as if he had gotten dressed in a hurry. He wore thick glasses; under the glasses were surprisingly vibrant blue eyes. His eyes and the flowers in the garden were the only things about him and his home that seemed fresh and youthful rather than faded and worn. He didn't seem at all surprised to see a stranger at his back door.

"Good morning, sir. I was wondering if I could speak to you for a few minutes."

"Certainly, but what about? Can it wait until my office is open?"

"*Vixi puellis nuper idoneus et militavi*," Peter said, reciting the first part of the code he had memorized two days earlier, a few lines from a poem written by Horace. Each of his contacts knew it as an emergency contact phrase.

Charles Toussaint's eyes sharpened. "*Non sine gloria.*" He opened the door wider, looked to make sure no one else was watching, and pulled Peter inside. Peter wondered if he was being pulled into a lion's den.

The inside of the home was well maintained—tidy like the outside but not as worn. The two men had entered a hallway. To the left was a narrow staircase. Beyond that were two small offices full of books, one on each side of the corridor. Toward the front of the house was a larger study, the one Peter had looked into the night before through the front window. Toussaint directed Peter up the stairs and followed behind him. At the top, they entered a small kitchen. Toussaint motioned for Peter to sit. Peter put his toolbox down and joined Toussaint at the table.

"Well, what do you want?" Toussaint began.

Peter hesitated, acutely feeling his lack of experience in intelligence gathering. The Frenchman laughed. "Don't worry, I'm only cranky because you disturbed my sleep. I often have visitors here until late in the evening, making it difficult to finish my work and get to bed at a decent hour," he said with a yawn.

"What sort of visitors?" Peter asked.

"Sources." He smiled.

Peter relaxed a bit . . . but only a bit.

"Would you like some breakfast?" Toussaint asked.

"No, thank you." Peter declined the offer even though he was hungry. He normally ate as much as Jacques and Genevieve combined, and even that was less than he was used to. The Olivier family had adjusted to years of wartime rationing; Peter hadn't. Despite the tiny breakfast he'd had that morning and despite the hunger growing in his stomach, Peter was leery of accepting food from someone who might be a double agent.

"You don't mind if I eat, then?" Peter nodded that Toussaint should proceed, and he did, fixing himself a small breakfast of bread and dried fruit. "Well, whoever you are," he said to Peter, "what can I help you with this morning?"

Peter launched into his prepared questions. "I'd like to know everything you can possibly find out about the German forces in the Calais region. How many are there? Where are they concentrated? Where are the nearest reinforcements? And perhaps most importantly, what do they expect to happen this summer?"

"Most of them expect an invasion,'" Toussaint said. "I'll find out what I can and send it in. That's the type of information I've been trying to find out for the past year, and my system seems to work fine . . ." He trailed off, but his eyes seemed to ask Peter what he was doing in his home when he had no new requests.

"Well, there are some very specific things General Patton's office would like to know. I have a few charts, and I'd be much obliged if you could fill in as much as you know about where the Germans are the strongest." Peter opened the toolbox he was carrying and pulled out several maps McDougall had given him.

"Goodness, I don't actually go out to the beaches. I haven't left Calais for more than a year. I haven't even been to the harbor since November. I don't know how much you were told, but the intelligence I provide normally deals with what very few officers have told me. They don't discuss tactics with me, just politics—and even that is a rare occurrence."

"Well, in that case," Peter said, "General Patton would be very interested in finding out what each of the men you work with thinks—and how much his opinion seems to matter with the other officers. How soon do you think you could figure all that out?"

Toussaint slowly chewed a piece of fruit. "Things like that take time. Some days some officers say things they should never say to one of their own junior officers, let alone to a Frenchman. Other days they won't say anything remotely related to the war. Hauptmann Wenders often comes to discuss gardening with me. Occasionally he brings something to drink, stays late, and lets things slip. He's really my best source, but those visits when he opens up don't occur all that often. He doesn't get drunk often enough to expect useful information soon.

"Oberst Hanke comes to ask legal questions. He says it's in the interest of maintaining good relations with the occupied subjects. Oberst Hanke occasionally complains about his Führer, but he doesn't discuss the detailed tactics you're looking for." Toussaint paused to take a bite of his bread.

"Does he say what he expects to happen with the Allies?"

"Yes. He thinks the invasion will come here and come soon, but he doesn't think it will succeed. He is in favor of keeping reinforcements spread out, just in case the attack occurs elsewhere. I don't know what the other officers with any influence think. Oberst Hanke doesn't get along with most of them. But that's due to his sour personality; none of his fellow officers would deny he's brilliant." Toussaint took another bite of bread.

"This Oberst Hanke, what exactly does he say about the Führer?"

"He says the same thing all brilliant military men say when clumsy politicians become too involved in what the good soldier feels is his task. He's not involved in any conspiracy, if that's the direction you are headed."

Peter frowned, feigning disappointment. "Do you have any other regular visitors?"

"Yes, Standartenführer Tschirner and Obersturmführer Prinz, his aide, both of the Gestapo, visit me regularly. Standartenführer Tschirner has never yet let anything useful slip. He says he comes for the same reasons as Oberst Hanke, so he can better understand what justice system the French people have been accustomed to in the past. I think he really visits me to find out what the army is thinking. Dangerous business he's involved in, spying on his own army. He's a ruthless man, but thus far he hasn't suspected me and seems to find me useful for some reason. To be honest, I dread his visits. He's a cold man, an evil man. I pray that if I am ever arrested, it won't be by him. The German Army and the Milice are both kind in comparison."

Peter nodded, unsure of what he should say next. Most of Toussaint's information wouldn't really matter since the invasion would come elsewhere. *But I can't let Toussaint think that what he's saying isn't a matter of life and death*, Peter thought, beginning to think that Colonel McDougall should have looked for someone with good acting experience rather than someone with one barely successful foray into covert operations. Fortunately, Toussaint himself steered the conversation in the right direction.

"Why are you here? Requests for information about German troop placements and what their officers predict could have been made through the normal channels."

"Yes, but codes can be broken."

"Then why didn't you just deliver a new code book?"

Peter leaned forward slightly, lowering his voice. "What is coming is far too important to risk a code being broken or a book being stolen. You know how well defended France is. A successful invasion can't take place just anywhere. I was sent to find weaknesses in German plans and then return to help plan the invasion. I apologize, but there's too much at risk for me to explain everything; details of the invasion are best kept quiet."

Toussaint stared at the stranger in his kitchen, his expression showing a mix of apprehension and awe. "How much do you know?"

Peter laughed, purposely letting some of his very real nervousness show. "Probably more that I should if I'm going to be trekking around Nazi territory. But these questions are best asked by someone who knows what the information will be used for."

Toussaint nodded. "Explain what you want me to do."

"I want you to keep track of what the men you have contact with are thinking. Make note of what they expect, monitor how they react to events that occur here, and notice how they respond to events that occur elsewhere."

"Meaning those false invasions Oberst Hanke expects."

"Perhaps," Peter said. "I was told to request that you continue using the same encoding technique, but in addition to your normal method of getting information to England, we'd like you to give me that same information if anything of importance comes up in the next week."

"So I'm to continue sending messages through Switzerland, and I need to get in touch with you as well?" Toussaint's tone indicated that he wasn't quite committed.

"I know it's twice the work and twice the risk. But getting things through Switzerland takes time. Not that I'm complaining—any system

that has lasted as long as yours is invaluable. But time is vital to the plans
we're making. I am a little worried about all the activity around your
home, so I'm not sure that meeting here again is practical. I'd like to set
up some kind of a dead drop. Do you go anywhere in town regularly?"

Toussaint leaned back in his chair. "I have to eat, and therefore I must
buy food. I also go to the church at least twice a week."

Peter was about to ask about convenient dead drop locations when he
heard a car drive through the street, coming closer and closer until it came
to a halt right in front of Toussaint's home. Toussaint rushed into another
room—his bedroom—with Peter following swiftly behind. He went to
the window and drew the curtain aside an inch so he could see the street.
"Standartenführer Tschirner and Obersturmführer Prinz," Toussaint said,
a scowl forming as he watched them leave their car. "This is the earliest
they've ever visited me. You had better stay in this room until they leave.
We usually talk in my study, but occasionally Tschirner sends Prinz up
to make tea or coffee." There was a loud rap on the door downstairs. "I'll
try to make it quick." Toussaint left Peter and went downstairs to receive
the two Gestapo officers. Peter slipped off his shoes and tiptoed into the
kitchen to retrieve his toolbox then returned to the bedroom. He closed
the door behind him then thought better of it and left it open a crack.

Toussaint greeted his visitors with enthusiasm and invited them in.
Peter was relieved that they were speaking in French rather than German
and that he could hear every word they said. *If Toussaint is the double agent,*
Peter thought, *now would be an easy time for him to betray me.* Peter had
played his part and tried to make it obvious that he knew details about
an imminent invasion of Calais. In addition, Toussaint believed Peter was
alone and unarmed. Peter smiled, wondering what Jacques was thinking
and planning right then. He opened his toolbox, grateful for Genevieve's
foresight in greasing the hinges just that morning for him. He gently
released a lever, and the bottom of the box smoothly separated from the
top, releasing a compartment that contained Peter's Colt M1911.

The conversation downstairs had progressed beyond the initial
apologies for disturbing Toussaint so early and had turned to the weather.
Only two people were speaking: Toussaint and a voice Peter assumed to
be Tschirner's. The second voice was deep and powerful; its intonations
made Peter feel like he had stepped from a Tunisian summer into an Idaho
winter. Even without seeing him, Peter knew the man was evil.

"Monsieur Toussaint, the urgent matter that brings us to your door
so early began two days ago. An American bomber was shot down. We

believe most of the crew was killed, but one of my most trusted colleagues, Hauptsturmführer Schneider, found a parachute caught in a tree. The cords had been cut, and the user of said parachute was gone. Late that evening, Schneider rounded up someone who confessed to helping cut an airman down and bandaging his wounds. The man said he was assisted by an old man he did not know; he himself had fled when he heard a patrol, leaving the airman with the stranger. Schneider found blood in the area around the tree, so he requested dogs. The dogs led Schneider to a nearby farmhouse. In the barn, he found that two people had been hiding in a pile of hay. One of them had been bleeding, but the dogs couldn't track the scent from there. Whoever was hiding managed to cover their trail, so Schneider questioned the owners, and they told him that one of their acquaintances had been hiding there that afternoon and fled with the airman on a bicycle. They gave Schneider directions to another farmhouse."

"They confessed and gave directions just like that?" Toussaint's voice asked.

"Schneider stopped by headquarters and spoke with me before going to the second house. I think he mentioned that the owners of the first home began their conversation with Schneider by pretending to be surprised that someone had been hiding in their barn. But Schneider has his ways of getting the truth out of people." The voice contained a hint of admiration.

"It is methods like the ones Schneider uses that make so many of the people here harbor ill feelings toward Germany."

"Monsieur Toussaint, do you dare criticize the brilliant strategies Hauptsturmführer Schneider and myself have found to be so effective in managing Calais?"

"Standartenführer Tschirner," Toussaint said meekly, "I would never purposely criticize you. But you have asked for my opinion of how best to maintain order and cooperation. I'm simply pointing out that those methods tend to create hatred."

"But they also create fear. And fear is an effective means of achieving order."

"Yes, of course," Toussaint mumbled.

"Schneider left one of his soldiers and the dogs at the first farmhouse. Then he briefed me on the situation and went to the second farmhouse with two assistants. He had instructions to learn all he could and, if possible, bring in the airman and the people who were assisting him. I told him to do what was necessary to ensure that the Resistance wasn't warned. So often we capture one member of the cursed Resistance, bring them in, and get information from them. But by the time we break them, the few contacts they have are somehow warned, and we never get the chance to truly break the chain. Suspects disappear before we can bring them in, or someone tells us false information. Some of them—the stubborn ones—give us no choice but to kill them. Others attempt to kill themselves and often succeed.

"Hauptsturmführer Schneider understood the extreme importance of acting quickly to break the Resistance cell, and I was therefore expecting him to be gone for perhaps as long as two hours. When he was gone for three hours, I personally went out to investigate. I found him and his assistants dead. The airman and the residents of the home had fled. I left an agent hiding there just in case anyone comes back, but most members of the Resistance know better than to return.

"Yesterday we rounded up a few people who knew the owners of the first house, the house with the barn. They have told us nothing, and I'm beginning to believe they have nothing to tell. Unfortunately, the second farmhouse is in an isolated area. No one seems to know the owners or know with whom they associate, so our investigation has again been stalled. I turned it over to the army, but I'm not expecting them to dig up any additional information."

"Can you get no additional information from the owners of the barn where the airman hid?" Toussaint asked.

"They caught a mysterious illness and died yesterday. They were able to tell us the location and a first name, nothing more. They couldn't even give us a surname."

Peter could guess what *a mysterious illness* really meant. Based on Toussaint's silence, he guessed that his host, too, suspected the prisoners' unfortunate fate.

"Monsieur Toussaint, would it be too much for me to ask for some tea?" Tschirner asked.

"No, of course not. I'll go make it at once. It will take a while though; I haven't started a fire yet this morning, and I'm out of gas for the stove."

"No, no, I wouldn't want you to be troubled. I need your expertise. Obersturmführer Prinz knows where everything is."

Peter heard Prinz's footsteps come up the stairs. He peered out of the crack between the door and the frame and watched the German soldier open the correct cupboard for the teakettle. Prinz looked like the ideal Aryan soldier. He had fair hair, pale blue eyes, and a robust, athletic build.

He looked taller than Jacques but slightly shorter than Peter. He set about lighting a fire in the small stove then opened another cupboard and grabbed a container of tea. *He's very familiar with Monsieur Toussaint's kitchen*, Peter thought.

* * *

Prinz glanced around the familiar kitchen. Nothing had changed in the two weeks since he'd last used it. Though Prinz didn't relish the more mundane tasks he did for Standartenführer Tschirner, he did them with exactness. Anything less than his best effort was simply not good enough.

He had been born and raised in Austria in the southern province of Carinthia. He had eagerly joined the Hitler Youth then used all his skill and ambition to gain a position in the Einsatzgruppen, the SS. Fresh out of training, he had been assigned to Warsaw. It was there that he had begun his career of terror. At the time, Obersturmführer Zimmerman had been Tschirner's most trusted assistant. But Zimmerman was too squeamish for Tschirner's needs, too sympathetic to young Jewish girls, too reluctant to torture members of the Polish underground. Prinz had no such weaknesses. He had proven himself capable of following Tschirner's orders with exactness when they arrested an unfortunate baker who had been secretly listening to the BBC at night. The baker and his family were long since dead. Prinz had killed them—after they had begged him for death. Shortly after the episode, Tschirner had transferred Zimmerman, and Prinz had been his replacement.

After Tschirner had recovered from his near assassination by a Polish Resistance sniper, Prinz had joined him in Calais. In Warsaw, hatred and a feeling of racial superiority had allowed him to be cruel to the Poles. *Accursed race*, he thought. He had been equally merciless to the members of the French Resistance who fell into his hands. There was less racial hatred involved now, but power and torture were addictive. He felt no remorse over the lives he had ruined, no regret for the brutality he had used on even the innocent. His only source of shame was a secret he kept hidden from everyone: he was only three-quarters German. His maternal grandmother had been a Slovene, and Prinz was polluted with Slavic blood. His secret shame had made Prinz even more determined to stamp out all opposition to the pure Aryan race and to the Führer who led it.

The tea kettle whistled. Prinz prepared three cups and set them on Toussaint's silver tray. He carried the tea service downstairs, where

Standartenführer Tschirner continued his conversation. "Early this morning I sent Obersturmführer Prinz to the land office to find out who owned the second farm house, the one where Schneider was killed. We had the location and the first name of the owner: Marcel. Marcel something. Prinz had to wake up the clerk, and he looked up the appropriate address. But the files had been broken into, and the file we needed was missing. The clerk admitted to closing a little early yesterday, but he swore all was in order yesterday evening when he'd left. If the clerk is to be believed, sometime between yesterday afternoon and this morning someone broke into the office and stole the very record we needed."

Prinz served Tschirner first then began preparing a cup for Toussaint. He had done it often enough that he remembered Toussaint's preferences: no sugar, a great deal of cream, if cream was available.

"What can I do to help?" Toussaint offered.

"I understand that one of your specialties is in real estate law. I'd like you to go through your records and see if any of them involve this property." Tschirner handed Toussaint a piece of paper with an address written on it.

Toussaint thanked Prinz for the tea and agreed to help. "If the property has been sold or been involved in any legal issues since I began practice in 1934, I will find the owner's name and report to you immediately. Can I assume you already checked the tax office?"

"The tax office caught fire yesterday," Tschirner reported, a frown on his face. "The fire was put out before the office completely burned, but all the records were destroyed."

"An air raid?" Toussaint asked.

"No, arson."

* * *

As the conversation below turned to Toussaint's garden, Peter looked more carefully around the man's bedroom. The sounds from the street were beginning to pick up, but Peter still kept his shoes off so he would make less noise. He looked under the bed, but there was nothing there, not even clumps of dust. A small end table stood beside the bed. It supported piles of books but nothing else. The closet was open—Peter assumed Toussaint had dressed in a hurry before answering the knock on the door and had never closed it. The closet contained little more than clothes. But the bottom of the closet was lined with a rug. Peter thought that odd—a rug in the closet and no rugs anywhere else in the room—so he carefully moved Toussaint's two extra pairs of shoes, one shoe at a time, and lifted the rug. Under the rug were several loose boards. Peter quietly removed the boards and surveyed the hidden materials: a small camera, film, cellophane, razors, clamps, flat glass sheets, and several jars of chemicals.

Peter had never created one himself, but he was confident he was seeing everything someone would need to make a microdot, an image that could be shrunk to the size of the dot on an *i*. How Toussaint's communications made it through France without being detected to the British embassy in Switzerland was no longer a mystery. With every letter, Toussaint had only to write his report, prepare a microdot of the text, and then place it in his otherwise normal correspondence as the punctuation at the end of a sentence.

"I've been thinking about planting some new roses, but I've heard rumors that you expect a bit of action this summer," Toussaint said to Tschirner, their voices still audible to Peter.

"Find me the name; I wouldn't waste time on the garden if I were you."

"You are expecting an invasion too?" Toussaint asked.

"Not a successful one, but even unsuccessful ones can be messy," Tschirner said.

They were silent for a time. Peter assumed they were finishing their tea. When Peter heard them stand up, he quietly replaced the boards, the rug, and the shoes. "Monsieur Toussaint, it has been a pleasure, as always."

"The same, Standartenführer Tschirner. I assure you I will set all other cases aside, and if there is any information about this property, I will find it."

"I'll send a courier by tomorrow morning for your report." Peter heard the front door open and shut. He moved to the window and watched the obersturmführer start the car, a black Mercedes Benz, and drive himself and the standartenführer away. Peter breathed a sigh of relief, put his shoes back on his feet, and put his pistol back into its hidden compartment in the toolbox.

Peter met Toussaint in the kitchen when he came back upstairs. "Will you find any information on that property?" Peter asked.

"If I do, I will burn it. Standartenführer Tschirner has a tendency to round up everyone a suspect knows. Every time a German dies, a hundred Frenchmen disappear. I cannot join the Resistance. I don't have the skills, and I wouldn't want innocent people to be punished for my actions. But I will not betray them. We all have to do what we can. And to win this war, we will need the best efforts of everyone. I can't conduct guerrilla warfare, but I will do my best to make sure you get the information you need and that Tschirner doesn't get the information he needs."

"Thank you," Peter said with sincerity. "As for the information I'm asking about, I don't want to encourage actions that would make the Gestapo suspicious. I imagine they keep special tabs on a man with your connections."

"I haven't noticed people watching me, but I'm not trained in counter-intelligence. If they had good agents monitoring me, I wouldn't pick them out."

"Then it's probably best I don't come see you again," Peter said.

"That would be safer for me. I'll see what I can do for you in regard to invasion plans. There is a wooden bench on the south side of the Catholic Church, fairly sheltered from the wind. Check it Saturday night right before curfew then again on Wednesday, a week from tomorrow. If I have something for you, I'll leave a newspaper under the bench. There will be a microdot on the twenty-fifth line of the fourth page. If your field equipment doesn't include the proper means of reading a microdot, I assume you can wait for the information until you get back across the channel?"

"Indeed, sir. General Patton will want to do most of the planning himself. I'm simply to give him the proper intelligence and advise him as needed."

"Very well, then," Toussaint said.

Peter walked down the stairs, and Toussaint followed. They shook hands at the bottom of the stairs, and Peter felt genuine warmth in Toussaint's handshake.

"When you make it back to England," he began, "tell them to hurry. Things are getting worse over here. We need help, and we need it soon."

Peter nodded and wished Toussaint luck. Then he stepped outside and walked to the front of the home. He passed Jacques again, but as previously agreed, unless a complication arose, they were to meet again after they exited the town. Peter walked to the end of the street, turned right, and headed toward the outskirts of town just as the American Army Air Forces began their almost daily bombing of Calais and the surrounding area.

* * *

Jacques glanced at Peter. "The Papineaus have owned that house since before I was born. It's been in Marcel's family for generations. When did you say Toussaint began his practice?" They were riding bicycles back to the farmhouse. Both men were still in disguise, and both were a little edgy after passing through the German roadblock with forged papers and hidden firearms. The air raids seemed to make the Germans a little jumpy. They had the same effect on Peter; Jacques just tuned them out. As soon as the men had met up again, Jacques had asked Peter to report on everything that had happened inside Toussaint's home.

"It was 1934," Peter answered. "But he said even if he found something, he would burn it. I'm inclined to believe him. If he was on their side, he could have told Tschirner I was upstairs, and that would have been that."

"I can't believe the top Gestapo officer in the region happened to visit Monsieur Toussaint while you were there. Part of me started planning an assassination when he pulled up. He's been responsible for more deaths and suffering . . ." Jacques shook his head in frustration. "But that would have placed Monsieur Toussaint under suspicion, and the retaliation would be severe if Tschirner was killed."

"He sounded ruthless. Marcel's friend—the one who owned the barn where Marcel and the pilot hid—he and his wife are dead."

"Probably their neighbors and relatives too," Jacques said.

They rode along in silence for a bit before Peter spoke again. "Lucky that the tax office happened to burn down right before Obersturmführer Prinz went to get information about Marcel and Hélène."

Jacques looked over at Peter then back to the road in front of him with a slight smile. "Peter, you sound like you are asking me a question."

"Did you do it?"

"A little arson after a hard day's work of peddling cheese." Jacques shrugged.

"And the land office?"

"They had ridiculously easy-to-pick locks on the doors. And the file locks were cheaply made. I walked by and couldn't resist."

"Won't they still connect the Papineaus to you? You did marry their niece."

Jacques wasn't surprised that Genevieve had told Peter about Mireille. For Jacques, bringing up the past was painful. For Genevieve, it was therapeutic. "Yes, I did marry their niece, and the Papineaus are still like family to Genevieve and me. But few people know about the connection. We've all kept to ourselves since the war began. Most of our friends fled before the Germans got here, or they stayed just long enough to be drafted for labor in German factories. Standartenführer Tschirner can ask around the area, but few people are still around who know Marcel and Hélène. Maybe the Papineaus were confused about which social class they were part of; maybe they enjoyed each other's company so much that they didn't need other friends, but for some reason they weren't very social—even before the war. No one knows our families are so close."

Jacques allowed himself a few moments to remember his late wife's family history. He didn't know all of it, but he knew enough. It was a tale of two sisters: Hélène and Chantal. Both had stories that could have fit into a Shakespearean play—one a comedy, one a tragedy. The two had been raised in Paris by aristocratic parents who had been born wealthy but were quickly coming to the end of their inheritance. They had a good name, but they knew an end of money would also be the end of the social advantages their title gave them. Both parents came to view an arranged marriage to men of wealth as a necessity for both daughters.

Hélène, the eldest by two years, met Marcel Papineau one winter when he went to Paris on business. They claimed it was love at first sight. Marcel returned to Calais in the spring then wrote to Hélène and asked her to come join him as his bride. Hélène's parents were furious. Marcel was of a lower class, and although he had enough money to comfortably support Hélène, he didn't have quite enough to support her parents and the lavish lifestyle they had become accustomed to. Hélène married him anyway, and her parents disowned her. Marcel's business did well for a few decades then went sour when the Depression came. The two had been happy together through the rough financial patches and through the times of plenty, through peace and through war.

The other sister, Chantal, also fell in love with someone beneath her parent's aim. He was a university student, with a head full of ideas and pockets completely devoid of money. They spent a summer together, secretly seeing each other almost every day. He begged Chantal to run away with him, but she hesitated.

In the end, Chantal obeyed her parents, ignored her heart, and married someone of their choosing. With the marriage, her parent's financial security was cemented. Chantal's husband was twice as old as she and three times as rich as her family had ever been. Monsieur Desmarais, the man her parents had chosen, did well in business, and marrying into an aristocratic family appealed to him. He had never truly loved Chantal. At home, she was a beautiful decoration, like the oriental vases he collected. Chantal was never a cherished equal to him, and their daughter, Mireille, was an annoyance.

Monsieur Desmarais sent his only child to boarding school most of the year and was happy to send her to visit her aunt Hélène in the summer.

Too late, he realized that sending his daughter to live with his sister-in-law every summer made Mireille indifferent to money and title. Chantal, too, had influenced her daughter deeply when she had confessed that it was better to be poor and happy like Hélène than to be rich and miserable like herself. Mireille's father lost her, just as he was beginning to realize what an asset an arranged marriage might have been for his business empire. Monsieur Desmarais's loss had been Jacques's gain.

Jacques turned back to Peter. "Mireille and I had a very small marriage ceremony. There may be records of it somewhere, but Mireille's last name wasn't Papineau. I don't think they'll trace Schneider's death to Genevieve and me. But all the same, I'll be extra careful. Like I always am."

"And if they did track you down, what would they do to you?"

"Torture and kill me," Jacques said casually with a shrug.

"And to Genevieve?"

Jacques paused. He wasn't as casual when he began speaking again. "Probably the same. Or send her to a work camp. She's nineteen—young but probably too old to hope for mercy." He sighed. "And that's part of the problem. Genevieve just doesn't understand how dangerous this game is. She tries to tell me that most of the Germans are normal people just like me. Maybe she's right. Maybe 99 percent of them are decent. But that other 1 percent is vile enough to hurt an awful lot of people."

"Is that why you killed that soldier yesterday evening?"

Jacques glanced at Peter again. "He wasn't really a soldier; he was a Gestapo stooge. There's a difference. And he might not have been up to anything when I ran across him, but he was snooping awfully close to a dead drop site I used two weeks ago. He died for sins I'm sure he had already committed or soon would commit against the French people."

They rode along in silence for a while. Then Jacques continued, wanting Peter to understand. "Genevieve is smart. She always has been. But she sees what she wants to in people. When she wants to find good in someone, she usually does. That's why she was so upset about yesterday. And that might be a nice trait to have in a normal society, but it can be a dangerous one during wartime."

"Isn't danger a part of life during war?"

"Yes, but it's also a part of death. Genevieve is competent with a bomb and a good shot with a pistol or a rifle—our father saw to that. And she can sneak around in the fields or in town better than anyone else. We would play games when we were little, and she could sneak up on me, and I wouldn't hear a thing. I'm sure she could sneak up on any Nazi soldier as well. But I'm not sure she could pull the trigger when she got there."

* * *

Peter and Jacques returned to the farmhouse still partially disguised. Genevieve stared at both of them for a bit then turned to Jacques to ask him about their latest batch of maroilles cheese. The disguises had delayed her for approximately three seconds. The difference in the two men's height had helped her and so had Peter's eyes. Even with the make-up that aged the surrounding skin, Genevieve doubted she would ever forget those dark brown eyes and the thick lashes that surrounded them. *And will those eyes ever stop making me feel giddy?* she wondered.

Genevieve had been about to start more laundry. Her brother went into the cellar to see to the cheese. Peter offered to help with the laundry again and spent the rest of the morning scrubbing shirts, pants, socks, and tablecloths while Genevieve wrung them out. She was grateful for the help and pleasantly surprised that although the American's presence still made her feel a little dizzy, conversation between them was easy.

When Peter and Genevieve were finished washing, they hung the clothes on the line. There was a strong breeze, and Genevieve had trouble pinning up a particularly long tablecloth without it dragging on the ground. The wind caught it, and both of them reached for it as the white cloth threatened to blow away. Genevieve caught it first, and then Peter caught her hand in his.

He smiled and released her hand. "Sorry, I guess my aim's a little off when it comes to renegade tablecloths."

Genevieve felt herself blushing and quickly turned her eyes from Peter's face to the clothespins, wondering if her heart had really skipped a beat or if it had just been her imagination.

* * *

Later that day, Jacques and Peter went over their plan for the upcoming rendezvous with Mademoiselle Murat.

"I think you should go as a German gefreiter. There are plenty of those around; you'll blend right in and have a perfect excuse to gawk over a beautiful French waitress," Jacques suggested.

"But my German is very limited," Peter said. "I wouldn't pass as a native speaker."

Jacques pondered for a while. "It might still work. I'll be your hauptmann, so you won't have to speak much. My German is good enough; it's not as good as Genevieve's, but I could pass for a Sudetenland conscript. You can speak French when you talk to Mademoiselle Murat but pretend not to know it so well."

Jacques had Peter try on a blond wig. Then he showed the American how to use some paste from the make-up kit to lighten his eyebrows. Jacques made Peter practice his salute in the German style, and then they reviewed a few German phrases together.

As they worked, Genevieve began to sing in the kitchen. It was a slow, bittersweet love song.

"She has a good voice," Peter said. "Does she sing often?"

Jacques looked toward his sister in surprise. "I haven't heard her sing anything for years, unless you count the children's songs she sings with Birgit. Mireille and I used to call her our little canary, but that was a long time ago." He turned from the direction of the kitchen, puzzled.

Jacques's mind wandered back to the last time he'd heard his sister singing in the kitchen. It had been May 14, 1941. Mireille had been sick again. For several days, she'd woken feeling nauseated. By midday she had felt well again, but Jacques was growing extremely concerned. He hadn't known what was wrong, and he hadn't known what to do. It hadn't been that long ago that Jacques had seen his father slowly die of a mysterious illness. Seeing Mireille like that brought back all the dark emotions, chief among them a feeling of helplessness. He'd opened the door to their bedroom quietly after finishing his morning chores with the cows.

"Headache still?" he asked when he'd seen she was awake. He'd gently sat on the bed next to her and felt her face with his hand.

"Mm," she'd replied softly, leaning into his hand. "I'm sure it will go away soon."

Genevieve had been downstairs, singing as she'd kneaded bread dough. "Shall I go quiet our canary? The noise can't be good for your headache."

"Oh, let her sing." Mireille had forced a small smile. "I like listening to her. I hope our children do the same thing when we have them."

Jacques had lain down next to her. There had been few things Mireille had wanted more than a baby. Jacques had also wanted children, but they'd been waiting for what seemed like a very long time. He'd gotten into the habit of avoiding the subject because all too often any conversation about babies ended with Mireille in tears. Even Genevieve had learned to avoid mentioning anything that related to infants. "Yes, someday we'll see if they like to sing," he'd said hesitantly.

Mireille had turned her head and smiled impishly at him. "I think we'll see in December or January."

Jacques's head had spun around, surprise and wonder filling him as he'd looked carefully at his wife. "You think so?"

"I'm more sure of it every day."

Jacques had grinned then softly kissed his wife. "That's wonderful," he'd said, kissing her again. "And that's why you've been sick?" She'd nodded. He'd been relieved that nothing was wrong and elated that instead everything was right. With his left hand, he'd carefully felt his wife's stomach. It had felt the same as it always had to him, but knowing that there was new life growing inside had changed absolutely everything.

Jacques's memory was a bittersweet one, like the song his sister was currently singing. Being told he was going to be a father had been a high point. The day might have been the best of his life, but instead, it had been the worst—the morning's joy drowning in the evening's excruciating sorrow. That had been the night Mireille had been hit by a car. She had died in his arms, her body crushed, her breathing weak and then gone. Jacques had never been the same since; nor had Genevieve. The little canary had not sung for three years.

"Maybe she can feel that liberation is near," Peter suggested, giving a reason for Genevieve's transformation and bringing Jacques back to the present.

Jacques focused on Peter, thinking about what he had said. "Liberation—that would take a miracle. A very, very large one. Or thousands of small ones."

"Well, for the first miracle, I need to convince a café full of people that I'm from Germany."

"Will that be a small miracle or a large one?" Genevieve asked, coming out of the kitchen.

"Are you doubting my abilities to create a disguise?" Jacques said with a smile. He usually smiled when he teased Genevieve but just then there was something more to his upturned lips. He had noticed the way she'd looked at Peter when she'd come into the room, and Jacques suspected it wasn't the impending invasion that had set her singing again. He also noticed that she was wearing her hair down today; normally she pulled it back out of her face for her household chores. *Is Genevieve falling for the young American lieutenant?* Jacques wondered. Jacques wasn't sure how he felt about that but decided it probably wouldn't matter as long as he made sure Operation Sinon was completed on time and Peter sent back to England quickly thereafter.

"No, Jacques," Genevieve said, "I don't doubt your skill, just Peter's German."

"All I have to say is *ja.* The rest is just clumsy French," Peter said.

"Can you remember to speak French clumsily?" she asked.

"Of course, mademoiselle. I am a professional member of the United States Army, trained in the intelligence specialty. I can remember to be clumsy when my role calls for it."

Jacques tried to guess how Peter might feel about his sister but couldn't decide. Peter was being friendly, but Jacques didn't think he was flirting. He handed the American a German uniform and sent him upstairs to change. "Well, Genevieve, how does he look?" Jacques asked when Peter came back fully in disguise.

"I think I prefer him with dark hair," Genevieve said.

"That's not what I meant," Jacques said as he began piecing together loose hairs and pasting them onto his face as sideburns.

"I know. You wanted me to compliment you on yet another job well done. Peter, have you been in a French café before?"

"No. This is only my second trip to France, and the first trip wasn't long enough for even a lunch break." Peter automatically rubbed a spot on his left arm. Jacques guessed it was a scar from his previous mission.

"How did you learn to speak French?" Genevieve asked Peter.

"My uncle was over here during the last big war. He never says much about what he did, but he came back to Idaho with a Distinguished Service Cross and a French wife. He and my dad farmed together, and we were pretty much one big happy family. My aunt and uncle didn't adopt my cousin until five years ago, so my aunt had lots of time to devote to her nieces and nephews. She thought we should all learn French . . . so we all learned French. I can count on one hand the number of times she's used English to communicate with me. And if we didn't say something perfectly, she'd make us repeat it until we got it right. She also had us read a great deal of French literature, in French, of course.

"I've also picked up a little German, most of it this spring from old textbooks. I had a lot of downtime and thought it would be useful to learn some. I'm not very good yet, but I understand more than I can speak.

Where did you two learn English?" Around the Olivier farm, the three communicated most often in French, but English accounted for a sizable percentage of their conversations.

"At school. We had several different teachers. Most of them were stuffy and dull, but our favorite was a Scotsman named Howard McDougall," Genevieve said.

Peter looked at Jacques. "McDougall? Colonel McDougall?"

"Do you think I would trust him if I hadn't known him before the war?"

"He wasn't very good at explaining grammar," Genevieve said. "But with all the stories he told from Greek and Roman mythology, he was entertaining."

"How long did he teach you?"

"Five years. From 1933 to 1938." Jacques said as he used some powder to make his cheeks look hollow. He was also wearing a wig. "We kept in touch after he went back to England. Oh, and Peter, you should probably take your shirt off. We'll change when we get to town."

* * *

Peter watched Genevieve riding ahead of them with her bicycle basket full of clean laundry to be taken to customers in town. She'd told him earlier that if Jacques had his way, she would never leave the farm. It would hurt the family economically, but Jacques would willingly make the sacrifice. Peter could understand Jacques's reasoning. He thought that, given the same circumstances, he would do the same for his three sisters.

Genevieve, however, refused to be caged up. Jacques usually insisted on Genevieve going into town with Marcel and Hélène Papineau or with their other neighbors, Louis and Anne LeBras. Then she wouldn't be alone if she ran into trouble. Tonight was an exception to the rule, and Peter could tell Genevieve was thrilled with her new freedom. She still complied with another of her brother's attempts to keep her safe: a pair of thick glasses that made her eyes seem tiny and, hopefully, less attractive to young German soldiers. As she approached the city, she turned around and waved to her brother and Peter. The two men hid their bicycles in a stand of trees about a mile from the city and changed from their street clothes into their German uniforms.

Walking through the checkpoint in German uniforms was hardly a problem for them. They nodded, saluted, took their papers out of their pockets, and were quickly waved through without an inspection. Walking to the café was a unique experience. Jacques kept them walking at a brisk pace, which deterred other people from talking to them. But Peter doubted anyone wanted to; several civilians actually crossed the street to avoid them. They walked through a residential area, through a business area, and through several areas too thoroughly bombed for Peter to tell what they had been in better days. He had seen devastation and destruction in London, but the damage to Calais was much worse.

When they arrived at the café, Peter was surprised to find it whole, as if the war had somehow skipped over it completely. The smell of freshly baked bread mixed with the smell of the street at the café's entrance, inviting the two men inside. It was a little larger than Peter had expected, and it was two-thirds full when they entered. The majority of the patrons were German, but there was a significant number of French citizens as well. Jacques and Peter sat at a table on the far side of the room, where Jacques could see the entrance they had come through and where Peter could keep watch on the back door.

Marie Murat, their contact, was more than beautiful. Her blonde hair was pinned on the top of her head, and it glistened in the dim light of the café. Her eyes were blue, her lips red, and her body seemed proportioned to perfection. Every motion she made was graceful; every word she spoke brought a smile to the patrons she addressed. A few of the German officers in the room looked like they were having serious conversations, but even they stopped to talk with her when she brought their food or drink. Peter had a difficult time taking his eyes off her; so did at least a quarter of the other patrons.

She came up to them after they had been sitting for only a few moments. She addressed them in French, but Jacques pretended to know only German. Marie began again in slow German. Peter couldn't tell how good her German was, but he suspected she had been given plenty of opportunities to use it. Jacques ordered, and Peter said he wanted the same thing. They had practiced that phrase in German. While they waited, Peter gazed around the café in curiosity. There were a few French patrons who sat and spoke with German patrons, but for the most part, the French kept to themselves. One exception to the rule was the stout owner of the café, who greeted both French and German guests with familiarity and warmth. It appeared his only duties were greeting customers and taking their money. Marie did all the serving, and there was a cook in the back room.

"What did we order?" Peter whispered in French.

"Just a sandwich. The special for the day. And water. German soldiers normally drink beer, but in honor of my favorite religious fanatic, I'm letting our cover slip ever so slightly."

Peter smiled his thanks. "How did you know I don't drink alcohol?"

"Your army file said you are a Mormon. Mireille met some Mormon missionaries on a train to Paris once. She and a school friend sat with them to practice their English. She and her friend offered to order them wine, but they couldn't drink that. So they offered brandy then coffee then tea. She and her friend came to the conclusion that Mormons could only drink water."

Peter laughed softly. "Actually, we're not quite that limited in our choice of liquids, but beer is on the prohibited list. Did Mireille learn anything else about Mormons?"

"No. She invited them to her house, but her father promptly turned them away. He was always rather rude to anyone who didn't have a title or a lot of money."

"Did you ever meet him?"

"No. I'm quite sure it would have been beneath his dignity to so much as shake my hand."

Of the two closest tables, one had been empty when they'd arrived. Three low-ranking soldiers occupied the second. They left as Marie brought Jacques and Peter their sandwiches, giving them a greater degree of privacy.

"*Merci*, mademoiselle," Peter said as she placed his plate in front of him. Then he lowered his voice, "*Vixi puellis nuper idoneus et militavi*,"

She paused then laughed. "I love it when young German soldiers quote poetry to me, but I prefer it when they remember at least an entire stanza." She gave Jacques his meal and left to clear the nearby table.

Jacques shrugged and picked up his food. Peter wondered what had gone wrong. He mentally reviewed the papers McDougall had given him. According to OSS, Marie Murat was an active and intelligent contact. Peter didn't think she would have forgotten the code phrase. He had assumed that even a double agent would finish the phrase and find out something about the new contact before calling in reinforcements. Jacques motioned for him to eat, and Peter did, though without really tasting the food. Marie brought their bill but only smiled and thanked them for coming in. No code phrase. But when Peter picked up the bill he saw it written in neat, orderly handwriting. *Non sine gloria. Meet me in the market at the Place d'Armes tomorrow at noon.*

They paid, left the café, and headed back to their bikes.

"You Americans are so impatient. Did you expect her to answer right away?"

"Yeah, but I guess I shouldn't have, huh?" Peter said, recognizing his error. "Tomorrow at noon. Are you familiar with that market?"

"I delivered cheese there yesterday. I suppose I'll drop some off tomorrow too. You'll have to go as you were tonight so she recognizes you."

Peter nodded.

Their passage through the checkpoint leading from Calais to the countryside was fairly routine. The oberleutnant in charge of the checkpoint insisted on looking at their papers and asked Jacques what their business outside the city was. Jacques, in the uniform of a hauptmann, pretended to be insulted and told the lower-ranking officer to mind his own business. The oberleutnant obeyed with a stiff salute.

They were a mile down the road, past sight of the checkpoint and about to retrieve their bicycles, when they ran into another delay. As the two men walked along the green fields at a purposeful pace, they noticed a lone jeep coming toward them, moving toward the city. "They're slowing down," Jacques said. "If they stop, just keep your mouth shut and pretend you're unable to talk."

The jeep pulled to a stop a few yards in front of them. They were approaching a bend in the road; the trees that hid their bicycles were just ahead. Jacques waved the car on, but two Gestapo men got out of the jeep. "Heil Hitler." They saluted. Jacques replied in the same manner. Peter lifted his hand in the Nazi salute, feeling dirty as he did so, but he followed Jacques's advice and kept his mouth closed. Like an attentive German gefreiter, Peter clicked his heels together and brought his Karabiner rifle to his side.

Peter didn't pick up everything that was said because the conversation was in German, but he understood most of it. The Gestapo obersturmführer asked Jacques what they were doing out so late—they weren't headed toward any army encampments, and it was nearly twilight.

"We are on a special patrol," Jacques said.

The obersturmführer asked about Jacques's accent, and as planned, Jacques told him he was the son of a German man and a Czech woman. He had grown up speaking Czech as a first language, and that was why his German was somewhat imperfect. The obersturmführer then turned to Peter and asked him to identify himself. Jacques told the obersturmführer Peter had been captured by Russians near Stalingrad. They had tortured him and cut out his tongue. Peter doubted the obersturmführer believed either of the stories, but he knew Jacques didn't really care if his tales were taken at face value. He was just trying to buy a little time.

The obersturmführer motioned for Peter to come forward and show him his tongue, or lack thereof. His assistant, holding a rifle loosely in his hands, appeared relaxed and looked on with amusement. Peter nodded to the obersturmführer, catching Jacques's eyes as he did. Almost instinctively, Peter knew what Jacques was planning. He approached the obersturmführer then grabbed his rifle with both hands and swung the butt into the side of the man's head. At the same time, Peter saw Jacques's knife flash through the air and land in the second Gestapo man's chest. It couldn't have gone more smoothly if they had rehearsed it a dozen times. Neither of the Gestapo men was dead, but Jacques quickly changed that by retrieving his knife and slashing it across both of their necks.

"Are all Gestapo agents that careless?" Peter asked. He was appalled by what they had just done but also amazed that it had been so easy.

"They wanted us to trip ourselves up. They probably thought we were real soldiers going on an unauthorized field trip. Looting, courting country girls, that sort of thing. He was being cautious because of my rank."

"What do we do with their bodies?"

"We'll load them back in their car then throw them in the canal." Jacques glanced at Peter. "We had to kill them. We need to use your disguise again, and they've seen it."

Peter nodded, already trying to push it out of his mind.

The landscape surrounding Calais was laced with canals; a shallow, narrow one was only a few hundred yards from the grove of trees. They put the bodies in the back of the jeep, then Peter climbed into the front passenger seat, and Jacques drove the jeep off the road and toward the canal. When they arrived, they threw the bodies into the canal. There was little doubt that they would be discovered eventually, but Jacques didn't want the bodies to be discovered in the grove he often used for hiding bicycles and bits of disguises.

They drove the jeep back to the road and closer to the town entrance. Then they inspected each other's clothes for blood—surprisingly, there was none on Peter's German uniform. Jacques had done more of the dirty work, and it showed in a few stains on his sleeves. By that time, the lighting was poor enough that only a close inspection would show the stains; nevertheless, Jacques didn't want to upset Genevieve again, so they changed back into civilian clothes before retrieving their bicycles and riding back to the Olivier home.

* * *

When they returned to the farmhouse, Genevieve was ecstatic. "They read a verse from James over the BBC. Hélène and Marcel are safe!"

"That's great," Peter said. "I didn't think we'd hear anything this soon." Jacques smiled. Peter could tell he was relieved, but he could also tell that Jacques was surprised. Neither of them had really been expecting the three refugees to successfully make it across the channel.

"They read, '*For he that wavereth is like a wave of the sea driven with the wind and tossed.*' Do you think that means they had a rough ride?"

"They couldn't have had a very smooth one. We didn't send them in a very large vessel, and it was loaded to capacity," Jacques answered.

Peter wondered if they had all arrived alive. The American pilot had been in bad shape. He thought, however, that it would be unwise to suggest that the signal might have been sent even if fewer than three of them had survived the voyage. Besides, he was enjoying the smile on Genevieve's face. It had real happiness in it, not just the customary politeness of the first day he'd met her.

"Now we just have to wait for the war to end, and they'll be back. Maybe tomorrow I'll go see how Hélène's garden is doing," Genevieve said. "Oh, but that would be foolish. If you ran into Nazi trouble there, it's bound to still be under observation. I'll steer clear of their house until the Germans are driven out. In the meantime, I think we should celebrate the Papineaus' safe journey to England." She smiled again and disappeared into the kitchen.

"Well, I'm glad someone has faith in the Allies' ability to liberate Europe," Peter said. Jacques raised an eyebrow and gave a half smile. "Do you think they all made it?" Peter whispered.

Jacques shrugged. Genevieve came back into the room then, a smile still lighting her face. "I'm not sure how she got it, but one of the ladies paid me for her laundry with some flour and a chocolate bar. Perhaps we can split the chocolate and have a modest celebration dessert?"

Chapter Seven
Keeping Secrets

Wednesday, May 31

THE NEXT DAY PETER WANDERED back into Calais. Along the way, he noticed that the jeep they had abandoned the evening before was no longer where he and Jacques had left it. He didn't bother to check the canal where they'd left the corpses. He entered the city as a civilian then found the abandoned, half-destroyed building Jacques kept stocked with German weapons and changed from his civilian clothes into his German uniform.

The market Marie had mentioned was outdoors in an open square known as the Place d'Armes. War had not been kind to the buildings surrounding the square. Calais's ancient watchtower still stood, visible even from a distance, but many of the buildings had been damaged when the Nazis had moved in, and many others had been battered since.

Individual farmers and tradesmen had set up their booths in the square. Jacques was there with his patch and his limp, speaking to a vendor who bought and sold dairy products. Jacques had left his home about ten minutes before Peter so their entrances into Calais would not be connected. Peter wandered through the market and looked at what was offered. It was a large square, and he could imagine that in different circumstances it would have been full and busy. But food was not in abundance in wartime France. As Peter walked by, he could hear people complaining because the price of eggs had doubled in the last month and because there wasn't enough sugar to fill the amount granted them by their ration cards. Elsewhere, people were discreetly and illegally buying and selling ration cards and other high-demand items. Everywhere, purchases were complicated with wartime scarcity.

Peter saw Marie Murat precisely at noon. She had a basket hanging from one arm with a loaf of bread and some fruit. Her clothes were simple, but they flattered her figure. The two made eye contact, and she turned slowly away and began walking. Peter followed at a leisurely pace, stopping briefly to examine a few spring vegetables, very aware of the fact that half the male eyes in the marketplace were following Marie's every motion. Peter knew others would notice if he followed her too closely. Out of the corner of his eye, Peter saw Jacques and knew he was aware of all that was going on. Peter fully expected him to follow at a safe distance.

When Peter left the square, Marie was half a block away, looking into the window of a dress shop—one of the few completely undamaged shops on the block. She saw Peter, made no acknowledgment of it, and began walking again. She stopped again to have a conversation with a fair-headed, skinny boy who looked like he was about nine years old. Peter was too far away to hear what they were saying to each other, and Marie's back was to him, so he didn't know who had started the conversation. He did see how it ended. Marie tore her loaf of bread in half and handed part to the boy. The boy smiled and began walking toward Peter while tearing a piece of bread off with his teeth. The boy changed directions and darted across the street when he noticed Peter—yet another civilian hoping to avoid contact with a German soldier.

Ahead, Marie turned a corner, and when Peter followed a few moments later, he saw her walk into another building halfway down that block. The street was narrow. Two bicyclists could have passed each other, but only barely. A normal automobile wouldn't have fit. The street was quiet— Marie and Peter were the only ones on it.

As he approached, he noticed that the door Marie had gone through had no sign. Peter didn't know if it was a residence or the back door of a shop. He walked slowly, pretending to study the buildings to his right and to his left. Really, he was waiting for Jacques to catch up. When he saw Jacques limp past the turnoff, he followed Marie.

She was waiting just inside. The door opened to a small landing at the bottom of a flight of stairs, and she was sitting on the bottom step. She looked Peter up and down, a playful smile stretching across her face. Then she motioned for him to sit down next to her. He complied, catching the scent of her tantalizing perfume and admiring how elegant she looked, even sitting on a stair.

"Well, what do you want?" she said.

Peter hesitated, unsure how to begin, but she noticed his discomfort and smiled again. Peter sighed and relaxed a bit.

"I've been told that you have several good sources in the German Army. I'd like to know where their troops are stationed along the beach, where their reinforcements are, and how long it would take those reinforcements to arrive if they were called into action."

"You speak very good French," she said. "But it's not your first language, is it? Are you American or British?"

"Does it matter?" Peter asked.

"You're only asking me to risk my life," she said, piercing Peter with her clear blue eyes. "I have been helping the Allies loyally for the past three years, but I would still like to know exactly what I'm getting into before I agree to sacrifice any more than I already have. I'm certain the Allies will protect me as long as it isn't too inconvenient for them to do so. But the Allies don't control France right now; the Germans do. I'd prefer to live through the war unscathed." She paused then smiled. "I'm not trying to be a hero; I'm just trying to survive. And for me, survival depends on my knowing whom I'm working with. If you want information from me, you will have to give me some information about yourself. For all I know, you really are the German soldier you're dressed as, and you're trying to get me to confess to something."

Peter smiled. "You already have confessed to something—three years of loyally helping the Allies. But don't worry; I'm American. From the army. Fairly new to the intelligence section."

"I suppose that will do for starting our relationship. And your name?"

Peter paused, realizing he had no alias. "Lieutenant Smith."

Marie giggled at him, her melodious laugh filling the stairwell. "If you prefer to remain anonymous, just say so. Don't make up a new name on my account. My name is Marie."

"My name is Peter."

"Is that your real name?"

"Since I was born."

"Well then, Peter, why do you want to know so much about where the German troops are stationed?"

"Well, I can scout out their current locations, but I need help finding out where the reinforcements are and how long it would take them to get to the harbor."

"Why do you want to know so much about German reinforcements?" She was teasing him, and he was enjoying it.

"Mademoiselle Murat, from what your files say, I think you're smart enough to figure that out yourself."

She laughed softly. "You may call me Marie. And I'm flattered that US intelligence files have labeled me intelligent. Perhaps I should ask a different question. Are you trying to plan an invasion?"

Peter nodded.

"For when?"

"This year."

"Can't you be a little more specific?"

Peter shifted his position on the stairs. "I'd rather not be. I've been told not to be."

"Do you know?"

Peter nodded again.

"Very well. You want to know troop numbers and their positions. Reinforcements and estimated time until they would be effective." She looked at him carefully. "You should know that if I find all this information out for you now, it will look suspicious if I ask all the same questions in two month's time. That's why I was hoping for a more specific time frame."

"I'm sorry, but I can't give it to you. We're planning now, so we need the information now. I guess we're hoping that not much will change between now and then. Can you help us?"

She nodded. "Don't worry. I know how important this invasion is going to be. There are few things I'd like more than to never hear German spoken in the café again. I also know that the beaches are heavily fortified. Everyone wants the invasion to come. But are you sure it can be successful?"

"Is anyone sure of that?" Peter sighed and leaned back against the steps, supporting his weight with his elbows. "I am fairly certain that without good information it won't succeed. Which is why I'm here—to get good information."

"From me." Marie leaned back on the stairs with him and smiled flirtatiously.

"Something like that," he said, turning toward her. "How hard will it be for you to get that type of data?"

Her hand gesture suggested it would be neither time-consuming nor difficult. "German soldiers ask me on dates at least daily. I'll just say yes to a few of the loose-lipped ones with access to an automobile and get them to drive me around to the encampments. It astounds me what some men will do to impress me. They're happy to brag about how many men they command, how many more they have the authority to call in, what they plan to do to the Allies when the invasion starts. It's really just a matter of finding a few good sources and getting them a little drunk."

"What's your background?"

"What do you mean?" she asked.

"I guess I'm just curious about you. How did you learn to get information so effectively? Why are you willing to risk so much to defeat the Nazis? What made you come to Calais?"

"I've learned my skills from experience," she said, her playful tone gone. "I know the war for you Americans is only two and a half years old, but for the rest of us, the Nazis have been around, at least on the periphery, for a very long decade. I'm French. That's why I'm willing to take risks if it will defeat the occupying army. And for your last question, I came to Calais because a dear friend from school came here often. She told me it was beautiful and the people were wonderful, so when I needed a change, I moved here. Then the war started, and things have been difficult, but at least I know what's going on in Calais. I guess I've stayed because the Germans might be worse somewhere else."

"What school did you go to?"

"The Versailles School of Liberal Arts for Young Ladies. Have you heard of it?"

Peter shook his head.

"It's a rather prestigious school. But I suppose since you aren't from around here, I'll make an allowance for your ignorance," she gently teased.

Peter laughed softly. "I'll try to remember the school from now on. And its student."

Marie tilted her head to one side. "And your background? How did you get involved in the war?"

Peter shrugged. "My brother was killed at Pearl Harbor. I joined the army the next day. I don't think I knew what I was getting into, but at the time, I didn't really care. I was angry and eager to sign the paperwork."

"Do you regret it?"

Peter thought for a few seconds. "No. I should have gone about things a little differently than I did, but I think it was something I had to do." Marie nodded her understanding. Then Peter turned back to business. "How soon do you think you can have information for me?"

She thought a few moments. "Why don't you meet me again in four days' time? I'll be here at noon, or I'll leave you a note here," she said as she pulled a loose brick out of the wall and then replaced it, "with an alternative time or place. I may not have all the information you require by then, but I should have something."

Peter nodded. "Thank you, mademoiselle. It was a pleasure to meet you, and I look forward to seeing you again." *Who wouldn't look forward to seeing such a beautiful woman again?* he thought. "Would you like to leave now, and I'll wait a few minutes and then leave?"

Marie nodded, and they both stood. She leaned forward and kissed Peter on both cheeks. Surprised, he stiffened. She gave him another smile. "I suppose that form of farewell hasn't established itself on the other side of the Atlantic yet. Pity." Then she left.

Peter sat back down to give her time to leave the area. The room no longer smelled of perfume. It smelled old and musty. There were cobwebs hanging from the ceiling and from the splintered banisters on the stairs. Leaning against the stairs had gotten his uniform dirty. *Funny,* Peter thought, *I didn't notice the dirt or the smell when she was here.*

Marie Murat was beautiful to the point of intoxication. Peter wondered what she would find out. He also wondered what she would have to do to gather her information. He frowned at the thought of her becoming friendly enough with a Nazi soldier for him to share classified information with her.

Peter was lost in his thoughts when Jacques pulled the door open. "Good meeting?" he asked.

Peter shrugged and nodded.

"Okay, then, let's go. You've been sitting there for fifteen minutes. I was beginning to think she had stabbed you."

* * *

Marie was nearly to her apartment, but she was still smiling to herself. She liked the American. She was used to the effect she had on men, and she could tell Peter was no exception. *Open admiration,* she thought. *That's what she had seen in Peter's eyes. A nice change from the usual lust.* She'd already put Peter into a category: American, idealistic, kind, chivalrous, brave, almost boyish in his innocence.

Marie Murat had a history of falling for the wrong type of man. At age sixteen, she'd burned all bridges with her parents and left their home to elope with a man twice her age. He had promised her the world, and she had been willing to leave her parents and live in poverty to be with him. Marie had taken the train to Paris, and he'd met her there. At the train station he had revealed his secret: he was already married and wasn't willing to leave his rich wife's estate. Devastated and desperate, Marie had been fortunate enough to gain the sympathy of a restaurant owner, and he had given her a job.

Marie had spent the next several years in Paris, rarely without a boyfriend. Few of the men she'd aligned herself with had been any better for her than the first. She had arrived in Calais with a black eye, a dislocated shoulder, and absolutely no self-esteem. Calais had been better for her than Paris, but it hadn't been without its share of heartache. Her most recent boyfriend had been gentle with her, and she had truly loved him. She'd admired him most of all for his passion—his passion for his work, his passion for the ideas he believed in, and his passion for her. They had been together for three years; he had died very recently, and now she was alone again. Alone and unsure of the future.

Marie's thoughts darted back to Peter. *Don't get involved with an agent,* she told herself, *even if he does seem nice. Spies have very short life spans.* She had four days to gather the information she needed; she was already planning the best way to do it.

* * *

When Peter returned to the farmhouse, only a few minutes before Jacques, Genevieve had company. There was a smiling five-year-old girl with her in the kitchen. And the kitchen smelled awful.

"Welcome back," Genevieve said with a smile. "We're just bleaching Birgit's hair. Her roots were starting to show, and they're a little dark, aren't they, darling?"

"Black like the night sky, but we want my hair to be blonde like Aunt Anne's," the little girl said.

"That's right, darling. And do you remember what the rules are in our beauty salon?"

"No men in the beauty salon!" Birgit giggled. Genevieve smirked.

Peter left the kitchen as Jacques walked through the front door. "What does your sister use to bleach Birgit's hair out?" he asked.

"Something that smells horrid," Jacques said. "Louis and Anne both have fair skin and fair hair. It looks a little less suspicious for them to have a blonde child following them around."

"Did she come to buy cheese?" Peter asked, wondering if there were any downed airmen hidden at the LeBras farmhouse.

Jacques looked into the kitchen and waved to the girls before returning to the parlor. "I don't see the basket she usually brings the coins in, so probably not. She comes over often, usually not on illegal business. Genevieve's the closest person to her in age for a good mile. Anne and Louis probably get boring for a five-year-old full of energy. And the LeBras family isn't as talented at disguising people as Genevieve and I are."

After the hair dyeing was completed, Genevieve converted the beauty salon back into a kitchen and prepared a small feast of bread, cheese, the last of the chicken they had been rationing out for the past three days, and a jar of preserved pears. The four of them took it outside to eat, despite the clouds and the wind because no one wanted to eat in a kitchen that still smelled like hair dye.

Peter discovered that Birgit, her hair and eyebrows freshly bleached, was exceptionally bright for her age. She noticed every butterfly and every bird that flew by and could name them. She knew what type of vegetable all the plants in the garden would produce, and she could remember exactly how many German soldiers had been in church the previous Sunday. She laughed at everything Genevieve said and smiled and rolled her eyes at nearly everything Jacques said. Birgit didn't ask who Peter was but spoke with him like she had known him for years. When Peter asked about it later, Genevieve said she had told Birgit that Peter was a cousin visiting from Paris. It wasn't the first time Birgit had met an "Olivier cousin" visiting from Paris. She knew not to mention anything about visitors to anyone besides the LeBrases and her friends, Jacques and Genevieve.

When the food was eaten, Birgit wandered around the garden in search of bugs, and everyone else lay on the old picnic blanket and stared at the clouds. For a brief time, Peter found it was almost possible to forget they were in the middle of a very serious, very large, and very bloody war.

After a bit, Birgit came back, her facial expression indicating that she was bored.

"I know what we can do," said Genevieve. "Peter can teach us that game the Americans all think is so wonderful."

"Baseball?" Peter asked.

Genevieve nodded. Birgit smiled, clasped her hands together, and bounced up and down as she looked from Genevieve to Peter and back again.

He hesitated. "Well, baseball takes about eighteen people for a real game. We could probably play a game with half that many, but with only four of us . . ." Genevieve looked disappointed. Birgit frowned and put her hands on her hips. He scratched his chin. "Um, four people is probably enough for a little batting practice, if you want to try that." The girls smiled.

"Can you start out with just three?" Jacques said with a yawn.

"Don't be lazy," Genevieve said.

"Someone has to keep lookout," was her brother's reply.

Peter found a board in the barn to use as a bat, and Genevieve wrapped a rock in several napkins and tied it to use as a ball.

"Well, the equipment's not the best, but I guess it will do," Peter said when they had rounded everything up. Birgit clapped in anticipation. Peter tossed the makeshift ball in the air and hit it about twenty yards away. It wasn't a very impressive hit, but considering the equipment, he was satisfied.

"Let me try!" Birgit exclaimed.

"All right." Peter handed her the bat, helped her place her hands correctly, and showed her how to swing. She practiced a few times while he collected their makeshift ball.

"Okay, I'm going to throw the ball to you, and I want you to swing and hit it." He gently pitched to her several times. Birgit swung each time but failed to hit the ball.

"Okay, Genevieve, why don't you throw the ball to us." Peter knelt behind Birgit and wrapped his arms around her to grip the bat over her hands. She giggled. "Relax and wait for the pitch, Birgit," he said with mock seriousness as he eased the bat back. Genevieve's pitching was below average, but Birgit and Peter managed to hit the ball a few yards on the second pitch. Birgit laughed in delight.

"So this is what American boys do all day?" Genevieve asked, laughing.

"No, this is what American boys do on those rare, blessed days when they and their siblings and neighbors all get their chores done early. And the real games are a lot better than just hitting the ball around. I mean, I've never been to a professional game, but the high school games were exciting. I wish I could take you to one. I'd buy you popcorn and tell you which players were good and . . ."

"Someone's coming," Jacques said. "Birgit, come here. We're going to play a game called keeping secrets." Jacques pulled his eye patch from a pocket and put it on his eye. At the same time, Genevieve grabbed Peter's hand and started pulling him into the house. He kicked the ball into the garden, where it would be out of sight. As he looked over his shoulder, he could see a cloud of dust being stirred up along the road. In front of the dust was what looked like a military jeep.

"You'll have to hide under the stairs until we get them to leave," Genevieve said as she ran to the closet. Peter made sure his pistol was loaded and ready then crawled into the closet. Genevieve whispered for him to remain quiet and then put the panel over the hole. Peter heard her replace the cleaning supplies and shut the closet door.

* * *

Genevieve stepped away from the closet and waited, nervously looking around the room, making sure nothing seemed suspicious. After several minutes, Jacques, Birgit, and a German hauptmann entered the front door.

Jacques spoke first. "Hauptmann, this is my sister. We are the only people who live here."

"Mademoiselle," the hauptmann began, "perhaps you can be of assistance to me. We're trying to find the owners of a house about a mile from here. They have disappeared. We don't know their names or where they have gone, so we are asking the surrounding homes, but many of them are empty . . ."

"Many of our neighbors no longer live here, sir," Genevieve said. "Some of them moved to Southern France, others to England or Canada. If you could explain which house you are referring to, we will do our best to help you."

"This house was occupied, at least until a few days ago. If you've ever traveled that way, I'm sure you've noticed it. It has the most beautiful flowers I have seen in all of France."

"Which direction is it?" Genevieve continued the conversation, though she could have found the Papineau home while blindfolded.

"Along the road I just drove on, a mile farther east from Calais."

"I think I know which house you are referring to, but we didn't know the people who lived there very well. I can't even remember their names. Jacques, do you remember? Was it Cartier, perhaps? Neither of us goes that way very often. If we want to visit the beach, we just cut across the fields. And although we do leave our home once in a while, most of our travel is into Calais." Genevieve paused. "I'm sorry we can't help you more, Hauptmann."

"You said the name was Cartier?"

"It might have been, but as Genevieve said, we didn't know them well," Jacques stated.

The hauptmann paced around the parlor. "That's an odd smell coming from the kitchen. Did you burn something?"

"Spring cleaning, sir. We've had to be a little creative with cleaning supplies since the war began," Genevieve said.

"Hmm." She wasn't sure if the hauptmann was satisfied with her answer. "May I see your papers?"

Jacques and Genevieve handed their identity documents over to the German officer. He paced a little more, stopping beside Birgit and kneeling on the floor so he could speak with her easily. "You are a very beautiful child. What is your name?"

"Birgit."

"And, Birgit, where are your papers?"

"At home, sir."

"And how old are you?"

"Five, sir."

"My daughter was five when I last saw her. I remember her looking a bit like you. Beautiful blonde hair and brown eyes."

"Thank you, Hauptmann," Birgit said with some warmth.

"Where do you live, young lady?"

"Over there." She pointed in the correct direction, west, even though her home was not visible from the living room.

"Do you know many of the people who live around here?"

"I know Genevieve and Jacques, and my aunt and uncle."

"And that's all?" the hauptmann said with audible disappointment. "No visitors? Do you ever see men from England or from America? Men who tell you stories about flying airplanes?"

* * *

Birgit giggled. Inside the secret room, Peter was getting very nervous. He wished he could see what expressions or gestures Birgit was making. He knew she hadn't seen Genevieve pull out the back panel of the closet, but he thought Birgit might still know about the hiding place or mention something to the German that would lead to a more thorough search of the farmhouse. The suspense of hearing the conversation rather than seeing it was excruciating.

"Do your aunt and uncle ever have visitors?" There was a slight pause. "Do Jacques and Genevieve ever have visitors?"

There was another giggle followed by a reply. "Yes, of course, they have one right now," Peter heard Birgit say. Peter silently groaned. How foolish it was to trust a child to keep a secret, especially from someone who was being kind to her.

"Who, and where?" the hauptmann asked with great interest in his voice.

"Right here, of course."

Peter prepared to take aim at the hauptmann when he opened the closet's secret panel.

"I visit them all the time; I think I'm their favorite."

Relieved and surprised, Peter almost laughed. *Birgit is very good at this*, he thought.

"And, Birgit, are you their only visitor?"

"No, you are here. And sometimes my aunt and uncle come with me. But not all the time."

"And you don't know anyone else who lives nearby?"

"No, sir. I can't remember how things were before the war and before everyone moved away."

"Very well. Birgit, thank you for your help. Mademoiselle, monsieur."

Peter heard several more footsteps and the door close. Then everything was quiet. Peter heard the sound of a car driving away, followed by more silence.

Jacques's voice finally broke the calm. "Birgit, you played the game very well."

"Did I win?" she asked.

"Yes. And for winning, I'm going to find you a beautiful ribbon for your hair. Come help me look for one upstairs."

Peter heard their footsteps pass through the hall and over his head. Then the closet door opened, and Genevieve let him out.

"You were worried," she said with a smile.

"Wouldn't you have been?" he asked, still squinting, trying to readjust to the light.

"In your circumstance, I suppose I would, but I know Birgit. She is very clever. She doesn't understand everything that's going on, but she knows not to tell German soldiers anything useful. She certainly knows not to talk about visitors." Genevieve paused and smiled. "And I really doubt one German hauptmann could take down you or Jacques if it had come to that. There was another soldier in the car. But even if he had been inside, I'd bet on you and Jacques winning a shootout."

"More soldiers would have come to look for them when they didn't return."

"Yes, we would have needed to go into hiding had they found you or suspected us of not telling the truth. Jacques knows enough people that we could have managed. He would hate depending on others to keep him hidden from the Germans, and so would I, but we've both known it's a possibility for a long time. Sometimes I think it's not a matter of *if* we'll ever have to go into hiding but a matter of *when*."

"Well, your hiding has been postponed another day." Peter stretched his arms then put the cleaning supplies back in front of the closet's panel.

"I'm glad for that. He seemed nice," Genevieve said, referring to the German.

"Yes, that was one of the things that worried me. It's easy to keep secrets from an unlikeable enemy . . . a little harder when they seem like decent people." Peter shut the closet door. "When the war started, I hated them all. I imagined they were all evil, machinelike fiends. That was what they looked like in the newsreels, and it was easier that way."

"What made you change?" Genevieve's voice contained no judgment, no condemnation.

"Experience and my conscience, I guess." Peter said. "I met too many Italian civilians, and they told me about their husbands, sons, brothers. They were fighting against me, but they weren't evil, not if their families were to be believed. They were just victims of bad government. Then I met a few German prisoners. They weren't machines; they were human, and they were scared. And most of them didn't want to be at war any more than I did. They wanted to be farming or building things or taking care of their families. Hating them was the easy way, but it wasn't the right way. I had no more right to hate them than they had to hate me." Peter thought for a moment, reflecting on the younger, almost bloodthirsty version of himself. He was glad he had changed, but reawakening his conscience hadn't made the war any easier. "And you, Genevieve, have you ever hated them?"

Genevieve thought for a few moments. "Just the ones who killed Mireille and the one who attacked me. I'm trying to forgive them. It should be easy to forgive the dead, but . . ." She trailed off.

"But it's not?"

She nodded. "Especially the oberleutnant who came here. His intentions were so evil, so vile. How do you forgive that? I know I should—that's what Christians do. And I'm almost over the hate, but the horror and repulsion is still there every time I think about it."

"I think you're a very good Christian, Genevieve," Peter said, a little in awe of her ability to stay so innocent and wholesome amid such difficult circumstances. It was then that Peter realized that being around her made him want to be a better Christian too.

Chapter Eight
Sabotage

Thursday, June 1

THE NEXT DAY JACQUES AND Peter rode their bicycles to visit Monsieur Jean-Philippe Laurier, the last of the three agents Peter was to contact. Laurier's home was to the south of Calais, so Jacques and Peter took a route that stayed on the outskirts of the city. Jacques had given them both thick, dark beards and hair to match for the occasion, and they were dressed in ordinary civilian clothing. It was fairly early, and they saw few people on their way around the town. They did pass a few plane wrecks; the burned-up airplanes jutted out of otherwise normal fields. Peter hoped the occupants of each plane had parachuted to safety. The planes were a little like the bomb craters he saw in the city—jarring interruptions of what would have otherwise been a beautiful, peaceful part of the world.

They left their bicycles about half a mile from Laurier's home. They didn't want him to see two visitors, so they split up. Jacques left the road and moved swiftly through the field. Peter walked at a more leisurely pace along the road. He passed only one other house before Laurier's; most of the walk was along fields.

Peter knocked on Laurier's front door and waited. After a minute, he knocked again, but no one came to the door. He walked over to the garage. Jacques was there, but Laurier's car and radio were missing.

"McDougall said he reports by radio every Saturday," Peter said, a little puzzled. It was a Thursday.

"Maybe he's hiding it somewhere."

The two of them checked all the doors and looked through all the windows but decided not to pick any locks. Jacques had briefly gone through the home only days before. They rode back to the Olivier farmhouse with plans to try again the next day.

* * *

By evening, Peter was fighting boredom at the Olivier farmhouse. The afternoon had been a dull one for him. Genevieve went into town to collect laundry, with Louis LeBras as her escort. Birgit stayed in her home. Jacques made repairs around the house and worked on the cheese in their cellar. Peter weeded a few patches in the garden, studied his scriptures, and watched the American planes come in for an air raid.

By the time Jacques, Genevieve, and Peter were finished with supper and the evening BBC ritual, Peter couldn't hide his boredom any longer. He didn't mention anything out loud, but he couldn't help remembering part of his assignment was to make the Germans notice an increase in Resistance activity.

Jacques noticed Peter's fidgeting. "It's a good thing you aren't an injured pilot stuck in the Notre Dame of Calais. You have cabin fever after one afternoon of not doing anything. They often have to stay inside a small room for weeks at a time."

Peter recognized Jacques's statement as a well-deserved chastisement and nodded. *Patience*, he thought to himself. It was something he'd never had in great abundance.

"However," Jacques continued, "since you're bored, we might as well engage in something productive. The telephone lines are probably repaired by now from when they were last cut."

"I thought you said you weren't involved with that," Genevieve cut in.

"I wasn't, but if you said they were cut about a week ago, then they probably have them repaired by now."

"I guess I won't try to do any baking tomorrow, then."

Jacques wasted little time in getting his face-darkening make-up applied to all of them, and then the three rode their bicycles toward town. Even if it had been before curfew, which it wasn't, they would have looked suspicious riding into town dressed in all dark clothing with darkened faces. They rode a wide path around to the southwest end of town, stopping twice to hide from patrols, and then slowly slipped into the town center across one of the more narrow and shallow sections of the canal. Beyond that, the city wall was merely a pile of rubble. They stayed alert for patrols and cautiously stepped over the rubble heap.

Like the first time Peter had been in Calais after curfew, there was little visible activity. There were a few blackout curtains that didn't fit the windows exactly and a few open windows that allowed conversations or music to drift out into the street. For the most part, however, the city was quiet and dark. Peter had seen Jacques in action before, and his stealth was something Peter took for granted. But Genevieve also impressed him. She was as quiet as her brother while they crept carefully through the town, always staying deep in the shadows.

Jacques, in the lead, slowed as they approached the German Army headquarters for the city. The occupying army had taken over a group of buildings not far from the train station, near the Parc St. Pierre. A few guards were patrolling the area, but they were smoking cigarettes, probably to help them stay awake. Peter assumed the glowing end of their tobacco would hamper their ability to see in the dark, but even so, the three of them crawled slowly to their destination.

Jacques made eye contact with Peter and pointed to a storage depot. He spoke in a barely audible whisper. "They keep explosives in there. We'll need something to replace these." Jacques pointed to the bag he had packed with a variety of armaments. "Watch out for the patrol, but get together what the three of us can carry without being slowed down. Try to get a mix of detonators and explosives. Genevieve and I will join you in a few minutes."

Peter nodded and headed for the depot. It was not an elaborate building, just a red-brick rectangle. There was a guard smoking near the entrance. Peter watched him finish a cigarette and then slouch against the doorway. Keeping his distance, Peter made his way to the back of the building the guard was watching. There was no back door. Disappointed in the building's architect, Peter picked up a piece of rubble that had been scattered by a recent air raid and walked along the dark side of the depot toward the sleepy guard. He took a deep breath and hoped the guard was still slouched against the doorway with his face turned away. Then Peter peeked around the corner and saw the guard's back.

Peter glanced over at the main building and saw two shadows helping each other up to a second-story window. He wouldn't have noticed the Olivier siblings if he hadn't already known they were there. Peter also noticed a pair of guards walking around the main building and saw the guard near him straighten as they passed. Peter crept back around the corner into the darkness and waited until he thought the moving patrol was out of sight. He glanced around the corner and saw the guard slouch against the doorway once again. The guard seemed to have a hard time finding a comfortable spot, and he took his helmet off and slung it over his rifle. Then he rested his head in the corner between the door and the doorframe so he was facing the main building.

Perfect, Peter thought. He glanced about to make sure there were no other guards in the area and silently moved toward his opponent. *He obviously wants to get a little extra shuteye*, Peter thought. Using the piece of rubble, he helped the guard out with a blow to the back of his head. Peter caught the guard as he fell and lowered him to the ground. The door to the storage depot was locked, but the guard had a set of keys in his left coat pocket. The third key opened the door, and Peter dragged the guard in after him to keep the unconscious man out of sight.

The inside of the building did not disappoint him. *A spy in a munitions depot . . . I feel like a kid in a candy store.* He looked through the boxes and gathered a few potato masher grenades, some sticks of dynamite, a few timers, and some detonators. Then he wired some dynamite together and made a bomb that would go off in an hour. Peter was hardly a demolitions expert, but he had learned the basics in army training and a few extra tricks during his most recent OSS training stint. Peter was about to connect the timer to the explosives when he heard a noise. He hid himself in the corner behind the doorway. As a dark figure entered the room, he aimed his Colt at the shadow's head. He didn't shoot; it was Genevieve.

"Where is Jacques?" Peter asked quietly.

"The generator is on the other side of the building. He wants to work on that. He said to meet him by the bicycles. What do you want me to do?"

"Grab what's convenient to carry from this pile, then I suggest we relieve the Germans of all those excess supplies just sitting around in boxcars."

Genevieve and Peter both grabbed what would fit in their pockets and in the bags they carried. He set the timer on the bomb.

"Peter, you may want to set up more than one of those."

"All right, but why?" he asked.

"Not everyone that slaves away in German factories wants the Nazis to win this war. Duds aren't uncommon."

Peter took Genevieve's advice, set up the second bomb, and dragged the unconscious soldier to a row of cars parked between the depot and the main building. Then they left. The train station, or what was left of it, was near army headquarters. Allied bombing runs that targeted train tracks, airfields, factories, and supply depots had made it more difficult for the German Armies to stay supplied, but there were still some supplies coming in by rail and by ship. The line running from the harbor to the train depot was, for the night at least, in working order. Peter decided to remedy that.

He crawled under a boxcar, where he would be hidden should any patrols pass by, and started digging out enough dirt that he could put a few dynamite sticks under the rail. For good measure, he fastened a second bomb on the underside of the boxcar. Genevieve did the same thing on another boxcar about twenty-five yards away. After waiting for a pair of soldiers to pass, Peter went over to join her.

He was impressed with her work. "You're extremely useful to have around, Genevieve. I think that given the right circumstances, you could stop an entire company single-handedly."

She smiled. Peter couldn't see her face in the dark, but he saw a flash of white teeth.

"Anyone can stop an entire company single-handedly if they blow up the right bridge just when said company needs to cross it," she said.

After another patrolling soldier walked past them, Genevieve and Peter continued their work. For their bombs, they used a mixture of timed and pressure-sensitive detonators. When they had used half their explosives, they crawled away toward the east side of town. They were about a block away when they heard a loud explosion. Peter pulled Genevieve into a shadow and looked around for the rush of people he expected to see reacting to the noise.

"There goes either the generator or the supply depot," Genevieve said calmly. "That was too big to be a boxcar, unless the boxcar was filled with artillery shells."

"If reinforcements come to check it out, what direction will they come from?"

"Most of the senior officers live near the town hall in those buildings." She pointed to several buildings just within view. "The majority of the normal troops live closer to the beaches or several miles south of town." She smiled sheepishly at Peter, looking at his arms that were still wrapped around her. "Most people around here are used to hearing explosions in the middle of the night."

Peter nodded at Genevieve's information and relaxed his grip on her. Then they heard another huge explosion. Peter pulled Genevieve closer to him, out of the moonlight, instinctively wanting to protect her.

"There goes the other one." Genevieve sounded satisfied. They continued their journey to the rendezvous point. They saw more German troops on their way from the city than they had seen on their trip into the city, but they had little trouble remaining undetected. They continued the process of slowly and silently leapfrogging from one dark hiding place to the next until they reached the outskirts of town and crossed the canal. About that time, they began to hear airplanes.

"That would be the RAF on their nightly run," Genevieve said. "Or the Americans dropping supplies to Resistance members farther inland."

When they reached the bicycles, Peter sat down to wait for Jacques. Genevieve sat down right next to him. She sat closer than she needed to be, but Peter didn't mind. He noticed that she was shivering, even though he didn't find the night particularly cool.

"Are you cold?" he asked.

"Yes," she said quietly. Peter didn't have a jacket to give her, so he put his arm around her and pulled her close, assuming the canal water had splashed her more than it splashed him. He rubbed her arms with his hands, trying to create friction and warmth. After a few minutes, her shivering stopped, but she didn't pull away. The thought crossed Peter's mind that if someone like Genevieve had lived in Shelley, Idaho, he might have spent less time playing baseball and more time dating. Maybe.

They hadn't been sitting there very long when Peter heard someone coming. He whipped his pistol out and pointed it in the direction of the noise, pulling himself onto his feet in a low crouch. Genevieve tensed. Whoever it was, they were coming silently, so after the initial twig snap that caught Peter's attention, he couldn't tell how fast they were progressing. Then he heard a bird call.

"That's Jacques," Genevieve assured Peter. "We've used that signal before."

Jacques came into view then, grinning and breathing deeply, as if he had been running or was recovering from an adrenaline rush. Peter suspected it was both. "Well," he said between breaths, "I think that and the recent increase in air raids should get some attention."

Chapter Nine
Vintage Wine and French Soap

Friday, June 2

THE SECOND ATTEMPT TO VISIT Monsieur Jean-Philippe Laurier started just as the first had: the same disguises, the same route. They passed a few more patrols than they had the previous day. Peter wondered if that was a result of their sabotage work the night before.

When Peter arrived at the Laurier farm, he walked right up to the front door and knocked. He trusted that Jacques was already safely in the garage, hidden from sight. The door was opened immediately, and Peter suspected that Laurier had watched him walk from the street to the door.

"*Bonjour*, monsieur," Peter said cheerfully.

Laurier looked over Peter, sizing him up. He didn't say anything for a time; he just stared. Peter stared back. Laurier was tall for a Frenchman—taller than Peter by half a head. His hair was gray and thick. All of his hair was like that: the hair on his head, his eyebrows, his full beard, the hair on his arms. He appeared stolid and strong—strong both mentally and physically. Finally, Laurier smiled slightly. "Can I help you?"

"I was hoping to meet with Monsieur Jean-Philippe Laurier. Is that you?"

"It is." Laurier crossed his arms and leaned against the doorway.

"Good. Could I speak to you for a few minutes?"

"Regarding what?"

"*Vixi puellis nuper idoneus et militavi.*"

Laurier straightened and stepped aside to let Peter enter. "Ah, yes. *Non sine gloria*. Please come in. You are welcome in my home, although I do insist on all my guests disarming themselves."

"Is there a special reason for that?" Peter asked, entering the Frenchman's home. Peter didn't like to part with his weapons, especially since he was ready to trust Toussaint and Marie, leaving him suspicious of Laurier, the third and last agent.

"Experience," Laurier answered. Peter had hoped his host would elaborate more, but instead he pointed to a large wooden box. Peter reluctantly took out his trench knife and his Colt M1911 and placed them in Laurier's box. Peter would have preferred to keep them, but he wanted Monsieur Laurier to be cooperative, and he knew Jacques was only a few yards away. *Relax*, he told himself. *You've been planning this since McDougall's briefing.*

Laurier led Peter into his front room. It was what Peter and Jacques had expected to happen. There were several bookcases, a desk, three large armchairs, and two tables. All the furniture was made of dark wood that needed polishing. Both tables and the desk supported stacks of books, magazines, and other papers. The house smelled musty and was rundown, matching the home's outside appearance.

"This is the first time someone has come to me in person. Would I be correct in assuming the reason for this unexpected visit has to do with an upcoming invasion?"

Peter nodded.

"Will it be in Calais?"

Peter nodded again.

"And you would like me to tell you what I've observed of the German defenses and troop concentrations?"

Peter nodded the third time, with a smile. "That's exactly right, sir."

Laurier motioned for his guest to be seated.

"Thank you, sir."

"Well, if I'm going to tell you all about the current German defenses, I'd like a drink." Laurier left the room, and Peter heard a few cupboards opening. Laurier returned carrying a tray with a nearly empty, thick green bottle of red wine and two full wine goblets. Peter looked at Laurier very carefully when he returned, but his host didn't seem to have retrieved any weapons. Laurier handed a glass to Peter, balanced the tray on a stack of books resting on the desk, then sat down and appeared to relax as he sipped his wine.

"All right, then, when will this invasion come?" Laurier asked.

"I'm not supposed to disclose that, sir. Truth be told, I don't have the exact day, just the week." Peter set the wine glass down on a nearby end table without drinking any of it. He'd heard people say a little alcohol was good for the nerves, and Peter was certainly feeling nervous, but he didn't plan to start a drinking habit, especially not while on assignment.

"Do you not care for my wine? It's vintage 1928—I've been saving this bottle for quite some time. I've only one other of this quality, and I'm saving that for the liberation."

"I am sincerely grateful for your generosity, sir, but I don't drink alcohol. That, and I came here for information, not fine French dining. I think it's best if I keep my mind clear." Peter gently steered the conversation toward business, ignoring the knot in his stomach and hoping he hadn't offended his source. "Do you know how many troops are stationed within, say, an hour of the beaches?"

"It will take more than an hour to establish a beachhead, I would think."

"Yes, monsieur, but we'd like to know how many troops we might be dealing with in the first critical hour. I've got a map in my pocket; I was hoping you could help me fill in where the German Army is currently most concentrated. Then we'd like you to keep us informed of any changes that happen between now and the invasion."

Monsieur Laurier nodded his consent. Peter took the map from his pocket and cleared a spot on the coffee table between them. He stacked a few books together and put them on the edge of the table, accidentally knocking over a pile of papers when he set the books too close to them. Peter bent down to pick them up and noticed the papers he had scattered included a large pile of ration cards. *Enough to feed several downed airmen for days at a time, or enough to be a generous reward granted for cooperation with the issuing authority*, Peter thought. He wondered how Jacques could have missed them in his earlier search. He looked at them more closely, fingered the spot where his pistol should have been, then looked up just in time to see Laurier swinging a large wrench at his head.

Peter threw his elbow up and caught most of the force with his forearm, slowing the wrench slightly before it crashed into the side of his head. The momentum knocked him over into the table, and it and Peter crashed to the hardwood floor, scattering paper, ration cards, and books everywhere.

Laurier attempted a second blow. He stood over Peter and brought the wrench down with considerable speed. Peter picked up the coffee table and used it to knock Laurier's arm away. It didn't make him drop the weapon, but it did stop him from hitting Peter, at least for a few seconds. Laurier switched hands and swung again. Peter countered by kicking him, but Laurier hit Peter's shin with the wrench. Peter kicked him again with his other leg, forcing Laurier a few feet away and stalling him long enough for Peter to get back on his feet. He picked up the coffee table and used it as a shield to block the next series of blows. It turned out to be a decent shield, and a decent weapon. Peter used the table to hit Laurier's hand again, this time leaving him uncoordinated long enough for Peter to lunge at the wrench and wrestle it away. Laurier grunted and kicked Peter's shin, right where the wrench had struck. Peter lost his balance, and both men crashed to the floor.

Weaponless, Laurier snarled angrily and grabbed Peter's hand that held the wrench and slammed it down onto the floor. Then he did it again and again. The third time was too much. The wrench flew out of Peter's hand and slid behind him across the floor. Laurier tried to get past Peter to the weapon, but Peter drove his knee into Laurier's abdomen and pushed him the other way.

Laurier grabbed Peter's hair to force his head back but only managed to tear the wig off. It surprised Laurier. So did Peter's fist, which connected swiftly and firmly with his jaw at about the same time. Laurier was strong, but Peter suspected the man's endurance did not match his strength. Still, he managed to grab Peter's real hair and slam his head into the floor a few times before Peter finally gained the upper hand in their struggle. Peter briefly remembered the advice an OSS instructor had given him a few weeks before: in hand-to-hand combat, there is usually only one rule— kill or be killed.

Peter was about to punch his opponent again when he heard a crash and saw Laurier go completely limp. Peter looked up in surprise and saw Jacques fingering the broken wine bottle with a look of distaste.

"I didn't hear you come in; nice timing," Peter said as he sat up, panting. "But I really had everything completely under control."

"Of course you did, but I was getting a little bored waiting around." Jacques held out his hand, and Peter gladly accepted the help back to his feet.

They tied Jean-Philippe Laurier to one of his large armchairs and gagged him so he wouldn't be able to shout if he regained consciousness while they were still in the neighborhood. They wanted Laurier to tell the Nazis that American agents were snooping around Calais, asking about troop concentrations, but not until they were very far away. Jacques pocketed the ration cards. "Never know when we'll have unexpected guests parachute in on us," he said by way of explanation.

Peter slowly sorted through the papers on the desk and carefully picked a lock on one of the drawers while Jacques looked around the kitchen and bedrooms. None of the papers in French were significant, but Peter kept the ones in German, fearing his limited comprehension of the German language would lead to inaccurate sorting should he try to do it himself. Peter also went through the papers on the end table, where he had set his wine glass, and noticed something new: a white powder on one edge of the glass. At about that same time, Jacques returned from the kitchen holding a small brown jar.

"I think he was going to drug you," Jacques said.

Peter nodded in agreement. "He left a bit of residue on the glass. I guess when that didn't work, he moved to plan B. I don't know if it included dragging me out to the pond so he could drown me, but you were right about him trying to bash my head in." Peter folded the papers and put them in his pocket.

"Try? Judging by the blood on the side of your face, it looks like he succeeded."

Peter put his hand up to the right side of his face. Jacques was right; it was bloody. And swollen. And painful to touch. Peter winced. He pulled up his pant leg to examine his other bruise and found plenty of blood there too.

Jacques went into the hallway and came back with a hat. He tossed it to Peter. "Put that on; a face as swollen and bloody as yours might attract more attention than we want on the way home."

Peter wiped most of the blood off his face, put his wig and the hat on, collected his weapons, and hobbled back to the bicycles. It was a long ride home, partially because every push of the pedal with his right leg made him dizzy. He moved slowly, but even that pace was a challenge. Jacques seemed to understand what was going on, and he adjusted his speed to match Peter's.

The farmhouse was empty when they returned. Genevieve had gone into town with their neighbor again. Jacques offered Peter something to clean his wounds, but Peter was too tired to bother with it just then. He sat down in the living room and closed his eyes. After a few minutes, he drifted off to sleep.

* * *

Moments later, Peter woke when he heard the front door slam shut. Genevieve had just come home with a new load of dirty laundry. She dropped it on the floor when she saw Peter.

"Peter, what happened?" she asked, kneeling by his side.

"His head came in contact with a large wrench and then with a hardwood floor a few times," Jacques said from the kitchen.

"And where were you when all this was happening?" She sounded angry.

"Emptying the oil from the man's automobile and putting water in the fuel tank."

"Jacques, you're supposed to be better backup than that. What if the man had killed Peter while you were playing with his car?" She started to get up to give her brother a proper scolding.

Peter touched her arm gently. "It's not as bad as it looks."

"Well, it looks awful, and I haven't even seen it all yet." She carefully removed Peter's hat and fingered the cut. "There's blood everywhere."

"Heads just bleed a lot. And there's not blood everywhere. None on my arms or my chest or my legs."

"No, there is blood on your leg; it soaked through your pants." She got up and walked past Jacques, who was standing in the doorway to the kitchen eating a slice of bread as he watched, amusement showing in his eyes. Genevieve reappeared with a bowl of water, soap, and a rag.

"I can do it," Peter said. He grabbed the rag and dipped it in the water.

"No, you stay still and let me."

Peter didn't argue with her. Jacques finished his bread and said he was going to go milk the cows.

Genevieve started wiping the blood off Peter's face with the rag.

"That hurts. Can you start with the leg instead?"

"Ripping the scab off your shin won't feel much better," she said. But she did it anyway. She knelt down beside Peter's right leg and rolled his pants up above the wound, slowly peeling the fabric off the wound.

"You're right—it doesn't feel much better," he said.

"It will only get worse if we don't take care of it now."

Peter grunted a hesitant agreement.

"Your contact certainly blew his cover," Genevieve said.

He nodded then stopped when he realized the motion aggravated the pain in his head. "Yes, but it wasn't really blown until I escaped. He could have radioed in that he was met by an agent, worked with him, then saw him being arrested later that day."

"A report like that would have been suspicious."

"I suppose he thought I knew something worth risking his cover for. I'm fairly certain his Nazi bosses would agree. If you were he, or any other German spy, for that matter, how much would you risk to prevent a successful invasion?"

"I would never work for the Nazis," Genevieve said. "But I see your point. The Germans are in power now, and the odds are in their favor when the invasion comes. Anyone voluntarily working for them has a strong motivation for keeping the status quo."

Genevieve turned back to her healing work and was as gentle and thorough as she could be. The soap stung, but after a few minutes, the blood was only a small oozing line, and Peter could see what his wound actually looked like. There was a large oval bruise, and the skin had broken at its center.

"What are all these scars from?" Genevieve asked, fingering a series of scars on Peter's ankle and calf.

"Shrapnel in Sicily."

"Go on," she said when he stopped talking.

"I used to drive tanks. We had gotten used to fighting Italians, and they weren't putting up much of a fight. Then we ran into some German artillery. My tank was hit before we really knew they were in the area. The controls stopped working, and our lieutenant told us to get out of there. I was last in line. Our ammo started exploding when I was halfway up the ladder. I barely remember it, but my lieutenant reached down and pulled me out. I was in pretty bad shape, I guess—pieces of hot metal sticking into my back, clothes on fire. And German artillery hitting all around us."

"Was this the biggest piece of shrapnel?" Genevieve asked, pointing to the back of Peter's ankle.

"It's the biggest scar, but I think it was probably one of the smaller pieces originally; they just overlooked it for a few days."

"They missed a piece of shrapnel sticking out of your ankle? I thought American doctors were better than that."

"Well, they got twenty-two out of the twenty-three pieces—they weren't doing too bad considering how many other casualties they were working on." He watched her brow furrow in concentration as she studied his leg.

"I only count six scars here. Where are the others?"

"Some are on my other leg. The rest are spread all the way up to my back."

Genevieve wrapped a cloth around Laurier's work to keep it from bleeding any more. Then she moved to Peter's face.

She had a light touch, but it still hurt. Peter gritted his teeth. He would have preferred to sleep but didn't feel he could tell her to go away and leave him alone. Time after time, she rinsed the rag, sopped up some of the blood clinging to his hair, and rinsed the rag again.

"This water is turning pink," she said when she was nearly done. She got up to change it then came back to finish the job and remove the fake beard Jacques had given Peter earlier that morning. "Well, any scar will be hidden by your hair once the swelling goes down. Unless the cut on your ear doesn't heal properly."

"It won't be the first scar on my face."

"That's right." Her fingers found the scar on the other side of Peter's head. "Where did you get this one?"

"It's a souvenir from my last trip to France."

"Scars are odd things to collect, don't you think? When in foreign countries, most people collect postcards or dolls or coins. What is it from?"

"A bullet." He watched her flinch ever so slightly as he spoke.

"That's awful."

"Not really. It would only be awful if it had killed me. But it didn't."

Genevieve leaned closer to glance from the old scar to the new injury. He smiled at her careful study. She smiled back then shyly asked, "Tell me, Peter, do you have a sweetheart back in Idaho waiting for you?"

Peter laughed, remembering his few pathetic high school attempts to impress girls. "No, no girlfriend. I guess I never found anyone that was worth the effort."

"Does it take a lot of effort in America?" Genevieve asked.

"Not always, I suppose. I just saw my brother and my friends crash and burn enough that I never wanted to try."

"And after the war, do you plan to find a sweetheart?" She busied herself cleaning the rag in the bowl.

"Well, yeah, I'm a horrible cook. If I don't find a wife, I might starve to death."

"Is cooking the only thing wives are good for?"

Peter smirked. "Cleaning too, I guess." He was joking, and Genevieve knew it. Still, a comment like that deserved some type of punishment. She laughed and playfully punched his forearm. Peter inhaled sharply.

"How many other wounds do you have?" she asked after she rolled up Peter's shirt to see the bruise left by the wrench's first contact with him.

"That's the last one. And it's not a big deal. No blood even, just a little swelling."

She looked at it again and shook her head. "Get some rest, Peter," was all she said. Then she walked away, leaving Peter to wonder what, if anything, their conversation had meant. It surprised him that despite his earlier desire to sleep, he now found himself wishing Genevieve had stayed.

Chapter Ten
War's Other Casualties

Saturday, June 3

PETER OBEYED GENEVIEVE'S ADVICE TO rest, but the next morning, he wasn't sure he felt any better. If anything, his bruises felt more tender, his body more sore. He helped Genevieve with the laundry, helped Jacques with the cows, and found time to stare with fascination at the bright colors appearing on his skin where Laurier's wrench had struck him. The work gradually helped with the stiffness. Staring at the bruises made him hope Laurier was feeling just as awful.

In the late afternoon, the three of them began looking through the small stack of papers Jacques and Peter had taken from Laurier's desk. Of the three of them, Genevieve had the best German reading skills, so she did most of the translating.

"This is interesting," she said halfway through the first page.

"What is it?" Peter asked.

"About five months ago, an entire Resistance cell was arrested. We could never figure out who betrayed them. This letter says the enclosed payment is in return for the tip leading to their arrest."

The next seven sheets of paper were more of the same in reverse chronological order. Two of them were payments for tips leading to single arrests. One was for a father-and-son team. Four had led to multiple arrests, but the numbers were either not specified in the letters or the respective crackdowns were still in progress.

"Why would he keep these?" Genevieve wondered out loud. "Wouldn't they be a liability if discovered by the wrong person?"

"But useful if he was questioned by the Gestapo. They prove he is loyal to the Third Reich," Jacques explained.

Genevieve nodded slowly then continued her translation. She gasped out loud at the last note.

"What is it?" Jacques asked.

"I must have read that wrong; you read it." She handed the note to her brother.

Jacques slowly went through the translation in his head and then read it out loud.

Monsieur Laurier, It is with great pleasure that we enclose this token of our appreciation. As you suspected, your son, Louis, and his friend Gaston did, in fact, have ties to the traitorous Resistance. Your keen observation and prudent action has ensured that neither of them will harm the Franco-German alliance ever again.

With deep gratitude, Hauptsturmführer Schneider.

"You were reading it correctly, Genevieve. Some men are devils."

"He told the British that his son mysteriously disappeared in 1940," Peter said, remembering the information sheets Colonel McDougall had given him. "I guess his disappearance was only a mystery to some."

Genevieve stood up and walked outside. Peter followed her, leaving Jacques to carefully reread all the letters.

"Hey, are you all right?" Peter asked Genevieve. She was sitting on the steps leading from the kitchen to the garden, her elbows on her knees, her head resting in her hands. Peter sat down next to her.

"We knew some of those people, some of the ones who were arrested. I hadn't known they were part of the Resistance, but I remember them from school or from church." She paused then sighed. "I wonder if any of them are still alive."

"The Germans are bound to need forced labor somewhere in this war. They could be peeling potatoes for soldiers on the Eastern Front."

Genevieve continued as if she hadn't heard him. "How could someone turn in their own son? The letter said nothing about blackmail or threats. He just turned in his son for money. How could he do that? Families are supposed to stick together."

Peter thought for a moment before answering. "Hate and love are both very powerful emotions. Once you feel one for someone, it's hard to go back to neutral ground. When my father was twelve and my uncle was fifteen, they and my grandmother decided to join a new church. My grandfather was furious. He'd heard stories about the Mormon Church and wanted no part in it for him or his family. They delayed their baptisms but continued going to church when they could. When my uncle turned eighteen, he decided to get baptized, despite his father's feelings. My grandfather kicked him out and never spoke to him again. He disowned his oldest son—then died three years later without forgiving him. Maybe Laurier and his son fought, and Laurier turned him in during the height of his anger. Maybe one of them was tricked somehow . . ."

Genevieve sighed. "This war makes me weary. I just wish it would end."

"Yeah, me too. And every day I pray it will be over soon, but . . ."

"But what?" she asked, looking at his face for the first time since he'd followed her outside.

"Well, my mom always said the Lord answers prayers, but it's not always when or how we want them answered. I could pray all night for the war to end next week, but it still might not happen for years to come. I just keep praying. And I keep trusting that He hears and that He knows what—and when—will be best."

"I'm glad Someone knows what's best," Genevieve finally said. "But I don't understand why God lets such bad things happen."

"I've often asked myself that question, especially since enlisting. Why do bad things happen to good people?"

"Have you come up with an answer?"

"Not completely," Peter replied. "But I do know God loves us. He wants us to learn, and the best way for us to learn is for us to experience the consequences of our own actions."

"We didn't start this war. Why are we suffering through it?" Genevieve stared at a row of parsley.

"I think that's where faith comes in—sometimes you just have to trust the Lord even when things don't make sense. For some reason, allowing people like Hitler and Mussolini to do what they want for a while is going to work with His plan."

"What is His plan?"

Peter thought back to the time he'd asked his uncle much the same thing. He gave Genevieve the answer his uncle had given him. "For us to learn to make good choices. For us to be saved. For us to be happy."

Genevieve was quiet for a moment. "Why are some saved and some not saved?"

"Well, Christ suffered and died for everyone's sins. He paid the price to save everyone. Back in Sicily when my tank caught fire, I was partway up the ladder. But after the shrapnel hit, I couldn't climb anymore. All I could do was grab Lieutenant Madsen's outstretched hand. My lieutenant was probably the shortest person in the company, but he was strong. He'd gone through college on a gymnastics scholarship, and his specialty was the rings. He had the most muscular arms I'd ever seen. He grabbed my hand and yanked me out. And he saved my life. I think our redemption is a little like that. Christ is there, able and wanting to pull us to safety. We just have to reach out to Him."

"But what about people who never have a chance? What about my little brother who died an hour before the priest came to baptize him? Why did he have to go to hell? He never did anything wrong—he never had a chance." There were tears in her eyes as she spoke, and she turned away so Peter couldn't see them.

Peter gently put his hand on her shoulder. "Genevieve, your baby brother isn't in hell."

"Limbo, then. It seems like the same thing to me."

"He's not in limbo, and he's not in hell."

"The priest said he was," Genevieve said, her voice soft with emotion.

"I'm sure your priest is a good man. He must be to devote his life to God and help so many Allied airmen. But maybe he was misinformed." Peter noticed that Genevieve looked a little startled. He continued anyway. "Little children aren't going to be thrust into limbo just because they've never been baptized. How could that possibly be fair? God is smarter and more merciful than that." Genevieve looked at him, and he could tell she was a little uncertain. Peter fumbled in his pocket for his serviceman's Book of Mormon and flipped through the pages of the Book of Moroni. He stopped a few pages short of the end, at Mormon's letter to his son Moroni about infant baptism. "Here." He handed her the book. "This man explains it better than I can."

She looked at the book in her hands and began reading the first bit. "This isn't the Bible."

"No, but it is scripture." Peter still thought Genevieve looked a little hesitant. "Do you think I'm an evil person, Genevieve?" She shook her head with a little smile on her face, and he continued. "So do you think I'd give you an evil book to read?"

She shook her head no again. Then she gave Peter another half smile and went back inside, taking the book with her.

* * *

Obersturmführer Prinz looked across his desk at Monsieur Jean-Philippe Laurier. Prinz guessed that Laurier was normally a confident man, but this afternoon he looked nervous. Gestapo headquarters often had that effect on people. "Can you describe the man who contacted you?"

Laurier nodded. "Not quite six feet tall, brown hair, brown eyes. He was wearing a disguise, including a beard, so I'm not sure of his age. He has a scar on his left temple. I think I gave him a new one around his right ear. He was on the thin side, but he was strong."

"And what questions did he ask you?"

"He wanted to know about the troops and the coastal defenses. He also asked about reinforcements and how quickly they could get to the beaches."

Prinz twisted his lips to the side as he thought. The intelligence staff at the Fifteenth Army had recently said an invasion was imminent, based on the radio interceptions they were receiving. Most men in the army expected the Allies to land near Calais, but the new alert hadn't specified a location. "Did he say where or when the invasion would occur?"

"Here, but he didn't say when."

"And you are sure he was an American?"

Laurier paused then nodded.

"And how did he get away?" Prinz watched as Laurier's face colored in embarrassment.

"I don't remember. He knocked me unconscious and left me tied up in my chair."

Prinz glanced at the bulging muscles on Laurier's arms and shook his head slightly. Laurier looked like he could hold his own in a fight, especially when surprise was on his side. "And how did you escape?"

"Madame Rambures stopped by to ask a question. She saw me through the window."

Rambures. Prinz thought for a moment. The name sounded familiar to him. He had skimmed through Schneider's file on agent Laurier just before meeting with the Frenchman. Then he remembered. "Related to Gaston Rambures?"

"His mother."

Prinz smiled. He had always been impressed by how well Schneider manipulated his sources into betraying friends, neighbors, and occasionally family members. But convincing Laurier to turn in his own son and his son's best friend was perhaps the most dramatic of the betrayals arranged by Schneider. It had happened before Prinz was in Calais, but he had vigilantly studied Schneider's methods. According to the story, Laurier had been concerned that Gaston Rambures was a bad influence on his son, getting him involved in reckless activity with the Resistance and causing a severe rift between father and son. Laurier had been angry with his son, but he hadn't fully realized that by turning in Gaston, he was also betraying the wayward son he was trying to save. Since then, generous payments and severe threats had kept Laurier in line. He was one of the better agents recruited by Schneider, and now he had given Prinz one more piece of evidence that the big Allied invasion would come near Calais. It was all fitting together—the increase in air raids, rumors from the spies in England, all the sabotage work, and now American interest in the troops surrounding Calais. All pieces of a puzzle slowly being assembled to reveal the Allied plan for the cross-channel invasion.

* * *

After an early supper and the BBC's evening broadcast, the Olivier siblings and Peter sat around a lantern for a game of cards. They played piquet, a two-person card game. Peter had never played, so he watched the first round then paired up with Genevieve for the remainder of the game. Jacques couldn't decide if the two were sitting so close to one another to aid in their cooperation or if there was something beyond that. After careful study, he decided that for his sister, at least, it was something more than the game.

Curfew under Nazi occupation ran from 2100 to 0600 hours. Peter and Jacques planned on checking for any messages from Charles Toussaint shortly before curfew began, just as Toussaint had suggested. In case it was a trap, the two planned to look very different from the way they had the last time they'd made contact with Toussaint.

For Peter's disguise, Jacques used a wig with curly salt-and-pepper hair. "I know it's ugly, but older men aren't as suspicious as someone your age. And the hair is long enough to cover the bottom of your bruise," Jacques said. He applied a mustache and some make-up to add wrinkles around Peter's eyes. Jacques made himself look about the same age. When he was finished, he had fewer wrinkles, but his hair was completely gray.

"Well, Genevieve, how do we look?" Jacques asked.

"Old. Are you sure you don't want me to come with you?"

"Not this time," Jacques replied.

"All right, I'll wait up for you, then," she said.

It was still light enough that Jacques and Peter felt going through the checkpoint was the safest way to get into the city. They would wait for dark to exit through illegal routes. Their papers were good, but they knew the weapons they were carrying could be a problem if they were searched. Before entering the city, Jacques led Peter to a fairly remote section of the canal. There were guards in the distance who would notice them swimming across at twilight, but between the tree cover and the distance from the main road, no one saw them wrap their weapons up, dump them in a gunnysack, and then tie that sack to a rope that was connected to some rubble on the other side of the canal.

They backtracked a ways then entered Calais on the main road. There were four guards at the checkpoint—usually there were two. Jacques hoped the extra security was evidence that his five sabotage teams were having success. The guards carefully scrutinized Jacques's and Peter's papers and gave them both pat downs. Both sets of forged papers said the men were residents of Calais.

"What was the purpose of your visit to the country?" one of the guards asked.

Jacques hesitated. He knew they would ask something like that, and he usually had his response prepared in advance, but this time he was blank.

"We were planning a picnic for tomorrow. It will be his wife's birthday," Peter said.

"His wife? Then what was your purpose?"

"His wife is my cousin."

The guards were satisfied with Peter's explanation. They returned the papers and waved the two on.

"Thanks for the quick thinking, Peter. Usually I bring some firewood or food with me so 'my reason for travel' is obvious. I forgot to have a reason thought up today. I guess I've had a lot of things on my mind." *A lot on my mind*, Jacques thought. *That's an understatement.*

"I guess I've picked up a talent for lying on the run the last few months."

They walked along the canal until they were directly across from the bag that stored their weapons. The two checked to make sure no one was nearby, then Jacques grabbed the rope and pulled the gunnysack across the canal so quickly the sack was never completely submerged. They rearmed themselves and walked back into town.

They found the bench near the church without a problem. There was no newspaper, with or without a hidden report inside on the twenty-fifth line of the fourth page. Instead, Monsieur Toussaint himself sat on the bench. He appeared to be in deep contemplation. Jacques and Peter walked past Toussaint then turned into an alley.

"I thought he wasn't going to be here," Jacques said.

"Me too," Peter said. "Did you notice anyone else around?"

"Anyone else, meaning the Gestapo? No, but they can usually remain out of sight if they don't want to be seen."

Peter thought for a few moments. "Either it's urgent enough that he felt he had to see me, or he's been arrested, and they're trying to bring in his contacts. Unless we see trouble, I think I'd better go talk to him. Curfew is in less than thirty minutes—he might not want to be out past then."

Jacques nodded, agreeing with Peter. "I'll go look around the church and see if there are any obvious problems. I think you'd best walk around the block and see how many soldiers are waiting around. We'll meet here again in five minutes."

* * *

Neither of them found anything suspicious, so Peter left Jacques in the alley, walked up to Monsieur Toussaint, and sat next to him on the bench. "*Vixi puellis nuper idoneus et militavi,*" Peter said, since he doubted Toussaint would recognize him.

"Goodness, are you really the same person?"

"Yes, sir."

"Remarkable. I suppose you were a little startled to see me."

Peter nodded.

"I'm glad you came. I don't have anything relevant to report, but I'm in a bit of a spot. My house was destroyed in an air raid a few days ago."

"I'm very sorry to hear that; I truly am."

"Yes, it's a shame. I've spent decades collecting all those books. None of them are salvageable. And my garden—gone. But I know I really shouldn't complain. Others have lost far more than me."

"I'm glad you seem uninjured," Peter said.

"Yes, despite this awful war, God is merciful. I was here, praying, when it happened," he said, pointing to the church.

"And your photographic equipment, was it destroyed?"

"Yes, it's all gone. The pieces are so small that not even Tschirner would recognize them for what they are."

"You're not in any danger from the Gestapo, are you?" Peter glanced around as he spoke.

"No more than I was on Tuesday. I haven't talked with any of them since then. I sent Tschirner's courier away with my apologies. And like I said, I don't have anything to report to you. To be honest, I'm not sure how I can get a report through from now on, even if I do receive relevant information." Toussaint's shoulders were slumped even more than usual, and he seemed to have aged years instead of days since Peter last saw him. "I suppose if I thought long enough, I could think of another method, but microdots were so convenient and so difficult for anyone to detect unless they knew where to look."

"It's getting close to curfew. Where are you staying?"

"With friends, about five minutes from here. All the hotels are billeting soldiers."

Peter thought for a moment. "I think you should continue to send your messages to the Swiss embassy in Paris then to Switzerland and the British embassy there."

"The Germans will read any mail sent to Paris."

"Yes, I know. Hear me out. You report on a limited number of contacts, right?"

"Yes, Hauptmann Wenders, Oberst Hanke, and Standartenführer Tschirner. Those are the officers I have normal contact with."

"Do you have some paper and something to write with?"

Toussaint grabbed a pen from his pocket and felt in his pockets until he found a handwritten receipt for a clothing purchase.

"Here's how you can encode any information you learn into a letter. If it's about Wenders, write about your neighbor Winox. If it's Hanke, write about your neighbor Henri. If by some miracle Tschirner lets something slip, write about Tristan. Say there's been some illness going through the neighborhood and describe their war perceptions in terms of their health. A headache is an expectation of an invasion here; a stomachache is an expectation of an invasion elsewhere. If they have both ailments it means they expect invasions both here and elsewhere. Fear that they won't recover means they think whatever the Allies are doing will succeed. If they called the doctor, reinforcements have been requested. If the doctor prescribed medication, the reinforcements have been sent. If you mention that any of your neighbors were reminiscing about a favorite vacation to Southern France or Norway or Yugoslavia they took before the war, that's where they expect the attack to come. A light stroke suffered by any of your neighbors is a possible conspiracy; a serious one is an attempted coup. Do you follow me so far?"

Toussaint was still scribbling down notes, but he smiled and sat up a little straighter. "Yes, I follow you. If Oberst Hanke thinks an unsuccessful invasion will come here, I write that Henri has a headache, but he expects to recover soon. Something like that. What do I do if I have a new contact?"

"Talk about a female neighbor. The older she is, the higher her rank. A great-granny would be a generalfeldmarschall. A little girl would be a gefreiter or a sturmmann. If it's a contact you think we would recognize, try to give them a name. Make it rhyme with the real contact's name or have the same initials. I doubt that will cover all contingencies, but that's the best I can come up with on the fly.

"It would probably be unwise to use the system too much," Peter continued. "Only use the system to indicate a change in what they expect, and you may want to include a lot of other information in your letter so the report isn't the main focus. And we'll know what's really going on, so no need to report on what we're doing. We would, however, still appreciate your report on how the Germans react to everything."

"Once things start, they probably won't have time to discuss gardening or legal cases with me," Toussaint observed.

"You're right, of course. Either way, we hope to have Calais liberated soon. Then there won't be a need for any more reports. When I get back to England, I'll make sure they know of your sacrifices to help us. On behalf of the Allies, I offer my sincere apologies for your home." Peter wasn't sure he really had the authority to formally apologize on behalf of anyone, but it seemed like the right thing to say.

A soft smile formed on Toussaint's face. "No need to apologize. Just hurry up and win this war."

The two men shook hands again. Then Toussaint stood up and walked back toward his friend's home. Peter watched him until he was out of sight then returned to Jacques in the alley.

"Well?" Jacques asked when Peter returned.

"His house was bombed. That's why he came here. He didn't have anything to report, but we needed to figure out a new way for him to get information to us. I just made something up. I hope it works if he ever has to use it."

"I think we should verify that his house was really destroyed," Jacques said. "The British aren't the only ones that send false information through their spies. It's possible—not likely, but possible—that he doesn't buy the bluff that you're going to help plan the big invasion."

Peter nodded his agreement.

It wasn't completely dark yet, so the two slipped into an uninhabited, half-destroyed building and waited for darkness to envelop the streets of Calais. Jacques laid his head back against the least damaged wall and closed his eyes. Peter kept his eyes on the street. The volume of foot traffic quickly dwindled as curfew approached. By 2100 hours, there were no civilians and only a handful of soldiers within sight.

"Jacques, would you be mad at the Americans if they bombed your house during an air raid?"

Jacques didn't change his position as he answered. "No, I'd be mad at the Germans for starting this war. Although I might think less of the Americans or the British if they missed all their legitimate targets on the same raid. Why do you ask?"

"Toussaint didn't seem upset. I assume it was an American raid that hit his home. If it had been a British raid, he probably would have been in his bed sleeping. I'm sure he knows I'm an American, but he still seemed willing to help."

Jacques opened his eyes. "It's a smart man who can recognize an ally even when things go wrong. And you're assuming his home really was bombed."

"I guess we can confirm that before the night is over."

* * *

Some time passed with Jacques deep in thought. He was surprised at how much Genevieve had changed since Peter's arrival. Jacques remembered how powerful love had been for him, but for him, it had never been so fast. His love for Mireille had grown slowly, steadily, over a period of many years. Like a tree, he had always thought, growing gradually and developing strong, deep roots.

It seemed he'd had too much on his mind lately. So many old, buried memories brought to the surface again—and the pain they brought with them seemed just as fresh as it ever had been. Old memories, old beliefs— they had crowded his mind all day, left him unprepared at the checkpoint and uncharacteristically philosophical as he sat waiting with Peter.

"Peter, do you believe in God?"

"Yes," Peter said.

No hesitation, Jacques noticed.

After a pause, Peter turned the question back to Jacques. "Do you?"

"Yes," Jacques said, but he knew his voice lacked certainty. "Well, maybe I just used to."

"What changed?"

"The whole world changed, Peter. War came. My wife died. And now I've broken so many commandments I know I'm past saving. It used to be nice to think that there was a heaven. It was someplace my parents were, someplace Mireille was—even if they weren't here with me, at least they were somewhere. But now . . ." he hesitated. Jacques had given little thought to religion since the war began, but now, as he sat there, all he had been taught as a child came back to him clearly. "Now I think it would be easier if everything just ended with death. I don't want to be stuck in hell with all the Nazis, trapped there away from Mireille and everyone else who's good."

"Jacques, no one is past saving."

Peter seemed to genuinely believe what he had just said, but Jacques was unsure. "I don't know about that," he said. "I'm certain you're not past saving. Sure, you've been a soldier and with that comes shooting and killing. But you haven't enjoyed it, and you've only killed when necessary. I was like that for a while. I only killed when I felt it was needed to protect my family or win the war. But, Peter, I've changed. I like war. I want it to end, but I like killing Nazis. I like the thrill; I like the challenge. Sometimes I even like the sound. Usually I don't worry much about my soul, but after I gave Birgit a ribbon the other day, she said I was good. I'm not sure why she said that or why it had such an effect on me, but I knew she was wrong. I'm not good, not anymore."

"From her point of view, you are. She could be right."

"She just doesn't see all the evil lurking under the surface."

It was too dark for Jacques to see Peter's face, but his voice sounded kind and confident. "Children sometimes see things more clearly than we do, don't they? The goodness she sees in you is really there, Jacques. I think the reality is we all have at least a little good in us and a little evil too. War tends to bring that evil side out in full force, but as long as there's an ounce of good left, there's still hope. Like the scriptures say, Christ's hand is stretched out still, even in the midst of punishment and chastisement."

"Stretched out with what?" Jacques asked sincerely.

"Mercy and forgiveness."

"I hope you're right, Peter." Jacques paused, feeling briefly hopeful. But the more he thought about it, the more Jacques felt that his path had already been set. Changing it now was impossible. He spoke again. "And if you're wrong, I hope I'll get a spot in hell right between Hitler and Himmler so I can shove brimstone into their faces for all eternity." That was the end of their conversation, but it wasn't the end of Jacques's thoughts. *Only those who still have hope in salvation can believe such a change is possible*, he thought.

* * *

Peter was surprised. Jacques hadn't struck him as philosophical or religious. But he remembered some of the things Genevieve had told him and had the impression that the Jacques he now knew was very different from the Jacques who had existed before the war.

They waited in that wreck of a building about an hour past curfew. By then it was as dark as it would get. They quietly slid through piles of rubble and the shadows of buildings until they arrived at where, until a few days ago, Charles Toussaint had lived. The agent had been telling the truth. The home was completely destroyed.

"Back to your house?" Peter asked Jacques.

He nodded.

They started back to the east side of town, staying out of sight and moving slowly. They passed several patrols but encountered no other obstacles on their way to the canal. They headed for the stretch of water they had pulled their weapons across earlier so that they would be able to reset the rope and gunnysack and use the same method again. The two men forded the canal as quietly as they could. Once on the other side, Jacques wrapped the end of the rope around some rubble and hid the sack.

They were standing up from replacing their shoes when Peter heard a noise. It had been a soft noise, like someone stepping on a pile of leaves. He looked at Jacques, who nodded. He had heard it too. Jacques pointed at Peter then pointed east. Jacques went north. Peter crouched and started walking, listening as intently as he could.

The noise did not repeat itself, but about a minute later, Peter heard someone speaking German. He was speaking slowly enough that Peter could understand what he was saying—he was commanding someone to put their hands up and turn around. Peter knew the voice wasn't directed at him. He moved slowly toward the noise, trying to be silent.

"What are you doing out so late, old man?" the German voice continued.

Peter peered around a tree and saw a single soldier with his rifle fixed on Jacques's back. The soldier was only five yards away. Peter switched his pistol from his right to his left hand and grabbed his trench knife because during basic training, Peter had been told the hilt could double as a club. *Time to test that piece of knowledge*, Peter thought.

"You had better answer me, old man," the soldier continued.

Peter carefully closed the space that separated them and knocked the soldier on the back of the head, right below the helmet line. The soldier fell to the ground, and his helmet fell off. Peter's second blow with the knife left him unconscious. Jacques turned around with his weapon drawn then put it away when he saw the situation was under control.

"Thanks," he said. Peter nodded. They made it the rest of the way to the Olivier farmhouse without incident.

Genevieve was asleep when they returned. She had been waiting for them, but when her brother and Peter came in, she was hunched over, her head resting on her arm, her arm resting on the kitchen table. Peter's Book of Mormon was opened to the last page. Jacques gently shook her shoulder.

Genevieve yawned. "What took you so long? I thought you were just seeing if there was anything at the dead drop."

"We ran into some complications," her brother said.

"Would you care to elaborate?" she asked. Jacques complied, giving her a quick summary of the night's activities.

When he was finished, Genevieve yawned again. "Sorry. I'm not bored, just sleepy."

"Me too," Peter chimed in.

"Always wise to get a good night's sleep when you can," Jacques said.

They finished their conversation and went to bed.

Chapter Eleven
Blood, Tears, and Fire

Sunday, June 4

JACQUES SAT AT THE KITCHEN table with Genevieve and Peter and stifled another yawn. He'd had a bad night. His thoughts continued to distract him—just as they had been distracting him the evening before. He had been thinking about Genevieve at the checkpoint and had almost slipped up then. He had been contemplating the fate of his soul after crossing the canal, and that had nearly led to his capture. *You've got to stop thinking about things you can't change*, he thought, *you can't afford to make any more mistakes—not if you want to keep ahead of the Nazis.*

Jacques finished his breakfast, bringing his mind back to the present. "Last meeting today?" he asked, addressing Peter. The American nodded; the meeting with Marie Murat was at noon. "Are you sure it's necessary?" Jacques continued. "We already know Laurier was the double agent. Wasn't that your main assignment?"

"Yes, but Marie's information could still be useful. We'd like to keep track of troop movements. If she can tell us how the troops are concentrated now and how they're concentrated next week and next month, it could be valuable no matter where we invade."

Jacques nodded. "You're right. I'm just imagining what a challenge it will be to hide that hideous bruise on your face."

"I thought you could disguise anyone and anything," Peter jested.

"I can. I just said it would present a challenge."

"So one more meeting, and then you'll go back to England?" Genevieve asked. Jacques noticed a hint of sadness creeping into her voice.

"That's the plan," Peter said. "I just want to get this last bit of information before I go."

"How does a woman get detailed information on German troop concentrations?" Genevieve asked.

Peter shrugged, so she pushed again. "Do you really want to trust information someone's picked up by sleeping with the enemy?"

"That's a bit of an assumption, don't you think? Our contact is highly educated and seemed very cooperative at our last meeting," Peter said in Marie's defense.

"Cooperative, huh?" Genevieve cleared a few dishes from the table and went to the sink.

"What's that supposed to mean?" Peter asked. He grabbed the rest of the dishes and followed her. Genevieve took the plates but didn't meet his eyes.

"Would you be going to this meeting if the contact weren't a ravishing beauty?" Genevieve asked.

"Yes," Peter said. "Our contact last night was a balding middle-aged man, and we thought his information was equally important."

Jacques saw Peter looking at him for an explanation about his sister's sudden mood change, but Jacques had moved to the window and was staring outside, pretending to be uninterested in the conversation between the two of them. In reality, he wasn't sure what was more amusing: Genevieve's obvious jealousy or Peter's inability to pinpoint it. His amusement soon faded, replaced by apprehension. "Birgit's coming," he said.

Genevieve moved to the window. "It's awfully early for her to be coming over."

Jacques nodded and watched her come. She knocked on the kitchen door then entered, as was custom. She had a smile on her face as usual. And hanging from her arm was the cause of Jacques's apprehension: a basket.

"Good morning," Birgit said.

"Good morning, darling," Genevieve replied. "How are you today?"

"I'm still sleepy. Aunt Anne and Uncle Louis let me stay up late last night, but they didn't let me sleep in like they usually do Sunday morning. Aunt Anne wanted me to come buy some cheese first thing this morning. She said she just needs one wedge, and it's very important that I come right away, before breakfast, even."

"Yes, dear, why don't you go pick some flowers while I find some cheese for you."

Birgit smiled and went outside to find her flowers. When she was gone, the smile on Genevieve's face disappeared. "They've never requested a specific pick-up time before, let alone only one day to make arrangements."

She looked in the basket. "Three. We can't hide three of them here very easily, and we can't send them to the Papineaus."

Jacques was silent for a moment. "I can't take them to England tonight; there's not enough time to find transportation. And you're right, we can't hide them here. Not safely. But I'm sure the LeBrases wouldn't have requested we pick them up tonight if it were possible for them to keep the men longer. We'll have to figure something out."

"Why would they pick them up if they couldn't safely hide them for a few days?" Genevieve asked.

"A lot could have changed from when Louis gave the signal to the actual pickup," Jacques said as he sat down at the table. He put his elbows on the table and rested his head in his hands, squeezing his temples as if he could somehow force a solution to form.

"We have a radio transmitter under the stairs where Peter's been sleeping; we could request someone come in tonight to pick them up," Genevieve said.

"That bulky old relic? We've already used it twice from here. With my rusty skills on the radio, the Germans will probably pinpoint the transmission's source before I'm a third of the way through. It will already be risky when we radio in to send Peter back across the channel. I'd rather not push our luck any further."

"I could leave tonight with the airmen," Peter said. "That will cut down the number of uses."

"It would, but I doubt they'd be able to pick you or the airmen up tonight. They don't like shorter than forty-eight hours' notice. We'd have to radio in now and wait until tomorrow. Then we usually have to radio back to confirm—another risk, even if we manage to haul the radio to a different location without being seen." Jacques paused. "Things were so much easier a couple years ago. The patrols weren't as experienced, and there were fewer of them."

They were all quiet, searching their brains for a solution. The only sound was Birgit, outside still, singing a children's song. Genevieve finally broke the silence. "I guess we could try to keep them here for a few days. They could hide in the cheese cellar. The Germans have taken so much of the cheese that it's almost empty anyway. As long as they're not injured, it might work. The cellar has been searched before, but we might get lucky. We could try burying the cellar door under a pile of hay or something." She didn't sound very convinced.

"I think I have a better plan," Jacques said. "I have a contact in a line that takes downed airmen to Paris. Then they move south and cross the Pyrenees into Spain."

"Is the line secure?" Genevieve asked. Her brother knew she was protective of the men shot down over her country and didn't care to trust them to just anyone.

"I don't know. It was in February. I don't love the plan, but I think it's better than the alternatives. I'll have to travel to Brunembert today—that's where my contact lives. I'll leave right after I fix Peter's face. Peter, you'll have to go to your last meeting alone."

Peter nodded.

"Is that safe?" Genevieve asked.

"Do you have any better ideas?"

Genevieve didn't say anything for a while. She looked at her brother then Peter, the corners of her mouth turning down into a frown.

Jacques stood up and gently touched her shoulder. "Genevieve, I imagine Birgit is ready for her bit of cheese."

Minutes later, they sent Birgit home with a single square of cheese. Then Jacques got to work on Peter's face. When finished, the side of his face was still visibly swollen, but the discoloration was hidden. Then the three left—Peter to his rendezvous, Genevieve to attend Mass, and Jacques to Brunembert to make contact with another Resistance line.

* * *

"Is it difficult to ride a bicycle in a skirt?" Peter asked. Genevieve was wearing a pale blue blouse and a long, chocolate-brown skirt, her Sunday best. They were halfway to town, and she hadn't spoken to him at all. That was a little unlike her, so Peter asked the first question that popped into his head.

She glanced at him. "It depends on the skirt. If it's too full, it can get caught in the gears. Too narrow and it's hard to pedal." She fell back into silence.

"Genevieve, I did something to make you angry, didn't I? I'm sorry. If you tell me what I've done, I'll promise not to do it again."

She looked over at him, surprised. "Oh, Peter, I'm not mad at you. I'm just worried."

"About today?"

She nodded. "I don't think it's wise for you and Jacques to split up. You both should have backup."

"If you have another idea, I'm willing to listen to it." He slowed his pedaling as they approached the site where they would split up.

"That's the problem; I'm not sure what to do. We don't have any better plans." She slowed her pace to match his.

"If it makes you feel better, you know Jacques works without backup the majority of the time. And I'm not as experienced as he is, but I've gone solo before too."

"I know, but I still don't like it." She looked from the road to his eyes. "You'll be cautious, won't you, Peter?"

He told her he would be, and he certainly meant to follow her advice. He hid his bicycle in the clump of trees and watched her pedal into town. After passing through the checkpoint, he found the same abandoned building he had previously used and changed into his uniform. He hoped no one in a similar uniform would try to have a conversation with him in German.

Peter saw plenty of patrols, more than he remembered from the last time he was in town during the day, but fortunately none of them tried to speak with him as he made his way to the alley and the staircase. When he arrived, it was a few minutes after 1200 hours. No one was in the room, but Marie had left a note behind the loose brick. It simply said, *My place as soon as you can.* She had also written her address, but Peter already knew where she lived.

He easily found his way to Marie's apartment. It was near the center of town, so there were plenty of people around, but Peter didn't see anything out of the ordinary. He knew someone in the crowd would no doubt see him going into the apartment building, but he doubted anyone would find it strange. German soldiers could go where they pleased.

The inside of the building was old but well maintained. There was a hallway and staircase in the center, with apartments on either side. Marie's home was on the second floor, along with three other apartments. No one was in the hall to watch Peter knock on her door.

Marie opened the door, and Peter thought she looked more beautiful than ever. It was the first time Peter had seen her with her hair down. It cascaded gently over her shoulders, curling slightly at the ends. Red lipstick enhanced her lips, which formed a pleasant smile. She didn't say anything to him at first; she just motioned for him to come in.

"Hello, Marie. It's good to see you again," Peter said. "Did you get the information we requested?" he asked as he set his German rifle, a Karabiner 98k, by the door.

"Oh, you'll be amazed at all the things I have found out. These Germans, they talk too much." Marie's voice sounded almost like a song.

"Do they suspect that the invasion will come in Calais?"

She hesitated. "Yes, many of them suspect. Most of them, even. But not all."

"We plan to win with manpower, not with surprise."

"Good, because I don't think you will have complete surprise. You will need your manpower." She walked to the table in the center of the room and motioned for Peter to come with her. "These are some maps one of my friends in the German Army let me borrow. They're a little outdated, but I know where changes have been made."

Together they studied the maps. Marie said she had to return them, so Peter took notes on a piece of paper. He knew his cartography skills were rough, but he felt the map he drew and the notes he wrote would be valuable to someone in Allied intelligence. Marie was wearing her intoxicating perfume again, and it would be a lie to say that Peter's concentration was unaffected each time she put her hand on his shoulder as she showed him the positions of German soldiers near the beaches. After that, they went over the information she had learned about reinforcements. She hadn't learned as much about reinforcements as she had about current troop positions, but she had more information than Peter had expected.

"Marie, thank you," he said as they finished up. "I'm amazed at the quality and the quantity of your information. I hope you won't suffer adverse consequences from gathering it."

She shook her head. "I might have to go on a few more unpleasant dates, but I'll manage." She again kissed Peter on both cheeks to say good-bye. Then she kissed him on the mouth. It wasn't a light kiss. It made time stand still and his head twirl and his heart pound, and he couldn't help but kiss her back. Marie's arms reached around him, and Peter closed his eyes and let her hands make their way down his back. But then he felt Marie pull his pistol from its hiding place in the small of his back. He opened his eyes in time to see her cock it and point it at him.

* * *

Marie stepped back, out of Peter's reach. Her late boyfriend, Hauptsturmführer Schneider, had taught her that trick. She had used it most recently in April when she had infiltrated a cell of committed Communists and helped Schneider round up the entire group. Marie wasn't really a

Nazi, but she had truly been in love with Schneider. They had met in April 1941. Within a month, she had begun working as a double agent, reporting whatever Schneider requested by radio to the Allies. In return, Schneider had given her his love and his protection. Now he was gone, but Marie still felt trapped. She had chosen which side of the war she was fighting on, and it was too late to change her mind now. She knew the consequences of desertion from SS service, especially now that she lacked Schneider's protection.

Marie smiled sadly, keeping the handgun pointed at Peter as she walked sideways to the wall bordering the neighboring apartment. She used the palm of her hand to make four distinct raps. "You're so quiet," she said. Peter didn't respond. "Do you know why the apartment next to me is empty? There used to be a little family living there. They moved away long before the bomb cut a hole in their wall. The father was sent to a work camp in Germany. The mother moved in with a German officer. I don't think she loves him, but her children were hungry, and he fed them. So don't take it personally. Like my neighbor, I'm just trying to survive. The Germans are in power, and they pay better. Like I warned you before, I'm not a hero. I would betray my own mother to keep out of a German prison."

"That's not saying much, since your mother disowned you when you were fifteen," Peter said as the door opened and Obersturmführer Prinz and Sturmmann Weiss walked into the room. They were armed, and their weapons—a submachine gun and a rifle—were pointed directly at Peter.

"Sixteen actually," Marie continued. "And you're right, betraying my mother would be of little significance. But I did betray a dear friend from school once. That was the turning point, when I had to decide whose side I was on. It was painful," Marie explained. She had reported her friend to Schneider because he had asked her to. His approval and trust had been more important to her than her friend, and though she hadn't participated in an arrest, she knew her betrayal had led to deadly consequences. "I'm amazed you know my parents no longer claim me, yet you failed to recognize that the poem you quoted as a code phrase is about a man giving up all romance because he has been stung by a woman. That should have warned you not to trust me. Or perhaps the words of another Roman poet I studied in school say it more clearly: *The words of a woman . . . should be written on the wind and the fast-flowing water.*"

Obersturmführer Prinz handcuffed Peter and placed a thick wad of cash on the table. "Mademoiselle Murat, it has been a pleasure, as always."

Marie nodded and pretended to count her pay. She had liked the American more than any of the other men she had trapped for the Gestapo. *He seemed nice,* she thought sadly. Marie had relished his open admiration of her beauty, and she had enjoyed kissing him. She knew what awaited him and preferred not to think about it.

* * *

Obersturmführer Prinz and his associate led Peter down the hall, down the stairs, and out onto the street. There was a third man waiting in a jeep. The jeep hadn't been there when Peter had entered the building. The Gestapo men said nothing to Peter on the ride to their headquarters, nor did he speak to them. Peter knew there was no point in claiming he was innocent of spying. He assumed they had been listening to the entire conversation he'd had with Marie and knew he had been eagerly writing down information about their army. In addition, he had been captured with maps and other incriminating papers.

They didn't take Peter to the town center. That was military headquarters. They took him instead to the south end of Calais, to Gestapo headquarters. Once there, they still said nothing. They took Peter into an empty jail cell, ripped his blond wig off, removed his dog tags, and locked him in. The cell had a concrete floor and walls of concrete blocks. The door was thick reinforced wood with a small window at eye level, about one square foot lined with seven vertical bars. Peter was alone. Alone with time to reflect on how stupid he had been. *Stupid to go into Calais without any backup,* he thought. *Stupid to go to Marie's apartment instead of to a neutral meeting place. Stupid to trust her. Stupid to fall for her. Absolutely mindless to kiss her.*

The Gestapo didn't leave him alone to ponder his errors for long. Obersturmführer Prinz returned with two others. Peter stood when they arrived and carefully evaluated them. The sturmmann had helped Prinz with the arrest. He was half a head taller and sixty pounds heavier than Peter. Coarse, straw-colored hair swept across his broad, suntanned forehead. He looked down at Peter with disgust. The standartenführer gave him a similar look. Peter stared back with defiance. He knew he had been foolish to let Marie trap him, but that didn't change the contempt he felt for the Gestapo.

The standartenführer was about the same height as Prinz, with thick, dark hair graying slightly at his temples. His hair was oily, his complexion pale, and his eyes dark and hard. When the standartenführer spoke, Peter knew who it was. He recognized the evil in his deep, powerful voice. Peter had heard the voice five days before in Monsieur Toussaint's home. It was Standartenführer Tschirner. He looked Peter up and down and then spoke. "Soften him up," was all he said.

Prinz and the sturmmann grinned with pleasure.

Peter protested, trying to force authority into his voice. "I am an officer in the United States Army, and I demand to see your commanding army officer. I am under their jurisdiction, not the Gestapo's."

Standartenführer Tschirner paused on his way out of the cell and looked back at his prisoner with a cold smile. "You have no dog tags."

"I had them until Obersturmführer Prinz removed them," Peter said.

"Do you recall seeing any military identification on this prisoner when you arrested him, Obersturmführer Prinz?"

"No, sir," Prinz said with a smile.

"Then, as I said, you have no dog tags. Furthermore, you were arrested in the uniform of a German gefreiter. You are a spy and under my control. The German Army will never know of your existence. Prinz, Weiss, you may proceed." Tschirner walked away and closed the jail cell behind him.

Peter faced the two Gestapo men, his back against the prison wall. He could guess what was coming. He knew the odds were against him, especially with his hands shackled together in front of him. Prinz was slightly shorter than Peter, but he was more muscular. Weiss looked tougher yet, reminding Peter of a heavyweight boxer. He thought he still might have a chance until he saw the brass knuckles, chain, and nightstick they pulled from their pockets and unhooked from their belts. Still, he wasn't going to let them beat him without a fight. The gestapo men stepped toward him. Obersturmführer Prinz and Sturmmann Weiss grinned like evil jack-o-lanterns and began their work.

* * *

Genevieve dropped her bicycle and ran into the house. "Jacques! Jacques," she yelled, gasping for breath. She had never ridden her bicycle so hard. Her heart was pounding and her breathing rapid.

She had never really intended to go to church that day. Instead, she had followed Peter to the alley then to Marie's apartment. Her initial motivation had been mostly jealousy, but when she saw Peter in handcuffs, all that had changed. Genevieve knew Obersturmführer Prinz by sight. There had been no need for her to follow Peter after that—she knew where Prinz would take him.

"Jacques!" she shouted again. But her brother was not home. Brunembert was too far away. Jacques couldn't have even arrived yet, let alone returned. *Louis,* Genevieve thought. He was her next best hope.

Genevieve grabbed her bicycle again and rode through the fields that separated the two farmhouses. She pounded on the back door, but no one answered. She knew where the LeBras family was. They were in Calais attending Mass. Tears stung her eyes as she remembered. She suspected airmen were hidden somewhere on the LeBras farm, but she couldn't ask them for help. Even if they were healthy, which was questionable, she doubted they would blend in with the French population.

Genevieve turned away, numb, unsure of what she should do next. She knew the wisest course of action was to wait for help. Her brother had rescued five other people from the Gestapo prison of Calais. *Jacques did it before; perhaps he can do it again,* she thought. She had never rescued anyone. *But how long will I have to wait? And what will they do to Peter in the meantime?*

* * *

Peter's legs would no longer support him, so when Weiss released him, he collapsed onto the floor of the cold, damp cell. Peter's resistance to the beating had been successful for only a few minutes. Prinz had noticed the swelling on the right side of Peter's face, where Laurier had struck it a few days before. He had punched it, stunning Peter for a few moments— which was all the time it took for Weiss to get behind him and hold him, making the rest of Peter's resistance rather futile.

But even after Peter fell to the floor, the Gestapo men continued their work. After a time, Peter just stopped moving. It didn't matter anymore as blow after painful blow came. He tried counting them for a while, hoping that, like counting sheep, it would have a calming effect. It didn't. But gradually Prinz and his accomplice tired of their work, and Peter's first session in Gestapo hell came to an end. Prinz and Weiss left him alone without saying a single word or asking a single question.

Peter didn't know how long the beating had lasted. There were no windows to the outside world in the cell; he had no idea what time of day it was. He tried to concentrate on anything that would distract him from the pain that screamed at him from every part of his body. He felt small streams of blood trickle from the burst bruise on his temple, his broken nose, and his split lips, and wondered what would happen next. Would each subsequent session of torture be easier or harder to bear?

* * *

Perhaps three hours after Peter's first face-to-face encounter with Tschirner and Prinz, they returned. Peter heard them unlock the cell and come inside, but he didn't move. Moving made the pain worse. After a bit, Prinz kicked him in the back, rolled him over, and shoved him against the wall so he was sitting up, facing them. Peter noticed blood on the German's uniform when Prinz stepped away, and Peter knew the blood was his own.

Tschirner had brought a stool into the cell and was sitting on it. He didn't smile or sneer. He didn't show any emotion at all. He just crossed his arms and stared at his prisoner. Peter stared back, trying to keep his face as emotionless as his captor's.

Prinz, on the other hand, allowed his satisfaction at Peter's current condition to exude in his haughty, wicked grin. His expression of contempt angered his prisoner, and that anger woke Peter from the depressed, pain-filled state he had been in and brought with it a determination that he would not let them win. After a few more moments of gloating, Prinz grabbed a notebook. It was finally interrogation time.

Tschirner asked the questions. "What is your name?"

"Peter Eddy," he mumbled.

"Date of birth?"

"February 20, 1923."

"Rank and serial number?"

"Second lieutenant, nineteen-five-five-six-oh-nine-two."

Prinz scribbled it in his book. Peter assumed they would have to believe him, since he was telling the truth and since the Gestapo did have his dog tags somewhere, even if they didn't want to admit it.

"How long have you been in Calais?"

Peter didn't answer. The Geneva Conventions said he didn't have to.

As if reading Peter's thoughts, Tschirner continued. "Since you were captured out of your uniform, the Geneva Conventions do not apply to you. Not that it would matter if they did. You will cooperate, or you will be tortured and killed. How long have you been in Calais?"

Peter wasn't sure if Tschirner was right about the Geneva Conventions. He did, however, believe him when he said he didn't care if they applied to him or not—Peter got the impression that the Red Cross was not exactly welcome in the Gestapo buildings of Calais. Peter also knew if he told them he had arrived the night of May 28, they might link him with the pilot and the Papineaus and Hauptsturmführer Schneider's death. So he simply repeated his name, rank, and serial number.

Tschirner gave him a look of exaggerated disgust. Peter glanced at him then stared at the door behind Tschirner's stool.

"Why are you in Calais?"

Peter closed his eyes and leaned his head against the wall. "Peter Eddy. Second lieutenant, US Army. Nineteen-five-five-six-oh-nine-two."

Peter could hear Tschirner standing up. *Maybe he's leaving*, Peter thought. But he wasn't so lucky. Instead, Tschirner picked up the stool he had been sitting on and swung it into the side of Peter's head. It knocked him over. Peter opened his eyes, and Tschirner was calmly standing over him, still holding his stool in one hand.

"Why would the United States Army send someone so young?" Tschirner said, stepping back a pace. "Your mission must not be very important, or surely they would have sent someone with more experience."

Peter knew the question was clever bait—asking him to assure the Gestapo and Peter's own ego that his mission was valuable. Peter didn't bite. "Peter Eddy, US Army. Nineteen-five-five-six-oh-nine-two."

Tschirner calmly swung the stool at Peter again, aiming for the face. Peter turned and blocked the worst of it with his arms. He expected Tschirner to swing again, but he didn't.

"Lieutenant Eddy, how long have you been in Calais?"

One day too long, Peter thought. "Nineteen-five-five-six-oh-nine-two."

Tschirner didn't use the stool again. He kicked Peter in the chin with his boot. It knocked the back of his head into the cement wall behind him and stunned him, but Peter could hear Tschirner telling Prinz in German that he would send Siebert along and return in approximately an hour.

An hour, Peter thought. *I can survive anything if it's only for an hour.* Then Tschirner kicked him again, and everything turned black.

* * *

Jacques was just leaving Brunembert. He'd had an easy time finding his contact, a man known to him as René. They had met briefly one year ago, in Colonel McDougall's office in London. McDougall was their only connection, and he had introduced them to one another for emergencies like the one Jacques was currently having with the three stranded airmen and a very tight deadline.

Where Jacques excelled at creating disguises, René was a master forger. René had taken an hour to create permits that would allow him to drive his truck to Calais and back that day as well as the papers that would give him access to fuel. Jacques had felt slightly uneasy with the delay, but overall, he knew the truck would save them time. *And if any of the airmen are injured,* he thought, *it might save their lives.* In addition, René had allowed Jacques to observe, teaching him a few new forgery ticks. It was a skill Jacques was happy to improve.

Jacques's bicycle was now in the back of the truck, squeezed between several large wooden barrels. The barrels were huge, big enough for a man to hide in. That evening, they would hide three fugitives as the airmen continued their journey to freedom.

René was a quiet man. As his contact drove, Jacques's mind wandered. He couldn't stop the thoughts from coming. It had been years since he had thought anything was impossible. He did many things that others thought crazy and improbable, but he didn't think of them that way. He was confident that he could accomplish each of the missions he set out to complete. He considered them difficult, challenging, sometimes unlikely to be successful, and occasionally a tad foolhardy, but never impossible.

But now there was an impossibility. Changing himself. Repenting. Becoming good again. The road from Brunembert to Calais stretched out ahead of him. Jacques leaned his head on the truck window and closed his eyes, thinking. Peter had said it wasn't too late to change, but how could Peter be so sure? *It's too late for me,* Jacques thought. *No one would forgive me for all the horrors I've done.* Frustrated, he tried to clear his mind completely. He didn't want to think about the impossible. He succeeded in pushing away all his thoughts, and the gentle bounces of the truck meeting the uneven road eventually lulled him to sleep.

* * *

In Jacques's dream it was June 1938—the last time he had thought something was truly impossible.

Jacques had just finished taking care of the cows for the evening. Genevieve wasn't home from the Papineau home yet, which he found irritating. Normally she had dinner ready by the time he was finished with the cows. Hungry, Jacques grabbed the last of the bread and ate it, not bothering to wait for his little sister. As he finished, he remembered that it was Saturday, so he went out to the water pump to clean himself so he would be presentable for Mass the following day. The cool water was refreshing on his hot, dirty skin. He was naked to the waist and soaking wet when he heard his sister's laugh.

Jacques thought about giving Genevieve a lecture on how the vegetables wouldn't weed themselves but sighed instead. The day wasn't over yet. There was no reason to ruin her laughter. His sister was, after all, only thirteen, and the year had been a difficult one. Jacques dried his face and turned around. Genevieve wasn't alone.

"Hello, Jacques, how are you?" Mireille Desmarais asked. Jacques stared at her, his mouth open. She came to Calais every summer, but she was a week early this year. Her regular letters to Jacques had said nothing about a change in schedule. Mireille's curly blonde hair was down, free to move gently with the evening breeze. She was wearing a new dress, red, with little white flowers on it. She was studying him carefully, her whole face joining with her mouth in that smile he loved.

He noticed with satisfaction that Mireille seemed impressed with his build. Like most men of eighteen who spent the majority of their day in manual labor, Jacques was toned—his muscles weren't large, but they were well defined. "Hello, Mireille," he said, still staring at her.

Genevieve sighed. "Are you two just going to stare at each other all night? Jacques, you are so boring. I want to show Mireille the garden I'm planting."

That particular year, the garden actually benefited from Jacques's efforts more than from Genevieve's, but Jacques let Genevieve take credit and managed to find his tongue. "I was just about to change clothes. You'll still be here in a few minutes?"

"Of course," Mireille said with a smile. Genevieve rolled her eyes and dragged Mireille to the garden.

Inside the farmhouse, Jacques put on his best clothes and carefully parted and slicked his hair, imitating the businessmen he saw in town. When he returned, Genevieve had finished her tour of the garden. Mireille turned toward Jacques as he came out the kitchen door and gave him a wink.

"Oh dear," she said.

"What is it, Mireille?" Genevieve asked.

"I have a present for you, Genevieve, but I forgot to bring it. It's still at Hélène's home."

"A present for me?" Genevieve asked with excitement. The Olivier family was not wealthy, and presents were rare.

"Yes, I can't believe I forgot to bring it. Oh . . . I'd hate for you to wait. I'm very anxious to see if you like it, but I'm very tired after traveling all day. It's up in the loft—what if you were to go over to the Papineaus and have Hélène help you find it? We'll follow you in a while."

Genevieve glanced at Jacques for permission—their father had died six months ago, and Jacques was now her legal guardian. He nodded his consent, eager to be alone with Mireille, even if it was just for a few minutes. Genevieve quickly left, excited to find her present.

"When did you arrive?" he asked Mireille. They could still hear Genevieve singing as she rode her bicycle back to the Papineaus' home.

"Just a few hours ago. I tried to get away immediately, but you know how Aunt Hélène can be."

He took a slow step toward her. "That was sweet of you to bring Genevieve a present. All she got for Christmas was a few pieces of candy and some yarn."

"I'm just glad I remembered to forget it." She laughed, stepping toward him. The present was a new dress with stockings and shoes and a two-hundred-year-old golden necklace, a cross with a dozen different gemstones. "It turned out to be a good distraction."

Jacques smiled. "I think you're still the smartest girl I've ever met. And you're even more beautiful than I remember." Mireille blushed at that, which made her look even more lovely. "Did you have a good trip?"

"Yes, but I wish I could have been here earlier. I'm so sorry about your father. I wish I could have been here to help you . . . It must have been so hard for you. I miss him." Mireille slipped her hand into Jacques's as she said this.

Jacques turned serious. "Hard for me, hard for Genevieve. I'm trying to be a father and a mother and a brother to her, and I'm doing a rotten job at all of them."

"She looked happy when I saw her. And she must have grown a good three inches since last summer. What are your feeding her?"

Jacques smiled and gently ran the fingers of his free hand through her hair. "Actually, she does most of the cooking. It's the same things over and over again, but she's up to five dishes now. When Papa died, it was just two."

"Maybe I can teach her a few new things."

"I think we'd both like that." Jacques paused. "I've missed you, Mireille. Every day I've missed you."

Mireille kissed him softly. "I'm here now." Then they kissed again. It wasn't their first kiss—that had been nearly two years ago. But it was their first kiss in ten months, and it was fresh and tender. Partway through, Jacques abruptly pulled away.

"What is it?" Mireille asked.

"I should get you back to Marcel and Hélène," Jacques said, suddenly rather cool. "I'm sorry."

"Jacques, what's wrong?"

Jacques was already a few paces away. He stopped and looked down before answering. "What's wrong is that I've finally figured out what I want most in this life, and I can't have it."

Mireille stepped toward him. "What is it that you want?"

"You."

"And why are you so certain you can't have me?"

"Because in six or seven weeks, you'll go back to Paris. Then your father will marry you off to some stuffy, rich aristocrat, and I'll never see you again. Or if I did see you, you'd belong to another man." Jacques's voice trailed off. The last thought was particularly painful.

"Actually, I don't think I'll be going back to Paris. I plan to stay in Calais permanently. Marcel and Hélène said I can stay with them until you propose to me. Then we can get married and live happily ever after."

Jacques dared a glance at her. "Mireille, this isn't a fairytale. We love each other, but that doesn't change the reality that we're from different worlds. Beside, you're only seventeen."

"I'll be eighteen in two weeks."

"Your father will come for you or send someone for you."

She smiled at him, walking toward him with small steps. "On my way out of the city, I mailed him a letter telling him I was eloping with a student from Valencia. My father will be looking for me in the wrong country."

Jacques shook his head and took a step back as she approached. "Mireille, even if your father doesn't come, it's not possible. I don't think you understand how poor I am. I have a house, an acre of land, and a few cows. That's all. And I almost lost that this year. Taxes came due right after we buried my father, and I didn't have the money. I had to sell the piano and all my mother's jewelry to pay them. Genevieve cried about the piano for two weeks straight. For a few days, I thought she'd never speak to me again."

"She's lucky to have a wise brother who knows an instrument isn't as important as a house."

Jacques coughed to clear away the emotion sneaking into his voice. "Mireille, can't you see it's impossible for us to be together? You are heiress to a title and a huge fortune—you can't just throw that away. With me, there would be no butler, no maids, no cooks, no summer home in Marseilles. You'd have to wear the same clothes for years and make them and wash them yourself. I could never give you even a fraction of what you've been given your whole life."

"You think I care about any of that?" Mireille said, her smile gone.

"If you don't now, you will someday."

"Do you really think I'm just a shallow rich girl?"

Jacques looked at her then looked away. "No, you're not shallow, Mireille. You are the most wonderful person I have ever met, and I love you. If it weren't blasphemous, I'd worship you. But you are rich. And I am very, very poor."

"You're right, Jacques," Mireille said, matching his serious tone. "I am a spoiled rich girl for ten and a half months of every year. And if I return to Paris, my father will marry me off to someone as rich and stuffy as he is. But for six weeks of every year, I'm just a normal person. And those six weeks are what I live for during the other forty-six. I don't want wealth and privilege. I don't want to be a pawn in one of my father's business deals. And working on a farm doesn't scare me. What I want is love, and I've found that here. I love you."

Jacques turned toward her as she spoke. He believed she loved him, but social norms of the time still told him that marriage could never be. "It's impossible," he said. "You can't tie yourself to me."

"Nothing is impossible, Jacques."

He wanted to believe her. She would probably be happy with him for a few months, he thought, but could she be happy with him for decades, for a lifetime? Her blue eyes pleaded with him, begging him to believe her. Jacques had known Mireille since they were five and four years old. She had always been rich, but she had never been concerned with material possessions, not in the entire time he had known her.

She stepped toward him, just inches away now, and put her hand on his shoulder. He gently brushed her hair away from her cheek. "You could be happy with me?"

Mireille nodded. "Yes."

"You're certain?" Jacques asked, wanting to believe her.

"Very."

"For how long?" he asked.

"For eternity. And you owe me the other half of a kiss."

The rest of Jacques's doubts melted away.

* * *

Nothing is impossible, Jacques. A bump in the road knocked his head into the window, waking him. He sat up straight, surprised he had fallen asleep. *Nothing is impossible.* The words echoed through his mind.

He glanced over at the man driving. René wasn't his real name. Jacques knew that, and he knew René knew he knew. Still, Jacques trusted him. He wouldn't have drifted off to sleep if he didn't, nor would he be introducing him to the LeBras family or trusting him with downed airmen. *Nothing is impossible.* Mireille's words ran through his head again. She had always been right, hadn't she? A few minutes later, Jacques decided that after a three-year silence, it was time to pray again.

* * *

When Peter regained consciousness, his head was submerged in ice-cold water, and he was choking. He tried to lift his head out of the water, only to feel strong hands shove him farther under. He tried to resist, but his hands were tied behind his back now. He tried to get some type of leverage with his feet and legs, but his legs were tied together and pulled behind him, so all of Peter's weight rested on his knees. Just when he couldn't hold his breath any longer, he was pulled up. Peter gasped for air. Prinz was crouching nearby, watching with a smirk on his face. Weiss was in the background, a similar look on his face. He couldn't see who was behind him, but Prinz looked at whoever it was and nodded.

Down Peter went again. It was so cold it made his head hurt even more than it already ached from Tschirner, Prinz, and Weiss. The pain in his lungs, however, was far more intense. They had only pulled him up for a few seconds; Peter hadn't caught his breath from the first time they had shoved him underwater. Struggling was no use. Peter tried to hold his breath, but this time he couldn't. He inhaled water and started coughing, swallowing more. Finally, they pulled him out. He coughed up water and breathed in blessed air. Then he was shoved down again.

Peter tried relaxing this time. It helped for a while, but not for very long. The next time they pulled him out, he spat up water again. Peter felt the man behind him begin to push him back under.

"Siebert, hold for a moment," Prinz said. Then he looked at his prisoner. "How long have you been in Calais?"

Peter hesitated too long. They shoved him back under the water. He tried struggling again, but it was difficult to do so with his hands and feet both tied behind him. He ended up with another lungful of water before the next break.

When he was done vomiting water, Peter looked at Prinz and told him he had been in Calais a little less than a month.

"Who have you been staying with?"

"No one," Peter said between gulps of air. "Hid . . . in . . . the . . . fields."

Prinz raised an eyebrow, and Siebert shoved their prisoner into the water again. This time they held him under so long he lost consciousness.

Peter woke up on the floor, choking and wheezing. Siebert had actually released him. When Peter was done coughing, Prinz asked him where he had really been staying.

"In . . . a . . . barn. By . . . Monsieur . . . Laurier's . . . farm. That . . . street."

Prinz made a face, trying to decide if he was hearing the truth. He wasn't convinced, so he signaled, and Siebert lifted Peter up on his knees again and shoved his head into the water. Peter's lungs burned. His head ached. He wanted to give up but told himself he couldn't. *You can't let them have Jacques and Genevieve and Birgit. Don't tell them anything.*

On the floor again, Peter heard Prinz's questions in between his coughing and gasping.

"How long have you been in Calais?"

"Just . . . under . . . month."

"Where have you been staying?"

"In . . . a . . . barn, by . . . Laurier . . . home. South . . . of . . . the . . . city."

"Are you the spy who robbed him and tied him up last Friday?"

Peter didn't answer immediately. Prinz motioned, and Peter was back under water. He held his breath as long as he could, but each recurring punishment was shortening the time he could hold out until the inevitable lungful of water. Siebert pulled Peter out while he was still conscious, and after Peter had disgorged most of the water from his lungs and stomach Prinz began repeating his questions.

"Where in Calais have you been staying?"

"In . . . a . . . barn, by . . . Monsieur . . . Laurier's . . . farm."

"Are you the spy who visited him on Friday?"

Peter nodded his head, conserving his breath.

"Weiss, go inform Tschirner."

Peter watched the Gestapo man leave the room. Then Prinz continued his questioning. "Who are your contacts?"

"Alexandre . . . Dumas . . . and . . . Victor . . . Hugo."

Picking names from French literature had worked for Peter once before. It didn't work this time. Siebert shoved him back under the water. When Peter was released, Prinz asked him for his contacts again.

"I'm . . . not . . . going . . . to . . . tell . . . you," Peter said, knowing the result of his statement would be another round of drowning.

Prinz smiled and leaned in so his face was inches from his prisoner's. He slapped Peter across the face then taunted him. "Oh, Lieutenant Eddy, I think you will tell us. The only question is *when.*" He motioned to Siebert.

Peter was under the water for so long that he thought they were going to let him die there.

* * *

Genevieve had paced away most of the afternoon, waiting for her brother to return. He hadn't. Nor had Louis. Finally, Genevieve decided to act. She left home with a set of fake identity papers that said her name was Madeleine Petit and a small bomb hidden in a basket of cheese. She left her glasses at home and strapped her Enfield MK1 revolver to her thigh. Genevieve entered town from the south, following a crowd of people and managing to avoid an inspection.

She waited until twenty minutes before the Gestapo sentries changed shifts then approached one of the guards. She told him she had a suspicious neighbor to report. The guard led her into an office with plans to call his commanding officer, but before he could make any arrangements, the bomb Genevieve had hidden only a few yards from the gate surrounding Gestapo headquarters exploded. The guard went to investigate, and Genevieve slipped out the door and into the building's basement, where she knew the prisoners were kept. By the time the guard was done inspecting the bomb site, his shift would be finished, and he would assume his replacement had taken care of the informer. Genevieve didn't know exactly how she was going to get out of Gestapo headquarters, but she had twine in her pocket for tying up guards, she knew all the building's exits, and she would have Peter to help.

Now in the hallway, Genevieve listened carefully. "I ask you again, who are your contacts?" the voice on the other side of the door was smooth, like velvet.

"I'm . . . not . . . going . . . to . . . tell . . . you," she heard Peter say. At least she thought it was Peter. The voice was strained—like he was having difficulty speaking. She was standing right under the little window in the thick door, but she wasn't tall enough to see into the room without something to stand on. *What are they doing to him?*

"Oh, Lieutenant Eddy, I think you will tell us. The only question is *when*," the smooth voice said. Genevieve heard muffled sounds. *Splashes?* Instinct told her it was vital that she act, and act soon. Still, despite how much she wanted to help Peter, she was frightened. The Geheime Staatspolizei was notoriously cruel; whatever they were doing to Peter, they could easily do to her. She hesitated for a few seconds, and then love overcame fear as she slowly turned the doorknob and pushed the door in.

Inside, she quickly surveyed the room—two guards, their prisoner, a large bucket of water, like one she would use for washing clothes. Peter's hands and feet were tied behind him, and the larger of the two guards was holding his head under the water. She held her Enfield revolver with both hands and pointed it at the largest guard. Her hands were shaking, but at this range, there was little risk of her missing her target.

"Cut him loose," she ordered. Her voice was trembling almost as much as her hands were. The guard looked at her weapon and obeyed, freeing Peter's arms and legs with a knife. Peter, however, was no longer conscious, so his head remained under the water.

Genevieve was alarmed. "Pull him out!"

The large guard looked at Prinz, who glanced at his watch and shook his head ever so slightly. The sturmmann stood up and stepped away from Peter's body, back against the far side of the cell from Genevieve, next to Prinz.

"Pull him out, or I'll shoot," Genevieve threatened.

The sturmmann looked at Prinz and stayed where he was.

Genevieve knew she didn't have time to argue with the Gestapo guards. She knew that a shot from her old revolver would attract too much attention—if she could bring herself to pull the trigger. Besides, shooting one or both of the guards wouldn't save Peter. So she made her decision and transferred her weapon to her left hand. She kept it pointed in the general direction of the guards and used her right arm to pull Peter out of the water. His unconscious body was heavier than she expected, and her grip on him slipped. He slid down to the ground, lying on his back, still not breathing.

Genevieve gasped as she took in the physical marks of Peter's torture. Swollen, red patches covered his face and neck. She glanced up at the guards, who were still standing calmly against the wall. She fleetingly thought she might be able to pull the trigger more easily now that she had seen what they'd done to Peter. More pressing was the matter of how to get Peter to breathe again. *Get him off his back*, she told herself.

Great physical strength was not one of Genevieve's assets. Genetics and wartime rations had seen to that. She would need both arms to turn Peter over. She hesitated, knowing what would happen if she put her weapon on the floor. If she put it down, there would be no chance of escape. All her exit plans had involved Peter being alive and conscious, but now all those plans were useless. If she didn't set her weapon down, Peter would die. She could have Peter, or she could remain free, but she couldn't have both. So she placed the Enfield revolver on the floor and pulled Peter's arm over his head so she could roll his water-logged body onto its side and then roll him onto his stomach. Before she had finished, the two guards had drawn their weapons and stepped toward her. She hadn't expected any other outcome.

"Hands up, mademoiselle." The silky smooth voice was Obersturmführer Prinz's. His Mauser was pointed at her face, and her own weapon was under his shiny black boot. Genevieve obeyed. As gravity began to drain the water out of Peter's mouth and throat, he began to cough. He was alive, but Genevieve was certain that the rest of his life, and the rest of hers, would be very short and very painful.

* * *

Peter's brain was fuzzy. *Don't tell them, don't tell them.* The phrase had been the last one to go through Peter's mind before everything had again gone black. Now it was all his brain could remember. *Don't tell them,* he thought again. *Don't tell who? And don't tell them what?* he wondered.

He was still coughing, gasping for air. The skin lining his nose and throat felt raw, like it was burning. He gradually became aware of how cold he was. The floor was wet, as were his clothes. Objects came into view then—the water bucket, Siebert's boots. Then Peter remembered everything that had happened that day. *Why aren't they asking me any questions? And why are my hands untied?* he wondered. *Who cares? Just be grateful you can breathe again.* So Peter stayed as he was, breathing and lying still so as to not attract attention to himself.

Peter heard the door open and someone walk in. "You're late, Weiss," Prinz said. "No matter. Siebert, I think it's time we inform Standartenführer Tschirner of our most recent development."

Peter watched Siebert walk out of his range of vision. He was concerned. *What recent development? Did I break and forget what I told them?* Peter didn't have long to wonder what the development might have been before he felt the end of Prinz's boot striking his abdomen. Peter grunted and slowly turned his head to face Prinz. *That's strange,* he thought, *Prinz's gun isn't aimed at me.* Peter followed Prinz's arm to the corner of the room where Genevieve was standing with her hands fettered behind her back. Despite the steady ache in his lungs, he momentarily forgot to breathe as terror flooded over him. "No," he whispered.

* * *

Obersturmführer Prinz was enjoying himself. Lieutenant Eddy was obviously pained to see that his accomplice had been captured, and the young French girl was practically paralyzed with fear. He brought his boot back to kick his American prisoner again, wondering how many strikes it would take to cause permanent damage. Lieutenant Eddy had some time ago stopped fighting back, but he gritted his teeth and took his abuse in silence. This prisoner frustrated him. *He should have broken by now,* Prinz thought. *He should be in tears, begging me for mercy and offering me anything I want.* Prinz kicked him again. Eddy squeezed his eyes shut and clenched his jaw, but that was the only reaction Prinz could elicit.

"Stop, please!" That was the French girl, crying out in desperation. Prinz ignored her and kicked Lieutenant Eddy again, harder than the previous time. He got only a mild reaction.

Then Prinz had an idea. Physical pain didn't seem to be the key to breaking Lieutenant Eddy—not when he was the recipient. *But what if the pain were directed at someone else?* He walked toward the scrawny French girl and put his hand around her thin neck. She had made his day when she'd shown up in the jail cell. He thought he probably could have disarmed her immediately, and even if not, she hadn't been aiming her weapon at him. Knowing Weiss was on the way, Prinz had pretended to cooperate, and he had found it so very entertaining to watch her knowingly seal her own fate.

"You are no longer in a position to ask for anything," he told her. Then Prinz grabbed her shoulders and threw her to the ground by the American. Now he could keep his weapon aimed at both of them. He carefully watched their faces. To Prinz, love was a weakness, a weakness both the American and the French girl obviously suffered from. It was a weakness he fully intended to exploit.

* * *

Genevieve's knee hit the concrete floor when Prinz threw her to the ground. With her hands in shackles, she was unable to break her fall. Peter caught her in his arms before her face ground into the floor. Still, a soft cry of pain escaped her lips.

"Are you okay?" Peter asked her. He had somehow managed to reach out as Prinz threw her to the floor and was now working his way into a sitting position. His hand brushed over hers. It felt like ice. "What has he done to you?"

"Just what you saw." Genevieve fought to control the waiver in her voice. "How did they get you?"

She could hear the pain in Peter's voice.

"I just wanted to help you, Peter. I saw them arrest you, and I was so worried—" Before she could say anything else, she felt rough arms pulling her away from Peter. She struggled against them, to no effect. Siebert and Weiss held her between them.

A man she recognized as Standartenführer Tschirner walked confidently into the room. He kicked Peter rather forcefully in the chest, forcing Peter onto his back so he was looking up at the Gestapo men. Genevieve despaired as she looked more carefully at how beaten he looked. The wound on the side of his head was wider, and blood was seeping from the split, mixing with water from his hair and dripping onto the prison floor. Still, Peter appeared outwardly composed, looking up at Tschirner with calm contempt as Tschirner connected one end of a chain to Peter's wrist and the other end of the chain to an iron socket in the wall.

"Let's cut out the normal introductory questions, shall we? We all know you came to Calais to prepare for the invasion," Tschirner began. "I want to know where and when the invasion will take place. If you don't tell me quickly enough, you will watch us cut off this mademoiselle's fingers one by one. Then her ears, her toes—we'll move on from there if necessary. To begin, Obersturmführer Prinz, why don't you show Peter Eddy, second lieutenant, US Army, one-nine-five-five-six-zero-nine-two, that we are quite serious."

In one fluid movement, Prinz pulled a switchblade knife from his pocket and exposed the blade. Siebert changed his grip on Genevieve so the back of her neck was exposed. Prinz let the blade sink into her skin. She could tell it wasn't deep—just deep enough to hurt and draw blood. Genevieve's eyes filled with tears, and she trembled as Prinz used the knife to extend the length of his cut. She bit her lip to keep from screaming out loud. She knew things were only going to get worse, but she was willing to suffer quite a bit for France and sacrifice perhaps even more for Peter.

"Stop!" Peter pleaded. "Please, stop. I'll tell you what you want to know."

Prinz pulled his knife away from Genevieve's skin. He stepped into her line of sight, a look of disappointment on his face. She could feel a small trickle of blood running down the back of her neck.

"Peter, don't tell him," Genevieve cried with resolution, noticing how desperate his eyes looked. "There are too many lives at risk—" The rest of her words were cut off as Siebert put his hand over her mouth. His hands were coarse and dirty, his nails were broken and stained, and his actions were rough and violent. Genevieve winced.

Tschirner seemed satisfied with the desperation in Peter's voice and with Siebert's methods of handling Genevieve. "Where will the invasion come?" he asked, leaning over Peter and placing his boot on the American's chest.

"Here," Peter said. "Calais." Genevieve shuddered as he answered.

"I want more specific information."

Prinz lifted his knife again and stuck it lightly into Genevieve's neck. She felt it draw blood.

"Wait!" Peter cried. Prinz withdrew his knife. "The plans aren't finalized, but there will be several landings to the east and to the west of the harbor. Paratroopers will be dropped a few hours in advance to take the main roads and the docks and hold them until the regular army joins up with them. We want the harbor; that will be the focus of the invasion." Genevieve's heart sank. Such details, she knew, could allow the Nazis to thwart any invasion attempt. *Peter, what are you doing?* she thought sadly. But she knew what he was doing—he was trying to protect her.

"Where are the diversionary landings going to be?" Tschirner continued his interrogation.

"Diversionary landings?" Peter asked.

"Yes, I've heard rumors that there will be several false attacks before the real one. Where will they be attempted?" Tschirner continued in a dark, calm voice.

Peter paused. Prinz looked at Genevieve with evil anticipation and grabbed one of her fingers. Genevieve tried to silence Peter with her eyes. *Don't tell them, Peter. Please don't tell them,* she thought. But Siebert was still preventing her from speaking.

"Norway, the Balkans, Le Havre," Peter said.

"Who will be the commander on the ground?"

"General Patton."

Tschirner paused. "When?"

Peter glanced up at Genevieve. Prinz's knife was resting against her right index finger. She managed to shake her head at him, but he spoke anyway. "The fourth of July."

"Why then?"

"Enough moonlight for the paratroopers to see by. And we Americans are a little sentimental about that day. It's our Independence Day."

"Yes, you Americans are entirely too sentimental," Tschirner said, looking at Genevieve. "I will check the date of the American Independence Day. If you have lied to me, you will find her head—separated from her lovely neck—on the floor next to you within the hour."

Tschirner motioned that the interrogation was over, at least for now. Prinz exited, and Siebert and Weiss dragged Genevieve after them. *What have I done?* she thought. *I've just made things worse—I was exactly the leverage the Gestapo needed. We're both as good as dead, and now the invasion will fail.*

* * *

Peter watched them drag Genevieve away. He was terrified of what they might do to her, and though he wanted to go to her and free her from the Gestapo guards, he knew it was physically impossible. The chain that connected him to the wall was strong, and the torture had left him weak. Tschirner was the last to leave the cell. He sneered at Peter then kicked him in the side of his head. It didn't knock Peter completely unconscious, but it was several seconds before he could see anything, and when his eyes began to discern light, the room wasn't standing still. Peter turned on his side and heaved. His stomach was empty; nothing came out. He had never before felt so sick, so powerless, and so hopeless.

Torture. It isn't always physical. As Peter lay there on the prison floor shivering in his wet clothes, he thought about Genevieve. *Please*, he prayed and begged, *please don't let any more harm come to her because of my mistakes. Let them drown me, torture me, or execute me, but please don't let them hurt her anymore.*

Odd, it had only been a week, but he felt like he'd known her much longer. He hadn't fully realized it until he had seen Prinz throw her to the floor, but he cared about her deeply. The memory of Marie's kiss crossed his mind, and he shook his head in despair, wishing he had never kissed her. Despite her beauty, she wasn't the right girl. *Even if she hadn't turned me over to the Nazis,* Peter thought, *she wouldn't be the right one. Why didn't I see it earlier? Genevieve was the one I should have kissed.*

Peter's body ached. His bones were bruised. His muscles were beaten. But what hurt the most was his heart.

* * *

Several hours later, Peter was half asleep, still shivering in his jail cell. He heard the door of his cell open again. He didn't turn around because he didn't want to know who it was. *Prinz with his brass knuckles? Siebert with a pail of water? Something new?*

Peter could hear two men speaking German. He didn't catch most of it—it was too fast, and the one speaking the most slurred his words together. He felt a gentle prodding with the end of someone's shoe and then heard orders for him to stand up. He ignored the orders. He wasn't sure he was still physically able to stand. The voice became more intense, and he heard a whip crack and felt it land on his back. It didn't hurt; Peter thought perhaps he was too numb to feel any new pain. The voice was almost yelling now, and Peter felt the whip hit him again. He didn't find the second stroke any more painful than the first had been.

Finally, the two men pulled Peter off the floor and unlocked the heavy chain around his wrist, replacing it with a pair of handcuffs. Peter glanced at the men through swollen eyelids. He didn't recognize either of them, the sturmmann nor the hauptsturmführer. The hauptsturmführer looked at Peter with disgust as he looped his whip and fastened it at his side. Then each of them grabbed one of Peter's arms and led him out of the cell. Peter found that his legs still functioned, although not without pain. The hauptsturmführer who escorted him was a little shorter than Peter himself. The lean sturmmann towered over them both. *This is your best chance for escape*, Peter told himself. He looked ahead to the stairwell. That, he felt, was the best place to try. If he succeeded, he would try to find Genevieve.

"Where are we going?" Peter asked as he hobbled along between them. He didn't expect them to answer, but he hoped to distract them. He was surprised when the sturmmann spoke.

"You are going to Paris," he said.

"Paris?" Peter repeated.

"Fresnes prison," the hauptsturmführer informed him. Peter had heard the name of the prison before. All the rumors surrounding the Fresnes Gestapo prison indicated that it was one of the worst places in Europe, though Peter wasn't sure it could be any worse than the Calais jail.

"Don't do anything stupid," the hauptsturmführer said as they reached the staircase. Peter looked at the hauptsturmführer more carefully, not because he had anticipated Peter's thoughts but because the voice now sounded slightly familiar. His own eyes were badly bruised, but he could see the golden brown eyes of the hauptsturmführer. The eyes belonged to Jacques Olivier. Jacques noticed Peter's gaze and winked. Relief flooded over Peter.

Genevieve, Peter thought. *Does Jacques know where she is? Does he know she's been captured?* Peter was uncertain if the sturmmann was a member of the Resistance or simply fooled by a disguise. Peter chose his next words very carefully. "Is the young woman that was captured shortly after me also being sent to Paris?"

Jacques seemed startled, but he recovered and looked straight ahead. *So he doesn't know,* Peter thought.

"Sturmmann Kuhn, how many people have been apprehended today?" Jacques asked.

Kuhn thought for a moment then replied. "Five."

"Any of them female?"

"One of them."

"Do you have her name?" Kuhn shook his head, so Jacques tried a different method. "Can you describe her?"

"Dark hair, dark eyes, petite figure. She was still beautiful the last time I saw her. I can't say what she looks like now. Sometimes the women look very different after they've been here for an evening." He finished with a knowing laugh.

"Kuhn, if she is connected to this prisoner, she should go to Fresnes as well. She might be useful leverage to get the information we need. Fetch the girl and meet me at the north entrance."

"Yes, sir."

Kuhn saluted then hurried down a different hallway, and Jacques and Peter continued in their original direction at a slow pace.

"How did Genevieve get into this?" Jacques asked in a barely audible whisper.

"I don't know the details," Peter admitted. "She saw me being arrested and said she wanted to help. They brought her in and threatened to slash her with a knife if I didn't cooperate."

"Did you cooperate?"

"They think I cooperated. Last time I saw her, they hadn't done anything serious to her, not physically."

"When did you last see her?"

Peter shook his head. "I'm not sure. Time's a funny thing when you're in prison. I've not been conscious the whole time. I think it's been at least two hours since I saw her, maybe as many as five."

* * *

Jacques nodded, still shocked that his little sister was in danger. He wished Peter had a better time line but understood why he didn't.

"Jacques, how did you know I was here?"

"Genevieve left a note saying she saw the Gestapo take you off in handcuffs. I thought she was with Anne and Birgit. I didn't go find her because I've never yet figured out how to make her look like a German soldier."

Jacques had returned from Brunembert with René and gone directly to Louis LeBras. The three Frenchmen had hidden the three airmen in the enormous barrels in the back of René's truck, and within minutes, René was taking them back to Brunembert. If everything had gone as planned, they had arrived there just before curfew and would leave for Paris at dawn.

After the airmen left with René, Jacques had asked LeBras about the strange deadline. Anne LeBras had been shaken up a few days before when some of her friends had disappeared. Worried about Birgit, Anne wanted the airmen out of her house; she had set the tight deadline. To put it bluntly, she had lost her nerve. She wouldn't even stay at the home while the airmen hid there, insisting that the entire family stay in town with friends until evening. *I guess I don't really blame her,* Jacques thought. *War can wear down the soul, and she's already endured it for almost four years.* LeBras had reluctantly agreed to honor his wife's wishes and end his work with the Resistance.

Jacques had almost returned home then but had gone into town instead. At the time, he'd assumed Peter and his sister were at the farmhouse, and he'd been curious about how they were getting along but also hesitant to disturb them. He suspected Genevieve's jealousy and Peter's attraction to Marie would come to a head, and he had planned to give the two of them time to quarrel and make up. And if they didn't make up, well, Jacques thought that might be for the best. Either way, Peter would soon return to England, and Genevieve would stay with her brother in France. Jacques had a nagging suspicion that living with Genevieve after Peter left would be difficult and depressing. He was certain his sister was in love but doubted anything permanent could work out.

In town, Jacques had gone to confession at the Notre Dame church, primarily to give the clergyman new instructions about the changed line but also for religious reasons. Only after those arrangements were made had Jacques returned to the farmhouse and found Genevieve's note, written in a code their father had taught them.

He sighed and shook his head. "Why didn't she wait for me?" But he already knew the answer. The fact that Genevieve had attempted to help Peter, despite great personal risk, shouldn't have surprised him. He looked carefully at Peter, hoping his sister wouldn't look as beaten as he did. "Can you see well enough to aim a pistol?"

"Yes."

"No broken bones in your arms?"

Peter lifted his arms to test them, wincing with the movement. "No."

Jacques thought Peter's voice sounded weak and strained, but his eyes seemed determined. "Right, keep moving around, and it will get easier to walk again," Jacques said as he unlocked Peter's handcuffs and handed him a Luger P08 pistol. Peter checked the clip; it was full.

They turned a corner, and Jacques spoke again. "So there were two double agents? Monsieur Laurier and Mademoiselle Murat?"

Peter nodded. Then a thoughtful look crossed his face. "Jacques, what school did Mireille go to before she married you?"

Jacques turned his gaze from the hallway to his companion. He thought it was a strange question, but he knew the answer. For many years, he had sent letters there at least once a week. "The Versailles School of Liberal Arts for Young Ladies."

"Did they study a lot of Roman poetry?"

"They studied a lot of every kind of poetry."

"Jacques, I think I know who betrayed your wife," Peter said slowly. Jacques stared back at him, taut and intensive. "It was Marie. She went to the same school. And she said she betrayed a dear friend from school right as she began her work as a double agent—a friend who visited Calais often and loved the beauty of the land and its people. She also started giving information to the British—false information, I suppose—the same month your wife was killed, May 1941."

Jacques turned away from Peter, knowing that his feelings would be written plainly on his face. He breathed in and out deeply, fighting tremendous emotion. He remembered how excited Mireille had been after running into an old friend at the Calais market. It had been a friend from school, and one term after studying Shakespearean tragedies, the friend had given Mireille the nickname of Juliet—on account of the prediction that falling in love so young would only lead to tragedy. Mireille had also given her friend a nickname, Ophelia, with a prediction that she would fall in love with a mad aristocrat. Mireille had laughed, telling Jacques how surprised she had been to hear someone yelling out "Juliet" from across the market. Jacques had never known Ophelia's real name. Mireille had spent the afternoon catching up with her friend, and Ophelia—Marie—had said she wanted to help fight the Nazis. Mireille had believed her and had made arrangements for Marie to meet Jacques and aid the Resistance in Calais. The night of the rendezvous had come two weeks later. Instead of an old school friend, there had been German soldiers and death. Mireille's life had indeed played out like a tragedy. Jacques felt anger, grief, and a thirst for revenge. He had lost his wife, his unborn child, his happiness, his faith, and his peace. And now his sister was also being threatened.

"She was going to have a baby," Jacques said softly.

"Mireille?" Peter asked.

Jacques nodded. "She had just told me that morning, the day she was killed. We hadn't even told Genevieve yet."

After a bit of time, Jacques turned and gently pulled Peter from the wall he had been leaning on. They started walking again and finally reached the building's north exit, the main entrance. The two men stopped in the shadows. Near the exit was the door leading to the guards' break room. The door was closed now, but Jacques knew it would be full of guards, even though the clock outside the room indicated that it was 0200 hours, the middle of the night.

"I expected Kuhn to be here before us," Jacques said quietly.

"Is Kuhn a real Nazi?"

Jacques nodded. "Yes, a rather simple one. Impervious to bribes but gullible." He pulled a wool cap out of his pocket and handed it to Peter, who put it on with gratitude. "I'm sorry I don't have any dry clothes for you."

"I'm sorry I was stupid enough to get captured. And I'm sorry Genevieve got pulled into this. I'm more sorry about that than I've ever been about anything. I'll do anything to help her—anything."

Jacques nodded. He could tell Peter was sincere. Then they heard footsteps. Just one pair. Peter hid his hands and his pistol behind his back. The footsteps belonged to Kuhn.

Jacques adopted an air of authority. "Sturmmann Kuhn, where is the other prisoner?"

"Obersturmführer Prinz arrived just before I did and took her to Standartenführer Tschirner's office."

On hearing the two names, Jacques felt a knot develop in his stomach. Outwardly, he displayed a perfect mixture of boredom and annoyance.

"Fine, I will go myself and make the arrangements with Tschirner. Prepare a vehicle for immediate departure to Paris." Kuhn saluted and started walking out the door. As he opened the door, Jacques could see four sentries posted outside. It was dark outside, dark and stormy. Dark enough, Jacques realized, to hide additional guards in the shadows beyond his vision. "Sturmmann Kuhn, what were they doing in Tschirner's office?"

"Finishing their paperwork before they enjoy the bounties of France. You know, wine and pretty women." Kuhn answered, saluted again, and disappeared out the door.

Jacques's hands started shaking. He turned and began walking as quickly as was prudent in the direction Kuhn had come from. Peter followed. Jacques knew exactly where they were going and led them deeper into the building. He turned a corner and paused.

"I don't think Tschirner will believe the orders I forged, but I'm going to give it a try. They have your name on them, but perhaps he'll agree to keep both of you together. If it doesn't work, you and Genevieve get out of here as fast as you can. I'll make sure Tschirner and his henchmen don't follow you."

Peter shook his head. "I think you and Genevieve should go; I'll hold them off. You can move faster than I can, and you know this building. I don't."

"Genevieve knows the building. Marcel Papineau's business was electrical systems, and he wired this building. We saw it being built from the foundation to the final coat of paint. She knows where to go."

"Jacques, I'm not in good shape. You'll move quicker than I will."

The statement was true. Jacques could see blood soaking through the hat he had given Peter only minutes before. "Perhaps, but based on your swollen eyes and what I can guess your arms look like, I don't trust your aim. I don't want you to waste all my ammunition."

"Jacques, don't be ridiculous. My aim will be true enough. And you have a better chance of getting Genevieve to safety than I do."

"That's irrelevant," Jacques said as he began walking again. Peter quickened his pace to match.

"I don't know what could be more relevant," Peter protested.

"Peter, did you know that McDougall gave me orders to kill you if there was a real risk of you being captured and interrogated? He said you know some things that he doesn't want the Nazis to know. He told me to follow standard procedure: if you were apprehended by more than three people or if you were apprehended inside the city, I was ordered to shoot you rather than rescue you."

"I didn't know that," Peter said. "But I'm not surprised. I just don't understand why you're bringing up your execution orders right now."

Jacques continued. "When the occupation began, I was horrified at the cruelty I saw in the actions of the Germans. That was just what I saw. The things I heard about were even worse. But in fighting a ruthless enemy, I myself became ruthless. I like you, Peter, and I trust you. But everyone captured either talks or dies; usually they do both. I would have followed through with McDougall's orders, either to prevent you from being broken or to end your misery. It's wartime, and that's just how it is. But I have a soft spot. Well, a few of them actually. One is only a memory, one is but five years old, and the other is my sister. My loyalty to them is even deeper than my loyalty to France." He paused and glanced at Peter.

"I still don't follow where this is going, Jacques."

Jacques stopped walking again and looked directly at the battered American. "Peter, are you blind? Genevieve would never forgive me if I left you behind or let you get killed. She's in love with you."

"In love with me?" Peter asked, confusion in his voice. "Are you sure?"

"Why do you think she's been singing around the house again after a three-year lapse? Why do you think you're the first person over the age of five that she's opened up to even slightly since Mireille died? Why do you think she was so upset that you were going to see Marie? And why do you think she risked coming to get you without waiting a few hours for my help?"

Peter looked overwhelmed. "And my mistakes led her to this," he whispered. "What a horrible way to repay her."

Jacques put his hand on Peter's shoulder. "We all make mistakes, Peter. You can't change the past. But you can shape the future."

Peter nodded slowly and followed when Jacques began moving again. They stopped outside an office door and glanced through the small glass window. Tschirner was sitting at a desk. Jacques and Peter could see the Nazi's profile; he was speaking to someone out of sight.

* * *

Genevieve waited for Standartenführer Tschirner to say something. Obersturmführer Prinz had taken her from her cell not long before and had brought her to Tschirner's office at the standartenführer's request. Tschirner had greeted her with silence, the suspense increasing her dread as she waited.

Finally, he spoke to her. "Two hours ago I sent details of the upcoming invasion to Paris and to Berlin by armed courier. You realize what that means, Mademoiselle Petit?"

Genevieve nodded and looked away, a few fresh tears trickling down her cheeks. *It means the invasion will fail,* she thought sadly. The fact that Tschirner believed her to be Madeleine Petit, the name written on her false papers, brought her little comfort.

"You are sure of Eddy's information?" Prinz asked his commander.

Tschirner nodded. "The Americans have little experience in espionage. Their own secretary of war once said, 'Gentlemen do not read each other's mail.' Naïve. With the British you can expect some type of a trick. With the Americans, resistance and then compliance. Americans are used to relying on their own strength, especially the young ones. Once their strength is broken, you can depend on the information you extract from them."

"What will you do with Lieutenant Eddy?" Genevieve asked softly, afraid of what the answer might be.

Tschirner glanced at Prinz, who answered Genevieve's question. "A slow, painful death after we've extracted all the information we want. We'll begin again tomorrow morning with piano wire and move on from there."

Genevieve shuddered. She had heard rumors that the Nazis sometimes used wire to strangle their prisoners. She had spent the last few hours awake in her cell, crying a lot and praying even more. The mercy she had prayed for didn't seem to have been granted to Peter. She had yet to ask any for herself. "And my fate—it will be the same?"

Tschirner smiled and allowed her to wait in painful suspense before answering. "Perhaps in the end, but in the meantime Sturmmann Siebert desires an hour or two alone with you."

Genevieve glanced at Siebert. He was sitting in a chair in the corner of the office. His size, his expression—he matched the mental picture she had given the god Hades. He looked back at her with clear, barbaric lust in his eyes. Genevieve physically flinched, backing away from Siebert until she bumped into Prinz, who shoved her into Siebert's lap. She could feel Siebert's hot breath on her temples and wished she were dead.

"Alone?" Prinz asked. "You aren't going to make the American watch?"

Genevieve cringed as he spoke. She struggled to get away from Siebert, but he held her firmly. Prinz laughed at her.

"Sir," Genevieve said to Tschirner, fighting to keep her voice even. "I would prefer immediate execution."

"Not tonight," Tschirner answered. "You seem to be Lieutenant Eddy's weak spot, so we won't execute you just yet. Sturmmann Siebert, you're free to do what you will. Just return the prisoner to her cell when you're finished."

Siebert left the office, dragging Genevieve with him. She thought of begging for mercy, but she knew it would have no effect. She also thought of trying to escape, but Siebert's grip on her was too strong, and her hands were still cuffed.

A few steps down the hallway, she heard something that briefly sounded like wind blowing through a tunnel, and Siebert suddenly released her. Hopeful and curious, she stepped away and glanced over her shoulder. Siebert's hands had released her so he could more effectively deal with the whip wrapped around his neck. Genevieve's eyes followed the whip and then stared at the Gestapo hauptsturmführer who held the other end. It only took her a few seconds to recognize him.

"Jacques?" she gasped. Her brother winked at her, and she almost fell to the floor with relief. Then she saw Peter, who gave her half a smile before smashing a heavy garbage can into Siebert's face. Siebert fell to the floor with a crash, no longer conscious. Peter searched Siebert's pockets for a key then unlocked the handcuffs that still held Genevieve's hands behind her back.

"All right, back to the north entrance. Pretend you're my prisoners if we run into any patrols," Jacques said. They turned to leave as Prinz appeared in the doorway of Tschirner's office. Within a second, his pistol was drawn. At the same time, Jacques ripped the pin from a grenade and threw it into the office.

Peter pulled Genevieve to the floor and tried to shield her from the blast. They were to the left of the door, Jacques to the right, when the grenade exploded. Prinz fell in the doorway, a single shot from his pistol firing harmlessly into the ceiling above him. Jacques came through the smoke, and the three of them headed farther into the building.

An alarm bell sounded. A few moments later, they heard the sound of running guards. Jacques led the others around a corner and down several flights of stairs.

They were on the ground floor when they ran into more complications. As they approached the intersection of two long hallways, they ran into two three-man patrols converging at the crossing. They ducked into a room, another office. The doorframe was set a few feet in from the hallway, and the door opened to the outside. Once inside, Jacques and Peter crouched in the doorway, where they were partially shielded by the door and the recessed walls, and began firing at the patrols.

"Genevieve, see if you can get out the window," Jacques said.

She turned to the window but couldn't open it. She grabbed a stool, broke the glass, and risked sticking her head out the window. She looked back and saw a bullet slam into the door only a few inches from Peter. But the window was clear. "I don't see anyone," Genevieve reported.

"Not yet anyway," Jacques said. "Peter, you and Genevieve use the window and get out of here. I'll catch up later."

"You can't hold off all of them by yourself," Peter said as four bullets hit within a foot of where the two men were crouched in the doorway. They both took aim and shot at targets past Genevieve's range of vision.

"I have a better chance of holding them off than you do," Jacques said.

"You also have a better chance of getting Genevieve to safety than I do."

"If you don't go now some of the patrols will make it to the window, and then none of us will get out," Jacques said as a bullet narrowly missed his shoulder. It left a hole in his clothing.

"I think we should stick together," Peter said.

"Two groups will be twice as hard to catch. We already had this conversation, Peter. Go."

Peter took another shot at a Gestapo guard. Genevieve heard a cry in the hallway, so she assumed Peter had hit him, but Peter only looked more worried. "Five more turning the corner." Peter looked at Jacques, who motioned for him to move to the window. "Do you have any more grenades?" Peter asked.

"If I did, I would have used them by now. Just go. I'm sorry things are going to end like this; it's just how our cards were dealt."

Peter looked at Genevieve. She blinked away a few tears and nodded in agreement with her brother. She didn't want to leave anyone behind. But she also knew that Jacques wouldn't change his mind and that time was working against them. The thought of leaving her brother caused her pain, but the prospect of losing both men was even worse.

Peter took a final few shots at the guards in the hallway. "Good luck," he said to Jacques. Jacques nodded and flashed his teeth like he always did in extreme danger. Genevieve took one final look at her brother and led Peter out the window and into the night.

* * *

The night was dark and windy with a light rain. Genevieve and Peter stayed close to the building as they edged away from the firefight. They could still hear the sound of gunfire for a while, but then the noise grew fainter and stopped—but Peter wasn't sure if that was because they were too far away or because the firefight had ended.

Peter heard footsteps. He and Genevieve both flattened themselves against the ground, into the shadows and the wet earth. A patrolman slowly walked past them. It took every ounce of Peter's self-control to quiet his muscles that were still trembling from cold, exhaustion, and stress. The guard walked past them then turned slowly toward them again. He said something under his breath and brought his rifle up slowly. Peter brought his pistol up quickly and shot the man. Even with the muting effect of the rain and wind, the shot seemed loud.

"Can you run?" Genevieve asked, helping Peter to his feet.

"I think so."

"Then we run for the gate. I can't see anyone there right now." She pointed beyond the building they were walking along. There was a tall fence around the entire Gestapo building. Prinz had brought Peter through a gate on the north side of the complex. The gate Genevieve pointed at was on the south side.

"Out the back door," Peter said under his breath.

Genevieve grabbed his arm and helped pull him along the building toward freedom. They stopped at the edge of the building and peeked around the corner. There were two guards there, with rifles slung across their backs. They looked fairly relaxed, but they also looked watchful. It was to be expected that they were fully awake; few people could doze through the sounding alarm. Peter checked his weapon; he only had one bullet left.

Peter again glanced around the south end of the building, searching for a way out. *I got us into this mess*, he thought. *I'll get us out of it too.* The fence was about ten yards away from the side of the building where the two of them were standing. The fence consisted entirely of vertical iron bars with two horizontal exceptions: one bar spanned across the base and another along the top. Between the horizontal bars were six feet of vertical bar with no grip. The fence was topped with looped barbed wire; climbing wasn't an option without wire cutters, and the only gate within eyesight was the large gate to the south.

At the south of the building, the grounds opened up into a large yard. There were two cars parked parallel to the gate and the road running past it. The cars represented an opportunity, Peter thought—not a great opportunity but perhaps the best chance they had. Both were military vehicles without a top, German versions of the American jeep. Peter would have to work with his back to the guards, and if he succeeded in hot-wiring one, he'd have to back it up before the two of them could go anywhere. Peter glanced around again. Short of digging a tunnel under the fence with their bare hands or going to the heavily guarded north gate, there was no other way out.

"What will we do, Peter?" Genevieve asked softly.

Peter had an odd thought. "We wait, just for a few minutes." Peter followed the impression, despite the knowledge that waiting increased the risk of another patrol finding them. After a few minutes, Peter noticed a truck driving up the road toward the gate. It stopped, and one of the guards from the south entrance ran to open the gate. Peter and Genevieve strained to hear. They couldn't make out the words but thought it sounded like the guards were laughing. One of the sentries waved the truck in, and the driver pulled the truck up to the middle of the yard, turned the engine off, walked around and opened the back to reveal some crates. The two men unloaded the crates and stacked them by the entrance to the building. They were still keeping a careful watch but weren't in too much of a hurry to complete their task. Now Peter and Genevieve had three guards to deal with instead of just two, but the gate was open.

Peter leaned toward Genevieve's ear. "I'll go pull the car around. Wait for me to back up then run for the passenger's side and get down on the floor." She looked a little startled, and Peter thought she was questioning his sanity. The cars were in plain view of all three guards, and Peter would have to cross twenty yards of open ground to reach them. He placed his pistol in her hands. "Use this if you have to."

Peter got back down on his stomach, clenching his teeth to suppress a grunt of pain, and snake-crawled to the eastern fence. Each time he moved an arm or a leg, his bruised body threatened mutiny. He thought of Genevieve and kept crawling.

He was grateful for the mud. Within yards he was coated in it, and it made a perfect camouflage. After reaching the fence, he crawled along it to the two cars. It took a long time. Despite the rain and the distance between him and the guards, Peter was concerned they would notice any sudden movements. Crawling from the building to the fence, he had been only in their periphery. Now he was crawling on ground they were regularly scrutinizing. He forced himself to move smoothly.

After an agonizingly slow journey that tested his patience and his pain tolerance, Peter reached the first car. He crawled past it to the second, where he would have slightly more cover from the gaze of the Gestapo guards. He slid past the front of the vehicle, where he was hidden from the guard's view, and moved to the driver's side door. Glancing over the top of the car, he could see the three guards. They were standing around talking, taking a break from unloading the truck. Two of them seemed to be keeping fairly diligent watch, but he could tell they weren't expecting to see anyone. Peter tried to pick up what they were saying, but they were too far away for his limited German to comprehend. Then he heard something else—airplane engines. He hoped the sound would distract the guards for at least a few seconds.

Okay, Peter thought to himself, *let's see if I can hot-wire a Nazi jeep before I get bombed by the RAF or shot by the Gestapo.* But he didn't have to hot-wire it. The keys were in the ignition. Peter allowed himself a smile of relief. Slowly, he opened the door and slid inside. One of the guards saw him and began to shout. Peter started the car, shoved it into reverse, and stomped on the gas. He quickly backed it around to the side of the building and pushed open the passenger's side door. Genevieve ran around the back and got on the floor on the passenger's side, just as she had been instructed.

Then Peter shoved the lever into gear, smashed the gas pedal, and after a brief spin-out in the mud, they were headed straight toward the gate. As they passed the corner of the building, Peter could see the three guards. One was running to the other car and was nearly there, one was running to the gate to close it, and the other was only ten feet away with his rifle pointed right at Peter.

The soldier fired, but Peter was moving fast enough across his field of vision that the bullet hit the windshield instead of him. The windshield shattered, and Peter felt a few pieces of glass sting his face. After all he'd been through in the last day, he wasn't about to let a few slivers of glass slow him down. He gave the car more gas and headed for the still-open gate.

The gate opened out onto the road. One of the guards had run onto the road and was pushing the gate in to close it. The third guard had just started the other car.

The guard had succeeded in closing the gate enough that Peter couldn't get through easily. He rammed the gate as he went out, but it barely slowed the car. It threw the guard on the other side of the gate to the ground. Peter turned the car to the left, toward the town. He didn't love the thought of driving through an air raid, past German Army headquarters with the Gestapo on his tail, but there would be more places to hide inside the city.

The other car pursued them, with two of the Gestapo guards inside. Peter turned on the headlights and sped up. He made a sharp left, then a sharp right, and they were inside Calais. Genevieve stayed low but moved from the floor to the seat. The Nazis stayed on their tail. Then they began shooting.

"Check the glove box for extra bullets, a flare gun, anything!" Peter said.

Genevieve reached over the seat and brought back a rifle. "Will this do?"

"Perfect! Are you any good with bolt-action rifles?"

"Decent, but I've never killed anyone before."

"You don't have to kill anyone. Just shoot the driver up enough that he stops following us; it doesn't have to be a fatal shot." Another shot hit the door at Genevieve's side. "And please don't let them shoot you."

She took aim, but right then they ran over a series of potholes created by bomb shrapnel. It slowed Peter and Genevieve's car some, and their pursuers closed the gap from fifteen yards to ten.

"Get down," Peter said. He pushed Genevieve's head down and made a last-minute swerve to the right. The car behind them squealed as it followed, but it lost little ground.

Peter could hear explosions going off about three blocks to the north. He turned a corner again, heading toward the explosions. Genevieve had been about to shoot when he jerked the car around, and her shot went wild.

"How am I supposed to shoot anyone if you keep turning so suddenly?"

"I'm turning again . . . now!"

As Peter straightened out, he looked back. The Gestapo car had dropped back a bit, but only a bit. A bomb exploded in a building that bordered the street they were driving on. The force of the blast pushed Peter's car off the road and slowed the pursuing car. Peter drove the car back on the road and managed to just stay ahead of the Gestapo. Genevieve aimed and shot. It missed. In the mirror, Peter saw the guard in the passenger's side aim his rifle, so he pushed Genevieve's head down and crouched low over the steering wheel himself. The Gestapo guard shot and missed. In the rearview mirror, Peter could see him reloading his rifle.

"I'm going to let them get closer so you can get him, okay?" Peter said.

Genevieve nodded. Peter eased off the gas, and their pursuers closed in nearly to their vehicle's bumper. Genevieve shot and shattered the windshield. They swerved slightly then resumed their chase. The guard finished reloading his weapon and aimed, but Genevieve shot first, and this time she hit the driver. The Gestapo car swerved, and the guard's shot missed. Peter punched the gas pedal as far down as it would go. Seconds later, another bomb exploded, closer than the first had been. Peter's jeep swerved and tipped on its side. He landed on the street, and in the back of his mind, he thought he heard a woman's scream. *Genevieve?* he thought. Then the world went dark again.

* * *

Genevieve gasped for breath. "Peter?" she called softly. She looked around. The car was on its side, and she was still partially stuck inside. She could see Peter lying in the street a few feet away. His face was turned away from her, so she couldn't see it. "Peter?" she called a little louder. She looked behind her, suddenly afraid that she would see one of the Gestapo guards descending upon her, but she could detect no movement from the other car. From what she could see, their car was more damaged by the blast than hers had been.

The crash had left every muscle in her body tense and sore. She forced her shoulders to relax and took a deep breath, gradually relaxing her other muscles as well. She was lying partially on the road. Part of the vehicle's body had collapsed, and she could feel the pressure on her right thigh. Genevieve tried, without any success, to bend the metal back away from her leg. She looked at Peter and could still detect no movement. "Peter?" she called again, but there was no response.

She carefully studied the piece of the car still pinning her into the jeep. Her leg was stuck in the narrow end of an angle formed by the seat and the crushed front of the vehicle. She felt her leg but knew the moisture she felt was rain, not blood. Working against gravity, she pushed her body away from the road until her right leg was free. Then she tumbled out onto the road.

She winced slightly as she stepped toward Peter. She knew her thigh was going to show a deep bruise, but she ignored it for the time being. She looked at the Gestapo car—there was still no movement.

She leaned over Peter and could feel his breath on her cheek. Common sense told her the best way to wake someone who wouldn't respond to sound was to throw water on them or slap them. Peter was soaked through from the rain and the puddle he had landed in. If the rain falling on his face wasn't waking him, Genevieve doubted any additional water would. She looked at his face, so bruised and beaten. She brought her hand back but couldn't bring herself to slap him. Instead, she held his face and tried to block some of the rain.

"Please wake up, Peter," she said, fighting back tears. She thought she saw a slight movement in Peter's eyelids, but she couldn't be sure. "Please, Peter, we can't stay here, and I can't carry you, and I won't leave you. Peter, please come back."

* * *

"Peter, Peter!" Peter's eyes flickered open, and he saw Genevieve huddled over him, felt her hands gently holding his face. As he looked up at her, he saw her expression change from fear to relief.

"You're kneeling in a puddle," he said, glancing at the ground around her.

"Yes, and you're lying in one. You'll catch a cold if you're not careful."

Peter felt his lip twitch, and then he laughed. Genevieve gave him a strange look. "Is your head all right?" she asked.

"I haven't been knocked senseless, if that's what you mean. I just think it's funny that you're worried about catching a cold." Peter sat up with her help and rubbed his head. "How long was I out?"

"Just a few minutes, I guess. It felt like much longer."

A few minutes, Peter thought. *Too long for us to be out in the open.* His eyes gazed past Genevieve and focused on the weapon Jacques had given him. It was lying in the street, midway between himself and his wrecked automobile.

Forcing himself to his feet, he picked up the Luger and walked cautiously to the Gestapo jeep. The only thing moving was flames. Peter sighed with relief and walked back to Genevieve. Bombs were still exploding almost nonstop, but most of them were now far to the south.

"They won't be following us anymore, but we'd better get moving," he said.

Genevieve nodded. "Do you think I killed him?" she asked.

Peter looked at her. "The driver?" She nodded. Peter had no idea if her shot had been fatal or not, but he could tell Genevieve was worried that it had been and that she didn't want to be responsible for another person's death. "I think we should probably give the Royal Air Force credit for that kill," Peter said. Genevieve looked relieved. Peter took her hand and led her away from the wreckage. "Do you know of any safe houses where we can hide? I'm afraid your house might not be safe any longer."

Genevieve thought for a minute. "I didn't give the Gestapo my name or address. I had forged papers with an alias, but they might be able to ask around and find out the truth. We can hide in the cave the priest and Louis LeBras use as a dead drop for airmen."

They continued walking quietly through Calais to its outskirts. It was well into curfew—very early in the morning—so the streets were devoid of French citizens. Even so, the two of them stayed off the main roads and hid several times amid the ruins of what had been buildings. The air raid continued, but they remained safe from the bombs and hidden from patrols. They finally reached a stretch of destroyed city wall then crossed the canal. It was cold, but they had been in the rain long enough that they were wet and cold anyway. As they left Calais, Peter was exhausted, but he also felt elated to be free and physically able to walk.

Genevieve led quietly as they left town. The wind continued, and the rain picked up. After a few minutes, Genevieve began to stumble. Peter stepped up to walk beside her and slipped his arm around her waist to support her. She didn't say anything; she just leaned into Peter and kept forcing one foot in front of the other. They walked along the road but stayed several yards away from it.

About a half mile out of town, Peter heard a car, and they dropped to the ground. The vehicle drove past them at a leisurely speed. There were four men in it. One drove, and the other three looked into the fields on either side of the road.

"Do you think they're looking for us?" Genevieve asked after they passed.

"Maybe."

"We don't have much farther to go." It took a lot of effort to get up. Peter's body had nearly reached its limit, but they both managed to start moving again. They walked for a few more minutes, hid themselves again when the same car came back along the road returning to town, then got up and walked another mile. The night began to grow light, and Peter noticed the horizon changing colors, indicating that the sun would soon rise.

"It's here," Genevieve said as they approached a small hill. At the hill's base were several trees and a few large rocks. Genevieve moved a plot of sod aside to reveal a trapdoor. She opened it and stepped down into a hole that was nearly her height. Midway down, there was a tunnel. In the dim light of dawn, she felt for what turned out to be a candle and a match. Peter ducked down into the hole and pulled the sod over the trapdoor. They had to crawl through a narrow opening, but then the cave opened to an almost six-foot-high ceiling. It reminded Peter of a mine. The floor and walls were dirt. Splintered wooden beams supported the ceiling. The walls didn't form a perfect rectangle by any means, but the area was about ten feet by twenty feet.

The cave was far from bare. At least a few of the pilots and other airmen who were taken through the line had changed from their uniforms into plainclothes in the cave. And there were blankets. Peter grabbed a thick flight jacket and handed it to Genevieve. She took it but didn't move to put it on, though she was shivering from the cold.

Peter decided to give her a moment to pull her thoughts together. He removed his wet shirt. The lighting was too dim for him to examine the past day's damage to his torso, but he felt some of the newly formed scabs come off with the shirt. He replaced it with a dry RAF shirt. He found a pair of pants and moved behind Genevieve's line of sight to change into them. His bruises were starting to stiffen again, he realized. The pants were too large around the waist, but the length was about right.

Genevieve was standing in the same position, still shivering. Peter took the candle from her and placed it in a rough wooden candleholder on the wall. Then he took the coat from her and threaded her arms into the sleeves. She was staring straight ahead, but Peter got the impression that she wasn't seeing anything. He gently examined Prinz's work on the back of her neck. Rain had washed most of the excess blood from her wounds, leaving two thin scabs. One was about an inch long, the other about three. There wasn't much he could do for them, so he left them as they were. Next, he grabbed a blanket and gently dried her face and her hair. Then he wrapped it around her.

"Genevieve," he said softly. "How is your knee?"

She closed her eyes for a few seconds. When she opened them, she was looking at him but through tears. "Oh, Peter," she said, and started to sob. "My brother is dead, and the Nazis are going to rule France for the next thousand years. What does my knee matter?" She cried harder and slid to the floor, burying her face in her hands.

Peter knelt down beside her, something rather hard to do considering all his body had been through. He found her face with his hand and brushed the hair off her forehead. "Hey," he said when she looked up. "Hitler's days are numbered. France will be free again, and it will happen soon."

"But you told them about the invasion. They know where and when." She shook her head and held back a sob. "Tschirner sent the information to Paris and Berlin through couriers. They know, and they'll stop the invasion. It can't possibly succeed this year, and by next year Hitler will have the coast so fortified no one will ever be able to take it."

"Genevieve, they still don't know what's going to happen. The invasion isn't coming in Calais. I don't know where it will come, but it won't be here. And I don't know when the landing will be. The fourth of July is just a date I pulled out of my head."

She looked at Peter with surprise. "Really?"

"Really," Peter said. "I don't have the information they want."

Genevieve's face showed relief for a few seconds. Then sorrow. "But Jacques is . . ." He knew she couldn't bring herself to say *dead*. She started sobbing again. Peter sat next to her and put his arm around her, trying to comfort her. She buried her face in his shoulder, and he held her while she cried. She cried with grief, exhaustion, and a hundred other emotions. Peter wanted to say something consoling, but he didn't know what to say. So he just held her and gently ran his fingers through her hair. Eventually her sobs slowed, and her breathing became more normal. Then her breathing relaxed even more, and she fell asleep. Peter said a prayer of gratitude, thanking the Lord that she was safe and that he was safe with her. He also pleaded for strength to do whatever he had to do next. *Please, Lord*, he said, *help me deal with whatever is coming. Give me the strength and wisdom to do the right thing.*

When Peter was sure Genevieve was asleep, he kissed her gently on the forehead and laid her down on a soft jacket. He wrapped another blanket around her legs; then he lay down next to the cave's entrance and fell asleep.

Chapter Twelve
Redemption

Monday, June 5

THE MORNING WAS MOSTLY GONE when Peter awoke. The candle had burned out, and the cave was black. He felt awful, and as the previous day and night's activities flipped through his head, he wasn't surprised.

Genevieve was still asleep. Peter couldn't see her, but in the absolute silence of the cave, he could hear her breathing softly. He was still exhausted; he wondered what had awakened him. He sat up and looked around the cave. It was completely dark—he couldn't see anything, but he could sense that something wasn't right. He felt around for his Luger and held it ready.

Peter heard something outside. Genevieve's breathing continued uninterrupted; she had slept through the noise. He felt the ground ahead of him and crawled into the tunnel. His body was bruised beyond anything he'd before experienced, and he found it difficult for his stiff body to crawl with a pistol in one hand. When he got to the end of the tunnel, the trapdoor suddenly opened, and he was temporarily blinded by the illumination.

The day was overcast, but his eyes still took a few seconds to adjust. When they did, they were staring at a pistol only a few inches from his face. Peter looked past the pistol to the man holding it. He was a member of the German Army. He said something in German then took Peter's pistol and motioned for him to get out of the hole. *At least it's not the Gestapo*, he thought. Then a rather pessimistic voice inside his head said, *The army will turn you over to the Gestapo. It's just a matter of time.*

Peter climbed out of the hole and stood before the oberleutnant. Peter looked around. It was windy and still raining lightly. The oberleutnant and another soldier had come in a German military jeep, parked only a few yards from the hill. Peter looked closely at the second soldier. He had seen the man before—on a boat, in a storm, on the English Channel. It was Gefreiter Himmelstoss. Peter thought he didn't look as pale as he had looked that night, but he looked just as young. The oberleutnant called him over to translate. Peter didn't bother to tell the oberleutnant that he already understood most of what he said. Himmelstoss came. He didn't recognize Peter at first, but then his eyes widened with remembrance.

Through Himmelstoss, the oberleutnant asked Peter if he had been alone in the hole. Peter wasn't sure what to say. Regardless of what he told them, he was sure they would check. Lying wouldn't work, but Peter couldn't bring himself to tell them that Genevieve was still in the cave.

"There is no one else who will harm you in the cave," Peter finally said.

Himmelstoss raised an eyebrow slightly. The oberleutnant didn't see the gefreiter's expression, but he said something to Himmelstoss, who walked to their car, grabbed a flashlight, and proceeded to check the cave. The oberleutnant motioned for Peter to hold his hands out, and he handcuffed him. Then the oberleutnant made sure Peter didn't have any hidden weapons. His pat down wasn't purposely rough, but each of his movements managed to exacerbate a bruise or cut. Peter gritted his teeth and waited for what he felt was inevitable. Genevieve would be brought out at gunpoint, and both of them would be driven back to the building they had just escaped from.

* * *

Gefreiter Himmelstoss came out of the hole by himself. He had seen Genevieve but had chosen to leave her as she was. Himmelstoss was not a Nazi. In fact, he thought Adolf Hitler was the worst thing that had ever happened to his country. Himmelstoss was also not a fool. He had a mother and two sisters living in Hamburg. For their safety, he had accepted his draft into the army and almost always obeyed his orders. But the woman in the cave had looked harmless, and for some reason, Himmelstoss believed the American when he told him the girl was not dangerous. Himmelstoss liked France and liked the French people. His biggest regret was that he was in France as a soldier. He would have preferred to come as a student.

Back outside, he stretched his back and told his oberleutnant the cave was clear. He directed their prisoner to the car. The oberleutnant drove. Himmelstoss sat in the backseat with the American. He kept his rifle pointed in his direction. The prisoner, he remembered, was dangerous, although at the moment, he looked rather broken.

"Mercy for mercy; now we are even," Himmelstoss said quietly.

"Thank you," he said with sincerity. "Was she awake?"

"Yes. Awake and frightened. I told her to stay there."

The American looked thoughtful, relieved, but also melancholy. "How did you find us?"

"Luck. We planned to eat lunch on the hill. There are no puddles on the high ground. Last night's storm moved the grass over the trapdoor."

The American looked back toward the hill. Himmelstoss had the impression that his prisoner was more worried about the young woman than he was about himself. When he turned back to Himmelstoss, he asked another question. "Will I be turned over to the Gestapo?"

Himmelstoss was slightly surprised by the question. He detested the Gestapo and was proud of the fact that he was not directly a part of their reign of terror. "We are not SS; we are honorable soldiers. You will go to a POW camp." Himmelstoss hoped the American would understand the distinction between a normal soldier and an SS minion.

"And if they demand custody?" the American asked.

Himmelstoss thought he finally understood. His prisoner looked like he had been dragged behind a Messerschmitt during takeoff then stomped on by a parade of Hitler Youth. That morning the Gestapo had alerted army headquarters that there was an escaped prisoner. Himmelstoss looked at the man sitting next to him and realized they had just recaptured the fugitive.

Himmelstoss's gaze shifted from the American to a small dark object arching out of the bushes on the side of the road onto the pavement where they were driving. It exploded when it hit the ground a few feet ahead of them, and he knew it was a grenade. The car swerved off the road and flipped over. Himmelstoss and his prisoner were thrown out of the car, and the last thing he remembered was his world going black.

* * *

Peter landed in a patch of mud. The wind was knocked out of him, but nothing felt broken. He lay there for a moment without moving. He could see Himmelstoss lying completely still only a few feet away from him. The oberleutnant was stuck under the car, unconscious. As Peter fought to fill his lungs with air again, he gazed up into the sky. The clouds were thick and peaceful. Despite the drizzle of rain, part of him wanted to just lie there forever. But he knew it was unlikely that he would get a break like this again. It was time to find some energy and get going.

"Didn't mean for the car to flip over, but I guess the end result is satisfactory," Peter heard a voice say. He looked toward the voice and couldn't believe his eyes.

It was Jacques Olivier.

He limped over to Peter and extended a hand to help him stand up. Peter took Jacques's hand, half expecting it to be an illusion.

"I thought you were dead," Peter said rather hoarsely as the Frenchman pulled him to his feet. Jacques was still in his Gestapo hauptsturmführer's uniform, but his make-up had been washed off. The lines around his eyes looked tired and worn, but there was excitement there as well. He had a bandage tied tightly around his left thigh. "I was positive you were dead, Jacques."

Jacques shook his head and looked at Peter with amusement. "I thought you had more faith in me than that. I've escaped from trickier situations before." Jacques walked back to the jeep and retrieved Peter's Luger. "This is the second time I've had to supply you with a handgun," he gently teased. "I wish you'd do a better job keeping track of your weapons."

Jacques found the keys to the handcuffs and unlocked Peter's shackles. He put them back to work by handcuffing one of the oberleutnant's hands through the broken passenger's side mirror and then connecting the other end of the handcuffs to one of Himmelstoss's ankles, locking them both to the car. He then threw the handcuff keys—and the car keys—across the road and into the bushes he had been hiding in. "You look awful, Peter."

"I feel it," Peter said, still a little dazed from the car wreck. "Jacques, how in the world did you get out?"

"I shot a guard right before he pulled the pin from his grenade. The grenade rolled right to me. Perhaps it was guided by an angel. I used it, switched rooms, then hid in the air duct for a few hours till they assumed I'd escaped. Then I borrowed a rope and some wire cutters, climbed over the fence, and walked away."

Peter stared at him, absorbing all he had just said.

"Lucky break. But even in hindsight, I'm glad I sent you and Genevieve off with a bit of a head start. I had complete faith in your ability to get her to safety."

"Genevieve—she still thinks you're dead. And that I've been arrested again." Peter turned and started back toward the hill. Jacques limped after him.

When Peter reached the hill, the trapdoor was still open. "Genevieve, are you all right?"

"Peter?" she asked softly. Her face came into the light a second later. "How did you get away? I'm so confused. Why did they leave me? How are you here again?"

Peter grabbed both her hands and helped her out of the hole. "I'll explain later; first there's someone else you should see."

She looked past Peter at the figure of Jacques. He was still a ways off—Peter knew he wouldn't have recognized Jacques if he hadn't know it was him—but Genevieve's breath quickened, and her eyes filled with tears. She felt who it was without really being able to see him. "Peter, is it really him?"

Peter nodded and replaced the trapdoor. Genevieve ran to her brother and nearly knocked him over when she embraced him. Peter watched with a smile and wondered if Mary and Martha had reacted the same way upon seeing Lazarus alive again. But Lazarus and his sisters hadn't had to worry about being arrested by passing Nazi patrols.

Like Peter, Jacques seemed keenly aware of how exposed they were. He put an arm around his sister's shoulders and, with her help, started walking back toward Peter.

Peter walked to meet them, looking carefully at Jacques's leg. Peter hadn't been moving all that quickly when he'd gone back to the hill, but he had still covered twice the distance Jacques had in the same amount of time. He suspected the injury to Jacques's leg was serious.

Jacques looked more closely at Genevieve's neck. "What happened to you in that prison?"

She felt the cuts on her neck. "That was Prinz making sure we knew he was serious. Peter managed to come up with a good enough story—I believed him until he told me otherwise."

"Did Tschirner believe him?"

"He must have, or I'd have more than a few shallow cuts." Genevieve smiled at Peter, then at her brother. "He sent couriers out with the information Peter gave him. He seemed to think that because Peter was an American, any confession would be genuine."

Jacques raised his eyebrows and met Peter's eyes.

"Is that what Colonel McDougall meant? When he wanted an American instead of an Englishman?" Peter thought back to his briefing.

Jacques nodded. "I think Tschirner came to the exact conclusion Howard wanted him to come to."

Peter gazed upward and exhaled deeply. "I'm glad something went according to plan." He looked around. "We'd better leave. Himmelstoss and the other soldier won't be unconscious forever. How is your leg?"

Jacques shrugged. "I'll manage with it. We can hide in Louis's attic till nightfall. First we need to stop by our home and get our extra papers and some new clothes. I don't think it will be under observation, but we'll be cautious, just in case."

"Jacques, we can't go to Louis—what if we're discovered there? What would they do to Birgit? Especially if they find out she's Jewish?"

Jacques looked at Genevieve and nodded. "You're right. And Anne's scared. I think she lost her nerve completely. I don't think it would be good for her to know we're in trouble. We'll stop by our house, and by then I'll have thought of something—I hope."

The three of them tried to keep well away from the road as they walked, but Peter still felt exposed. Based on the tense looks on his companion's faces, they felt the same. Fortunately, traffic on the road was extremely light, due in part to the wet, windy weather.

"Jacques, when did you manage to escape from Gestapo headquarters?" Genevieve asked.

"A little before dawn."

"How did you get out?"

"I hid till things calmed down, then I threw a rope over the fence, clipped the wires, and climbed over."

Genevieve nodded and looked at the sky. It was a bit after midday, and the sun was barely peeking through the clouds. "Where were you until now? Did you think we had gone back to our house?"

"I thought you'd be in the cave—it's closer to the city. But I didn't have a car, and I do have an injury and needed to stay out of sight, so it took me a little longer to get here. I also made a small detour in the middle of town. I guess I should probably tell you about it. Peter solved the mystery of who betrayed Mireille."

Genevieve's head shot around. She opened and closed her mouth, but no words came out. She looked from her brother to Peter and back again.

"It was Marie Murat—the very same person who sold Peter to the Gestapo. So I stopped by to pay her a visit," Jacques said.

Genevieve was quiet for a few seconds. "Mireille wouldn't have wanted you to kill her."

"I know. That's why I didn't. I just drugged her and shaved her head."

Peter looked at him, confused. "You did what to her head?"

"That's the traditional method of punishing women who sleep with the enemy," Jacques explained. "Whether she slept with them or not, I don't know, but she was willing to sell her country's freedom to them. A shaved head is a rather light punishment, but it will do for right now. It should warn others not to trust her. After the war, there will be time for further reckoning."

After a minute of reflection, Genevieve turned to Peter. "Peter, there's something else I'm still confused about. Why did that German soldier leave me under the hill? He saw me, he took you . . . It doesn't make sense."

Peter shrugged. "I once showed him mercy. I could have killed him, but I let him go. He was returning the favor."

"'Blessed are the merciful, for they shall obtain mercy,'" Genevieve quoted thoughtfully.

Jacques spoke next. "I must confess, Peter, when McDougall let me read the report of your first mission, I thought that incident showed a weakness in you. You had been soft when I wouldn't have been. But perhaps you can discern when to make an exception better than I can."

"You were merciful to Marie," Peter said after a few awkward seconds.

"Yes, I suppose you wore off on me. But I won't be expecting her to return the favor." Jacques laughed then quickly changed the subject. "Looks like it will stay wet most of the day."

"Good, maybe that will keep the Nazi patrols inside," Genevieve said.

"It didn't keep that one inside. Get down," Peter said, and everyone dropped to the ground. The car was still far off. Peter wasn't even sure it was German, but few trustworthy French citizens had cars with petrol.

They didn't get back up until a while after the car had disappeared. They were weary and grateful for the break, even if the break consisted of lying on the soggy earth. Eventually, they began walking again, and after more than double the usual amount of time it would take to walk from the town to the farmhouse, they arrived. It appeared deserted, but the three paused at the edge of the property near a cluster of trees.

"The Gestapo doesn't have my real name," Genevieve said.

"But they might have descriptions of you circulating by now," Jacques said. "Someone you do laundry for might recognize you if they have a sketch. Once they have your name, it won't be long before they have the farmhouse."

"I'll make sure everything is secure," Peter said. "Genevieve, will you watch the front door?"

"You're wounded," Jacques said.

"So are you." Peter walked cautiously toward the house. He raised his pistol and slowly opened the back door by the kitchen. All appeared much as it had when he'd left the day before. *The day before*, Peter thought. *It seems like it's been so much longer than a mere day.*

Genevieve's note was on the kitchen table. Peter picked it up and stared at it but couldn't recognize the alphabet it used, let alone the language. He placed it back on the table and moved from the kitchen to the living room. There was little light coming through the windows—the weather wasn't improving. There was no one in the living room, no one in the linen closet, no one under the stairs in the hidden chamber. Peter took care to be silent, but the stairs were creaky as he walked up to the top floor. There were two bedrooms upstairs. Peter checked under the beds, in the closets, behind the long curtains in Genevieve's room. The house was deserted.

While in Genevieve's room, Peter caught sight of his reflection in the small mirror that hung on her wall. He barely recognized himself. Monsieur Laurier's handiwork on his temple had split open again during one of his beatings. The rain had washed it mostly clean, but it was there, probably in need of stitches. He had a pair of black eyes—that was a first for Peter; even after his worst fights in grade school, he'd never had more than one at a time. Peter still had all his teeth, but his lips were cracked in several places. Another candidate for stitches was the deep cut on his chin from Tschirner's boot. Peter thought his nose looked crooked. There were bruises on the side of his head, on his neck, and on his face. Some of the bruises had burst during the rounds with fists, chains, shoes, and stools. They now showed scabs where the skin had ruptured.

Frowning at the sight of his face, Peter went back downstairs. He opened the front door, spotted Genevieve, and then heard the kitchen door open. Peter paused, and rather than wave the all clear to Genevieve, he carefully stepped across the room and hid just outside the kitchen. Peter knew Jacques was armed; he wondered who had slipped past Jacques's watchful eyes.

Peter peered around the corner and saw a little girl with bleached-blonde hair and large brown eyes walk in. He sighed with relief. Birgit looked around the room, and her gaze stopped when she noticed Peter. She cocked her head to one side, trying to recognize him in the dim light. She wasn't afraid; she was just thinking.

"Did someone beat you with your baseball bat?" was what she finally asked.

"I guess I look kind of like a monster right now, huh?"

"No, you look like a pair of monsters caught you," she said. Peter thought her unintentional references to Tschirner, Prinz, and the rest of the Gestapo were accurate enough. He went to the front door and signaled the all clear to Genevieve.

"Is anything wrong?" Genevieve asked when she came in, confused by the delay.

Peter shook his head and pointed Genevieve in the direction of the kitchen. She hesitated. "It's all right, I promise."

Genevieve looked around the corner. Her face lit up when she saw Birgit standing by the stove. "Come sit on the sofa with me, darling," Genevieve said. She held out her hand, and the two left the kitchen.

Jacques came in through the kitchen door. "Your leg is getting worse, isn't it?" Peter asked in English when Genevieve was out of earshot.

Jacques nodded.

"Do you know any doctors we can trust?"

Jacques sat at the table and thought for a while. "I rarely trust anyone. We can't really bring a doctor here—no sense in further endangering our neighbors . . . Genevieve will have to leave Calais. I guess I'll send her across the channel with you if we can arrange transport."

Peter looked at Jacques's leg. "Maybe you should come too, at least until your leg is mended. It's pretty bad, isn't it?"

Jacques shrugged. Peter pulled another chair around and gently propped Jacques's wounded leg up on it. Then Peter grabbed a knife from a drawer and slit Jacques's pants so he could see the bullet hole. It looked worse than Peter had expected.

"Is it really that bad?" Jacques asked. Peter looked up, realizing too late that Jacques had been watching his reaction rather than looking at his wound.

Peter didn't want to directly answer. "Did you examine it before? Does it look any different now than it did then?"

"I didn't have time to look at it. There were a bunch of Nazis searching for me. I just crawled into the air duct, and when I got out, I tied some stuff around it."

The hole the bullet had made was slightly visible, but the skin around it had swollen so the hole was more of a slit than a round circle. Peter grabbed a clean rag and some water and washed the blood off Jacques's skin as gently as he could. He could tell he was hurting his patient because there was sweat running down Jacques's forehead, but he didn't complain. Under all the blood, the skin was brownish red, growing darker closer to the site of impact. What worried Peter the most was the nauseating smell the wound emitted. Peter had smelled something similar a few times before when animals had been injured on the farm. But in each of those

cases, by the time the injury was bad enough to cause a stench, they'd had
to put the livestock out of its misery.

Genevieve walked into the kitchen and put her hand on her brother's
forehead. "Jacques, you have a fever," she said with concern. She looked
at the bullet hole in his leg then at her brother's face, and finally at Peter.
"It's infected, isn't it?"

Peter nodded. "We need to get him to a doctor."

"I won't make it through a check-point like this, and I think it would
be unwise to ford the canal again."

"Do you have any disinfectants around here?" Peter went to the sink
to wash the rag.

Jacques didn't say anything.

"Nothing stronger than soap. We used up the last of our iodine about a
month ago when some British pilots were shot down," Genevieve said. "We
haven't been able to get any more since then. We don't even have any liquor."

"I guess we'd better bring a doctor out here, then," Peter said from the sink.

Jacques thought then shook his head. "No, it's too risky."

Genevieve squeezed his shoulder. "Jacques, we have to do something.
This doesn't look good, and I can tell Peter is worried about it, and that
makes me worried too."

"Peter worries too much. And so do you, Genevieve."

"Jacques, will you stop shrugging this off; you can't just pretend you're
not wounded," Genevieve said.

Peter squeezed the excess water from the rag and turned back to the
Oliviers. "I'll go into town and find a doctor. We can use some of Monsieur
Laurier's ration coupons to bribe him if you don't have cash."

"We have cash, but you don't know the town."

"I'll go," Genevieve said.

"No," Jacques and Peter said at the same time.

Genevieve looked at each of them in turn, a hint of defiance in her
eyes. "I'm not completely helpless. I'll wear a disguise. I appreciate your
chivalry, but there isn't a better alternative. I'll attract less attention than
either of you will in your current conditions."

"I can show Peter where Doctor Chirac lives." Peter turned around to
look at the small voice. He had momentarily forgotten that Birgit was in
the house. The three adults had slipped from English to French at some
point along their conversation because Jacques was feverish and speaking
French took less effort for him.

"Birgit, that's a very kind offer. But we might be out a little past curfew, and that's not good. We can't have a pretty little girl like you breaking the rules."

Birgit frowned at Peter's rejection of her help.

"Actually, I think Birgit has a good idea."

Genevieve and Peter both looked at Jacques in astonishment, wondering if the fever was making him delirious, but he continued. "Birgit, you can lead Peter to your Uncle Louis, and Louis can show Peter where to find the doctor. Peter, you can bring the doctor to meet us. I'd rather not meet here—it's too close to the LeBras farmhouse, and if something went wrong they'd be questioned. We'll meet in a home a little farther down the road. It's the first house you saw when I brought you here."

Peter nodded. The plan made sense to him. They would meet at the Papineaus' home. The LeBras family would be farther from danger if they ran into trouble.

"Are you sure it isn't being watched?" Genevieve asked.

Jacques shrugged. "We both know enough hiding places around there to stay hidden for a month, maybe more. I think we'll be all right. You'll probably have to help me get there and keep a lookout. But you've done that before."

Genevieve nodded.

"Peter, if you're going into town, you had better wash your face. No need to shave. We'll make a beard for you before you go to cover up as much of your skin as we can."

"And his eyes?" Genevieve asked.

"I have an old pair of slightly tinted glasses that might make them less noticeable. Will you get my kit?"

Genevieve and Peter went upstairs together, she to get the kit and he to wash his face and change into civilian clothes. At the top of the stairs, Genevieve put her hand on Peter's shoulder. "How bad is his leg?"

"I don't know," Peter said, looking away.

She grabbed his face, gently finding a spot without a bruise, and pulled it around to face her. "Peter, please. How bad is it?"

Peter studied her face for a few seconds. He knew what he wanted to tell her, but he also knew she wanted his honest opinion. "I wish I could tell you not to worry. I'm not a doctor, so I don't really know. But it's infected already, and the way it smells, and he has a fever . . . I think he might lose his leg if we don't get him some help soon. I wish I knew what to do, but I don't think scrubbing it with disinfectant will solve the problem, even if we had something to clean it out with."

She looked down and blinked back a few tears.

"Hey, keep your chin up," Peter said as he wiped the tears from her eyes. "You're going to make it through this war. And you're going to be stronger because of it."

"Perhaps, but will anyone I love still be alive with me?" She turned and walked into Jacques's room to get his disguise kit.

Peter watched her, not answering her question, afraid the answer might be *no*.

When she came out again, she handed Peter a towel and told him to be careful not to make his cuts bleed again. It was good advice. Peter tried to follow it but didn't quite succeed.

After he washed up, he knelt down and prayed. He expressed gratitude that Genevieve was safe and pleaded for Jacques. Peter had grown up hearing scripture stories of miraculous healings by Elijah, Jesus, the apostle Paul, and others. He had always believed that the power to heal was real and was again on the earth, but he had not yet been ordained an elder and given the Melchizedek Priesthood and the power to administer to the sick. Before he left for war, it hadn't seemed that important. That had long ago changed; he could think of a dozen incidents in Northern Africa or in Sicily when he had yearned for the power to heal the wounded and restore life to the fallen.

Since he had gone away to war, the Melchizedek Priesthood had seemed important but unavailable. Organized branches of the Church were hard to find. But the biggest obstacle was that Peter didn't feel worthy to be trusted with the priesthood. He had been a soldier, and he had killed. Now he was a spy, and he not only killed, but he also lied. He did those things to help good triumph over evil, but the nagging feeling that he wasn't good enough to have the priesthood had kept Peter from approaching any of the few branch presidents he'd met as a soldier.

Peter thought of Jacques and wanted to kick himself. Other warriors had found ways to fight in wars and be faithful servants of the Lord. Peter knew his circumstances were no excuse. His doubts had made him less useful to God and less useful to those he cared about.

Peter fought back the feelings of guilt and self-loathing that had been building since the previous day and plead with God again. *Father*, he prayed, *I know it's too late for me to go back and change the past. I'm sorry I haven't been better, and I promise that I'll work harder from now on. I'm sorry I've been so distant—I didn't feel I was good enough to approach Thee with my thoughts and feelings. I'll do better from now on. Just please don't let*

Jacques suffer because I've been weak. Peter ended his prayer with a simple plea. *Please help me know what I should do.*

* * *

When Peter came back downstairs, Genevieve was bandaging her brother's leg for the trip to the Papineau home. Jacques had a pile of dark brown hair that he was forming into a beard on the table. It matched Peter's hair color almost exactly. As Peter looked at the Oliviers, he felt a wave of guilt for all the suffering he'd brought to them in the past day and a half. He knew they didn't blame him, but he also knew that, in truth, if he hadn't been there, their cover wouldn't have been blown, Genevieve wouldn't have emotional scars and two cuts on the back of her neck, and Jacques wouldn't have an infected hole in his leg.

Jacques motioned Peter over and began sticking the hair to his face. "This will hurt when it comes off. It might pull some scabs off with it."

Peter shrugged. "I've been through worse." As Jacques worked, Peter pushed his thoughts aside and began concentrating on the task before him. Jacques smeared several layers of cream over Peter's face. First he used some yellows and greens to mute the purples and reds. Then he applied some thick flesh-colored cream over Peter's bruises and powdered the rest of his skin. Jacques handed Peter forged papers, and he put them in his pocket. Then Jacques gave him a pair of thick glasses. They blurred Peter's peripheral vision a bit, but he could see what was directly in front of him quite clearly.

"Well, Birgit, how does he look?" Jacques asked.

"Like a man with a beard and glasses."

"Child, you are supposed to tell me you can't even recognize him."

"But I can still recognize him. His nose is still the same—I think it's broken. So are his shoulders, and the bruises on the side of his neck. And his lips are still puffy and cracked."

"Thank you, Birgit. I feel very handsome now." Peter wrapped a scarf around his neck to hide a few of the bruises.

"I'm sure Genevieve still thinks you're good looking."

"Birgit, hold your tongue," Genevieve said as a blush rose in her cheeks. She had been reloading Peter's pistol for him, and one of the bullets fell to the floor as she spoke.

"Birgit, Genevieve and I have to go away for a while," Jacques said. "It won't be safe for you to come to our house or to tell anyone you ever knew us. Come give me a hug good-bye."

Birgit looked at Jacques, and her face fell. "How long will you be gone?"

"We will be back when all the German soldiers leave."

"But will they ever leave?" she said through tears. Her whole life they had been part of her surroundings. She had no memory of life before the war and before the occupation.

"Yes, darling, someday they will leave, and then we'll see each other again." Genevieve bent down and gave Birgit a hug. "You be good."

"I will be."

Then Birgit went over to Jacques. He pulled her to his lap, held her, and whispered in her ear. "Be brave," he said softly. "Thank you for believing I'm good." She sniffled and nodded.

"Come on, Peter, I've got to take you to meet my Uncle Louis." Birgit grabbed Peter's hand and led him to the door.

"Wait, Peter, take this." Jacques handed him some money. "Tell the doctor we'll pay him that much again when he comes. And take my bicycle, since you and Genevieve have left yours who knows were. And for heaven's sake, eat something before you fall over." Jacques smiled then handed Peter half a loaf of bread. That was his way of saying good luck.

Peter met Genevieve's eyes. "Good luck," he said. For a few seconds, looking at her made him feel at peace, but only for a few seconds.

"The same to you, Peter. Be careful."

Peter nodded, put a hat on his head, and allowed Birgit to lead him out of the farmhouse. There were only a few hours of daylight left, so he grabbed the bicycle and walked with Birgit across the field as fast as her little legs could go. Peter looked back and saw Jacques and Genevieve starting out in the other direction. Jacques was leaning on Genevieve for support and limping deeply. Peter pulled his eyes away. He knew the best way of helping them was to follow a young but clever child across the field then allow a trusted stranger to direct him to another stranger he couldn't trust. It was complicated, but it had to work.

"Wait here," Birgit said when they neared the house. "I'll make sure we don't have any guests who wouldn't like you."

Peter nodded and stood in the shadow of some trees, finishing the bread he had been eating on their walk. He thought it odd to be eating at a time like that, but he hadn't eaten anything since breakfast the day before. He needed the energy.

The LeBras farmhouse was about the same size as the Olivier farmhouse. The clotheslines were empty, probably because of the wind and the nearly nonstop drizzle of rain. There were a few rabbits and chickens in cages under a small A-frame barn. The paint, like the paint on most of the homes in Calais, was a little old. The garden was well kept, with the exception of a bomb crater that grazed one side of it. *That particular air raid must have nearly taken their house down*, Peter thought. Peter looked more closely and could see marks from where shrapnel had cut into the side of the wooden home.

After a few minutes, Birgit came out of the house with a broad-shouldered man. He was of medium height for a Frenchman, with fair hair and weather-beaten skin. Hard work had made his body strong; wartime rations had made it lean. He strode with confidence toward Peter.

"Bonjour, stranger." LeBras's bass voice boomed across the garden.

"Uncle Louis, I told you he's not a stranger. His name is Peter, and you need to take him to the doctor because Jacques is hurt."

"Yes, I remember, Birgit. Why don't you run along into the house and help your aunt clean the kitchen?"

"But, Uncle Louis, I don't like cleaning the kitchen. I want to help Peter."

"Birgit, go," he said firmly.

She dropped her eyes and pouted to see if her uncle would change his mind. When she looked up again, he motioned toward the house with his head, and she sighed.

"Good-bye, Peter," she said. "Take good care of Jacques and Genevieve."

"I will, Birgit. Thank you for your help."

LeBras waited until the door closed; then he began in a quiet voice. "Are you armed?"

"Yes."

"With what?"

"A Luger." The gun was under Peter's jacket, tucked into his belt.

LeBras nodded. "Where are you from?"

"The United States."

The next question quickly followed. "What part of the United States?"

"Idaho," Peter answered with equal speed.

"And where is Idaho?"

"The northwest part, almost in the corner."

"How long have you been here?" LeBras maintained his even tone, but one corner of his mouth was pulling into a slight smile.

"A little more than a week. You left a light on the beach for us when I came with Jacques."

LeBras nodded. "Will you describe what a football looks like?"

Peter made the shape with his hands. "It has pointed ends with lacings across the top, like this . . ."

"Who is in charge of kicking the football?"

"The punter, I guess. You throw it more than you kick it in the game."

LeBras was smiling fully now, but his rate of interrogation did not slow. "And who is in charge of throwing it?"

"The quarterback."

"What team did Joe DiMaggio play for?" His pronunciation was off, but Peter still recognized the name.

"The New York Yankees."

"What was hung in the church to warn Paul Revere that the British were leaving Boston?"

"Lanterns: one if by land, two if by sea."

Louis LeBras paused, rubbing his chin with his hand. "Well, either you *are* an American, or you're a very good mole. I don't trust you, but I'll take you to the doctor's home. I don't trust him either. He knows medicine, but I don't know anything about his political leanings. I advise you to be cautious. You can't trust anyone these days—especially people who look as if they have plenty to eat, like our friend the doctor."

Peter nodded.

"What happened to you?" LeBras asked.

"What do you mean?"

LeBras gestured toward Peter's face. "Jacques has done a good job hiding the bruises, but I can still see them—who gave them to you?"

"A few Gestapo thugs," Peter answered.

"Is that what happened to Jacques?"

"He was shot in the leg by the Gestapo. He hasn't been assaulted like me, but his leg is badly infected, and he has a fever."

"If you've been with the Gestapo, I doubt you've heard the latest war news."

"What news?" Peter asked. "We haven't listened to the radio since Saturday."

"The Allies took Rome yesterday," LeBras said.

Peter felt a smile spread across his face. "That's the first good news I've heard in quite a while. I wonder if my old squad was with them."

"Did you fight in Italy?"

"Just in Sicily. I was injured and transferred after that."

LeBras nodded with a bit of respect. "Come on. Follow me on your bicycle."

Peter silently obeyed. As they left, Peter saw Birgit looking at them through the window. He gave her a thumbs-up sign, and she smiled and waved.

LeBras and Peter made good time into town. The guards at the checkpoints looked briefly at their papers, but the soldiers were more interested in staying dry than in being thorough. It wasn't raining hard, but the wind made it seem worse than it was. Peter was grateful for the weather's effect on the guards, since he was armed and since he knew his bruises were visible if anyone looked closely. His hat blocked most of the rain, but the make-up Jacques had used wasn't completely waterproof.

Doctor Chirac's home was on the east side of town, a few blocks south of the harbor. There were German patrols out, but they were paying little attention to the few French civilians scrambling to avoid puddles and get out of the rain. The bikes LeBras and Peter rode made the water splash up and soak their pants. Peter hoped the Olivier siblings were somewhere warm and dry by now, but he doubted it.

They reached a small apartment complex, and LeBras stopped pedaling. "Since his house was destroyed in 1940, Doctor Chirac lives in the flat on the top floor. His is on the south side. I wish you luck, but I must leave now. Be cautious."

"Yes, sir. Thank you for your help. I just have one other favor to ask of you."

"What is it?" LeBras asked.

"The Olivier cows. We're going into hiding, and they'll need a new home. Will you take them or find someone who will?"

LeBras nodded with a smile, turned his bike around, and began to pedal off. Peter watched until he turned a corner and disappeared from sight. Peter doubted LeBras would sleep at all that night; he would be on the lookout for danger out of fear that Peter was a mole or that he had been captured and turned. Peter was determined not to let that happen. The LeBras family, especially the daughter, would remain safe even if it meant his death.

Peter took a deep breath and walked into the group of flats. Doctor Chirac lived in number eight. No one else was around when Peter knocked on the door. He didn't have to wait long for the answer; a rounded, middle-aged woman opened the door almost immediately. Her hair was pulled up tightly into a bun, tight to the point that it lifted her eyebrows and forehead. The hair was a faded brown with gray streaks. Her face seemed stern but also showed curiosity. "Yes?" she said.

"Is the doctor home?" Peter asked.

She nodded and motioned for Peter to stay where he was. She closed the door, leaving Peter outside, and he heard her footsteps patter away from the door. The rain continued to fall, the wind to blow, and the night to grow darker as Peter waited. A few minutes later, Doctor Chirac answered the door.

"Someone called for a doctor?" he asked. He had a round, boyish face with a full head of light brown hair.

"Yes, sir. I have a sick friend who needs medical attention as soon as possible."

"Where is he?"

"Outside of town a bit."

Doctor Chirac frowned. "I don't leave town this late."

"We're willing to pay you well." Peter took out the money Jacques had given him.

Doctor Chirac's eyes widened.

"We'll give you this much again after you see him."

Doctor Chirac paused. "What is wrong with your friend?"

"He—uh, he fell on a piece of metal, and it punctured his thigh. He has a fever, and I think his leg is infected. If you could come right now, I think it would be best for him . . ."

"Right before curfew. I'll earn every bit of the money you pay me." He motioned for Peter to come inside, and he complied. "Sit down."

"Aren't we going to leave now?" Peter asked.

"Do you want me to go without the proper instruments and medicine?"

"No, sir."

The doctor told Peter to sit again, and this time Peter obeyed, sitting on a dark red chair. The room was furnished with expensive but well-worn furniture. The bookshelves displayed a mix of books: mostly science and philosophy. Thick rugs hid most of the dark wood floor. The room smelled of bread and tobacco.

The woman who had answered the door, Doctor Chirac's wife, was sitting across from Peter. She was knitting very slowly by lamplight. But she wasn't looking at her work; she was staring at the stranger in her living room. Peter smiled and nodded to her. She continued to stare. It made him nervous. Peter didn't think she would be able to see many details in the dim lighting, but her gaze made him uncomfortable, like she was trying to remember his face so she would be able to describe it later. Peter hoped she merely found his crooked nose amusing.

He was relieved from her gaze when Doctor Chirac came into the room again, carrying a small black bag. Peter immediately stood up, hoping they would leave at once. Doctor Chirac saw Peter's hurry, sighed, and began walking to the door.

"Good night, madam. I take it for granted that you will wait up for me?"

"Of course, my love."

Peter thought there was something spooky about that woman and that sitting room. It made the hairs on the back of his neck stand up, and he was glad to leave. "I came here on bicycle. Do you have one you can use?" Peter asked as they walked down to the street.

Doctor Chirac nodded. "Of course I have a bicycle. Is it far?"

Peter shook his head, afraid that if he told the doctor the truth, he would refuse to come. The doctor wouldn't make it back before curfew. Peter was willing to sneak the man back into his apartment, but he wasn't sure Chirac would be willing to risk a late-night appointment for a stranger.

At the outskirts of town, they were held up by a larger-than-normal German patrol in a covered truck. Peter could see them checking papers and hoped they weren't performing searches because the pistol he had tucked in the back of his belt would be apparent in most pat downs. Peter tensed as he neared the truck. The doctor seemed unaffected. *But he isn't doing anything illegal, or at least not yet*, Peter thought.

There were five soldiers present at the checkpoint. They were all sitting in the back of the truck, trying to stay out of the rain and wind. They asked for Peter's papers and gave them only a superficial glance. None of them wanted to come out into the unpleasant weather, so none of them searched the two men.

Next they examined Doctor Chirac's papers. "I hope you don't have to go far, Doctor. Curfew is in an hour," the Nazi soldier said in passable French.

"Not far, oberleutnant. But duty calls—the sick need my aid, so I will go out in this accursed weather and risk my health to improve theirs."

The oberleutnant nodded. Peter glanced at the other soldiers. They appeared relaxed. As he looked at them, his fake spectacles blurred the faces of the doctor and the oberleutnant. Peter felt like something had passed between them in their brief encounter, but he wasn't sure what. He shrugged it off. They had probably met before. *Besides*, Peter thought, *Jacques needs a doctor*. So after they passed the checkpoint, Peter continued leading Doctor Chirac to the Papineaus' farmhouse.

* * *

Genevieve came into the Papineaus' front room with a towel and dried her brother's face. She had found the towel, a blanket, and Marcel's Webley & Scott pistol quite easily. As a child and teenager, she had spent much of her time at the Papineau home and still knew where almost everything was kept.

He's getting worse, she thought as she covered Jacques with the blanket. Still, she tried to be brave and gave him a smile. Then she began tinkering with the broken radio the Papineaus had used to contact the Allies. It took her some time, but she eventually got it to work again. But after ten minutes of trying, she was unable to raise anyone. She finally pushed the radio away in frustration. She looked at her brother for commiseration and was surprised to discover he had been contemplating a very different subject.

"How long have you been in love with him?" Jacques asked her.

Feeling herself blush, Genevieve attempted to put him off. "What makes you think I'm in love with anyone?"

Jacques wasn't fooled. He rarely was, especially when it involved his sister. "Several things, including the color of your face right now. But I got my first clue when you started singing again." He paused, studying her face. "I always thought I'd want to strangle anyone you fell for. No one could ever be good enough for my baby sister. But I like Peter. You could be happy together, I think."

"But I don't know how he feels about me . . . What if he doesn't feel the same?" Genevieve asked, suddenly very serious.

"Some men fall in love quickly and realize exactly what's happening as it happens to them. Others fall in love equally quickly but don't realize what has happened to them until the change in their heart is complete."

"And Peter?"

Jacques smiled. "I think Peter is in the latter category. You shouldn't fret. Just give it some time."

Genevieve nodded, hoping her brother was right.

"Give the radio ten more minutes," Jacques suggested. "If you can't get through in that time, go keep a lookout. Two knocks on the house when Peter comes. Three knocks if someone else shows up. If the unexpected happens, I want you to hide until you're certain it's safe. We can try the radio again after the doctor leaves."

Genevieve tried the radio again without any luck. She glanced at her brother. She could tell he was in pain, but he forced a smile for her as she slipped the pistol in her pocket and left the house.

* * *

Doctor Chirac asked question after question on the way through the countryside. Peter gave him vague answers, wishing the doctor would mind his own business. Peter kept looking around, but the road appeared deserted. Finally he stopped and pulled his bicycle to the side of the road. They were nearly there, but he still didn't trust the doctor.

"Where is your injured friend?" he asked.

"Not too far away," Peter answered.

"Well, if you are in such a hurry, why have we stopped?"

"Doctor, there is a very good man who needs your help. I want you to give me your word that as a doctor you will treat him to the best of your ability. You won't consider politics or anything else."

Doctor Chirac glared. "Don't insult me. I am a professional. I never let politics interfere with my work."

"Are there any other doctors in Calais?"

"None that see civilians."

Peter wasn't reassured, but he didn't know what else to do. He silently prayed for guidance but received none. He didn't feel like he was making a wrong choice, but he also didn't feel the quiet confidence he was hoping for. He remembered that for the last few years he had routinely distanced himself from heavenly guidance and the guilt he feared would accompany it. He concluded that it was only natural for it to be slow in coming now that he wanted it back. *You've only just begun your penance*, Peter reminded himself, *so be patient*. Peter couldn't see anyone following them, so he got back on his bike and rode the rest of the way to the Papineaus' house.

It was quiet when they arrived. It was also dark. The sun hadn't completely set, but nearly all of its remaining light was hidden by the clouds. No light shone through the blackout curtains that still covered the windows.

Peter slowly walked to the front door. The door didn't latch properly, so he gently pushed it open. Jacques and Peter had broken the lock on their last visit to the Papineau residence.

Inside, few things had changed since Peter had last seen the home. Perhaps the only differences were that the houseplants now looked wilted, and there were dried bloodstains on the floor. The bodies of Schneider and his men were gone. Jacques, wrapped in a blanket, was lying awake on a couch. There was a hurricane lantern burning on the floor beside him, currently the only source of light in the house. His hair was sticking up at odd angles, Peter assumed from an attempt to dry it. Jacques looked pale, and despite the thick blanket, he was shivering. Genevieve was nowhere to be seen.

Peter raised an eyebrow in inquiry. Jacques knew what Peter was asking, and as Doctor Chirac examined the bloodstains on the floor, Jacques pointed outside and gave Peter a thumbs-up. Peter smiled with admiration. Even while feverish, Jacques had the sense of mind to keep a lookout on duty.

"Doctor Chirac, here is the patient I told you about." Peter guided Doctor Chirac away from the bloodstains that had distracted him since entering the house and directed the doctor's attention to Jacques.

"Let's get him on the floor. It will be easier to work on a completely flat surface."

Peter grasped Jacques under the shoulders, and Doctor Chirac supported his legs as they lowered him to the floor.

Doctor Chirac knelt on the floor next to his patient and began unwrapping the bandages. When finished, he very carefully studied the wound. "I thought you said he had fallen on a piece of metal? This looks like a bullet wound to me." Doctor Chirac turned toward Peter.

Peter stuttered for a second. "Um, I, uh, well, I didn't want to alarm you or anything, and the bullet is mostly metal, so I, uh . . ."

"You lied."

"Yes, sir—but we needed help, and I wasn't sure you would come if you knew it was a bullet wound."

"For the amount of money you are paying me, I would have come."

Chirac turned back to his work, seeming content that he had made Peter admit to lying. He took a bottle from his bag and drenched a cloth with it. Then he set about cleaning Jacques's wound. Based on the grimace spread across Jacques's face, Peter doubted the doctor was being very gentle.

"You," Doctor Chirac said to Peter, "hold this lantern so the lighting is better."

Peter obeyed, though he didn't think the lighting really improved very much.

Peter had never been very squeamish. He attributed that characteristic to his older brother. There was a small pond on their parents' farm, and the two brothers had passed by it everyday on the way to and from town. Almost every afternoon when they were in elementary school, and somewhat sporadically in the mornings, Robby would find some kind of creature—a tadpole, a beetle, a worm, an occasional mouse—and the boys would very scientifically dissect it with their Boy Scout pocketknives.

Their younger sisters would occasionally scream and tell their mother that the brothers were being cruel to animals, but Robby and Peter both did very well in their high school biology classes.

Despite his normally strong stomach, Peter found watching Doctor Chirac work on Jacques's leg a very unpleasant experience. Jacques never cried out; he kept his teeth tightly clenched the entire time. Sweat poured down his forehead as Doctor Chirac used a pair of forceps to extract the bullet from Jacques's leg. The doctor pulled it out with triumph and held it close to the lantern to examine it.

"You were shot by a German weapon?" Chirac asked.

Jacques didn't hear the doctor. His eyes were squeezed shut, and he was shaking slightly. Doctor Chirac was cleaning the forceps, so Peter put the lantern down and moved to Jacques's side. Peter unwrapped the scarf that had been hiding the bruises on his neck and used it to wipe the sweat off Jacques's forehead. Peter was still on his knees when he heard a noise outside—three very distinct knocks on the side of the house.

Jacques's eyes focused immediately. "That's the signal—someone is coming."

Peter immediately reached for his pistol, but his hand didn't grip it in time. When the doctor heard Jacques, he picked up his medicine bag and swung it with all his force into the side of Peter's head, right into the spot Laurier and Prinz had both pounded within the last few days. To Peter, the room suddenly seemed to spin. Dazed, he fell on his side, and his pistol slipped from his hand. Doctor Chirac, who had stood when Genevieve knocked, kicked Peter's gun across the room and pulled a small revolver from his bag. He was standing almost directly over Peter. As he brought his handgun around so it was pointed directly at Peter's heart, Peter kicked Chirac's hand, and the gun fell to the floor. Then he kicked the doctor's knees, knocking him to the ground. Peter rolled toward the nearest weapon: the doctor's handgun. As he moved, Peter heard a car pull up in front of the Papineau farmhouse.

Jacques had started crawling for Peter's Luger. Rather than rushing for his own gun, Doctor Chirac scrambled to his feet and kicked Jacques in the leg, right where his infection was the worst. Jacques cried out in pain. Doctor Chirac's teeth flashed as he grinned in demented pleasure. He pulled his leg back to kick Jacques again, and Peter pulled the trigger on his revolver. He hit the doctor in the thigh, and the man fell to the floor just as the door flew open and three German soldiers burst into the room.

One of them yelled something. Peter thought the soldier was probably telling them to surrender. But Jacques had reached the Luger by then, and neither Jacques nor Peter wasted time firing several rounds off. Two of the three Nazis fired their weapons before they were killed, but neither of the bullets had been aimed at Peter. All three of the soldiers fell to the floor. Peter could feel a trickle of blood running down the side of his face into his fake beard, but he knew it was from Chirac's precisely placed strike with his medicine bag, not from any new bullet wound. Peter sat up in relief.

The three German soldiers were all from the group that had stopped Doctor Chirac and Peter on the way out of town. One was still conscious, but Peter could tell he would die soon. Peter pulled the man's rifle out of his reach and left him. Next Peter checked on the doctor. He had been hit in the crossfire and was dead.

Jacques wasn't moving. Peter stepped over to him and saw a red hole in his back. He grabbed his scarf from the floor and pressed it over the wound. Then he gently turned Jacques over. He was still alive.

Jacques looked up at Peter with dazed eyes. "I got shot again, didn't I?"

Peter nodded.

"Funny, my leg still hurts so badly I can't feel anything else."

The back door flew open, and Peter swung around with his handgun to shoot the intruder, thinking he should have checked outside earlier.

It was Genevieve.

Peter lowered his gun, and she lowered hers. Then she noticed her brother lying on his back behind Peter. She let out a cry then ran and fell on her knees at his side.

"Oh, Jacques, I should have been here."

"I told you to warn us and then hide until the shooting stopped. My plan was right, as usual. It kept you safe."

"But it didn't keep you safe," she sobbed. Jacques brought his hand up to wipe her tears away. Genevieve grabbed his hand with both of hers and held it next to her cheek.

Jacques tried to say something, but instead he coughed. He coughed again, and Peter noticed blood in his mouth. "I think I finally made my peace with God . . . on the road back from Brunembert. Like Paul, except he was going to Damascus." Jacques closed his eyes. When he spoke again, his voice was softer. "Do you think I'll go to heaven?"

"Yes, but please don't go now," his sister pleaded.

Jacques opened his eyes again. "Mireille is in heaven."

"But I'm here, and I need you. France needs you too. You can't go now."

Jacques coughed again. This time Genevieve noticed the blood, and her eyes widened in alarm. "Peter, he'll be all right, won't he?"

Peter didn't say anything.

"Jacques, you can't leave! Don't leave me, please."

"I don't think it's my choice anymore," he said. He looked at Peter. "Take care of her." It was part question, part command, part plea.

"I will," Peter said.

Jacques looked from Peter back to his sister. "I love you, Genevieve."

"I love you too, Jacques."

He lived for a few more minutes, but he didn't say anything else. His breathing grew more and more labored as his lungs filled with blood, and then the breathing stopped. Genevieve continued to sit by him and hold his now-lifeless hand. She cried quietly. She had thought her brother dead the day before and had mourned for him then. Peter could tell mourning for him the second time wouldn't be any easier. He blinked back the tears from his own eyes and began preparing to leave.

Peter knew the Papineau farmhouse was still under Nazi suspicion. They couldn't spend the night there. Not wanting to leave any evidence of what had just happened, and needing a task to distract him, Peter loaded the bodies of the Nazi soldiers into the back of their truck, pocketing their identification papers because he knew military identification might come in handy later. Then he added Doctor Chirac's body. While Peter was loading the corpse, he noticed the doctor's papers. In addition to his identification, he had a sheet of paper with a handwritten note on it:

Being taken out of town against my will. Possible Resistance meet-up. Please follow at a distance.

That was why the three German soldiers had followed them. Peter crumpled up the doctor's papers in anger and frustration. *He hadn't been taken out of town against his will*, Peter thought. *He had gone along for the chance to earn triple his normal pay.*

Back inside, Genevieve hadn't moved. She looked up when Peter came in. She had stopped sobbing, and though tears were still streaming down her cheeks, she was calm. "I guess we need to leave now?" she asked.

Peter nodded and helped her to her feet. She looked vulnerable and broken. Peter put his arms around her and held her for a moment, resting her head on his chest.

"Can we take him back to our farmhouse and bury him there? I can't bear to just leave him here. . ."

"Yeah, I'll get him."

Peter picked up Jacques's body and loaded it into the German military truck. They drove back to the Olivier farmhouse. There, Peter carried Jacques into the house and left him with Genevieve. Peter next drove the truck, with the remaining bodies, back toward town. He had been planning on rolling it into a canal but instead noticed a fresh crater—someone's bomb had missed its target. He rolled the truck into the hole then lit it on fire. As it burned, Peter thought of what he'd lost.

He walked away from the truck about half a mile, paused, and then did something he hadn't done since early elementary school—he fell to his knees in the mud and wept. Peter had always been taught that men of his generation didn't cry. But just then he felt less like a grown man and more like an abandoned child.

Why wasn't I warned? he prayed. *Did I just not hear what I was supposed to do?* Tears of anguish slipped down his cheeks. Only a few days ago, he'd told Jacques that no one was past redemption, but now Peter had doubts about himself. Jacques was dead because of Peter's mistakes. Genevieve had lost her brother—all the family she had—and would have to flee her home. That too, Peter knew, was his fault. There was no one he cared for more than Genevieve, and no one he had hurt more. He hadn't meant to carve a path of misery and pain through her life, but that was what he had done. There didn't seem to be any way he could make things right again for her. The damage was irreparable.

Peter lost track of time as he knelt there in the mud, but after a desperate, sorrowful prayer, a memory came to his mind that changed his perspective. It was from seven years before. Peter had been coming back from the potato field after a long day of weeding. As he passed his aunt and uncle's home, he'd stopped because he could hear his brother practicing for a solo he would be singing in church the next day. Robby had a good voice but very little training, so their aunt Anne-Laure had been his accompanist and his coach for several weeks. As Peter remembered that day, he could almost hear his brother's voice. *Fear not, I am with thee; oh, be not dismayed, For I am thy God and will still give thee aid. I'll strengthen thee, help thee, and cause thee to stand, upheld by my righteous, omnipotent hand. When through the deep waters I call thee to go, the rivers of sorrow shall not thee o'erflow, For I will be with thee, thy troubles to bless, And sanctify to thee thy deepest distress.* Peter also remembered what he had felt that day. He had known that what Robby was singing was true—and he had known it without any question or doubt.

A second memory came to him then, one that was more recent. Peter remembered how he had felt after reading the letter his father sent him while he was in the hospital. Bob Eddy had written that he prayed for Peter, that he was proud of him, and that he loved him. Where Peter had thought there were angry and bitter feelings, there was instead love. *Have I made the same wrong assumption about my Father in Heaven?* Slowly, Peter realized he had. Somehow he had forgotten what he had known so clearly as a fourteen-year-old boy. The Lord never deserts His children. Even in their darkest trials, He is there to help and comfort them. As Peter came to that understanding, a warm feeling of peace spread over him, confirming his thoughts.

He paused for some time, letting the words of the hymn run through his mind again and the feelings of acceptance and love run through his heart. He continued to pray, but this time gratitude replaced his sorrow. *The Lord has been with me*, Peter thought. *He kept my brain clear despite the lack of oxygen while Prinz and Siebert tried to force me to identify my contacts. He made someone leave the keys to a Gestapo jeep in the ignition, arranged for the gate of Gestapo headquarters to open, and softened Himmelstoss's heart.* Peter realized the Lord had also performed a miracle for Jacques. Peter wasn't sure how it had happened, but Jacques had changed. A week ago, he would have killed Marie, Himmelstoss, and Himmelstoss's oberleutnant. Today, however, he had died at peace with his conscience. That change, Peter thought, was the greatest miracle of all.

Finally, Peter stood and began walking back to the Olivier farmhouse. The walk back was quiet, giving Peter time to plan ahead for the coming days. He still mourned the loss of his friend, but he took comfort that Jacques was no longer separated from his wife and sweetheart. Peter also took comfort and hope in the knowledge that his Father in Heaven remembered and loved him. Peter knew he still had faults, but God would never give up on him. He would welcome Peter back every time he sincerely turned to Him.

The weather began to clear a bit as Peter dug a grave near a tree on the edge of the Olivier property. It wasn't six feet deep, but it was close. Considering the state of Peter's body, the effort to dig the grave was a sacrifice, but one he was happy to make. Genevieve and Peter wrapped Jacques in the quilt Marcel and Hélène had given him and Mireille on their wedding day and laid him to rest in the middle of the night. Like most funerals, it was quiet. Both Genevieve and Peter recited their favorite scriptures; then Peter sent Genevieve inside while he covered Jacques's body with dirt. Peter smoothed the soil and replanted the tall grass he had carefully dug up. If anyone came by the home the next day, they would have to stand directly on the grave to recognize it.

Genevieve was asleep on the couch when Peter went back into the house; he went up to her room to bring down a blanket. He draped the blanket around her and took extra care to tuck it around her toes and her shoulders. He would have carried her up to her room, but Peter was exhausted physically and emotionally, and seeing her safely sleeping was comforting. Peter sat down against the wall, where he could see the kitchen door and the front door at the same time. He could also see Genevieve. Peter watched her sleep and thought about her, her brother, and all the other villains and heroes he'd dealt with in Calais.

Chapter Thirteen
D-day

Tuesday, June 6

PETER HAD PLANNED TO STAY awake all night in case the Gestapo or German Army came to the farmhouse, but he didn't make it. He woke when the sun shone through the kitchen window onto his face and found himself spread out on the floor, his right arm stinging with numbness because he had fallen asleep on it. He pulled himself up and frowned as the blood pulsed back into his arm. It, like most of his body, was still tender. He walked quietly toward Genevieve. She was still sleeping. Peter watched her for a few seconds, admiring the contrast between her dark eyelashes and fair skin. He felt an urgency to leave Calais, but he also wanted to give her more time to rest.

There were things to do before they left, so Peter went outside to check on the cows. LeBras had already taken them. Peter was glad for that; he didn't want to deal with them. He went into the cellar and grabbed as much cheese as he felt two people could easily carry then took it into the house. He glanced at Genevieve's sleeping form then turned the small radio on, keeping the volume low, to see if there were any additional updates about the campaign in Italy. Peter packed food, spare clothing, and water into two bags as he listened then washed his face, removing the remnants of the beard Jacques had made for him. As he dried his face, he glanced at the kitchen doorway and saw Genevieve watching him.

"Peter, where are we going? I feel like everything is all wrong. Jacques is gone—really gone this time." She bit her lip and wiped fresh tears from her eyes. "Jacques seemed to think we could get a boat and meet the Royal Navy off the coast. Yesterday I fixed the radio at the Papineaus' house. I knew all the right passwords, and I was on the correct frequency, but no one would answer. How can we get to England if the Allies won't respond? It's like they've forgotten all about us."

Peter was about to suggest they try the large two-way radio under the stairs when something on the smaller radio caught his attention. "*Radio Berlin issued a special bulletin this morning, stating that the long-awaited British and American invasion began when paratroops landed along the coast of Normandy. Radio Berlin also reported fighting between German Naval forces and enemy landing craft. Thus far, there has been no Allied confirmation of the attack.*"

Genevieve looked at Peter with surprise. "Do you think it's really started?"

Peter thought for a moment then nodded.

"The real invasion?"

"McDougall said there would only be one." Peter knew there were things McDougall hadn't told him, but he was sure McDougall had told him the truth about that. "But with a little luck, maybe the Nazis will think it's just a feint, that the real invasion will come here instead."

"Tschirner believed you."

Peter nodded. If Tschirner believed the lies he'd told in prison, and if Tschirner convinced his superiors to believe them too, then maybe Peter's mission would be a success after all. He thought of McDougall's words: "*Your mission will be one more piece of evidence tying the Fifteenth Army to Calais, one thread weaving its way through all our other schemes.*" Peter thought that if the German Army still anticipated an attack near Calais, they might not rush all their troops to the one just starting in Normandy. His eyes fell on the bags he'd started packing. "I think we should make the nearest front line our new destination."

"Normandy? It's more than two hundred kilometers away from here. And we'd be heading into a battle."

"Maybe Louis can get us a ride. Or help us find Jacques's contact in Brunembert."

"Maybe," Genevieve said quietly.

He could see the fear and uncertainty in her eyes. He walked over to her, gently put one arm around her waist, and ran his other hand through her hair. She had been through so much already, but their journey wasn't yet finished. "Do you still have the false papers Jacques made for you?"

"Yes, two of them."

Peter gently held her face in his hand and wiped away the tears that had begun to creep down her cheeks again. "Then are you willing to try it? An escape through the front line?"

She thought about it for a minute. She looked down, then at Peter, then down again. "Yes, but I've never been to Normandy."

"Didn't you tell me you found new places interesting?" Peter said, trying to be cheerful. She nodded but still looked sad and hesitant. "Genevieve, I know the last few days have been horrible for you. I think we should leave soon, but if you need more time, we can wait."

"No, we can leave now—there are a few things I'd like to bring, but I can be ready in a minute or two." She paused, looking around the home she would be leaving behind then looking at Peter. "It's just that I'm not very brave, Peter."

"Of course you are—I don't think I've ever met anyone more courageous than you, Genevieve."

"No—I was terrified the entire time I was in prison and most of yesterday too. I thought you might die when I saw you in your jail cell. You weren't breathing, and there was blood everywhere—all over the floor and all over you. It terrified me. And I heard their plans for you afterward, when I was in Tschirner's office—it was horrible, Peter. I didn't think there was any way you'd survive what they were going to do to you. And I was horrified of what they might have done to me. And now the invasion has started, and I should be thrilled, but instead I'm scared." She looked up at Peter. A few faint lines had appeared between her eyebrows and around her lips. Peter couldn't tell if they were the result of grief or worry.

"Genevieve, what is your definition of courage?"

Genevieve thought for a few seconds. "Doing hard, dangerous things and not being afraid to do them."

Peter shook his head. "Genevieve, being brave is doing hard, dangerous things *despite* being afraid to do them. Blowing up boxcars, breaking into prison, standing up to the Gestapo, leaving your home—those are all very courageous things."

"Not if you're terrified the entire time."

Peter pulled her closer to him. "Especially if you are terrified the entire time."

"But you're never scared."

Peter was quiet for a few moments. "No, I am sometimes. I try to hide it, but it's still there. In prison, I was scared I wouldn't be strong enough, that I'd give something or someone away. When I was arrested yesterday, I was afraid I would never see you again." He paused then continued quietly. "And I fear I'm falling in love, and I don't know what to expect or what it will be like—or how much it might hurt."

"You think you're in danger of falling in love?" she asked.

"Yes," Peter said.

"It's not supposed to be scary," she said, smiling for the first time that morning. "After all you've been through, surely you're not going to let love frighten you?"

Peter shrugged, looking away.

"All you've been through . . . You've been through some awful things, Peter. Will you be all right?" she asked as she gently placed her hand in his. It was her right hand, and Peter could see a small scab on her index finger from Prinz's knife. He thought about her question for a few moments. Would he heal from this mission? Physically, Peter knew the answer was yes, but mentally and emotionally . . . Jacques hadn't been his brother, but Peter's role in the events leading up to his death made losing him just as hard as hearing that Robby's ship had been destroyed.

Then Peter remembered the feeling of peace he'd had the night before. He smiled and looked into Genevieve's beautiful brown eyes. Her skin was smooth now, the worry lines gone. *If the Lord can forgive me,* Peter thought, *and if Genevieve can love me, then maybe the future will be blessed after all.*

"You know, I think I will be all right," he said.

She smiled softly. A little uncertain, Peter leaned toward her and gently met her lips with his. She was still smiling when he paused and opened his eyes, so he kissed her again.

Over the radio, the announcer began reading a special bulletin from General Eisenhower's headquarters, confirming the Allied invasion. But none of that mattered right then. Peter was kissing the woman he loved, and nothing else—not even the fate of the world—could distract him from the beauty and joy of that moment.

Author's Notes

OPERATIONS SINON AND SWITCHBLADE ARE, of course, completely fictional . . . but they could have easily happened. Operations Fortitude North, Fortitude South, Ironside, and Zeppelin all took place. The information Peter reads in McDougall's office about these operations is factual. As a result of Fortitude South, the German Army met news of the D-day invasion with disbelief and slow reactions. The German Fifteenth Army didn't move from the Calais region to the real front in Normandy until the end of July. Radio Berlin was the first to broadcast news of the invasion, and SHAEF issued an official communiqué only hours after the amphibious landings began.

Throughout the book, references to those with a rank of general are real, historical individuals. Those of lower rank are fictional. With any mention of real, historical figures, I have tried to keep their involvement as true to history as possible. General von Rundstedt did predict that the invasion would come near Calais, and General Patton was in command of the fictitious Dover invasion force.

I have made an effort to accurately describe firearms, limpet mines, airplanes, vehicles, and other equipment as they were in 1944. Spy gear, such as L-pills and microdots, existed at the time of this story.

The description of Calais and the surrounding countryside is largely factual. Maroilles cheese and lacemaking are common to the area. Calais was surrounded by canals, hedgerows, and a wall. There is an outdoor market at the Place d'Armes, a Notre Dame cathedral, and a medieval watchtower. During World War II, the Germans did set up their army headquarters near the train station. The beaches would have looked as they are described in this novel, though without Olivier's narrow mine-free path. The description of the city's wartime devastation is also accurate.

Residents of the city had to deal with rationed food, curfews, air raids, checkpoints, and round-ups for forced labor in Germany. In fact, there was an air raid in the Pas-de-Calais the night of June 4–5. The homes of the characters and Gestapo headquarters are a product of my imagination.

Details of the Gestapo and Abwehr are factual, and the Gestapo methods described in this book have been documented by historians. Prinz's home province of Carinthia was the source of more death camp guards than any other province in Germany or Austria, and many of its inhabitants were of mixed Slovene/Austrian ancestry. Fresnes prison was a real place. Having one's head shaved was a common consequence for French women who collaborated with the Nazis, although it was more common after liberation than during occupation.

If you have any questions about what is fact and what is fiction, please contact me on my website: ALSowards.com.